THE GRASS ROOF
Younghill Kang

and THE YALU FLOWS
Mirok Li

The Norton Library

W·W·NORTON & COMPANY·INC·

NEW YORK

COPYRIGHT © 1975 BY W. W. NORTON & COMPANY, INC.

THE GRASS ROOF copyright 1959 by Younghill Kang

First published in the Norton Library 1975 by arrangement
with the Asian Literature Program of The Asia Society

Books That Live
The Norton imprint on a book means that in the publisher's
estimation it is a book not for a single season but for the years.
W. W. Norton & Company, Inc.

Library of Congress Cataloging in Publication Data
Kang, Younghill, 1903–1972.
    (The Norton library)
    Reprint of the 1966 ed. of book one of Kang's work
published by Follett Pub. Co., Chicago. Originally
published in 1931 by Scribner, New York. The second
work is a reprint of the 1956 ed. of Li's work published
by Michigan State University, East Lansing. Originally
published in 1946 under title: Der Yalu fliesst.
    1. Korea—Social life and customs. I. Li, Mirok,
1899–1950. Der Yalu fliesst. English. 1975.
II. Title. III. Title: The Yalu flows.
DS904.K3   1975   915.19'03'3   74-30257
ISBN 0-393-00766-9

Printed in the United States of America
1 2 3 4 5 6 7 8 9 0

INTRODUCTION

THE Norton Library, in association with the Asian Literature Program of the Asia Society, has published several distinguished Asian classics over the past decade: *The Burman: His Life and Notions* by Shway Yoe; *Letters of a Javanese Princess* by Kartini; *The Lost Eden* and *The Subversive*, the two Philippino novels by Jose Rizal; and *Alberuni's India.* Now added to this list of works which had either gone unpublished in America or had been long out of print are the two works brought together in this volume: *The Grass Roof* (Part I) by Younghill Kang and *The Yalu Flows* by Mirok Li.

The authors of *The Grass Roof* and *The Yalu Flows* write of their early childhood and young adulthood days in Korea at the beginning of this century, when Korea was going through a turbulent period after, in the words of Younghill Kang, "the people had been happy in the same customs, dwellings, food and manners for over a thousand years. Life in such country districts as mine was a long unbroken dream, lasting thousands of years, in which the same experiences, the same thoughts, the same life came unceasingly like the constantly reappearing flowers of Spring, whose forms and attributes were the same, although the individuals were changing."

But the unbroken dream was shattered, and Younghill Kang and Mirok Li were profoundly affected by the changes taking place in Korea. Isabella Bishop, an American traveller in Korea, wrote at the end of the last century, that Korea found herself "confronted with an array of powerful, ambitious, aggressive, and not always over-scrupulous powers bent it may be on overreaching her and each other, forcing her into new paths, ringing with rude hands the knell of time-honored custom, clamoring for concession, and humiliating her with reforms, suggestions and panaceas of which she sees neither the meaning or the necessity."

Bewildered and bombarded by a change that was robbing them of their humanity, every Korean faced conflict. When the proclamation was handed down by the Royal family (under Japanese influence) that the traditional topknot was to be cut off "in order to accomplish important tasks which are connected with our relations with many foreign countries," one official cried out, "You may cut off my head but not my topknot." Such intransigence was rooted in the belief in tradition, faith that it was in the past models that stability was to be found. Isabella Bishop arrogantly called it the "unspeakable grooviness, irredeemable, unreformed Orientalism of the Korean people."

But why change? Were not the Koreans being forced to accept concepts and values alien to their tradition? Were not these changes upsetting to the rhythm of human life, the rhythm of nature? Many Koreans may have recalled at this time the essay of Yi Kyubo (twelfth century), "On Demolishing the Earthen-Chamber." When he discovered that his sons were digging a hole in the earth to make an earth-covered chamber where "we may grow in it flowers and cucumbers during the wintertime, women may come here to do their spinning and weaving, without their hands getting chapped, for it will be warm even in winter inside this earthen chamber, like in the spring-time," Yi Kyubo replied, "That it is hot in summer, and cold in winter is the way of Heaven. It is against nature to impede its workings by artificial means. . . . Why should we upset the seasons and do the spinning and weaving in the cold winter? It is the same with flowers. It is right for the flowers to bloom in spring and fade when their season is over . . . to cross the working of nature to suit our purpose is to upset the prerogatives of Heaven."

If security was found in nature, in its rhythm, in mountains and valleys, it was also in living life according to the Confucian code of conduct—the five relationships: ruler and subject, father and son, husband and wife, elder and younger brother, friend and friend. Harmony was to be found in playing the role "correctly." While the Confucian Chinese could be expedient, the Korean was guided by constancy. As two of the most famous Korean sijos go:

> Though this frame should die and die,
>   though I die a hundred times,
> My bleached bones all turn to dust,
>   my very soul exist or not—
> What can change the undivided heart
>   that glows with faith toward my lord?

Chong Mongju (1337-1392)
translated by Richard Rutt

> Don't boast of your new dresses,
>   Peach tree and plum tree in blossom.
> Look at the pine and the bamboo,
>   Green, green in sun or snow,
> Those noble, lofty princes—
>   *They* don't change with the weather.

Kim Yu-gi (c. 1675-1700)
translated by Peter Lee

Koreans were also influenced by Taoism and Buddhism

and their native beliefs; however, it was largely the Confucian influence that the reformers were confronting. Koreans have been accused of being the *most* Confucian of the countries under the influence of China, the most rigid—"overburdened by Confucian dignity," as James Scarth Gale put it at the time. In the fifteenth century, the same century that the Korean language (hangul) alphabet was invented, the Korean official, Ch'oe Pu, was caught in a storm off the coast of Cheju-do (an island off the southern tip of Korea). Ch'oe Pu, a man of the Yi Dynasty, when Confucianism became institutionalized, wrote a moving human record remindful of the official who chose to lose his head rather than his topknot. Shipwrecked off the coast of China, and after much hardship (including proving he is not a Japanese pirate in disguise), he is then taken to the Court.

In *Records of Drifting Across the Sea* (translated by John Meskill) Ch'oe describes what happens when he is ordered to remove his mourning dress and appear in festive dress to give thanks to the emperor for his graciousness.

The Chinese official says: "You will now put on the hat and clothes, go into Court, and acknowledge the Emperor's graciousness. You must not be slow."

I pointed to the mourning hat on my head and said, "In my mourning, if I wear brocade and a light silk gauze hat, will I be easy in my heart?"

Li Hsiang said, "If you were beside the coffin, your father would be important. Now you are here; know only that here is the Emperor. When the Emperor is gracious it is a great breach of ministerial courtesy if one does not go and thank him. That's why, by our Chinese code of etiquette, if a prime minister goes into mourning and the Emperor sends a man with a funeral donation, though [the minister] is in deepest mourning, he must put on festive dress and hurry to the Palace to bow his thanks. Only after that may he change back into mourning dress.

"Imperial graciousness must be acknowledged. To acknowledge it, one must be inside the Palace. To get inside the Palace, one may not be in sackcloth. It is a matter of expediency, like giving a hand to a drowning sister-in-law. If you fall in with the festive mood now, you will be bowing to circumstances." [The reference is from Mencius: As a rule that is to say, one would not touch the hand of a sister-in-law, but if she is drowning it is well to ignore the rule.]

I said, "When the awards were received yesterday, I did not receive them personally. How would it be if now, at the time of the acknowledgement of graciousness, I again ordered my staff and those below them to go and bow?"

Li Hsiang said, "When you received the things, there was no elaborate series of bows, and it was all right to delegate someone. But now, the Ministry of Rites and the Court of State Ceremonial have discussed the matter of your acknowledging graciousness and have already put in a memorial that says, 'The Korean barbarian official Ch'oe Pu and others . . .' You are the head of the list. Can you afford to be absent?" [All non-Chinese—even those from a tributary—were barbarians to the Chinese.]

I could do nothing but lead Chong Po and the others behind Li Hsiang and walk to Chan-an Gate. Still I could not bear to put on festive dress. Li Hsiang himself took off my mourning hat and put on a light gauze hat. Not only that, he said, "When state business comes up, there is a way to rise from mourning and return to duty. You will now go in through this gate in festive dress; when you have finished the rite of acknowledgement and left through this gate again, you will change back to mourning dress. It will be only for that short while. There can be no complete regulation without exceptions."

Six centuries after Ch'oe Pu (who was executed as a result of factional disputes in which Confucianism played a part) had made his way across the Yalu back to Korea, Mirok Li crossed the Yalu out of Korea, first to China, then Germany. Younghill Kang crossed the Pacific to America. During the years they were growing up they and their people were placed in situations that brought discomforts similar to what Ch'oe Pu had experienced. As

Ch'oe Pu bowed to have his mourning dress removed to survive, Koreans abandoned traditional beliefs to survive. Many must have held their heads as Younghill's grandfather had and questioned whether "a scholar of Confucius must bow to the learning of the West." How many children sent to schools of the "new learning" (a school of science and technology) must have felt the discomfort Mirok Li did, who was told by his mother: "This new civilization which is so alien to us, just does not suit you. Think of the earlier years. How easily you learnt the old classics and poets."

"All the ancient forms of the east have been flung to the winds in exchange for the inextricable confusion that we see today," James Scarth Gale observed, but these autobiographies speak to us at a time when we *all*, all the world's children, are confronted with a rapid change, are questioning values and look "back" nostalgically to when life was simpler, or believed to be simpler, certainly "deeper," as one of my Korean friends once commented. (Max Morath, a contemporary musician, says: "The past is a good place to visit, but I wouldn't want to live there.") Mirok Li's friend, a musician said, when Mirok Li, after a rest at home, returned to school to pursue courses in science and math:

"Wouldn't it be wonderful if you were to live here and we could always make music like this? You would not have to work nor trouble about anything; you could live happily, as a human being should live. You could ask your friends to come and see you whenever you wished, and talk with them about the heavens, and the earth, about the world and about human hearts. You might have a hut built in the mountains, and there you could listen to the splashing brooks and watch the passing clouds. Your mother would be happy, and you would live serenely, and I could remain with you forever."

But there was to be no turning back, no turning from

the strength of Japan, the strength of the West. In *The Yalu Flows*, Youngman tells Mirok Li that "Japan has now reformed, and has many trains and steamers."

> "People say there are now six civilized nations in the world . . . England, America, France, Germany, Russia and Japan."
> "And where does our country stand?" I asked with astonishment.
> "Not among the civilized by a long shot," was his dejected reply, "because we have too few railroads."

Kang writes in Book II of *The Grass Roof* (*not* included in this volume), that after the annexation of Korea by Japan, the framework of Korean society had collapsed, security was gone, the classical tradition was scorned. Even a child of eleven cried out that "Everything is wrong. Life is spoiled now." Kang's father said, "For every good that science gives man, it gives him two ills," but Kang himself was encouraged by the "new generation" and thought that Korea could regain freedom by acquiring the knowledge of science, and the old Confucian school receded to the past in his mind. Receded too were the words of his grandmother, who was herself a Buddhist: "There is a heaven above and earth below, Amidst these two dwells man, He is the noblest creature of all . . . Let not your life fritter away meaninglessly. You must train yourself to be good and useful and prepare to make others happy, so always study hard the wisdom of Confucius." Laws of gravitation and Boyle's law now attracted Kang. He had his hair cut off, dishonoring the family, wore a Western hat, and directed his steps toward Seoul and the Western learning:

I was wearing straw shoes made by my father. On my back, I carried an anthology in two volumes of great Chinese and Korean poets written in my crazy-poet uncle's calligraphy, a notebook, and pen and ink. On my shorn head was the Western hat given by Park Soo-San. And now I was on the highway leaving the village behind me, my face towards Seoul. . . .

There he went to the Japanese school for his "Western learning" but he found the Japanese "as superficial about their Western learning as they were about the Chinese classics. I saw in order to get my education I must go to America right away." His first step, however, took him to Japan where he went to a school with the hope that he would learn how to lead his country. After four years in the school he wrote, "The whole thing I have learned in this school, I thought, is how more and more people can be killed, at one time." He returned to Korea briefly, to a world of azaleas and poetry, to a new look at his Korean heritage, and on a Buddhist pilgrimage exchanged his Western shoes for the "comfortable elastic grass shoes of my country." But it was the end of his childhood utopia. His friend said, "Nothing can be done, the disease of the so-called civilization is upon us."

Life was not "perfect" for all Koreans before the impact of science and technology, or the "so-called civilization." It was—and to an extent still is—a rigidly class-conscious society with little room for mobility or egalitarianism. Women were in an inferior position in the Confucian system. Younghill Kang's uncle considered women somewhat beneath the dignity of a classical scholar. "Longevity, Wealth, Male Children" are the words painted on the bride's sedan. Mirok Li's mother prayed 100 days to the Mirok Buddha for a boy—after having had three girls!

A folk ballad, a tragic one, relates that life becomes so unbearable in the husband's household that the wife attempts to return to her home by disguising herself as a monk but she is not recognized by her mother, her father, elder brother, or elder sister-in-law. "Alas, where will I go?/You hateful match-maker?/How much profit did you receive for/Pushing me into this cruel fate?" The ballad is a reminder that a married woman was not to return to the home of her parents, no matter how unfortunate her married life. And there is the poignant picture of a wife sitting before a mirror, imagining herself playing another role than that of a sad and isolated woman. And then one day that woman scrapes off the acid paint or mercury and eats it, and thus ends her plight. "Widow knows what widow is crying about," says the Korean proverb.

In the inner court, however, the place of women could be quite different than her social status and rights would indicate. Witness the grandmother in *The Grass Roof*, the mother in *The Yalu Flows*. It is not out of place here to mention the institution of the Kisaeng, the women entertainers, who were accomplished women, wrote poetry, could sing and play an instrument. While it was and is an institution to serve men, it did provide women with the opportunity to have a less restricted life than women confined to the home.

Confined to the home as she was, however, Osini, Mirok Li's sister, revealed a wisdom and sensitivity grounded in the Korean tradition. She questions her brother's "new education," and in doing so expresses that humanism central to Korean culture:

One evening, while I was alone in the little "east room" on the Inner Court, Osini came to see me. "These books are so strange," she began with disapproval. "They contain no classical words and no sentences of any profound meaning. Do you believe that they will one day make you a wise man?"

"I hope so," I answered.

"And what do you learn from these books?" she asked with an air of superiority, fingering one page after another.

"I think it is a pity for you. You are, after all, gifted; you have read Tsung-yong. You have learnt many old poems by heart, and have even copied Yulgok's anecdotes. But now, with this new learning, you are wasting yourself on worthless things."

Osini was an intelligent girl. She liked reading and knew many of the anecdotes and novels written in the old style; her speech was rich in classical Korean words unfamiliar even to my mother. People considered her the cleverest of us children, and indeed she was the only one who often found fault with me. She thought my handwriting miserable, my language without beauty or dignity. For this reason I tried to avoid talking with her.

"It is just that the new learning is something different," I told her at last: "it teaches you how to build railways which will enable people to travel over thousands of miles. It teaches you to estimate how far off the moon is, or how to make use of the power of the lightning to produce light."

"That does not make you a wise man," she said with concern.

"These are the new times," I continued, "brighter ones after our long, dark sleep. A fresh breeze has awakened us. Now it is spring, after a long winter. That is what they say."

For a long while Osini seemed lost in thought and hardly listened to me. "And how far is it from us to this country which they call Europe?" she asked me at last.

"That I haven't learned yet, but it must be many times ten thousand miles."

"Once upon a time the Princess Sogun married into a country without flowers. It couldn't be there, could it?"

"No, that was only the land of the Huns."

"Do you believe they have flowers like our forsythia and azalea?"

"I do not know."

"Do you believe they have a south wind there? Do they sit in the moonlight drinking wine in order to write poems?"

"I cannot tell."

"Then you don't know anything worth knowing," she summed up disappointed.

A word should be said about the language in which these works were written. Neither was written in Korean! Younghill Kang wrote in English—not always with a complete understanding of the language: why should he have? He inappropriately draws on French words (garçon) and uses geisha rather than the Korean kisaeng, "cowboy," which has a specific connotation for an American, "deb dance," "tuxedo," which have no cultural equivalents in Korean. Kang draws extensively on European literature for quotations to open a chapter; he had become —so to speak—a citizen of the world.

When *The Grass Roof* was first published by Scribner's in 1931 another Scribner's author, Thomas Wolfe of *You Can't Go Home Again* fame, reviewed it.

Kang is a born writer, everywhere he is free and vigorous; he has an original and poetic mind, and he loves life: again and again in this book is a person, a scene, an action are described in a few words of rich and vivid brevity. Thus, a man has "a face filled up with the dust of sorrows," an innkeeper is "a short, sincere little fellow with a fat chin," "a tall, very pale young man of twenty-five, so slender that in a silk dress he would look almost like a dragonfly" . . .

There are also the larger scenes and persons—the life of the family; that wonderful and ancient family of the tribe of Han which could endure poverty and hunger but which could not endure to be without poetry—"a man," the author says, "should not be ashamed of coarse food, humble clothing, and modest dwelling, but should only be ashamed of not being cultivated in the perception of beauty." Every one in that family wrote or quoted poetry; there were contests in the household to decide who was the best poet; and the final meditation of Kang himself naturally and spontaneously condenses itself at every point into poetry, of which his knowledge is great and fruitful. . . .

The scenes, the traditional customs, the observances of feast and season—of birth, death, marriage and harvest—of all these people in *The Grass Roof* are remote from Western experience, but what the reader must instantly feel about the people in the book is his kinship with them: they belong first to the family of the earth. We know them and recognize them. Kang, with his great feeling for life, his sense of time and human tragedy, has done something more than make a record for our curiosity of a world far from our travel and our sight; he has made a record of man's wandering and exile upon the earth, and into it he has wrought his vision of joy and pain, and hunger, and in this is the first and most lasting importance of his book.

Kang *did* go home again, but not to the "utopia" of his childhood. He held the position of presidency of a college in Seoul for a time and for a period after World War II he was an adviser to the American Director of Office of Civil Information in Korea. His last trip to Korea was in 1970 when he attended the International P.E.N. meeting and at that time was awarded a doctor's degree in literature at Korea University. However, most of the years after he left Korea were spent in various positions in the United States, including the Encyclopedia Britannica, the Metropolitan Museum of Art, Yale University Library, Long Island University. He also lectured widely in America, Europe and Asia. Wherever he was, his dedication, in his own words, was to "preserving the enduring values of human life and culture against the evil forces threatening them." It had been his wish to see *The Grass Roof* reprinted, and though he had authorized me to make the arrangements, I regret that publication did not take place prior to his death in 1972 and only Book I is included in this volume.

Like Kang, Mirok Li, whose original name was Yi Ui-gyong, never forgot his native Korea, though he left Korea as a young man never to return. He spent his life in Germany, where he arrived in 1920. Mirok was his "child name," which was given to him as a result of his Mother having been granted her wish—after praying to the Mirok Buddha for a male child.

In Germany, he was active in cultural organizations and his autobiography, written in German, received the kind of acclaim which placed him in the German *World Literature Dictionary* and the *Dictionary of Modern Authors*. Chung Kyu-Hwa, a loyal friend of the works of Mirok Li, and responsible for getting his works more widely known in his native Korea as well as in Germany, wrote that when Li died in 1950, "so intense was his longing for home that, on his deathbed, he could still recite the opening lines of the Korean national anthem: "Until the East Sea dries, or Mount Paektu wears away . . ."

The first English translation, by H. A. Hammelmann, was published by the Harvill Press (London) in 1954. The *Times Literary Review* (August 6, 1954) stated that Hammelmann's English language version of the original, simple German is "calm and fully expressive of the closely felt Korean scene that stirs the reader by its blend of intimacy and remoteness." Upon American publication by the University of Michigan Press in 1956, the *New Yorker* (November 17, 1956) called it "a classic distillation of the timeless essence of friction and growth."

The translation by Hammelmann does not include the fragments which describe Li's journey to Germany (on a boat with fellow student Koreans, Vietnamese, and Indians), though these have been included in Chung Kyu-Hwa's recently released German edition. They are omitted here because they begin another "voyage," one which best belongs in another collection. When Chung Kyu-Hwa sent me the German edition (August 1974) he wrote: "The people between the four oceans are brothers." (Confucius). Indeed *The Grass Roof* and *The Yalu Flows* are part of the human achievement that is the heritage shared by all of us, the family between the four oceans.

Bonnie R. Crown
Director, The Asian Literature Program
The Asia Society
November 1974

ACKNOWLEDGEMENTS

ACKNOWLEDGEMENT is due the National Endowment for the Humanities for a grant to the Asian Literature Program of the Asia Society which assisted the research of Bonnie R. Crown on the Korean tradition. Some of the introduction to this work is drawn from that work-in-preparation. Appreciation is expressed to Chung Kyu-Hwa for sharing information about Mirok Li which had not been available before and to Marshall Pihl, Jr. for translating from the Korean an article by Mr. Chung which appeared in *Munhak sasang* (Seoul).

The two sijos appearing in the first part of the introduction are from *The Bamboo Grove, An Introduction to Sijo*, edited and translated by Richard Rutt (University of California Press, California, 1971), a volume initiated and sponsored by the Asian Literature Program of the Asia Society, and *Poems from Korea, A Historical Anthology*, compiled and translated by Peter H. Lee, East West Center Book, (Unesco, 1964, 1974). The excerpt by Ch'oe Pu is from *Ch'oe Pu's Diary: A Record of Drifting Across the Sea*, translated by John Meskill, published for the Association for Asian Studies by the University of Arizona Press, Tucson, 1964.

THE
GRASS
ROOF

YOUNGHILL KANG

To Frisk:

> Awake from Winter's DARK ROADS;
> Come to the garden of Spring.

All the oriental literature quoted herein is from actual translations made by myself and Frances Keely. We have paid much attention to carrying over the spirit, the aesthetic pattern and the literal meaning from the original.

YOUNGHILL KANG

CONTENTS

In a grass roof idly I lay,
A kumoonko for a pillow:
I wanted to see in my dreams
Kings of Utopian ages:
But the faint sounds came to my door
Of fishers' flutes far away,
Breaking my sleep. . . .

(Old Korean poem)

Chapter 1

THE VALLEY OF UTOPIA

We are the music makers,
And we are the dreamers of dreams. . . .
Ode: ARTHUR O'SHAUGHNESSY

AT last the truth must be told about my life, and by my own pen, without boasting or pride because it has gained some success, without hidings or modesty because it has suffered failure. I swear it is true by the Bible, for I have seen in a Law Court the Americans swearing by this. I have had one occasion in my life to swear by stars and flowers, an oath more divine, more romantic, more adventurous. But that is another story. I shall relate here plain matter of fact, although it may seem novel and strange to a Western reader.

Yes, the life that I have lived, with all the joys and sorrows, is an interesting life, and I should be the author of the story, because this is the one life I know the best. I have always believed in heroes and I have thirsted to study the lives of all great men, such as Confucius, Christ, Shakspere, Keats, Li Po, and many others: innumerable names that are enrapturing my soul, stirring my heart, fascinating my mind, making my blood jump and my muse fly; but I know my own story better than theirs. I am not writing this to make anybody educated, or to put down any Babbitry, or to spread any new sort of gospel. My one aim is to tell you the life, the human story of one man, made up with the stuff called love, hatred, smiles and tears. All I can do is to tell this sincerely and frankly, for *life*, which includes such things as to travel very often in dreams in the castles of Spain, and again to worry where the morning breakfast will come from, has always seemed to me bigger than anything else; even bigger than *thoughts* extending from the devil-fight in the pandemonium of Yellow Springs, to the stars and clouds in the Green Void. I too would say with Ruskin: "This is the best of me; for the rest, I ate, and drank, and slept, loved, and hated, like another; my life was as the vapor and is not; but this I saw and knew: this, if anything of mine, is worth your memory."

I close my eyes, I recall my first memories, memories of the long ago. Some of them come into my mind more sparkling than others. All are vivid and novel and impressive, because they were the first things to reach me after I cried in the cradle; and where I was before, indeed I cannot remember. . . .

I was told by one of my aunts that I was born somewhere in Northern Korea, while my mother was on a trip to China with my father. Since I cannot verify my birth place accurately, it is safe to say that I was born in that village where I was brought up, not far from Asiatic Russia and Manchuria, in a hand-made house fashioned of stone, wood and clay, and covered with a grass roof that turned up slightly at the eaves like Korean women's shoes.

I know now that I was born in the year when the minds of the people were greatly perplexed. Everybody was worrying and talking about the coming war, prophesying that the Japanese would soon be over to kill all the Koreans. It was about that time when Japan was to declare war on Russia, and requested from the Korean government permission to use the roads into Manchuria, a request that was really a command, and was followed soon by military occupation.

They said that I was born on the tenth day of May, by the Korean calendar (which is about a month later than by the American), just as the sun came up and the cock crew: also that according to the Four Pillars of Destiny (the hour, day, month, and year of birth) I was born to be a wanderer all my life, with no home but the wide world. I never remember my mother, for she died a few months after I was born, but I fear she must have eaten only grass roots, and suffered every hardship, for the people were very poor just at this time. Besides the political anxiety which recalled my father from China, it had been a hard year for the crops at home, and the whole village was starving.

This village where I was born—Song-Dune-Chi, or The Village of the Pine Trees—was made up entirely of my own relatives, a clan by the name of Han, who were ruled by national ideals which had been handed down from father to son for innumerable generations. Our community had long been looked up to by others for its famous scholars and its olden-time clannish spirit, in a country for immemorial years under the iron thumb of tradition and ancestor worship, a country of which Napoleon said: "A giant is asleep. Do not wake him."

Our village was situated in a huge valley, partly poor sandy rock, and partly fertile soil, between high mountains, covered with pine and oak trees, and many high tall grasses. There were streams running down from each mountain hollow, joining the big river which murmured eternity's chant through the centre of the valley. A few miles farther on, this river passed through the market place where the people of my village went every five days for barter, and there it rushed into the sea. Except for the market place, the people were rural and isolated, and this mysterious water, constantly tumbling in, was the only far wanderer among them. My native village was the kind which all the great oriental sages have thought Utopia in itself. The people had been happy in the same costumes, dwellings, food and manners for over a thousand years, and were like the ideal state of Lao-Tze, where "though there be a neighboring state within sight, and the voices of the cocks and dogs thereof be within hearing, yet the people might grow old and die before they ever visit one another."

On the right bank of the river, bordered and interspersed by pine and weeping willow trees, was the village, and behind it, somewhat lower, the rice fields. On the left bank grew the millet and other grains, and farther over, against the opposite mountain, were to be found the deer, the hawks, the tiger cats and fabulous Dragons. I can remember in the mornings when the sun was getting up how its beams trembled on dew-shrunken foliage of the mountain, then poured down like sparkling bits of glass over the water in the valley—especially when the rice seeds were ripening in the fields. At such a time the whole world seemed to dance and glisten, for the color of the ripe rice was tawny, and lay rippling like a golden fleece under the eye. In the Spring, of course, this rice would be a clear young green, the color worn by brides in my country. But at all times the rice fields were a picturesque sight, for they were kept covered by water artificially, and mirrored the changes of the elements, reflecting the bright blue of the sky, taking on the colors of the slender rain, catching the dying sun in a blurred glass, and enhancing the mystery of the Yellow Dusk, or perhaps imaging the round moon above some scholar's roof.

But life was not all Utopia to the people in my village. Sometimes the river behaved like an evil Dragon. Even if the village did not have heavy rains, there would be floods which came from the mountains, where there had been a cloudburst. The hardest time for the farmer was during the months of August and September, when all the old crops had been eaten, and the new grain had not reached fruition. Then the only food would be potatoes and fish. This cost the father of the family only a few pennies per day, but often he did not have even so much as that. Then his family had to live on grass roots and rice hulls. I remember how one farmer, after hungering many weeks during the starvation time, went away and ate too much, so that he died. This is the same fate which overtook the Chinese poet, Tu Fu, and it gave rise to a saying in the East that there is a greater danger in over-eating than in under-eating.

There is a Korean proverb: "Scatter frost upon the snow." Often the Autumn floods would occur during the lean months, and then the almost empty store-houses, the cattle, dwellings, and every kind of valuable property, would be swept away by the river. The people of Han had an endless struggle for existence in spite of their beautiful surroundings amidst nature. I shall never forget a tragic picture I saw one time: an old man crying miserably, as he and his wife and children on the bank watched his house, his cattle and all his goods being carried away on the flood. What should he do now for the winter months?

Our home was not exempt from this miserable dependence upon the elements, but my family did not seem to mind their helpless poverty, since most of them were indulging in the mystical doctrine of Buddhism, or in the classics of Confucius, who always advocated that a man should not be ashamed of coarse food, humble clothing, and modest dwelling, but should only be ashamed of not being cultivated in the perception of beauty. The sage said: "Living on coarse rice and water, with bent arm for pillow, mirth may yet be mine. Ill-gotten wealth and honors are like to floating clouds." A man has no place in society, Confucius teaches, unless he understands æsthetics.

Many of the great men influencing my people, like Po Yi, or Chieh Chih Tuei, starved to death. Thus it was a point of honor with my family to suffer hardship, and to scorn all content except æsthetic peace. My crazy-poet uncle, the scholar of the family, cared little how his hair looked, or for dirt in his nose, but went right at it with his pen. He was a comical creature. Everything he said was poetry. If you mentioned any incident, he would quote: "Under such a situation a famous poet once said—" and then he would recite the whole poem by memory. In a few minutes he would give his own verse to fit the occasion, using the same rhymes used by the poet he had quoted. At one time he had lived at the capital, Seoul, where he had attained to high rank; and he had studied a long time in China. For him the New Year's gifts piled up, chickens, gloves, shoes, stockings, an occasional overcoat. Many respected such genius and would have died for him. My poor father, who would put days and days in working in the interests of public service which did not pay him a penny, never received these favors. Every time it rained my crazy-poet uncle wrote a poem like Li Po's. Like Confucius, he was "a man so eager that he forgot to eat, whose cares were lost in triumph, unmindful of approaching age."

My grandfather was making his own living away from us by writing poetry and selling caligraphy, and by divination. Professionally, he was a *poong-sui* (which means master of wind and water), a scientist who chooses by geomantic system the most propitious sites for burial grounds. It is a very respectable professional position, and only a great scholar of the classics would be able to master its intricacies. By scanning the horizon and by ranging over the country in the study of hills and plains, my grandfather could tell just which of the nine stars and five planets controlled the land. My grandmother one time told me that he had picked out many locations for those who were now, through the success of his efforts, famous and prosperous in society. One man, who was told by him that a certain burial ground would bring a *pak-sa* or famous doctor-of-letters to a son of the fourth generation, dug out his own great grandfather's grave and buried the ashes into the spot indicated, being ambitious not for the fourth generation, but for himself. And later, sure enough, he became a *pak-sa* or a famous doctor-of-letters. I still do not know how to explain it, for it certainly seemed to work out. Of course one explanation is that there is a spiritual force in the mountains helpful to the vitality, energy and destiny of the people who bury their ancestors correctly.

My family has always had its wanderers. Besides my grandfather there was my prodigal-son uncle. He could write very good poetry and was full of advice for the children from the sages; especially he was fond of advice from Confucius who taught the responsibilities of family life and devotion to fathers and mothers and elder brothers. But my junior uncle did not practise what he preached. He came back home only to ask for money, mount up debts and cause trouble. Later he had children by his wife, who of course, all lived with us, but he never stayed at home, nor did any work for them. He was a small, lively man with twinkling eyes full of the wine of life, and somewhat of a dandy in his dress. I remember him best as wearing a tiny black moustache which he carefully oiled and then rearranged with his fingers in order to make it look more beautiful than it was.

My prodigal-son uncle was my grandmother's youngest and her favorite until I was born. Because for a long time I was the youngest grandson, and because I was the eldest son of the eldest son and would pray to her spirit after she was gone, my grandmother was very partial to me. I remember her picking from her own bowl the choicest bits of chicken and putting them in mine. How eagerly she would watch me eat, as if she tasted them herself! I can only remember her punishing me once. That was because of a childish indecency: I asked the servant to give me food before the hour.

In spoiling me, she was assisted by Ok-Dong-Ya, my little cousin with the beautiful smile. Ok-Dong-Ya (meaning Little Jade Girl) was about my own age, a daughter of the crazy poet. She would save her candies often and then give them to me with that expression my grandmother had when she gave me her chicken. But she was not just copying my grandmother. I remember Ok-Dong-Ya even then as gay, tender, womanly. She was always full of imagination. She too loved the beautiful poets and would have me recite them to her. We understood each other. She preferred me, I think, to her own brother—a fat, good-looking, sarcastic boy, some years my senior, but almost too clever. With him I always fought. His name was Eul-Choon (meaning In-the-Spring-of-the-Year). My name was Chung-Pa (meaning Green-of-Mountain). He and I often fought over our favorite poet, or the meaning of a verse of the classics.

The livelihood of this whole family depended upon my father, who, in theory, was the master of the house, but, in fact, was the slave of everybody. He was a large, stout, heroic-looking man with a great black beard reaching half-way down his long white coat, in the style of the old-fashioned Koreans. In spite of his Homeric look, his eyes held an anxious, responsible expression. He was emotional, rather than reasoning, and had a strong sense of traditional duty. Since he was the oldest male representative of the family at home, he had to take care of his two younger brothers, and his sister before her marriage, and the brothers' wives and their children, besides raising me. He had to do everything for them, from roofing the long house with grass—an annual task—to making the children's shoes. Nor was there any division of labor. No one else felt responsible. That means, he himself was putting the roof on the house, or making the shoes for the children; no one else turned a hand.

There was a little income in the household from the salaries of my senior uncle, who in addition to his fame as a poet was a teacher of classics. The chief source for supplies was what my father made by fashioning tools of all kinds and taking them down to the sea to barter, for the whole community used very little money. The thing he made the most was a tool for gathering pine needles to cook rice with: he could do almost anything very well with his hands, and was an excellent binder of my poet uncle's books. (Always he had a deep respect for scholars, though he was not a great scholar himself.)

Sometimes during the hard months when food in the village was scarce, my father's position as head of the household was especially hard. One ghastly night of rain in flood-time the whole family sat up waiting for him to return home and bring them food. He had gone out in the night in his old straw raincoat to a particular rich man, miles away, who was reported to have poor small seeds of wheat. None but the very rich had food in the grain-house then. My father tried to get the wheat on credit, for he had nothing to trade with. The man refused to let him have the grain, not even a spoonful for my grandmother. My father went elsewhere and everywhere was refused. He could not even get a small tail of fish for my grandmother. So finally my father slipped back home and had to confess that he could get no food. The others went to bed, but he walked up and down, up and down all the long night, and he could not sleep. "It was not because I was hungry," he once told me with tears in his eyes. "I felt no hunger. But it was because I knew my mother was hungry and I had not been able to bring her food."

From the time he was only a child, my father carried the responsibility of the whole family. Although he had a living father, the geomancer, my grandfather was always away travelling, coming home just once in a while to see the family (which is how my uncles happened to be born). My grandmother was in many ways the most important one in our house. I know that she was much loved by my father. She was a tiny gray-haired woman of great energy. Most Korean women are small, but she was smaller than most. I think she was pretty. But I might be prejudiced in speaking of her; since my grandmother, however plain, would still look attractive to me. She generally wore the traditional white of middle-class Korean women, and was not at all particular about her clothes. I never remember seeing her powdering her nose, nor oiling her hair like other Korean women. The wives-and-mothers-yet-to-be of Song-Dune-Chi were all told to become like her. Besides being learned in every kind of wifely detail, she was capable of the work of a man in the fields when there was sudden need. But above all, she was a true Oriental woman. The quietism of Buddha, the mysterious calm of Taoism, the ethical insight of Confucianism all helped to make her an unusually refined personality. Because of her lonely life in the long-continued absence of my grandfather, and her bewildered fear of the "foreigners" (the Japanese and the Westerners who came in ever-increasing numbers to Korea during my childhood), and because she was a woman, she was most attracted by the emotional elements of Buddhism. No one else in our house was a Buddhist. My father was a Confucian; my crazy-poet uncle was mostly a Taoist; only my grandmother loved best the stories and sayings of the pitying Buddha. Yet she usually preached to me because I was a man-child the Confucian virtues of obedience, self-sacrifice and a deep love of the classics. I remember her saying: "There is heaven above, and earth below. Amidst these two dwells man. He is the noblest creature of all that God has created. Hé! it is a great thing to be the Master of all. Let not your life fritter away meaninglessly. You must train yourself to be good and useful and prepare to make others happy, so always study hard the wisdom of Confucius."

My grandmother loved the great literature of the past and sound scholarship was one of her ideals. But she did not want us to be a house of scholars. She knew that the more scholars there are in a household the poorer it is. There are several reasons for this. To be a scholar you are handicapped, you have to be honest. And furthermore a scholar is not expected to work in the fields. Poets in the Orient, although much respected, make no money. Both my uncles wrote verses for all occasions, for weddings, for funerals, for births. Yet they got no money in return. Nobody thought of offering them money, but only gifts, of wine and dainties. My grandmother was just as well satisfied that my father should not be a scholar. She said that she had made one great scholar among her sons, my crazy-poet uncle, who was officially very distinguished, and that now she wanted to make one more among her grandsons and the rest must be practical.

My crazy-poet uncle's library was remarkable. The walls of his studio-house were lined with sliding panels of bamboo. People all over the province borrowed his books and usually kept them, since he was absent-minded. From the beginning my uncle used to give my verses very serious attention: both mine and those of my cousin Eul-Choon. Mine, he said, were the better. Always he took greater pains with my education than with Eul-Choon's and everybody considered that I was to be the scholar of the family.

Here is one of my poems of childhood, written in Chinese, which I later translated into English:

> My world is full of many lofty hills,
> And down their side the sparkling streamlet trills;
> The many-colored birds fly swiftly by,
> The soft-toned feathered warblers of the sky,
> While in the winding, rippling mountain stream
> The dancing, curving fish of silver gleam.
> In Summer I go toward the greenwood tree
> And lie, and sing, and play, and watch the bee.
> In Autumn I go out and watch the moon
> And listen to the tree tops' sleepy croon.
> In Winter I look out upon the snow
> And wonder where those brilliant flakes will go.
> In Spring I watch to see the flowers rare
> Come up to scent the warm, entrancing air.
> For trees, and flowers, and clouds and birds of May
> Are now my friends and shall be, I do pray.

Chapter 2

THE ACHING AUTUMN SONG

Too soft for a grave-digger's tune,—
Bleak for that child Spring's mid-wife;
Mouldering impassively
Dearest leaves of life;
Burying Summer without voicing
Anguish for any leaf forgotten;
Neither sorrowing nor rejoicing
As next Summer is begotten.
                Autumn Rain: FRANCES KEELY

WHEE! Pee!"

This peculiar whistle I alone knew, and it came from Yun-Koo (or Jade-Lotus). It meant that Yun-Koo was standing outside the sugar-cane fence and the bamboo gate of our house, waiting for me to give him the signal as to how to adopt the situation. If I gave him a certain sign, it would mean, "Keep quiet and don't come in, because I am in a dangerous position"; or another sign, "The situation is entirely favorable: everybody hospitable."

No dignified adult would have approached the house in this way: no, but he would enter the gate, come up the path, and standing in the centre of the path, would clear his throat; or else, if nobody were in sight, would inquire in a loud clear voice, "Is Mr. Han at home?" No visitor would think of entering the porch without permission, because the doors were never locked, and it was considered unrefined to approach them without the permission of the master. If his courteous request were answered by a woman, the door would now be opened just a wee bit, and a modest voice would murmur, "He is not in"; if by a man the door would be flung boldly wide, and in ringing tones, the guest would be invited to come in, or directed to where he might find Mr. Han.

Yun-Koo was one of my own chronological associates, a small boy of seven or eight. When Yun-Koo called, I had been planning how I would become the greatest man in the country. It had to be; I had it all conceived in my mind. I knew that my grandfather was picking out his grave with a view to making one of his grandsons a *pak-sa*, which everybody considered would be I. I can never remember a time when I did not consider myself more highly than most of my associates. Already at the age of seven I often felt a dragon surge up in me prompting me to be too original, a habit which sometimes brought me in disgrace with parents.

One most dreadful example was on the occasion of the Annual Ancestor Worship. This was not the ordinary Ancestor Worship which goes on in everybody's home all the time, but was a festival for the worship of the Ancestor of the whole village, the first Han who lived tens of generations back. His tomb was deep in the mountains. There the whole village made solemn pilgrimage once a year, taking with them materials for a sumptuous feast. The Ancestor's tomb was in the heart of stillness and pure air and mountain pines. He must have slept in great peace for there was nothing around Him, but a stately monument or two, and His own house, kept by one man the year around, for this special service.

The annual Ancestor Worship was something like the Americans' Thanksgiving: it occurred after the Harvest, during the harmonious days of October, keen, warm, bright, sunny days when the oak trees were golden and scarlet, and the lazy river was jewelled with a cargo of treasure. It seems to me colors must be more vivid over there than in America. Certainly I have never seen anything in the West like those Korean Autumns. In the primitive parts of Korea, the forested mountain slopes dazzled the eye with bright color. Everywhere were the scarlet soo-yoo berries. The winding rivers and streams were a pure blue, and in the valleys and dales, the oriental houses, with turned-up roofs, sometimes of yellow grass, sometimes of a vivid green pottery, dreamed away behind their bamboo fences or their tiled walls.

Even the warm afternoons held the delicious taste of the first frost, and chrysanthemums were to be seen blooming in every yard. All sizes and all colors they were—chrysanthemum, that most beautiful flower to my judgment, a jealous flower, which is unwilling to share the Spring and the Summer with other flowers . . . so it chooses to come after all the others in the Autumn, nodding in the bright breeze. Its pungent aroma expresses its calm and mystical season; it is the last, and the perfection of all the flowers.

The feeling of the oriental poet about Autumn is a peculiar one. I can perhaps illustrate it in this way. Imagine the most beautiful mountains you have ever seen, the most beautiful trees, the most beautiful water, the most beautiful moon, the one perfect flower—and think of it all slipping away from you like a dream-utopia which you can never grasp to the hand, nor hold for very long; but while you are still infatuated with it all, the sighing winds of Autumn will turn to blasts, and the gorgeous leaves drop, one by one. . . .

I think of a Korean poem, which will probably not suggest as much to the mind of a Western reader as to an Oriental one, but I give it because it expresses the ardent sense of beauty in the passing hour:

> Chrysanthemum grows by the window
> Where the new wine waits to brew.
> The flower opens

> As the wine ripens;
> Friends flock;
> A full moon shines too.
> O Garçon! Tink-tink-a-tink the Kumoonko:
> Merrily, merrily sing the night hours through!

In the Ancestor's house, a selected group prepared the coming feast on the day before, and there everybody slept the night. During the whole afternoon before, the people kept arriving. Although the Ancestor's House was very large, it could not accommodate the entire multitude, and many went away to the nearest hamlet, or slept out under the stars. We boys had long awaited this occasion. We loved the all-day's march through the mountains, and the mysterious house at night, lit by the torches of those who were preparing food for the Ancestor, and for his descendants too, to be eaten on the morrow. Early in the morning everybody rose. First a great tray, larger than a wagon, was filled with all the best of everything, and carried by two men, who grasped the handles at each end and placed it before the Ancestor's tomb. All the mature and distinguished men of the village bowed down to the ground for several moments and my crazy-poet uncle read aloud in a moving and eloquent voice a prose poem of his own composition, written in classical Chinese in the best caligraphy on a scroll of the finest Korean paper, four feet long and four feet wide. As always, it began: "In the Fall of the year, gathered together, we pray to Thee" . . . and ended: "Bless us, and continue, Thou, to sleep in peace."

All the men were in clean white robes. Indeed the Korean native costume was for the most part white, though children and young women sometimes wore colored fabrics; it might be of silk, linen, or cotton, but was most often linen, generally made by the women of each household. We boys had just received our new double clothes for the Winter. Mine this year was a linen dress, slightly dyed in purple. I had a short jacket, very wide trousers, and a red ribbon tied around my waist, reaching almost to the ground; for the Koreans did not use buttons, but ribbons in their place. My overcoat was of light green silk. The *dong-chung*, or collar, had to be just so, and my grandmother, an accomplished needle-woman, had worked a long time to make it absolutely right. Children who have no society, no matter how wealthy their people are, will have no distinction in the cut of their *dong-chung*. My grandmother's *dong-chungs* were always considered of a remarkable cut.

After the service was over, the feast was served, but as it was done in chronological order, the children had still several hours to wait. The oldest men of the village were always served first, on low carved tables brought from the Ancestor's House. Great scarlet oak leaves were given them for napkins, and these too were placed on the wooden plates where the good things to eat were piled. Wine was served to the old men in silver drinking bowls, a white wine which looked just like crystal water, but which made your face red and your heart warm. Some of the boys whose parents had married them early, at fourteen or fifteen, were allowed to sit down at the tables with the grown men, and I remember, a group of old bachelors, of nineteen and twenty years, who found this hard to bear, but a man no matter what his age, was not considered grown up until he acquired a wife. I was not old enough to feel any interest in this example of chronological unfairness. In due order of time, I ate more than my fill, and wrapped up a large bundle in oak leaves and a scarf to take back to my grandmother—for the women and girls did not come to this festival, since only the married men were considered priests of the Ancestor.

In the afternoon of the feasting I invented the game which brought me into disgrace with parents. There were several beautiful mountain streams near the Ancestor's Tomb, which contained fish. We had not provided ourselves with anything to go fishing. But I discovered that by picking a long strong ribbon-like grass which grew in abundance on the banks, and catching a grasshopper and tying him to this grass, if you sat on a rock and were very quick, you might jerk the surprised fish from the water to your lap without the aid of a hook. I lined up the boys on either side of the bank, in their beautiful new clothes, some white, some light blue, or light green, others a more vivid hue, and soon I was the boss of a large fish-catching industry. "Ha! Here is one! Hurrah!" That cry went up continually. Unfortunately this game of deceiving the fish meant you hugged him to the breast of your new overcoat, and very soon our new clothes up and down the entire front were smeared with fish scales and mud. Even my distinguished *dong-chung*, one of my grandmother's most successful cuts, was spotted, and reeked of the fish. This little incident, owing to the number of boys I had involved, gave rise to the saying that there were fifty devils in me, not to be quelled in sight of the Ancestor's Tomb.

And—

"Whee! Pee!" Yun-Koo continued to whistle outside the bamboo house of our enclosure.

The gate was ajar. I could see him standing there. I gave him the sign with my hands which meant I would join him soon. I glanced back. There was my grandmother in the working-annex, stringing chrysanthemum petals on a thread. Already there were several dried strings hanging up on the wall, awaiting the time when they would be put into the New Year cakes. My heart thrilled as I caught the whiff of them, so promising and suggestive of the New Year festivities and the wine and the poetry with which they would be eaten. But just as I passed, without seeing me, my grandmother began to sing a sad song over her work. It was a song which was generally sung by women on a rainy day, but this day, though cold, was very bright, and the leaves on the trees were a cheerful ruddy brown. The song she sang was to a plaintive tune, and went something like this:

> O how sorry I am! How sorry I am!
> The wind is blowing! The wind is blowing!
> The rain is dripping, the rain is dripping!
> O my poor child, where are you to-night?

I looked in at her where she sat among the red and green peppers, the long white radishes, and the heaps of chrysanthemum petals.

> O how sorry I am!

My grandmother sang this rainy-day folk-song all unconsciously but it gave me a queer sensation for a moment. Outside again, the smell of the air reminded me of New Year's and I felt better. Eul-Choon, my fat sarcastic cousin, was raking leaves in the front yard, to be burned in the chimney for fuel, and scowled at me as I passed, because being older and bigger than I, he had to work and I did not. I joined Yun-Koo and there I found in the shadow of the bamboo fence Chak-Doo-Shay (or Ugly Knife) as well.

Chak-Doo-Shay, or Ugly Knife, had this peculiar name because he was particularly endeared to his grandmother and grandfather. He seemed to them too beautiful to live, and so they gave him the name of Ugly Knife. It was thought that evil spirits were at all times anxious to steal lovely children, to bear away to their spirit world to live with them. When such a fate was feared for a child, he was guarded by a repulsive name, such as Dog's Dung, or Ugly Knife, in order that evil ghosts might be frightened away from him. Of course this was only his milk-name. When he was old enough to be married, he would assume his deb-dance name, and it would be his real name henceforward. This Chak-Doo-Shay was the posthumous child of an only child, and at home he was like the emperor for power. He even smoked a long clay pipe when he wanted to, although he was just a small child, and children were not supposed to smoke. In all the village, he bowed to no one except to me,—Chung-Pa. We three, Yun-Koo, Chak-Doo-Shay, and Chung-Pa, were known as the triad, or triumvirate.

"We are going to hold a secret meeting," I told Chak-Doo-Shay and Yun-Koo. "Follow me, and don't say anything."

I led the way across the river. We used the primitive village bridge just wide enough for a wagon to pass, and which was nothing but two trees covered with boards and branches, where rocks, earth and grass were laid, so if you jumped up and down heavily in the middle, it shook like a swing. The far side of the river was the place where the village ghosts were worshipped once a year. Here was a temple built to the ghosts by the villagers, a lonely deserted summer house. We were being very brave to come here. Even grown people were afraid of the village ghosts. Behind the temple was the thick pine grove, so dense in parts we could not push through. I chose a comparatively open place among the pines, because it provided three large rocks.

"We are here to take binding vows," I said. "To be

the three greatest men in the country"—I paused as I had another idea—"Not in the country, but in the whole world." Yun-Koo and Chak-Doo-Shay looked a little doubtful, or as if they were smiling at me.

"In the whole world," I repeated, vigorously.

I caught them in the eye and tried to inspire them with my faith.

"Let us be modest as the bamboo, but let us be strong as these pines."

Oh, those pine trees of Song-Dune-Chi, more graceful and æsthetic than in the West! What poetic, yet straightforward look, what strength, what vitalizing smell, which always intoxicated me as I climbed to the top with other children to pick the sweet mellow gum to chew! When Winter blasts and winds blew and other trees were naked, all through the Eastern mountain and the Western valley, the pine tree still was standing like an eternal constant. You could not find that constancy in the other trees, the constancy of the ever-greening, the constancy of the ever-lasting, the constancy of the ever-beautiful.

Now I pointed overhead to those pine trees. The air in the Grove of Ghosts was dark from them and was soaked through and through with their strong smell. Gradually Yun-Koo and Chak-Doo-Shay looked at me with a kind of awe as I made them see what I meant. I told them to follow me in an extemporaneous song—it was the commonest kind in that country; men in the fields, women at the loom, little children at play, all made up songs and sang them, fitting them to folk-song airs. Mine was something like this:

Under the falling, falling long branches of the pine trees,
We three sit together, vowing to be the three greatest men in
    the world;
Our will is as strong as the rocks on which we sit.

Our minds are as enduring as the pine trees—though other
    trees are naked, these alone endure through snowy
    storms and heavy Winter blasts.
And our hearts are green as willow boughs on yonder side
    of the river.
Though hard the path, heavy the task, long long the day,
We-will-march-on!

We joined hands and danced around in a circle, singing it to a folk-tune. When we came to the last words,
"We-will-march-on," we dropped hands, and marched
in a straight and irresistible line forward.

Afterwards we marked our two wrists with the sign
which I still carry and shall have to carry for life. We
blackened white thread with Chinese ink, and put a
needle and thread through, but the ink remained behind,
so as to form a small black spot impossible to remove by
washing. By nice calculation, we made the spots on each
wrist the same. It hurt a little, but you are supposed to
have a hard time, in making vows.

As soon as Yun-Koo, Chak-Doo-Shay and I had made
our vows to be the three greatest men in the world, we
returned across the river to the other pine grove, where
the whole group of sixty or seventy boys usually played.
As we three entered the camp, silence fell over the children assembled there, for the leader alone was supposed
to speak when the group first came together for the day.
He then proposed the game to be played. Yun-Koo,
Chak-Doo-Shay, and myself passed through the group
and advanced as far as the "emperor's house"; there were
several houses in the Pine Grove which the boys had
constructed of pine and willow branches, around circular
holes dug in the ground, but the emperor's house was
high in a tree, and it was for Yun-Koo, Chak-Doo-Shay
and myself. I then gave directions for the day.

In my group I never was a follower, but always was a leader. Others must kiss the dust to me, and all must obey the orders which I dictated to Yun-Koo, the vice leader. He was my right-hand man. My left-hand man was Chak-Doo-Shay. We made an effective cabinet. Being the most executive, I could originate, and Yun-Koo could develop the details, which Chak-Doo-Shay was a deft hand to carry out. Yun-Koo was strongly built, domineering, shrewd, self-assured; he had a good head. Chak-Doo-Shay was tall, delicate, modest and sensitive; he could do almost anything well with his hands. I, the third, was well-built and agile, so that I was superior to anybody in my group in wrestling and in acrobatics— even in the senior group I could beat anybody but the senior leader; furthermore I excelled in telling stories and in making up games, so I was considered to have the eye of hypnotism, the energy of resource, and the mental superiority to make me the leader.

I now directed that the fishing nets be lifted. On each side of the Pine grove, streams entered the river, and in both streams we children had placed nets made from goldenrod stems. Every day we caught a number of small black and white minnows which were very good roasted by an open fire. The fish, I suppose, liked the smell of the goldenrod stems.

Around the fire which had been used to roast the fish I told one of the stories I had made up. It was a talk on the creation of the earth. I told them that *I* had been the creator, and that I had moved that big rock from a certain spot in the pine grove, and planted the big tree in front of that village. The details of the creation all came out of my own head, for I had not yet studied the Book of Changes, which explains various phenomena in the universe through sixty-four Hexagrams; neither did I know anything about the Book of Genesis. Some of the boys looked as if they really believed my story.

Whenever we wanted to, Chak-Doo-Shay and Yun-Koo and I withdrew to have a meeting to discuss defence, and to invent signs for calling parents when we were oppressed by an older group. But we did not always discuss defence. This day I told Yun-Koo and Chak-Doo-Shay a new saying of the Classics I had just learned:

"Though salt comes out of water, when it enters, it melts away; man comes out of woman, when he nears woman, he is destroyed."

These were the words I had heard my crazy-poet uncle using to my prodigal-son uncle. I heard them so many times, that now I knew them by heart. . . .

A cry went up down below while we were sitting up in the emperor's tree. The Seniors had advanced against our group. Eul-Choon, remembering my smile as I left the yard and perhaps the way I had waded through his leaves, had incited his leader to come against my group. I fought with Eul-Choon, my fat cousin. Now I heard Chak-Doo-Shay weeping with a badly hurt finger as he withdrew to seek comfort in parents. I could beat Eul-Choon, but the senior leader I could not beat; when the senior leader gripped me, Yun-Koo did not come to my help. . . .

So the day which had promised so well, ended in sorrowful defeat. Unable to collect Yun-Koo and Chak-Doo-Shay, again, I returned home by myself in the dusk, limping slightly, for the senior leader was very tall and rough. The air was now so cold that I shivered and regretted that I had not worn my interlined overcoat when I had left so blithely in the afternoon. But it was not my bruises which made me want to cry when I saw the wild geese in line against the sky, their images mirrored in

the flushed water of the rice fields. South they flew in
zigzag flight, with melancholy wailing. Soon would come
the first snow.

In the kitchen the fish-oil lamp was lit. My grandmother stood at the window, looking out at the desolate
rice fields with a sad expression. At first I thought it must
be on account of me. I slipped from the kitchen into the
first room. Ok-Dong-Ya was there, making bamboo dolls.
I came softly and she did not know I stood behind her.
She cut bamboo of the right length, and at one end
painted eyes, nose-holes and a mouth, with ink and
brush pen. Then she attached linen threads for hair,
braided them and tied on a ribbon. Afterwards she
dressed them in little pieces of beautiful silk. She would
put five or six against the wall and then would talk to
them in a low tone of voice when she thought nobody
was looking.

"Cheer up this evening. You're sad. What's the
matter?"

"Well, well, dear baby! Come to me and don't cry."

"What is the matter with Grandmother?" I whispered
in Ok-Dong-Ya's ear.

She started, and pretended she had not been hugging
her bamboo doll like a baby, but had been tying its ribbon. "The junior uncle has not returned. Grandmother
thinks he has run off again, and perhaps will not even be
back for the New Year."

There was a shadow over the whole house and I went
early to bed.

But not to sleep. Always I slept by myself in the crazy-
poet's studio, a separate house with separate fire and
even a tiny separate kitchen. In the studio were the
books, many hundreds of them, behind the thin wooden
panels of the hollow walls which contained nothing but

books. I loved my cozy room and the sense of the books all around me. I was even now learning them by heart. That night when others believed I was in bed, I read until late, and I thought how I would be a *pak-sa*. I awoke with a start to the sound of the Autumn rain. I seemed never to have heard it before.

O the Autumn, the Symbol of darkness in the heart, of mourning in the soul, Nature's executive official, cruel and tiger-like, marked by naked trees and cold sceptical skies! What can this remorseless hour have in common with tender Spring or bounteous Summer, or the tranquil fulness of harvest time! I heard the leaves shivering to the ground one by one. Why must they fall? Why?

To-night I feared the Autumn for the first time, like a great tiger prowling out there. I went to the window of the studio and put back the blanket (which I used in order that the grown people might not see my light and think I was reading too late), and I thrust my head outside, ready to cry. My grandmother stood at the door of the first room, with her coat over her head, looking out into the night. In a low voice that was more a wail than a song, she was singing the old popular air:

> O how sorry I am! How sorry I am!
> The wind is blowing! the wind is blowing!
> The rain is dripping, the rain is dripping!
> O my poor child, where are you to-night?

Chapter 3

POETRY, WINE, AND LIES

This bird of dawning singeth all night.....
Hamlet: WILLIAM SHAKESPEARE

My prodigal-son uncle was a great gambler and a drinker, and was always playing around with gisha girls in the market-place, or somewhere else away from home. Of course no gisha girls were to be found in our village, and if any came, my father, my crazy-poet uncle, and other respected men of the village would get together and make her go away. My poet-uncle considered women somewhat beneath the dignity of a classical scholar, and he would often warn my junior uncle against them. He said what a waste of time they were, and why didn't he spend his time in improving his knowledge of the classics.

The prodigal-son was over twenty, and he had not been married once yet. My father had only just got around to picking him a wife, for he had been recovering from the expenses of my crazy-poet uncle's second marriage. It took time, money, and occasions, to make good marriages, for of course no one in my family would want a wife that had not been carefully selected and long considered. A marriage was for life. The struggle to marry his two brothers to the best of his ability and one of his brothers twice over, was one of the reasons why my father himself never married again. So my uncle, the prodigal-son, was still unmarried, though my father had been arranging for a match to come off the next Spring and the gifts had already been sent to the bride.

I now think that it was because of the prodigal-son that my grandmother fell ill just before New Year's. He caused a great deal of heart-suffering and even privation among us, but somehow nobody seemed to blame the prodigal-son. My grandmother continually worried about his debts and his jail-sentences and his wild ways, and my father paid the bills when he had money, but as soon as the prodigal-son came home again it was all forgotten. It was just fate, they said,—not his fault. And he was much endeared.

My prodigal-son uncle not only hypnotized his family but everybody else. His companions used to tell the story of how he had been given a jail-sentence, thirty strokes with the birch switch, for gambling and disorderly behavior by the governor of the province. But while the county-beater was taking him out under a tree to receive punishment, they began talking, and my prodigal-son uncle entertained the county-beater with funny stories and he was so agreeable that they stopped in an inn to have wine first. The county-beater laughed so much and drank so much wine that by and by he was drunk. Then my prodigal-son uncle said: "Goodby, Kid. Sorry to leave you," and stepped off. When the county-beater got sober enough, he had to go back to the governor and report that he had given the required punishment.

My prodigal-son uncle had one very shrewd way of cheating at cards. Somewhere he had learned the Arabic numerals, and he bought his own pack of cards, and wrote the Arabic numerals, very small and inconspicuous, on the backs. This looked just like hen-scratchings to the uninitiated. Chinese numerals would look equally meaningless to Western eyes. Once he showed the trick to me. I remember well the long and very slender native cards, and the strange marks, 1, 2, 3, 4, etc. I thought them beautiful, fascinating and a little bit like black magic. This was my first taste of the Western Learning.

We felt very sorry about my grandmother's illness. The New Year preparations could not go forward without her. The village doctor was called in. This was one New Year's bill my father would not have to worry about. The doctor was not paid for his services any more than my crazy-poet uncle was paid for his poetry. Medicine was considered an avocation, not a vocation, and any good scholar was something of a doctor. Even my father was partly a doctor. But this man had been set aside by the village to specialize on the particular branch of the classics which told about medicine.

The doctor was a very tall thin man. You never saw so tall a man! He rode a mule. He could mount that mule just by lifting one of his legs, and then if he forgot to bring it off the ground, the mule would walk out beneath him. He had needles strung all around his waist, as a soldier carries bullets in a cartridge belt. This was the way it worked. If you had a head-ache, the doctor would stick you in the knee. If you had a stomach ache, the doctor would stick you in the big toe. There was a scientific reason for this known thousands of years back in the Great Age of Medicine, but the ancients had only put down the method without giving reason, so the village doctor himself would have been unable to explain why he used needles, and why his learning was so successful in many cases. He had studied his avocation by memorizing hundreds of verses which went like this:

When you have a head-ache, the pin should go right here. . . .

When you have a tooth-ache, the pin should go right
here. . . .

He chanted it just as any piece of didactic poetry
should be chanted. His mastery of this poetry corresponded to the eight-year medical course in the West,
but a Korean doctor studied much longer than that; in
fact a lifetime he considered was not long enough.

In spite of the doctor's attention, my grandmother
kept on being sick. Just before New Year's, my father's
sister, my childless aunt, came from a neighboring village, to take care of her and to superintend my fat aunt
in the New Year's baking and cooking. These two aunts
were very different.

My fat aunt was the wife of the crazy-poet, the step-
mother of Ok-Dong-Ya and Eul-Choon, and also the
mother of the fat baby, Cha-Dong, meaning "Next
Male." This aunt could not do anything well except manufacture babies. She had had too many servants in her
previous home; but that did not explain her intellect. In
fact she was somewhat slow in the head just as she was
in the legs. She did not even know how to tell a polite
lie on occasion, when it would have been kinder and
more courteous not to tell the truth. My family was a
diplomatic family and considered themselves gentle-folk
in all things, and often we were ashamed of her.

We had become very tired of my fat aunt's rice while
my grandmother was sick.

"Ai, Cha-Dong's mother must have played with mice
from the time she was the size of this," my childless aunt
said, as she jogged the fat baby on her arms the morning
after she arrived and brought order to the kitchen.

It was the superstition that little girls who played with
mice would never be able to cook well. The cooking of
rice is really an art, for though the same water, the same

kettle, the same grain is used, it will only taste right when cooked by an artist.

My childless aunt, on the other hand, could do everything well, *except* manufacture babies. All her gestures were amiable and ardent, and she moved with the rapidity of a magpie. Sometimes she was so quick in her movements that she stumbled over the shoes outside the door. In another woman, it would have been awkward, but everything about this aunt co-operated to make you think her beautiful, although she was not even very pretty. Her mind was bright too. She had mastered the art of divination just like my grandfather. If she had been a man, she would have made a good *poong-sui*, everybody said. But she was no good at all as a baby manufacturer.

She was about forty and never had had any children, though my grandmother offered up prayers for her at the Annual Worship of the ghosts many times. My scholar-uncle would read her prayer aloud from a list of other requests of the villagers, and my grandmother would murmur in an undertone, "Please, please," but it never did any good. Some Korean women can manufacture a beautiful baby every ten months, eyes, ears, hands, feet, all complete. Others try and try and can't make out anything. It was thought that my childless aunt may have been somewhat old when my father gave her in marriage. She had been quite an old maid, twenty-three or twenty-four, and her husband was a good deal younger. But in respectable homes all the girls were usually married late, at twenty-one or twenty-two, or even many times at twenty-five; but it was not so with the boys. Sixteen or seventeen was the average age for them, as the grandparents were anxious for their grandsons. Her husband could have divorced my childless aunt, but of course he didn't. There had never been any divorces in my family. We were too much respected. So my child-less aunt adopted two of her brother-in-law's children to be her own.

In the kitchen my childless aunt was so busy cooking for the New Year, together with my helpless fat aunt and the servant, that when I came in to watch, she bribed me to go out with one of the delicious pears which she had brought from her husband's farm five miles up the river. This was a fruit for which her district was famous. The pear was round and as large as a grape-fruit. Inside it was soft, sweet, but not too soft or sweet. It was better than ice cream.

"When you are a *pak-sa*, you must come to see me from the capital," she told me. "I will give you ten such pears. And one for each of the sons."

My father was making the lanterns to be hung on the porch outside. Without these no New Year would have been complete. They were made of carved teak-wood frames and decorated papers. Inside were placed candles of beeswax. To see them lighted from within so that all the gaily-printed flowers seemed to bloom was like some marvellous imitation of Spring, more beautiful because of the snow all around.

There was always snow for New Year, snow that lasted many weeks, not soiled as snow is in a big city or factory village. All the year around I waited for the first snow-storm, because it foretold New Year. Then my heart mingled with the joy of the flakes dancing down. Out-side the village was a little ditch which I hated. It had dirty ashes, refuse, old combs, old spectacle rims, old shoes. But when the snow had fallen, how I loved passing there! Then all was pure, and as long as the snow lasted, the country over there would be no dirty places. A tree grew near this ash-heap, also very wonderful under snow. It was the Yoon-Chi tree, a prodigious tree whose branches covered more room than a large house. Seven boys could barely encircle the trunk with their arms. Going up the tree were stone steps, put into the bark; out on its branches were built in many comfortable seats, and sleeping nets were hung where boys could spend the night, and there were bird nests too; it produced nuts the size of the smallest green peas, nuts much loved by magpies and crows. Under the Yoon-Chi tree was a stone platform, to which I once fell on my head so that I was sick for several days. This platform was where the farmers in warm weather used to spread out their straw raincoats and sleep during the noon-day sun; when under snow, it belonged only to boys and dogs, two classes of animals equally pleased with first snow-falls. Ah, that Yoon-Chi tree! It seemed to blossom when the snow came! It was covered with little flowers like a pear tree in Spring!

Another tree beautiful in the snow was the pine tree. It remained sharply green and each of its needles would be thrust through a cluster of snow-flakes. The glistening Christmas ornaments of the West are as nothing compared to this. There were of course many icicles on the houses, and the children were not allowed to pick these, because it was thought the crops would be good for the coming year in proportion to the number of icicles on your roof. Icicles on a grass roof were particularly nice, being crystal-clear and sparkling.

The river became frozen over, and one day I commanded the boys in my group to sweep the ice in order that all might be in readiness for the New Year. If you were a boy in the village of Song-Dune-Chi, you had to belong to a chronological group and your group bowed down to all in the older groups. If you were ever found separate from your group, the other children hazed you. All in my group bowed down to me and obeyed my word as ruler. If they did not, they got punished by officials in the group. My rule was Napoleonic. No disobedience was allowed. When one boy refused to obey me, we punished him by cutting holes for his hands in one of the silk-panelled doors, and giving him a heavy jug of water to hold while he stood thus for an hour. Afterwards we would not receive him back into the group until his mother made popcorn and candy to compromise.

Politics was our favorite game. We captured and punished the guilty. We had governors and county-beaters, who pretended to beat and who sometimes really hurt, and scholarly examinations to elect the officials and teachers. Each day I conferred one degree of pak-sa— only one, and it was not to keep. Just as the different villages all over the country would send yearly offering to the Korean emperor of their choicest products, tribute must be paid to me in the same way. The bright-colored boxes of yellow barley-candy acquired by any member of the group were brought first to me, carefully opened, but intact. I must have first choice, and later the correct apportioning was made by me. Yes, we played at governing Korea in the old way known to our fathers. As to the Japanese, they were not represented in these games of ours, though Japanese soldiers had been in the market-place since my birth; but nobody would consent to be a Japanese even in play.

Everybody seemed to have plenty of leisure for a good time during the New Year season. There were skating parties by night on home-made wooden skates. There was sledding (for this sport we used very comfortable straw mats, not so clumsy or dangerous as the Western sleds). Behind the tall walls of their homes chronological groups of sisters and girl cousins played on a form of high see-saw, shooting them twenty feet from the ground. They always rode standing, for they wore a good many clothes, and skirts were bulky; it would have been considered highly indecorous for a girl of any age to *sit* on a see-saw. They looked very graceful, shooting high into the air, in their gay light-colored clothes and their bright flying ribbons which harmonized with the snow. It was called an art to ride the see-saw well. My cousin, Ok-Dong-Ya, was very good at this sport. Here graceful, slender women showed to advantage, and the fat young women were out of luck. The young girls themselves were conscious of this and the thick-bodied ones would reduce by eating very little rice and as much *kim-chi*, or Korean pickle, as possible. Though some men like fat women, most of them prefer the others.

I heard my grandmother giving my fat aunt counsel once—because I often heard what my grandmother said when she did not know I was there. By keeping behind her just like her shadow and by being very quick, I could follow her around and escape notice for a long time. "Daughter," said my grandmother, "You are growing too fat. You must reduce."

Most fat women do not like to be told by others to reduce, but my fat aunt could say nothing, because my grandmother was her mother-in-law.

On the day before New Year's Eve, I still had no clothes for the great day, as my grandmother had been too sick to make any, and my fat aunt did not know how. Yet everyone is supposed to have a beautiful new suit for that occasion. I did not care; my mind was on the poetry contest. But my childless aunt's eyes were sharp. When I came into the kitchen with a brush-pen and a bottle of ink in my hand, she stopped me, looked at the front of my coat with her head on one side, and drew in her breath as if to say, "Eh, what shall I do with this big baby?" Only she did not say it because she was too polite. My coat was smeared with rice and *kim-chi*, and the threads were coming out where it was worn into a rag.

"Come, give your coat to me, little *pak-sa*," she said. "You are like your senior uncle! You do not value your clothes."

Now as I sat testing out my caligraphy for the coming poetry contest of the New Year, my little cousin, Ok-Dong-Ya came near me, throwing up something into the air and catching it in her hand.

"Wouldn't you like to have it?" she whispered, intent on her sport. "Wouldn't you like to have it?"

"What is it?" I asked.

"Oh, it is nothing."

She turned around several times more, tossing it into the air as if it had been a gay bird, and in the end threw it to me. "Here, you can have it!" laughed and was gone.

She had made a beautiful pocket for me out of purple silk, embroidered with yellow and pink chrysanthemums. The pockets of Korean children were separate from their clothes, and they wore them outside on their belts. Ok-Dong-Ya had made this one for me, because I had no new clothes to wear, but she was shy about giving it, so she acted in this funny manner. She had a spontaneous gay way with her always and was quite unconscious of herself. Often in the market-place she would laugh so merrily that people would turn to see this beautiful girl laughing; then she would be overwhelmed by shame and would hide her blushing face in her sleeve.

At last New Year's Eve came around, the long expected fête-night when nobody thought of going to bed, but sat up until the dawn, only dozing perhaps where he sat, or flung out on the warm mats of the floor in the heart of the tingling excitement, the beautiful lanterns, the piled up fruit and the wine bowls and all the holiday sweet meats. At half-past ten we boys left the snow and the skating, the bonfires, the fireworks which splashed into the sky like a constellation of stars joining in the carnival spirit; we blew out our candles, folded up the beautiful little paper lanterns which were our flashlights, and put lantern and candle in our pockets; then we assembled in the second room of my house for the poetry contest. It was large enough for over a hundred children sitting around on the warm floor which was heated underneath by the great fire in the kitchen. My crazy-poet uncle read us many New Year poems from the Chinese. One of them was this:

Under the inn's cold night, one man lies awake.
Why does the heart of the wanderer unspeakably ache?
He's a thousand lis from home on New Year's Eve!
Frost bites his beard, and a birthday comes at daybreak.

This crazy-poet was the examiner for many villages besides our own. Poetry examinations were very, very gay and important occasions in my country. At these examinations, if you were a contestant, you were given a large sheet of Korean paper too strong to tear. You wrote your name in one corner, rolled that, and sealed up your name, so that it could not be read until after the decision. This was in order that none might win by a "pull." The writers of the best verses enjoyed three weeks' wine and dainties, and people came to them and gave them subjects on which they must write poems. Many times I got the prizes for contestants of my own age. My earliest classical poem, my uncle told me, was written when I was three or four years old. It was a description of a snowy day written in Chinese, and might be translated: "Heaven and Earth lose their yellow darkness." This was spread around among the examiners as if it were a sign of coming wonder.

Now my senior uncle gave out rhymes for a poem of seven characters and we children bent over the little tables in front of us and drew with our brush pens on beautiful thin white paper. My cousin, Eul-Choon and I sought to rival each other. He was embittered because of my fame, and because my group was the more popular. (I belonged to a very young group, endeared to parents and considered clever, so we had no difficulty getting the best dens at night for dice and cards and poetry games.) I, in turn, grudged at Eul-Choon, because of his sarcastic tongue, remembering the time when he found us roasting beans on a charcoal burner and laughed at us for using a wooden bowl, and how his group oppressed my group without good cause.

As fast as we finished, we hung up the beautiful poems in our best caligraphy all around the walls. Mine, this year, my uncle said was the best. He picked out several of our poems to put on the pillars of the house to last the whole year.

Immediately after the poetry contest Eul-Choon and I ran to the kitchen before the goblets came in. We were allowed to eat the fruits and dainties of the elders, if we approached discreetly, but we were not supposed to drink wine. We had found previously that the best way to steal drink was with a hollow straw. Goblets were hard to get rid of, when you were discovered, but the straw you could bend up in your hand. This crystal wine was soft and sweet, but if you drank too much, you became tipsy. My grandmother, who had got up for the celebration, found me rolling on the floor, laughing so hard, that she knew I had been drinking wine.

She leaned down and gave me a little knock with her hand. She spoke to me so that nobody else could hear. "Hé! Do you want to be like junior uncle? He is no *pak-sa*. All the great poets and sages knew some obedience."

"Oh, no, Grandmother!" and I got up and showed her that I could walk straight.

But Eul-Choon, although usually a more conservative child than I, had taken so much that he could not walk straight, so he was whipped.

Now the elders came in to drink wine with those of their own chronological status, to talk and to quote poetry and to wait for the passing of the Old Year. Almost everyone cried when the Old Year passed away, thinking of his memories of youth and beauty, all his old joys and regrets. Each thought how he would never again see that Old Year, and how one by one the years dropped from his life, like leaves from an Autumn tree. This was the time, of course, when each added another year to his age (not on his birthday as in the West). So New Year's was everybody's birthday. But though all cried it was not a bad sort of sadness.

Only my father was not present at this festive time. Men with debts were supposed to pay them on New Year's Eve, and the creditors were afoot that night. This year my father had more debts than usual because of my prodigal-son uncle, who ran up a good many just before he left home. So my father fled the creditors by being away. Senior uncle, the crazy-poet, was left to entertain the guests.

But my father always came back for the Ancestor Worship, slipping in after the creditors had gone. Being an eldest son, he was the priest of the family, the post which I would occupy when I grew up and when my father died. For one night he was far more honored than my crazy-poet uncle, the family scholar. Second sons were rather carefree in Korea. They inherited no responsibility nor goods unless their fathers saw fit to endow them specially, and were very poor, like grandfather, who was a fourth son and did not have to come home to do any worship. Second sons got out of a lot, especially if they had some conscientious elder brother to take care of them.

After the passing of the old year, at the beginning of the new, the Ancestors were fed. This was done in the last room from the kitchen—our most formal room. A table had been spread with the best, and everything was done according to the Book of Rites, which has told the exact ceremonial arrangement for rice, meat, candy, salt, vinegar, and pepper. The spirit of the Ancestor would come before the cock crew. All men—my father, my uncle and my more distant uncles and cousins—stood in white ceremonial dress with flowing sleeves and tassels. Crouching down on hands and knees, all bowed until the forehead almost touched the ground. Some spectators overflowed to the porch. In the room next to the last room the women waited in silence.

After the service, everybody retired for three minutes, to allow the Ancestor to eat. When the cock crew all came back. It was said that the food weighed slightly less after the Ancestor had eaten than before, but I never had opportunity to measure this scientifically.

I think that the Ancestor's Table in our house was laid for my dead mother, but I am not sure, since I was more interested in the practical results of the worship than in the meaning of it. For immediately after Ancestor-Worship, we feasted upon everything that the Ancestor had left and more besides. Little children were not made to undress on that gay night. Women did not go to their husbands' chambers. People slept where they fell. But bright and early in the morning all changed to the new clothes. Hair, hands, nails, teeth, everything was made very clean. Newly dressed children would start out to give the New Year's greeting. You went to every house in the village, and all the adults whom you met, you bowed before, all the way down to the ground. "Quase-pyungan," you said, and they replied "Quase-pyungan." In the houses you were given delicious rice cakes, seven or eight different kinds, some soft as marsh-mallow, some hard as pie, and Korean pennies with their holes in the centre. You put the pennies in your pocket, which you carried at your belt, or you strung them on the ribbons of your dress. Sometimes you had to go home before you had finished making the rounds, weighted down by too much money, and it was all money for yourself with which to gamble in the game of *mukdong*.

When I got ready to dress in the exciting dark of New Year's morning, I found my old clothes laid out for me, which my childless aunt had washed and ironed and carefully mended. I went out of doors as dawn came creeping in and I joined the other children. Everybody had a new suit but me. Yun-Koo and Chak-Doo-Shay were particularly splendid.

"Where is your new suit?" asked Yun-Koo.

"And your new overcoat?" asked Chak-Doo-Shay.

I looked down at myself and I was shamed. I was silent. Han Chung-Pa, the boy destined to be a *pak-sa*, had no clothes for New Year's. Then I lifted my head.

"My new suit and my new overcoat are in the trunk, being saved for a Grand Occasion which is coming," I told them.

These were lies. Eul-Choon overheard me and laughed. Something went wrong with my New Year's Day. I came back home very early. In the kitchen, Eul-Choon was telling my childless aunt about my lies. She also was laughing.

"There is something of the junior uncle in our little *pak-sa* too!"

But to her I said vehemently:

"Those were no lies."

Then I stole off by myself to my crazy-poet uncle's studio and took down one of the folios, in order to lose myself just as he did in the wisdom of the sages and to forget our poverty.

My grandmother came upon me several hours later, still poring over "Confucius' Digested Conversations."

"You funny child!" she exclaimed, half to herself. She came in and sat with me, for she felt lonely on that day, too.

As we were sitting there and the long white crystal day was growing slightly flushed, we looked up suddenly both at once, and there was my prodigal-son uncle standing in the doorway. His memories of New Year must have been too much for him, and he had come back. But he was wearing at a jaunty angle a Western hat which he had procured somewhere. It was the first of its kind that I had ever seen.

Chapter 4

THE MARRIAGE OF THE PRODIGAL SON

Thou still unravish'd bride of quietness. . . .
Ode on a Grecian Urn: JOHN KEATS

MY junior uncle remained home long enough to be married in the Spring. We had prepared only two years for his wedding, which was a very short time. Some prepared for thirteen or fourteen years, and I have known cases where children were betrothed before birth. The fathers would come to an agreement over their wine cups. "If my wife has a girl, I will give her to your boy, providing your wife has a boy—or vice versa." The father, in theory, had the absolute right to dispose of his son or daughter as he pleased. But in practice a consultation took place in all respectable homes, and if the mother had a strong distaste for the match, negotiations would be broken off.

My grandmother was very active in choosing the wives in our home. When the question of marrying my junior uncle came up, she remembered a modest and beautiful girl in the village from which she herself came. She had heard much favorable gossip about this girl. But in order to see for herself, my grandmother disguised herself as a peddler of embroideries, in an old dress with an ill-fitting *dong-chung* so that she was not to be recognized. Then she went to the girl's house and observed for herself. She came home with a glowing report. The girl was as good as she was beautiful, and was a perfect artist at the loom.

Therefore we set about making the proposal for my junior uncle. The initiative proposal of marriage of course always came from the bridegroom's family. Sometimes matches were indirectly managed from a girl's side of the house by having one who was not supposed to be a friend at all spread good reports about the girl where the young man's family could hear them. Many women who owned beautiful girls had tried already to approach my grandmother in this indirect way to secure me for a son-in-law. But my grandmother always declared that she must look about her for a long time before she decided on the right wife for me.

To make the proposal for my junior uncle, we selected a good match-maker. A match-maker must be neither too high nor too low in society. Above all he must know how to bluff. We selected the brother of the tall village doctor for match-maker, and he proved to be a very good bluffer. He went to the girl's father and said what a good, clever, handsome and well-brought up boy my junior uncle was, always staying at home, always working industriously (never of course letting it out that he was the prodigal son). The result was that the girl's father, after consulting the family astrologer, accepted the match.

The date for the marriage was set by the astrologer in our family, by studying the Four Pillars of Destiny of my junior uncle and of his betrothed. For a date which might do splendidly well for one pair might be entirely wrong for another. It depended upon their ages, their names, and their Four Pillars of Destiny.

The astrologer in our family was a very great scholar, one of the greatest scholars in all Korea. He possessed the famous imperial degree called *pak-sa*, the degree I thought destined for me. Only a few *pak-sas* had been conferred during his reign by the emperor, so our astrologer was both very wise and very lucky, to obtain such an honor. His name was S-h-i-n-K-y-o; I spell it out of respect. He was called an uncle of mine, that is, he was my father's first cousin, for he was a descendant of my grandfather's brother who had been the eldest son of the house. He alone in all the village could dictate to my father who always honored his words very much. He lived next door to us in a large tiled house of more than twenty guest rooms, the house of the first branch, which had been divided in my great grandfather's time when my grandfather had moved under our grass roof. Our grass roof was at the fourth side of my uncle *pak-sa's* courtyard, and our back door faced toward his front. When I was very young, he was away in the capital most of the time, helping to educate the Princes, but whenever he came home, he treated me like a father, for he considered me the boy of highest scholarly promise in the family, and favored me even above his own children.

My uncle *pak-sa* set the date of my junior uncle's marriage for the April Moon. Then my junior uncle would be twenty-two and his fiancée twenty-one. My junior uncle was really his age; many fathers lied on the birth certificate about the ages of their sons, being in such great haste to have grandsons. I knew many young fathers, fifteen or sixteen years old, and still in the village school. The mothers of their children were large mature girls, several years older. My own age had been falsified by five or six years on the village records, and my father destined me for one of these early matches.

That year there was a special excitement connected

with the coming of Spring. Everybody in the village looked forward to my junior uncle's wedding. The date had been formally announced to the bride's house, on a beautiful sheet of white paper in my uncle *pak-sa's* best caligraphy. The chests had been sent to the bride-to-be by my father in the previous September. An artisan had come to make these chests in my father's own workshop. My father bossed the job, and saw to it that they were made in just the right way. Then the brass-smith came and decorated the chests with carved brass, and finally they were painted a bright yellow. My father and my grandmother picked out in the market-place the silks, cottons and linens to fill the drawers of the two chests, and some of the goods came from the house-stores woven on our own looms. These were sent to the bride that she might use them in making her trousseau. Some girls made their clothes for a lifetime during the period of preparation and never had to make any more, for the styles did not change during hundreds of years. With the chests had been sent two heavy silver rings, jointed together, the traditional present from the bride-groom to the bride-to-be. These were so heavy that when women worked they took them off and hung them on the ribbons of their clothing.

My junior uncle of course had nothing to do with the preparations. The polite way for a bridegroom to act was to pretend that he didn't know a wedding was coming to him at all. So my junior uncle never showed whether he was nervous or sorry or glad. He just fooled around home and wrote some didactic poetry, and was unusually obedient so that he seemed temporarily a re-formed man. We boys found him very agreeable, for outside the house he liked to observe us and make funny remarks.

Spring came very gradually. As the Winter retreated, you felt half-sorry to see it go. The snow melted reluctantly, and the sad white patches seemed to you like lost friends who would be missed as soon as they were gone away for good. You were reminded now of how beautiful the Winter had been, with fantastic gray branches under a fairy powder of snow and the blue intense skies; and how the atmosphere in the distance seemed full of tiny dazzling crystals and was as sharp as wine; now you forgot the dismal horror of the Winter blasts. The air was changing too. Oh, how surprised you were to see the plum-blossom one day! It came while there was still snow left on the ground. It was called the flower of first love. It was like snow, snatched up by the tree, given life and soul and a fragrance like immortality. . . .

You were beside yourself when you had seen the plum-flower. You could not leave; yet you could not stay forever watching because you had to go back into the studio to read the beautiful poets. And you could not bear to break off the plum-flower—there was something too sacred about it, for it was the first flower of Spring. So you ran back and forth, back and forth. . . . No more to sing the classical Korean song of the bamboo, recited during the winter months!

> Tree you are not,
> Grass you are not,
> Nothing is more straight than you.
> Inside why are you so clean?
> Bamboo, for this besides I love you,
> All four seasons you are green!

Poets turned to romanticism instead of classicism.

Then one day the wild geese came back from the South, in unswerving flight like an arrow across the sky, following the rays of the sun, and making a very different sound from their mournful wailing in the Autumn. Now that call snapped through the air like the salute of Life, the conqueror, full of rapture, full of strength, full of triumph. And in answer the grass became green, Earth uncovered herself, she breathed softly in the sun. Increasing, ever increasing, grew the glad noise of Spring. It was not the sharp cry of wild geese, nor the excited chirping of sparrows, it was not the barking of dogs, nor the cackling of hens, it was not the sound of the farmer-boy whistling on the farms, nor the woman humming in time to the beating of freshly washed flax, nor the girl singing at the loom, but all of these and more. It was the sound of the Spring, shooting up as from a gushing source below the surface of the earth, when the prison-wardens, Death and Winter, have suddenly said, "Now, I'll let you go." The water ran once more, the trees' bark was almost heard to crackle in budding, in the air was the whirring of tiny wings. The fat hen walked as if lame over the grass blades, very slowly, looking for still another dainty to peck. And how different came the perfume of Spring from that poignant and mellow smell of the Autumn! One made your heart ache with weeping, and the other made it dance feverishly like effervescing wine. The ghost of Spring floated everywhere like a frail smoke.

The garden was all a-twitter, as you wandered through it, and all day long looked as fresh as the dawn. There were little foamy flecks of green about all the trees, those old familiar trees. I say familiar, for you remembered them from your earliest years, all their contours and shadows. If you were the crazy-poet, you thought of that Korean poem:

> Years slip by like the water—
> Suddenly Spring comes again:

In the old garden, young life is green
With flowers of a long-ago fame.
Bring me flagons of new wine—
I'll be a Spring Gypsy to-day.

In our garden the high rocks were covered with recru-
descent moss, and even the fantastic water basins of
stone looked young again in spite of their great age. You
loitered there by the poet's stream and made a Spring
flute from a dandelion reed. You heard a humming in
your ears as of a bee; you struck wildly at the air; you
turned and saw Chak-Doo-Shay and Yun-Koo. . . .

Every year my crazy-poet uncle would retire into the
studio and write another volume of Spring poems. He
had a special drawer for them in the library. This year he
composed several on the famous line of an old Chinese
classic: "The Mountain-flower turns toward me with a
smile." This year I wrote a good many myself.

The bride's green dress was done, and her room was
ready. The whole house had been cleaned and decorated
anew. Poems were hung on all the doors, and pictures of
orchids and bamboo groves on silken hangings. The
painting was done by a distant uncle of mine, who was
a famous caligrapher. He had the degree of *chin-sa*—
that which the poet Li Po received. It was not so high
a degree as that held by my most illustrious uncle, the
pak-sa, for there were a number of *chin-sas* in the country, but in painting and in caligraphy this *chin-sa* was
superior.

At last it was only ten days before the wedding and
the time had come to begin the preparation of the wedding viands. All the village contributed their services.
Cook-soo was a very prominent dish: *cook-soo* made
from pickles, beef and pork and preserved pears, all
chopped up and put in chicken soup with noodles—a

delectable dish. *Kim-chi*, the pickle ingredient, was dug up from the ground. It was not exactly a vegetable, nor a pickle, but had a sharp vitalizing saline taste. Made from tender long vegetables, something like cabbage, it was preserved with salt, hot red pepper and sometimes fish, and put underground for a year in tall jugs six feet high. Of course a quantity of cows were killed: hundreds of fish prepared, and many thousand wedding cakes.

There were two main divisions of rice cakes made at the wedding, those made by the women and those made by the men. The rice cakes made by the men were cooked out of doors in the garden over an open fire on a plough-share washed very clean. I made the fire for the cooks, who were the oldest scholars of the village school, young men accomplished somewhat in painting and caligraphy. First fat was poured on the hot plough-share, and the cakes were made as breakfast pancakes are made in the West. While the cakes were still hot, pictures were drawn on them with a brush pen, pictures of dragons, chrysanthemum, plum-flowers, roses, in seven or eight different edible colors. Some boys were very clever at this. On other cakes were written characters meaning "Longevity," "Wealth," "Prosperity," "Happiness," "Have many male children," "Good luck," etc. These large round cakes were a beautiful white before painting, and had exquisite finish, as all those with defect were eaten by the cooks. There must be no spot or footprint of the spoon, of course. The cooks were never disabled by eating too many defective cakes, for there were many little boys sitting around them, waiting to be fed and watching their art, like Yun-Koo, Chak-Doo-Shay and me. On the outskirts of the group my junior uncle would come and stand, to make ludicrous remarks with a perfectly sober face. When he appeared everybody laughed, and he was told this was no place for him. "Go away! Go away!" He was not given a single cake.

The line most used on the wedding cakes was "Soo, Foo, Da Nam-cha" (Health, Wealth, and Many Boy Children). It was a line of poetry dating back to more than 2300 B. C. in the time of the good king Yao of China. A story was handed down about Yao, how he was told by an astrologer that he might have these three things, and he laughed at them as valueless. Living too long, he said, he would only gain the scorn of the younger generation, possessions meant endless care and endless responsibility, children brought anxiety and many times sorrow. Evidently wedding parties do not hold with Yao on these matters.

The wedding day dawned, a perfect day of April. Very early the wedding party started from our house to walk to the home of the bride, about five miles away. There were two dozen horses in the party, for the most distinguished rode on horse-back, at a slow pace. More than a hundred other men followed on foot. My junior uncle, in a new plain suit of white silk and a heavy horse-hair turban (his Western hat was discarded now), rode in the very front, on a magnificent horse decorated with red leather ribbons and bells. This horse was a musical horse and knew how to step daintily and to harmonize the bells. Every horse will not do at a wedding. This one belonged to my most illustrious uncle, the *pak-sa*, and had a social engagement book for months in advance as he was needed for weddings all over the country round. My junior uncle's two best friends—who would have corresponded to Yun-Koo and Chak-Doo-Shay in my own case—led the horse, and they had to keep up a dignified dance alongside of the accomplished animal, harmonizing their steps with his and with the jingling of the bells. Behind him rode my uncle *pak-sa*, and near him I was riding too. Eul-Choon had no horse, but my grandmother would not let me go without a horse and a leading servant, because I was the youngest child and the darling of her heart. Accompanying us were two dozen singers who kept up a loud and jubilant droning all the way. Besides being good singers, they were obliged to be strong men for they were to carry back the bride in the bride's sedan. It takes four men to carry the bride's sedan and they arrange the porterage in shifts, for sometimes brides are fat, although my new aunt did not prove to be one of the fat ones.

The bride's house was beautifully decorated with peach blossoms, just cut from the trees. As soon as my junior uncle arrived, he was given an entire new set of clothes, even stockings and underwear, all made by the bride's hands. Presently he appeared in his new formal overcoat and it was pale green. His friends gathered around him, and examined the sewing, and congratulated him upon getting such a clever needle-woman for a wife. They had done this however to my crazy-poet uncle when he was married, and my fat aunt was no needle-woman to boast about, but this was polite usage. A band of musicians was playing. The guests were given a grand feast, particularly my junior uncle. Ten men were required to carry the table which was all for him, a long table like a banquet table in America, but my junior uncle sat there alone, and in front of him was a pile of cakes, four feet square, a dozen roast chickens, and other things in proportion.

As soon as my uncle wiped his mouth and fingers with the napkin, the best pupils of the school in that village approached him, and offered him beautiful verses of their own composition, slandering him, and pretending to be hostile. He read them and replied at once in verses of his own, made up extemporaneously. In this he was very clever and quick but it was no more than was expected of such a scholarly family as ours. If he had shown himself unfamiliar with the classics, the boys were considered at liberty to seize all that was left on his table, and it would have been their right to feast on it as they chose. In the dialogue which followed my uncle proved himself master of the situation. The schoolboys said, "We want to take these things to our teacher," and my junior uncle said, "But I want to take them to my father and mother." So presently a whole wagon was loaded with them, and the oxen went off with their burden to my home. I planned that I would be very brilliant if I were ever put in the bridegroom's fix.

The wedding ceremony was solemn, like the worship at an Ancestor's Table. The bride's figure could just be discerned through the semi-transparent curtain hanging between her room and that of our wedding party. The couple had never seen each other before, face to face, and were not supposed to know each other by sight until the morning after their wedding night. This seems a barbaric custom to a Western reader, no doubt. But the Oriental viewpoint is different. My junior uncle and my new aunt were not two individuals brought together by egoistic passions, but merely representatives of Adam and Eve who fulfill their lawful duty. To choose your own wife, to consult your individual taste in the matter of propagation, was considered horrifying, licentious and uncivilized by the people in my ancient community. No man of breeding would dream of looking at his wife affectionately, nor speaking to her sweetly before others, even if he loved her for herself. Marriage was business, not sentiment. My new aunt's senior uncle, who was the eldest son and the priest of her family, performed the short and simple ceremony. He read words which went something like this: "This contracts you two not to forget each other for a hundred years. And now you are bound together always, for woe or for happiness." The cup of wine was given to the bridegroom, who drank a little and passed it through the curtain to the bride; she touched it to her lips also, and they drank of the same cup. Then the bride and bridegroom bowed to each other solemnly through the curtain.

My new aunt left immediately in the bride's sedan, which was kept by the village for that purpose: a red and green chair with characters painted upon it, meaning "Longevity, Wealth, Male children." It was a long journey for a frightened girl with only men attendants. In every village the carriers stopped and the people ran out of their houses to peer in at the bride and to say, "Oh, how beautiful she is! What a beautiful bride she is!" Of course they said the same thing about my fat aunt when she was married to my crazy-poet uncle, and she was rather a fat bride. But my new aunt really was beautiful. And how she cried! You could tell that she had been crying all the way when she got to our house. The brides always cried very much, and for some reason everybody wanted to see them doing it.

Sometimes the bridegrooms cried, if they were very young. I could not help noticing in those days that nobody I ever saw *liked* getting married. But my junior uncle did not seem to mind. He was just indifferent. He had arrived in advance on his musical horse, and was now with his friends, all of them rather gay young men who had been married a long time.

One of them fired a shot into the sky and shouted

loudly as the bride passed through the tall sugar-cane
gate. This was customary in order to frighten off any
evil ghosts who had followed her from the other village
to breed sickness and pestilence among us.

When the bride's sedan came up to the door of the
house, the right-hand lady and the left-hand lady were
waiting to lead her to her seat in the garden under the
blossoming fruit trees, and to be as kind to her as possible. They were chosen from the best and most beautiful
of Song-Dune-Chi. The bride's toilet-case, needle-basket
and such like small articles brought with her in the sedan
were taken into the house for her. One intimate recep-
tacle a bride always had, bringing it with her like a hat-
box: a small round bowl or basin, delicately fashioned
and decorated and given her by some very near relative.
It was a practical article for she might become nauseated
on the way, which was very likely to happen if the carriers had taken too much wine; or if they considered that
they had not been given enough, for then they shook up
the sedan purposely.

My new aunt was led into the garden over the silk
bridal path to the long picnic table, loaded with a feast
similar to that provided for my junior uncle in her village.
At this table she sat all alone except for the right-hand
lady, who fed her with small silver chop-sticks, and the
left-hand lady, who tried to converse with her. But my
new aunt only wept and cast down her eyes. All she
would eat was a little hard-boiled egg, only enough to
keep her from starvation. She sent all the food on her
table back to her mother and elder brother. This was
the orthodox way.

Throughout the garden at smaller and smaller tables,
according to their age and degree of importance, sat
women and girls of our village being feasted. Among

them, not far from Ok-Dong-Ya, was my new aunt's
maid-of-honor, her only attendant on her wedding journey besides her men relatives who were there as guests.
It was the bride's little sister. She had unusually long
hair for a little girl and I thought her beautiful. When
the bride cried, she cried too.

After the feast was over all the young girls of the village went with my new aunt and her little maid into my
junior uncle's new room, where the bride's chests, sent
the day before, were neatly fitted into the wall. (In Korean homes there was usually a place in the wall for
most things to go, so that a room might be spacious and
free.) Everybody examined my new aunt's trousseau,
and exclaimed and admired. They sat with her laughing
and talking until midnight.

Out in another room, my childless aunt was giving my
junior uncle certain instructions. I got behind the door
and listened and the next day was able to tell Yun-Koo
and Chak-Doo-Shay how to kiss the bride. My childless
aunt did not know I was there.

"When you go in, you must turn out the light," said
my childless aunt. "She will be sitting with her face to
the wall, at the screen of the mandarin ducks, beside the
pillow-of-two. Grasp her and put her under the comfort
when you undress her, because if you don't she will be
cold."

Then my childless aunt told him how to undress the
bride, a rather important piece of information, for she
was very mysteriously wrapped up, like a great parcel,
with long silk gloves on and even her sleeves tied down.
The last layer, according to my childless aunt, was not
to be taken off, for it was the wedding pajama, which
the bride had put on underneath everything before she
left home.

My junior uncle was embarrassed and kept saying,

"Don't talk, don't talk. I know all about that. I know how to handle her. That's easy."

At midnight my new aunt's relatives and her little maid said good-by to her, and left for home. My new aunt wept and wept at the parting and used up all the long silk kerchiefs which were laid out ready for her use. Two dozen there were—for a bride is supposed to cry hard at this time, whether she is sincere or not. But my new aunt wept so hard that my cousin Ok-Dong-Ya wept too with sympathy, and came out of the bride's room weeping, where I found her on the porch, behind a pillar, shaken with sobs.

On the first morning after the wedding, in front of my father and my grandmother, the little aunt sat down on her legs, although no chair was there, and inclined her head almost to the floor. Of course she did not drop forward on her hands and knees as polite boys and men do to a superior, or in greeting a contemporary equal; the women never did that. As I myself explain it, skirts being very full and stiff might lift up behind in an indecorous way.

Her bow was just formal greeting. This was no sure sign that she was going to be obedient to my father and my grandmother. Besides, all brides had to act obedient the first few days even if at heart they were as stubborn as that celebrated girl in China who was changed by the ghosts into a cow because she disregarded all manners toward her husband's family, and would not even lend one dress of her grand trousseau to her poor old mother-in-law who wished to go to a temple. There are three ways of speaking in Korea, the first, to an older and superior, the second, to equals and chronological playmates, the third, to children and dogs; brides are not supposed to speak disrespectfully even to dogs for the first few days.

Our grass-roofed house had eight pillars on the porch, each with a beautiful poem which was changed every New Year. One year a teaching of Confucius was posted on a pillar and my prodigal-son uncle used to point it out to us children: "Obedience is the source of hundred manners." (Then he would order us in words like the sages' not to smoke tobacco or steal drink, until you would almost believe that he was as good a man as my father, except that his actions in running up drinking debts for my father to pay made his ethical teachings seem hypocritical.) Since from her cradle my little aunt had been trained in the Confucian doctrine that "Obedience is the source of hundred manners," she was really sincere, and a far more obedient girl than you could find anywhere in the West. She was even good for my country.

As was the custom about three days after the wedding, my prodigal-son uncle was sent on his first long visit to his mother-in-law and his father-in-law. A bridegroom had to make this visit alone, staying several months perhaps. In the bride's village when he first arrived the bridegroom was likely to have a hard time after the big school boys got hold of him, for he would be skinned of clothes, and hung up by the feet. Then all the school boys would prick him with pine needles and demand the truth.

"What did you say to her first?"

"Did you bow to her?"

"Did you kiss her?" (If bridegrooms said no to this, they would only be more pricked.)

"Did you take off her clothes? What did you take off first?"

"What did you do next, and what did you do next, and what did you do next?"

They would prick and prick the bridegroom with dry pine needles loudly calling him robber and thief for taking the virginity of the most beautiful maiden of their village, until the bridegroom compromised by a treat of wine and dainties. Thus arose the humane custom of employing a detective, some little boy in a bride's family, to be the spy, and rescue a bridegroom by summoning father- and mother-in-law when the situation became too critical.

As my prodigal-son uncle set off on the white horse, my father counselled him about his associates.

"Among the flax, goldenrods grow straight," my father said, quoting a homely Korean proverb.

My crazy-poet uncle reminded my prodigal-son uncle how according to Confucius all surplus energy should be devoted to literary activity. As for my grandmother, she only folded her hands imploringly, and said, "Don't, don't!"

My prodigal-son uncle's absence gave the little aunt a chance to adjust to the situation, to wear just ordinary clothes and not to keep her face so thickly powdered as at first. She could be more at home with us; when her husband was there she was shy.

During the first few days after the wedding, she moved around quietly in the background, taking in the dainties to the men's dining room, passing the gourd of water to the women. The men never used these beautiful yellow vessels which came from the garden and made the most natural kind of cups; men's drinking bowls were always of metal. I wanted the little aunt to give me a drink from the women's gourd, because she was pretty, and I liked that kind of drinking cup, but my grandmother stopped her.

"No, no, child! Don't let him have that, or his beard

will never grow. Your senior brother-in-law wants to marry him early."

It was thought that boys who drank from the women's gourd would have feminine characteristics when they grew up; it being considered a sad thing not to have a beard. My family was just waiting until I could give them a grandson at the age of fifteen.

My little aunt's first piece of sewing in our house, I remember, was a *dong-chung* for my father, which she finished late one night when nobody knew, and which my grandmother praised highly. My little aunt and my father understood each other from the beginning. Both believed from the bottom of their hearts that "Obedience is the source of a hundred manners."

In the evenings now the maidens of the village crowded around my little aunt to ask her questions. They laughed and laughed and turned away their faces. They wanted to get some of her experiences, what she thought of being married, and whether she liked it. I heard them talking when they didn't know I was there. The maidens of Song-Dune-Chi used to talk in a very foolish way:

"I met so-and-so to-day and he smiled at me. Don't you think he is awfully cute? He will make somebody an awfully handsome husband."

"But so-and-so has the more beautiful husband!"

"Oh, I don't like fat men!"

"Don't you? Oh, I like fat men! I hope my husband will be some beautiful fat man."

Their imaginations turned always to their future husbands.

Once when she didn't know I was outside the door, listening, I heard Ok-Dong-Ya say: "My future husband? I want my future husband to be just like my cousin Chung-Pa. He must be good-looking, with eyes and nose and mouth and laugh like that, he must be full of fifty devils, he must be able to beat all others his age wrestling, he must be such a great poet and scholar that he is sure to become a *pak-sa*. I would rather have a poet-husband one day out of the year than a stupid man all the year round. But he *must* come back once a year, like my grandfather, so there can be some babies in the house."

She then said she would have three daughters and two sons, one son to take care of her, and one to be a crazy-poet, just like her father and her senior uncle.

Her playmates asked her:

"But aren't you going to have a third son, like your junior uncle?"

Ok-Dong-Ya shook her head. She did not say why because the little aunt was there and *she* did not yet know about junior-uncle, nor the debts and the trouble he raised in our household. No, two sons were enough, Ok-Dong-Ya said, two sons and three daughters. One daughter she would marry far to the East, one daughter far to the West, so that she might take a long exciting journey to see them sometimes; the third daughter, the daughter of her heart, she would marry close at home, so that she might see her every day.

Soon after this, my prodigal-son uncle returned, and it all came out that he had made many more debts for my father to pay during his long visit to his mother-in-law. Some of his debts the mother-in-law herself had paid, wishing to keep peace with our family. She respected our family name and village so much that she had no hard feelings against the match-maker for misrepresenting my prodigal uncle; certainly she had a very refined sense of values.

Chapter 5

DOMESTICITY AND VANISHING SPRING

I lived with visions for my company. . . .
Sonnets from the Portuguese:
ELIZABETH BARRETT BROWNING

Spring in the window where leisurely I robe!
Strolling suavely abroad I feast my eyes.
But the stream is outward bound
Where the melted flowers are strewn—
You may lead others to my paradise. . . .
(O flowers, don't go!)

THIS was one of the crazy-poet's favorite Korean poems, and I think of him when I quote it. He was a man supremely satisfied with life as it is. At heart he was a child. He was like his master, Lao Tze, the Old, or White-Haired Child. Everything in Nature was his friend: the cuckoo, the swallow, the nightingale, the white heron, the turtle, the rabbit, the dragon-fly and the fish, all were poets together with the crazy-poet, and not one ever tried either to imitate or to change the way of any other. *Laissez-faire* had always been my uncle's Taoist doctrine, in regard to himself and to other men. He did not try to be like my father, always thinking of grass for the roof, sandals for the feet, and rice for the babies, and he did not try to persuade my father to be like him and enjoy life, sitting under a tree by the poet's stream. The poet's stream was an artificial current of water passing the kitchen and the poet's seat, and ending out of sight in a drain. Bowls and flagons of wine were sent poets on this stream, and when they finished drinking, they just let the bowls float on, which eventually returned to the kitchen.

All this while the spirit of Spring was getting stronger as the second, the third, the fourth month went by. It

no longer hovered elusively beyond the reach, somewhere over a treetop; it had come to earth. Spring was
not only a breath of the air, it was under all the baskets
and the wine cups, it was between all the grass blades,
soaking through and through the ground, it lay at the
bottom of the clear stream, and everybody had it in his
heart. Everybody and everything was drunk. The little
leaves had grown big and waved luxuriously, the fertile
grass was at full height, the shady foliages of trees were
now the most marvellous, without one yellow leaf. The
flowers melted in your hand. Ok-Dong-Ya and I cried
to see it, as we picked the perfect branch to show to one
another, and the whole dissolved like mist leaving only
petals on the ground. Each person felt sorry that the
Spring was going and the Dragon Festival must come,
although everybody always enjoyed the gay Dragon Festival. Men tried to cheer each other up by saying,
"Don't feel bad that the Spring is getting late: be glad
that she is yours at last." I know many songs of regret
about this period. One is the song to the birds:

> Birds, oh birds, don't grieve for fallen flowers!
> Flowers are helpless when the winds assault.
> If the Spring too swiftly vanishes,
> Is it a bird's fault?

As Spring grew more intoxicating, the song of the frogs
swelled and swelled. Orientals love frogs as most Westerners cannot understand. Westerners are afraid of frogs,
thinking them weird or grotesque, and their very word
for the musical creature makes you feel a frog is something silly and absurd like a monkey or donkey. To the
Korean there is magic and poetry just in the sound of
the name, *kaguri*.

In the late Spring rain, when the world seemed as if it

were gasping and sparkling with pleasure after its
drenching, when all the leaves and grass looked painted
anew, the kaguri burst out singing. Then Ok-Dong-Ya
sped out of the house to see them. In the rain-filled low
places of the pine grove, and in the garden ponds, in the
rice fields and everywhere, the frogs were singing. She
clapped her hands and ran to the garden pond. Sitting
like a frog on the edge, she looked longingly into the
pool. She made up a song:

"Oh, frogs, I wish I were a frog and could jump in
there and play and sing with you! But alas, I have this
human body, and so I must stay outside. I cannot join
you."

She was very fond of soliloquizing like this. She would
capture a butterfly and put him under a basket with large
holes. Then she would look in at him and sing a song
which she made up: "O butterfly, your wings are so beautiful! Now won't you sing a song that will be as beautiful
as your wings?"

When she was in the garden, Ok-Dong-Ya looked like
one of the flowers, and seemed fed as they were on sunlight and rain, not human being's food. She was a very
beautiful child with face like painted ivory and fine black
eyebrows like down-feather. She always wore grass color
or rosy-red. She had a long plait black as a lacquer box
and tied with a cherry-colored bow. Chak-Doo-Shay,
Yun-Koo and I would come with our miniature dragon
boats to play on the pond. She would laugh and run
away.

Chak-Doo-Shay, with his artful fingers, was a fine
hand at making dragon boats. He carved them from the
same kind of wood used for wooden shoes; long, slender,
and delicate, with dragons for heads, which he painted
red, green, and yellow. When we grew tired of these

exquisite inanimate toys, we would chase the living dragon-fly. Sometimes we sought him with a light hickory frame on which we had collected spiders' web; or if we could find no spider-thread, we would hold up our fore fingers and call deceiving words to the dragon-fly, like the children in the old Korean poem:

> The little naked children
> With frames of spiders' thread,
> To and fro along the streams, shout:
> "Dragon-fly, dragon-fly, don't go that way or you will die.
> If you want to live, come this way, dragon-fly."
> Such is the world, n'est-ce-pas?

Especially my crazy-poet uncle was maddened during this season and always drank a good deal of wine. To some people the season of late Spring is the most poetic time of the year. They are feverish to enjoy every blossoming branch before it passes. It is a time of perfect rapture, and faint melancholy, as in the Korean poem:

> Why is the Spring growing late on the clear stream by the grass roof?
> Snow-white the fragrant pear blossom, the willow's gold is weak.
> In ten thousand cloud-strewn valleys, the ghosts are wailing.
> Ah, Spring too is a wraith.... (O why!)

My crazy-poet uncle would go to the forest and to the solitary ravines with a bundle of brush pens and some Korean ink. There he would compose on green oak leaves. When he got all straightened up, he would write out the whole poem on India paper, to be bound and placed in our library. His leaf manuscripts would many times be found two miles down the stream. Some ignorant woman might be wrapping meat and rice in oak leaves to go into the fire, and suddenly she would run to her husband, saying: "My! My! Oak trees can write!"

Then he would identify the characters as being those of the well-known crazy-poet of Song-Dune-Chi, and the leaves would be treasured in the family possessions.

To my fat aunt the crazy-poet was a mystery. He had never cared much about women, for he cared only about his beloved poets and about making up poetry; how indeed was a man like my uncle, the Poet Laureate of a whole district, to look for intellectual sympathy and companionship in a wife? He had allowed my father to marry him again from a sense of the social and biological necessity of it, but he only wanted women to keep out of his way for the most part. So he was always making my fat aunt cry, because she feared she had offended him. Somebody, I am afraid, was always making my fat aunt cry, she appeared so sincere, good-natured and awkward in every situation. But she seemed to like to cry, and if nobody else did, she made herself cry by singing over and over folk-songs in a sad tone of voice.

She would stop crying, when my grandmother came around. But she liked to have the little aunt for audience.

"My feet are sore, my legs are aching! I have been working all day on just one mouthful of rice-soup!" As she thought about it, the tears came rolling down, making wet spots as big as cherries on the bamboo carpet. "How hungry I am! How tired I am!" She reached for a pear, sobbing between bites: "Oh-h-h-h! How tired I am!" (But now and then she forgot to sob because the pear tasted so good.) "Oh, how my husband condemned me to-day! It is a terrible thing to be married to a man who condemns you and with everything he says quotes a poem."

My grandmother came in at this time and overheard her. She said in annoyance: "Daughter, what are you complaining about? You have the finest poet in the country round for a husband, and yet he is not a bohemian. He is very nervous, very sensitive. You should study harder to please him."

All Korean women are not like cows, but my fat aunt was very much like an innocent cow; and as she could not weave nor sew, my grandmother felt that she was not an asset to the family. Indeed both she and the crazy-poet were completely dependent upon others, but my grandmother never thought of it in that way.

Yet my crazy-poet uncle was so very absent-minded! One day my father was away from home and my grand-mother went to market. She told my crazy-poet uncle about the clothes which were drying on the banks of a farther stream, and about the rice grains which were spread out in the garden to sun. While she was gone, a heavy thunder-shower came, but my uncle was so busy writing poetry that he did not hear the thunder nor see the lightning. The grain was lost in the mud and the clothes were washed away down the stream. How dis-couraged my grandmother was! Yet my grandmother never blamed my crazy-poet uncle for his absent-mind-edness, which she considered a credit to the family. But the fat aunt did not have the excuse. Oh, that fat aunt was awkward in the kitchen! She did everything wrong and several times almost cut her fingers off in slicing vegetables for *kim-chi*. When she tied the ribbon bow around her baby's foot, it was no more graceful than if around a potato.

"My! Older sister, you are just like this baby!" little aunt said, laughing, as she retied it for her. "You need somebody to help you, don't you?"

The other smiled solemnly and a large fat tear ran down her face.

She was always making blundering mistakes with re-

gard to her crazy-poet husband too. If he wanted a pair
of stockings, she would pull everything out of the wedding trunk and pile them in the middle of the floor. When
the crazy-poet, who had not much patience, condemned
her, she would go and card flax, sighing, while her sniffs
kept time to the click of her shuttle. Presently she would
begin to sing sad songs about a beautiful cast-off concubine.

My fat aunt *always* cried more than usual in the Spring
about the time that my uncle deserted his bed every
night to spend the moon-lit hours with the muse. Then
it was hard for her. She could not understand why a man
should lose his sleep, no matter how beautiful the night
was. She would come out of the room in the morning
with a long face:

". . . (sniff) . . . I haven't done anything, and he went
out to the studio and spent all night!"

She would complain like this to the little aunt. If my
grandmother overheard her, she would shake the cau-
tioning finger:

"Darling, be careful! Never make that nose-noise
again when you are sleeping with him. Your husband
is very nervous."

So my fat aunt would cry and cry and think she had
made the nose-noise whenever my uncle went into his
studio for the night.

One night when the moon came up and my uncle
jumped out of bed and ran to the studio to write, my fat
aunt waked too and ran after him.

"O dear! O dear!" she sobbed—"Did I do it again? I
didn't mean to. Come back. I won't make the nose-noise
again." (All these words I heard from the next room,
where I lay in my bed. Then I peeped out and saw my
uncle and aunt in their pajamas.)

"O God! What a stupid woman this is!" soliloquized my uncle. "She has made me forget my rhyme! What was it? I had it in my head as I came out. Oh me! Where are the beautiful women at the capital? Where are they? Lan-Hyang [Orchid Perfume] who could write exquisite poems and paint gorgeous characters, Yu-Cha (The Willow Child) who danced like a reed in the wind, who sang to the words of my poems, and who gracefully entertained wandering bohemians, so they wouldn't be lonesome! Where are they now? They knew how to value a poet. I look around me and what do I see—only a wife!"

Here my crazy-poet uncle, still clutching his brush pen, dashed out bare-foot and in his night-suit toward the rice fields. . . .

Chapter 6

THE GARDEN OF THE LOTUS BLOSSOM

And there were gardens bright with sinuous rills
Where blossom'd many an incense-bearing tree;
And here were forests ancient as the hills,
Enfolding sunny spots of greenery.
      Kubla Khan: SAMUEL TAYLOR COLERIDGE

MY grandmother felt very dissatisfied with my crazy-poet uncle's match, but now nothing could be done about it. Match-makers were often reviled for misrepresentation. A clever one always kept a loop-hole by which to escape. The match-maker of our village once had a difficult client to marry, a boy who was almost entirely blind. So he went to a very very far place and explained to the father of the girl that this boy was an excellent match, hard-working and a good student, of a first rate family willing to do everything for him—in fact there was only one fault to be found with the match. He did not say what that fault was. Then the father of the girl became very eager, and asked, what was that fault, for certainly the other details seemed good. The match-maker replied, "Oh, no! There is one objection which will be insurmountable."

The father grew more and more impatient.

"What is it? What is it?"

At last the match-maker said, "I will tell you, it is too far." "Far" was an idiom for blind, because in my country it is considered impolite to call personal defects by their true name. As "it" is the same as "he" in Korean, this was equivalent to saying, "He is too blind." But the father did not understand it in that way, and he said, "Oh, that makes no difference!" The match-maker continued to say, "Too far, too far!" until the father was crazy to conclude the match, which he thought must be very good on account of the match-maker's feigned reluctance. After the marriage when it was discovered that the boy was almost completely blind, the family of the bride felt that they had been cheated, and bitterly reproached the match-maker. But he was all prepared, and said to them, "Didn't I say 'too far! too far!' ?"

This match-maker could not have been sued in a law-court, because he had left a way out. And my grandmother could not sue our match-maker either, for she had listened to the lying words of women who came from the same village as the fat aunt. There was one friend in particular, with whom the fat aunt used to waste her time gossiping. This friend was a tiny little woman who curled her tongue around five times when she spoke and that was almost continuously. Once when these two—the fat aunt and her friend—were washing clothes on the rocks, some distance from home, a Japanese soldier came down the stream.

In those days the dull blue military clothes of the Japanese were still an unfamiliar sight to the white-clad people of my remote village. My fat aunt and the little thin woman were badly scared, and did not know what to do. Then up jumped my aunt bare-foot, and she ran back home so fast she did not know how she reached there. The next day her feet were all wrinkled up, so that she could scarcely walk, and when Ok-Dong-Ya giggled and followed her around, asking "Mother, what is the matter with your feet?" she was ashamed of her cowardice. The other little thin woman ordinarily moved very fast. When she fed chickens, you could not believe your eyes. I

never saw a woman go over ground so fast. Now she was
here, now she was there! (Her brain wasn't like that
though, for she had no more intelligence than a feather.)
When my fat aunt fed the hens, *she* took all day. Yet
when that Japanese soldier came, she proved to be a
superior runner to her friend, for the little thin woman
just had strength enough to get to the nearest rice field,
where she put her head in among the tall grain, so no one
could see her face, but all her back was still on the street.
So the next day she boasted to the fat aunt.

"*I* wasn't afraid of that Japanese soldier. *I* almost hit
him on the head with my washing stick. But *you* ran
away."

My father and my crazy-poet uncle laughed at my fat
aunt's fears of the Japanese soldier, but my grandmother
was always disturbed when the Japanese were mentioned. My people always spoke of them as "the savages,"
and they were thought to have no civilization. They were
a new race compared to the Koreans and their morals
were not like ours. Among his chronological drinking
friends, my father used to tell a funny story about a Japanese who lived for twelve years in the market-place five
miles below our village. Suddenly he invited my father
to his house for a celebration. Jumping up and down for
joy, he said:

"I have a son! I have a son! Come to my house for the
celebration."

"But is your wife here?" my father asked.

"No, my wife is at home. She has a son."

My father still could not understand.

"Then you have been to see her recently?"

"No, not for twelve years."

"And you have a son?"

"Oh, yes! But I left a younger brother at home. Now I have a son!"

According to the Japanese this younger brother had only done his duty with great piety and family devotion. In our country to have sex intercourse with a sister-in-law even if your brother had died, was a crime punishable by death and was not even mentioned in polite society. Your sister-in-law was considered as your own daughter or sister. It is hard for the Western mind to conceive how fully my father accepted the wife of his youngest brother into his immediate family. Her welfare and her children's welfare were as dear to him as that of his own children. He made no difference. In return, she gave him every service in her power, and would have forgotten loyalty to her own blood for her adopted brother, and her mother-in-law. In this the little aunt was not unlike Ruth in the Bible.

Very often of course there was a conflict in family loyalties. For instance, there had been a law-suit in my family several generations back because a blood-daughter of Hans had betrayed a favorable burial-place in the mountains to her husband's family. This alien family had made use of our family secret, and had appropriated our spot, which was destined, the scholars in my family knew, to bring a *pak-sa* to a descendant of the ancestor buried there. We went to law about it, but the province lawyer had been bribed. We lost irretrievably that particular site, and did not have the satisfaction of seeing the defendant whipped in court. The spot that was going to make me a *pak-sa* was kept a profound secret.

My fat aunt was sometimes divided in *her* family loyalties, which brings me to a famous fight which once occurred between her mother and our grandmother. The crazy-poet's mother-in-law was a very rich widow who owned many pear orchards near the village of my childless aunt. My grandmother and this woman never got on well together, although you would not think it to hear them talk face to face. Each in her heart felt that she had been cheated by the match-maker, and that the other's child was not good enough for her own. They would come around in front of each other, and no women could be more polite and well-bred, but as soon as they turned to each other the back, their expressions changed as if they had swallowed poison. My grandmother never said it out loud, but you knew inside she was jumping up and down, clenching her fist and thinking, "I hate this woman!" The widow was not so good at controlling herself as my grandmother, for she did not come of so ancient, honored and noble family, and she sometimes let biting, sarcastic words drop down, particularly when my grandmother made excuses why the grandchild should not visit her at more frequent intervals and for longer periods. But my grandmother had no intention that the fat baby should be spoiled by this woman as the fat aunt had been spoiled, until he was able to do nothing with distinction and had no sense of manners in social intercourse. In his other grandmother's home he would not even be forced to use his spoon and chopsticks properly, my grandmother believed.

The widow was unusually anxious to quarrel with my grandmother just now, because she felt that my grandmother had made longer preparation and had bought more cows and chickens and above all more clothes for the wedding of my prodigal-son uncle and the little aunt than for the crazy-poet and her daughter. The fat aunt's mother was also curious about my junior uncle's wife, and so she made going to market an excuse for stopping overnight at our house.

The rich woman arrived in her splendid ox-cart with solid wooden wheels and two closed compartments. She was drawn by a magnificent black ox with long shining horns, and on the ox's back, her chauffeur was sitting. Her personal maid walked behind. Since maid and chauffeur walked most of the way, and easily kept up with the ox-cart, you can see it was a slow form of travel, but they had lots of time.

This black ox was Eul-Choon's delight. He had previously discovered that it was a very great fighter and could beat all other oxen, being particularly well-fed and carefully tended at home. As soon as they came, Eul-Choon always bribed the driver with tobacco from the barn, then unharnessed the black ox and took him out, unknown to the widow. Behind the barn my cousin would sharpen the horns of the black ox until they were like swords. This was cheating of course, and was cruel besides, but it made the black ox irresistible in battle. Then in the village, Eul-Choon would challenge the oxen of other cowboys. After they had joined in combat oxen could not be separated by stoning them nor by hitting them with sticks. There is only one way to separate fighting oxen: to take your Winter coat, your Summer one will not do, wet it in the creek and cover your ox's eyes, while the master of the other ox does the same. They only stop fighting when they cannot see anything. It was a dangerous sport, but Eul-Choon won a good deal of money this way; the widow never knew why her ox seemed so fagged after spending the night in our village.

The fat aunt's mother was a good-looking woman of beautiful figure, and exquisite dress. Her entire girdle was richly bejewelled, and she wore a jade ear-pick around her neck. I cannot understand it, but she was not at all like her daughter, the fat aunt, who was so sad, honest and incapable. The rich woman was very executive and knew how to manage her servants. Eul-Choon and I visited her during the Summer sometimes—but not if my grandmother could prevent it. In her own home, the widow would take one straw from the carpet, and carry it all the way out to the kitchen furnace. If she found another straw, she would take it out in the same careful manner, although she did not generally find two in the same day. Then with her finger she would go around to hunt for dust. If she found the least speck she was very angry, and would take the finger immediately to the servant who was responsible for dusting.

"Do you see it, as I see it? What is the matter with you this morning?"

But the fat aunt was not at all like her and hardly knew dust when she saw it. Eul-Choon never bothered to tease his step-mother, the fat aunt, but he was sarcastic with the rich woman when he went to see her. He knew that she was not used to children and he would try her patience in every way. Purposely he would play in sandy places where his white stockings might become permeated with dust. Then when he took off his sandals at the door and walked over her shining carpets, he enjoyed the excitement. Being her guest, she could not rebuke him. But her grand house was no-man's land. My grandmother said she could not see a man's point of view, and hence made a specially bad mother-in-law. Although she had been a widow quite long and was young and beautiful, nobody had ever dared to raid her. The custom of raiding a widow may seem like a strange one, but it was the only way in which she could get married again, for Korean women never took a second husband unless carried off and compelled. Indeed some widows welcomed raiding, for ladies who have once been married generally like the state.

Before the crazy-poet's mother-in-law came to our house, the floors were always carefully swept, every speck of dust was sent to exile, and the better rug, a soft straw carpet that gleamed like white satin, was laid down over the regular matting, so that the whole floor felt cushioned. The best things to eat were made ready, no matter how poor we happened to be. All children were dressed in clean clothes and instructed to be extrapolite. When she came, my grandmother was more solicitous about her comfort than about my uncle *pak-sa's* guests who came from the Capital.

"Is it warm in here for you? This seat is cooler. Do have this spot on the floor."

Koreans of course used no chairs, but sat on the clean soft floor surface.

The widow would say: "No, this spot is all right. It is very nice, cool and elegant, thank you."

At dinner in the women's dining-pantry, next the kitchen—where the dainty and unusual feast was served in the correct style to the rich woman, my grandmother would say: "I am sorry this meal is so coarse and not at all nice."

The widow would reply: "How do you train your daughters to cook like this? They do far better than my servants."

You could never have guessed from action or words that the two mothers-in-law hated each other. They did not go at it with kicks and bites because they were too refined. But their polite words were all the time fighting. They waited until the men had gone to bed, before they began the real issue. This was because when the sun was in the sky, men were dominant and women kept quiet and dared not show their true selves, but night and the moon belonged to women and then they became strong.

The rich woman seemingly had gone to bed. That night in the deserted kitchen my grandmother and my fat aunt were folding up the new linen which had just been bleached and washed and was not yet made up into clothes, when my grandmother discovered small holes all through the new linen.

"Daughter, what is this? See what you have done. As you washed, you carelessly picked up sand in the bottom of the stream. Then when you beat the clothes with your washing stick, you made these little holes all through the new weave. Now all our long labor is lost. What shall I do with you? How often do I have to tell you about such things?"

The tears began rolling down my speechless fat aunt's face.

My grandmother, who was very tired, and feared that she would lose her temper, said:

"Well, daughter, go to bed."

The fat aunt went out, shaking with sobs. Then by and by the kitchen door opened and the fat aunt's mother came in, fully dressed and with all her jewels still upon her front. She had been sitting up for this opportunity.

"She has not learned to do things," began the rich woman sulkily, "because in my home most tasks have always been performed by the servants. She is only a child and since she is willing to learn, much ought to be overlooked."

"But, it is very unfortunate," said my grandmother plainly, "that she has not had proper education; she seems unable to learn."

In my country having servants was no excuse for blundering ignorance like that of my fat aunt's on all occasions. When she came to our house, she did not know in setting a guest's table, on which side to place the wine and on which side to place *kim-chi*.

Couldn't my grandmother be a little more kind, the rich woman suggested? More considerate of her daughter's disability? And then wasn't it possible to replenish her daughter's wardrobe a little now and then? The cloth had been scant at her wedding, the rich woman implied.

Both these mothers had long held a grudge. The rich woman considered ours too poor a house for her daughter; my grandmother did not consider the fat aunt well-bred enough for a scholar and crazy-poet like my uncle. Now they went at it, not with blows but with words. The angrier my grandmother got, the cooler she became, and her words were ever soft and smooth as if she were speaking before a great governor. But the widow was heated, and tried all the time to add the fuel when my grandmother would have extinguished the flames; *her* voice grew higher and higher. From out of my bed in the crazy-poet's studio, I crept to the kitchen-door to listen. The air between the two mothers crackled just like lightning. The rich woman suggested that the fat aunt did not get enough to eat in our house nor enough clothes for her back; my grandmother's hands trembling with rage as she held up the new-woven cloth with tiny holes all through, and the fish-oil lamp bore witness to the latest evidence of the fat aunt's hopeless stupidity.

The fat aunt very soon rushed out, with the tears streaming down her face. She did not know which way to turn. In appearance she was with her mother-in-law, in heart she was with her own mother. She was so confused that she walked around the room picking up imaginary crumbs. When her mother began about the grand-child which she was never allowed to keep, my fat aunt grasped the broom and swept the floor with all her might.

"Daughter," said my grandmother, trying not to be irritated, "don't sweep the floor at midnight. You should never sweep the floor with your pajama on."

Then the fat baby in his little pajama ran out from a near-by room where he had been put to sleep on his tiny mattress. He was full of holiday good spirits and came in laughing and jumping. He thought it was New Year's at the very least, and imagined that he had heard fire-crackers.

In the meantime the voices of the widow and the fat aunt had awakened the crazy-poet. He only stopped to grab his long clay pipe and to put on trousers for of course he could not come out before the women in his pajama. Purposely he grasped the long clay pipe. He was very angry with his wife and his mother-in-law for making such a noise before my grandmother. But you cannot slap women on the face. He carried the clay pipe in order to beat on the table. As soon as he entered, everybody kept quiet except the baby. All were afraid of him except the baby. The baby ran up to him and clapped hands and laughed, but he pretended not to see it. This was my uncle's fastidious manner. He was polite, even without his clothes. In Korea it was very improper for a young father to notice his own child. When it played at his feet, he looked the other way. Of course he never stepped on the baby and went very care-fully around it or over it, but it was considered unpar-donable boastfulness to eye your own child.

The crazy-poet went straight to the table and beat on it with his clay pipe.

"What's this! What's this! What's this!"

He beat so hard that the clay pipe broke, and the bowl rolled down on the floor. The baby laughed and put it to his mouth. Then my grandmother ran to the baby, persuading it to give up the pipe. The fight was broken up. The rich mother-in-law retired, and the fat aunt ran after her, wringing her hands.

But my grandmother was still so angry that she could not sleep. She remembered all the rich woman's words with an aching heart. In order to be alone and to recover serenity, she took out my two dogs, Dalksali and Poo-hung, for a walk in the garden. As she came into the quiet garden, still breathing hard, even the frogs were scared by her angry spirit and dashed themselves into the pool. Gradually she surrendered herself to the serenity, the calmness, the quietude of the garden. It was one of those oriental gardens where little streams entwined their way through green grass and moss, and every flower and fruit bloomed in season and made the only changes there for a hundred years. Nowhere could life be found gentler, fairer, more exquisite than in an oriental garden like my grandmother's, just a few steps beyond our grass roof. How many plum-flowers of February breaking through icy obstacles my grandmother remembered to have seen in that garden, how many pink-red peach blossoms of March, how many frail cherry branches so easily changed to dust in the bright showers of April; what swooning wisteria in May, what strong, cool-bodied iris growing in the shades of June! No wonder the Chinese poet, Li Po, thinking homesick thoughts, spoke thus:

> I have been long from home,
> How often did the roses bloom?

But an oriental woman never left home. How much more poignant a garden was to her! Only my grandmother knew what dreams had haunted the lonely hours of her motherhood. What anxious solitude was hers, she who had been so long widowed by a living husband! What patient self-denial! To her the garden murmured sweet silent music which held the associations of a lifetime. And hark! she heard the monastery bells, and to her it was as though the flowers before her were distilling those sounds of benediction. Stooping over the pool, she saw the dripping heads of the lotus, the symbol of life, triumphant over all that is foul, ugly, loathsome and rotting, rising to ineffable beauty and purity out of the mud. Suddenly she was awakened to the land of beauty, purity and religion; she felt that her fleshly body had fallen into the rot. What anguish was hers! As she looked at the stars in the sky, at the lotus blossoms in the pond, she thought, "Ah, I made a mistake to fight with her! It was not beautiful, it was not pure, it was not religious to quarrel like that." To my grandmother religion was not belief only, nor narrow creed, not a set of principles only, nor salvation. But it was life—a passion which ran through her blood like fire in her vein. She spread out her arms, gazing at the guiding stars through the branches of the willow trees.

"O Stars! Guide me to symbolize my life like the lotus in the solitary pond!"

At last her anguish of self-condemnation gave way to the pale melancholy of Buddhistic traditions. . . .

What she felt was not exactly what you feel when you go up to the eighteenth floor in an elevator without stopping; it was not exactly embarrassment, as when you have sat on a piece of squash pie at some American picnic; it was not exactly pain, as when your teeth are pulled out by a dentist; but it was a reluctant letting go of all things, such as her love for her crazy-poet son, and her instinct of motherhood to fight for him, her irritation at the fat aunt for her stupidity, and the necessity to in-struct her how to pinch and save and bicker with the market-man over the price of fish every day, and then that still burning ache caused by the rich woman's sar-casm over our impoverished gentility. Now in her land of religious Utopia beside the lotus pool in the garden, my grandmother could forget her domestic trouble, and all the agonizing pains and tears that simple human life brings from day to day.

Yet she believed thoroughly in the domestic life, even as she mounted into the world of Buddha. She believed in raising children, and in getting her children and grandchildren married. It seemed to her that the only progress possible was through the domesticity of life. But somehow she could not bear this time to see the night go and the dawn break.

"Don't come—I don't want you!" she thought as a wan streak came. "I don't want to be seen. The sun shames me."

And it seemed like a man's hand upon her soul, calling it back. Night, the time of her woman's supremacy, was ebbing. She could no longer rest with perfect under-standing upon the dark. But she raised her eyes to the pine tree outlined against the rosied sky.

"O let my heart be inspired by that tall pine tree!"

Then she stooped down and washed her face and hands in the dew, like a rite of purification, and went into the house.

Always to my grandmother, the garden was a place for meditation and prayer, even when she came there in the heat of the day to do her spinning under a cool tree. Only to my uncle it was a land of the muse. Many a beautiful poem in my grandmother's heart was lost to literature through failure to be written down; not lost to the universe, for according to the Buddha's teaching, that could never be, but lost to the human ear.

When they met that morning, the rich woman and my grandmother were more polite than ever, and from their bland and amiable brows you would never have guessed of the storm which had passed over them in the midnight.

Chapter 7

THE FEAST OF THE HAUNTING GHOSTS

Drop yon blue bosom veil of sky, and show me
The breasts o' her tenderness:
Never did any milk of hers once bless
My thirsting mouth.
The Hound of Heaven: FRANCIS THOMPSON

THE two dogs which my grandmother took into the garden for a walk were very good friends of mine; I loved them more than Yun-Koo and Chak-Doo-Shay. Poohung was the name of the large serious one, which means Hoot-Owl. I gave him that name because he looked like that, and was too serious ever to deceive. He had pretty, gentle, sincere eyes and a strong tall body on which he let me ride. He very much resembled a wolf, but was more kind and brave in his temper than wolves. No dog could beat him at fighting. He had a good trick of catching wild chickens and all kinds of edible birds, and these he would always bring to me, meaning that I should give him the tails and the heads, which he thought were the only edible portions because he had never been fed anything else. He did not know that the body was expected to be eaten, but he always waited until he was given his share, heads and tails.

Once some wild school-boys came by night to get our chickens. They brought with them heads of chickens, knowing Poohung's peculiarity. He gruffly accepted the heads and seemed very friendly until they tried to go away with the chickens. Then he barked twice with something in his mouth. This was a trouser of a boy's leg. My grandmother heard, and she came and got back all our chickens. No Japanese could come around our house while Poohung was there. Poohung heard everything and would bark once for a member of the family, twice for a stranger.

His companion was a small comic dog, named *Dalksali*, because he had so much hair that he always collected sticking needles or *dalksali* in great quantities when he went to the woods. He too caught game, but only small birds, and always by deceit. He had no sense of square-dealing, like Poohung, who would announce to a bird in a deep voice: "Look out! I am going to catch you. Race for it!" Dalksali on a hunt could wiggle anywhere because of his size, and he gathered up straws and sticks and barks until he looked as if he were made entirely out of these. Like a bundle of leaves or a piece of hay, he would sometimes sit up in the tall grass and wait for a bird. He would sit up so quiet and so disguised that the birds came and almost sat on his nose: then snap, he had them. After it was all over, he would sing out, in a tenor voice: "Yang! Yang! Didn't you know I was here?"

He practiced deceit consciously too. I have often watched him jump in the stream, then roll in the leaves and sands. After this he became like an old sandy log. Indeed he could look like anything except a dog—he never looked like a real dog, because he seemed to have no feet nor head nor tail, for all was covered up by hair a foot long. You had to look in at least six inches before you could find any eyes at all, and he must always shake his head before looking out at the world.

Whenever it rained, he became somebody else. He would shrink. The first time I saw him wet, I did not know him, but thought he was another creature. Rain got his hair down.

In spite of his shrewdness, he too like Poohung thought that heads and tails were the only edible portions. These dogs did not know many luxuries. The dogs I have known in America are millionaires compared to them. I did the best I could for them.

They had no regularly assigned portion of the family meal. They were supposed only to get what was left over. This seemed to me very unfair toward them, for there never was anything left over—not since my fat aunt came to live with us. At that end of the kitchen furthest from the rest of the house was a deep step. When you went down this step, you were no longer standing in the kitchen on the mattings, but on the bare earth. Here were the two furnaces, fed by straw, wood and leaves, which heated all the house, through the hollow flues in the floors—one furnace for the men's part of the house at the front, and one for the women's at back. These stone furnaces also did the cooking, and there were many little ovens, reached by standing on the earthy floor, as well as the tall hot shelf which extended up into the kitchen for the cooking of fish and of meat. I would place myself by these little stoves just before the meal was taken in to the men, food which was carried in for each on light individual tables just like individual trays. Here I waited until the little aunt, who was sharper than the other women, left the room.

Before the little aunt took in the tables, I knew that she would run off and hide for a moment. The first time she did this, I was curious and followed her. She went into the Sacred Chamber of the women and way down under a basket, she hid and powdered her nose. Women always did such a thing secretly. A woman who powdered her nose before men would be considered indecent and so-phisticated, trying so obviously to make herself attractive that she was no better than a gisha girl. They powdered as much as gisha girls though, young newly-married ones like my little aunt. My fat aunt rarely powdered her nose; Ok-Dong-Ya would laugh and remind her to do so when there were guests. But I could steal anything from under my fat aunt's very eyes and she would never notice. The little aunt knew, and that is why I waited until she ran off and hid; she always was very careful about that now that her husband, the prodigal-son uncle, had come back. She powdered a good deal more when he was there, for she did not know him very well yet and felt formal.

While she was gone, I would snatch choice morsels of fish and meat from the dishes which were about to be taken in to my father and my uncles, and give them to Poohung and Dalksali. My little aunt was quick to discover this. One day she took me aside into the store room next to the Women's Sacred Chamber. She was so frightened, she was trembling:

"What shall I do? Oh, what shall I do?" she whispered, shaking her finger. "You have given all the fish to Poohung and Dalksali. I have nothing to take in to your father and your senior uncle and your junior uncle. It is too late to go to the market. Oh, dear, how ashamed I am! What shall I do?"

She was so distressed, that after that we compromised. She must treat the dogs like members of the family, I made the bargain, by giving them plates too, at the beginning of the meal. Then I said I would not steal for them any more. Hereafter the little aunt always fixed two plates for Dalksali and Poohung at the same time that she fixed plates for my father and my uncles, and she put them in a secret place where only I could see them.

I did not give Poohung and Dalksali their food at once; but first had some fun with them. I would tie a bone on the end of a string, suspend it in the furnace room, and start it swinging. Poohung would come in, leaping for joy, waving his tail and dancing his paws. When he saw the bone, he would say, "Wong! Wong!" which in his language meant: "I want that right now!" His eyes and his head and his tail would swing just like the swinging bone, and he would be actually hypnotized by the sight. Dalksali was funnier though, because when he swung his head from side to side, he had to throw the hair out of his eyes each time, so if I made the string go fast sometimes he got drunk. Then he felt huffy, and would sneak out of the house and into his house and Poohung's, which had a little grass roof, in miniature, just like our big one. Poohung had the better temper, and never got angry.

Sometimes when I gave Poohung his daily dozen in the kitchen it brought on a disaster. He broke a clay pot once, and my grandmother did not like that. When she scolded him, my poor sincere dog felt so badly, tears came into his eyes just; he was very sensitive. Both dogs carried things for me and minded me when I spoke. But sometimes Dalksali would only pretend to mind. If I told him to go home, he would take a roundabout road through the rice fields or the long grass by the stream, so that I could not see him, but he would be wiggling along after me all the while. If I caught him, he would turn around quickly and pretend that he had been going the other way ever since I spoke. He was deceitful with the basket too. If I gave him a basket to carry home, sometimes he would stop on the way and examine it. If it had something he liked, he would refresh himself before taking the basket further. Poohung was not like this, he never cheated, but always delivered the goods straight and got the receipt, whether it was berries from the woods, books from school, or fish from the market.

In Song-Dune-Chi after the Dragon Festival, Summer was in full swing. This Festival commemorated Chu Yuan, the great Chinese minister, who committed suicide because his prince would not take his advice, in the fourth century before Christ. It came on the fifth day of the fifth month, and was the sharp demarcation between late Spring and Summer. Before that time the people ate many green tender shoots of trees, weeds and vegetables which were considered nonedible and grown up after this period.

Under the trees now shade was complete; there were no more sunny dots as when the leaves on branches were young. The perfume from the fields brought a rich feeling of luxuriance, particularly after the heat of the day. In the evening, the breeze blew from mountain to mountain, and the bright moonlight streamed down on the river which forever and ever seemed to roll onward as clear and crystal as the sky overhead, to enter into the blue waves of the wandering ocean. From the pine grove would drift the sound of drum, string and flute, for every night the whole village danced and sang and wrestled together until the hour of morning. As we boys danced, singly, taking what steps our souls prompted, we kept up the simple refrain, "Chotta! Chotta! Chotta!" (Happy! Happy! Happy!) to the varying music of the orchestra. One song which all were very fond of singing to the accompaniment of the Pine Grove Orchestra was the Korean folk-air:

> Green mountains are natural, natural,
> Blue water is natural, natural!
> Natural mountains, natural streams,

> Mountains above me, rivers around me,
> > [I too am natural, natural!]
> Here where a natural body was grown,
> Even old age will be natural, natural!

When the visiting villages came, there were contests in playing the harp, in singing and in wrestling.

Mid-summer eve was another subject my crazy-poet uncle liked to write about. On such evenings as these he would have drinking parties with my *chin-sa* uncle and other chronological friends, in which they discussed styles of poetry. My uncle always held that it was divine duty for a poet to interpret beauty, elegance and rapture to those who could receive it. He was never materialistic about poetry and did not bring poverty very often into the discussion. When he did, he dismissed it with a bitter expression, such as "Poverty is a son of cow!" (This in my country was swearing.)

There was one great poet among my uncle's friends, Kim Sagat, so named because he used a long farmer's hat. Kim Sagat was a perfect Bohemian, and a very big flirt. He was always interested in pretty young ladies. Once he saw a pretty girl at the well and shut one eye at her. This young lady was so honest that she told her mother-in-law and her mother-in-law told her husband. Then her husband came after Kim Sagat.

"Why did you shut one eye at that young lady who was going to the well?"

Kim Sagat said:

"Oh, I always do that to everybody. I can't help it."

So all the time he was talking to the husband, he had to keep opening and shutting one eye so that the other would think it was habitual process, and he told my uncle under the pine trees that he got very tired of doing it, before the husband was satisfied.

Then the poets would tell of a long series of adventures on their way to the capital and how they had been entertained by the scholars in this and that place. They would lament how short life was to play with the muse. The big world was a kind of house, they said, where we lived but temporarily, dreaming a little joy, dreaming a little romance, dreaming a little adventure, but we were soon sped on our way in order to make room for the other guests. "Why not enjoy ourselves?" they would end up. "The Spring has gone, but the Autumn has not yet come."

My uncle would look up at the moon and remind them that the moon was a diary where they might see the reflection of their former good times and all sweet memories of the past. Referring to the Chinese poet Li Po, my uncle recited an old Korean poem to the moon:

> After Li Po passed away,
> Deserted, lake and mountain lay.
> Her lonely circling, the moon
> Found very mournful now to be.
> Li Po is here no more, O moon,
> Why not come frolic with me?

My illustrious uncle *pak-sa* sometimes joined my crazy-poet uncle and his friends in order to take part in the poetry discussions, but on those evenings, the drinking suffered, because in Korea only chronological equals were supposed to drink or to smoke face to face. So my crazy-poet uncle and my *chin-sa* uncle, whenever they poured another drink from the silver flagon to the crystal goblet would have to turn their backs for a moment unobtrusively on my *pak-sa* uncle—the way Eul-Choon and I had to do when we stole drinks—and it did not make for free and easy discussion.

The women did not mingle with the men in the Summer evening, but had their dancing and joy-making in their own yards beside the gardens. Men's world and women's world were just as different as the cat's and the dog's. They never fought of course, but meeting, they went around each other furtively, pretending hardly to look, and it was generally considered that they had very different interests and desires. But when I grew tired of masculine society in the pine grove, I would go to find my grandmother who rested beside her quiet old garden. Although she rested, her hands were always busy, and in front of the goldenrod fire, while enjoying the cool of the evening, she would be spinning, or preparing fresh vegetables for the next day. The spinning wheels were left out overnight. No one thought of thieves, and with the exception of wild school boys after chickens, thieves were unknown. My grandmother's attitude toward thieves was not American. "Never catch a thief," she would say. "It is impolite because it places him in an embarrassing position. And how would you like to be caught and placed in such a position?" The correct procedure, if you thought you heard a thief, was not to run toward him with a stick, but to clear your throat or make a loud noise, so that he knew you were listening. He would be equally aware of propriety and would go away.

Mosquitoes hated the goldenrod smoke of the midsummer fire, but its fragrance was sweet and mellow. Crouched before its blue vapor, my grandmother would tell us old stories about the stars, and would tell them as if they were facts.

On the seventh day of the seventh moon, two bright stars come close together, so that they seem to meet. One of these, said my grandmother, was the cowboy, and the other, the weaving girl, his loving wife. They could meet only one day out of each year, because when they were together, they neglected the duties of their proper spheres. The cowboy forgot to tend his cows and the weaving girl to weave. So they could meet only on the seventh day of the seventh moon. At all other times they were separated by the distance across the milky way.

"On the seventh day of the seventh moon," said my grandmother, "why do all the magpies disappear?"

"Why do they, Grandmother?"

"They go up the milky way, to build the bridge for the weaving girl to cross to her husband, the cowboy."

"And see?" continued my grandmother, lifting her palm, as the soft rain spattered in large drops, and preparing to put the spinning wheel under the Odong tree which formed a natural shelter, "why does it always, always rain on that night?"

"Why, Grandmother?"

"Because the weaving girl and the cowboy are so glad to see each other for one night, that they just cry and cry."

On the morning after the seventh night of the seventh moon, we might ask my grandmother:

"Grandmother, why is that magpie's head all bitten up?"

Then she would reply:

"Do you know why? That magpie didn't go up to build the bridge, and when the other magpies came down, they punished him. And if you don't do your duty, you will be punished too, just like that magpie."

Sometimes I sought out Ok-Dong-Ya and found her sitting on an old mossy rock by the river, talking to herself, and watching the river of stars go by in the water. Poor Ok-Dong-Ya! Like my grandmother in her passionately religious moods, her heart too was always full of a poetry which she could not express. But unlike my grandmother she was not born to be patient but to long ever for personal joys and thrills of delight and per- haps—for the human soul is strange enough—for the deeper experiences of struggle and sorrow denied most well-bred oriental women except through motherhood. But all Ok-Dong-Ya's rebellion came later. Now she was a carefree child in the lap of nature, and crooned a little song in which she pretended to be a firefly.

We spoke our thoughts in low voices, or perhaps in silence we swung our fox-glove stalks which glowed with the fireflies we had caught and placed in each rosy bell to make a little lantern. Once on a near-by rock we saw my prodigal uncle playing with a gisha girl who had wandered up from the sea.

My sarcastic cousin, Eul-Choon, liked to be witty at the expense of girls on Summer evenings. One of his favorite methods was that of deductive logic, which girls did not recognize at first. In speaking to one of Ok-Dong-Ya's friends, he referred to her as "darling little white nose."

"I don't know but one other like you in the village," he said. "I can't decide which has the more beautiful nose. When you come to the well in the morning, show your face a little, don't hide it; I want to compare."

The girl laughed at him, but she could not refrain from dressing up a little for the beauty contest when she went to the well in the morning. But when she got to the well she found all the men and boys of the village gath- ered about a Chinese with a long queue, a jingling Chi- nese orchestra and a white-nosed monkey which Eul- Choon had seen come in the night before, and this girl was very angry.

A typical mid-summer eve amusement with my cousin Eul-Choon was to raid the girls when they went in the water by night. Korean girls may not wear bathing suits by day. The Japanese do not feel as the Koreans in this respect, and the exposure of the bare thigh in both men and women was one of the things that shocked my people when the foreigners began to come in larger numbers from the island Empire. But on hot and moonless nights the young Korean girls would go in the beautiful natural pools with only their birthday suits on, and my cousin Eul-Choon knew about this. He would give them plenty of time to get undressed, to get into the water, then taking the most playful boys he would go very slowly and softly through the willows to the water's edge. From behind the willow screen they would drop sand and gravel in the pool where the girls bathed and watch the result. The distress of Ok-Dong-Ya and her friends was pitiful to see. They did not know if it were raining or hailing, or if it were the Japanese. Some would stay in the water, others would dart out, to seize their clothes and creep away into the rice fields, like the pale ghosts.

Chak-Doo-Shay, Yun-Koo and I did not play such tricks on girls. We were their friends. So we would frustrate the older boys by arriving there first. Then we threw in just a little sand and a little gravel, and cleared our throats, so that the girls could get away before the real attack came.

About this time I became a cowboy. It was late for me to take up this occupation since most of the boys in my village had herded cows from the age of six, but my family had allowed me to do as I pleased up to now, in order that I might study with my crazy-poet uncle as much as possible, Summer as well as Winter. We usually employed a cowboy outside the family, paying him not with money but with food and clothes. Even during this Summer my grandmother saw me become a cowboy with reluctance and only because she was afraid I was not growing fast enough, since in a year or two now, she wished to begin to prepare for my marriage. She felt that she must see me married before she died. I was to take precedence over my cousin Eul-Choon because I was the son of the main branch.

All the cowboys of Song-Dune-Chi had a waiting ground and an hour of assembly. We met in the field behind the pine grove, by the river, just after sunrise when dew was still on the grass and the day was delicate in the sky. We all lined up like military soldiers, sitting on our cows' backs and wearing each a big bamboo hat to protect him from sun and rain. Besides our mounts we each had one or more cows which we managed with leading cords. I rode on my largest and favorite cow, a slow wise good-looking animal with long curved horns, and I drove on leading cords three smaller cows. Korean cows are larger and slenderer than American cows, and their milk bags are much smaller; milk as a rule, in Korea, is only for calves and babies. The leading cords of the cows, which fitted firmly over their heads and were attached to wooden pegs through their noses, were decorated with bell-like leaves made of iron. As the cows shook their heads from side to side, these leaves made Chinese music—a sound monotonous without giving monotony.

We were led out of the village by the emperor of the cowboys. He was one of the older boys. (I was never the emperor, because I was a scholar and poet, and was only an amateur cowboy.) Yun-Koo and Chak-Doo-Shay's families employed professional cowboys that year, but my two friends sometimes went along just for luxury, since a Summer day spent in the mountains was really sport. It was the same with my dogs, Poohung and Dalksali; Poohung always accompanied me; Dalksali, when he was not too lazy. The mountains were a fascinating place to wander, and each hollow was different. The emperor of the cowboys chose varying hollows from day to day, sometimes the hollows of the West mountain, sometimes those of the East. Every hollow had a clear stream, and here the rocks were different from those in the valley. In the broad river-bed they were smooth and white and round, while in the mountain hollows the rocks were sharp, rough, wild, with an adventurous aspect. We approached up a long winding road just wide enough for an ox cart to pass. Such roads had been travelled by innumerable generations of cowboys, some of them my direct forefathers. They were not like village roads. There was grass growing upon them and they seemed very deserted and quiet. One side of the mountain was always in the shade, and it was rare that a soft wind did not blow down the hollow. So it was all very comfortable, riding along with greenness everywhere, to the rhythm of the stream and of the musical leaves which swung upon your cow's head as she walked.

A king might have envied the emperor of the cowboys. As soon as he had assigned duties to the other boys, such as guarding the exits of dangerous hollows and watching the borders of farms where a cow might do damage, he was free to wander wherever he pleased, to pick up fruits, to hunt for crabs, to play checkers, sitting on raincoats made of rice straw, such as we all brought with us, or to fish all day, for the streams were full of fish that had crept up from the sea. In Song-Dune-Chi poets, scholars, cowboys, everybody liked to fish. There are many native poems regarding this passion:

> Fast asleep in my grass roof,
> The birds sing me awake. . . .
> Behind those plum flowers the raindrops shine,

The sun begins to sink.
Garçon, bring fishing rods quick!
It gets late to fish.

Not being prominent as a cowboy, I had to do some work. But I generally found congenial associates, or a book to share my duties with me. Always there were picnics. Given salt, you may dig potatoes from some farm; you may catch salmon and trout; when beans are ripe, you may roast them and they are very good. But the most delicious picnic dish is that of cooked pine shoots. You take the tender ends emerging from bunches of pine needles and prepare them by the stream, taking off their hair, washing them very carefully and placing them between thin heated rocks. Sometimes I ate so many picnics that I could find no place for supper, and my grandmother would ask anxiously if I were sick.

This Summer for the first time, as well as I can remember, I planned definitely to become prime minister of Korea, the post of a poet and scholar. I would address my cow in very much the same way as the cowboy in a certain old Chinese poem.

South Peak is bare;
White rocks shine there. . . .
I wish the Golden Age of Shun and Yao were here!
One flaxen singlet on my back I wear;
I herd the bull-calf; brightly stars appear
In the long velvet night; dawn's light gets near. . . .
By Tsang-Lang creek, where rocks show clear
(Though fish a foot and half are there)
Through fresh forenoon and far into the night,
I herd, this garment scanty and threadbare.
My yellow calf, which pants up yonder hill,
You fellow, I shall leave you, to be Prime Minister;
You'll whet your horns on stone outside the Eastern Gate,
And in some splendid grove of evergreens can wait.
My flax shirt, heigh! has many a fray!

Now, herd, grow strong on slender silken grass—
Tse's future minister is of this company.
Into Tsoo Kingdom you shall go with me.

As I gazed commandingly into her eyes I would say:
"Cow, you will some day be grateful to me, for I am
going to be prime minister of the country. Look at me,
know who I am. Follow me!"

Then when the cow became attracted by grass and
refused to listen, I would shake my fist to her face, and
lift up her head by the horns. "Listen to me!"—At last
we would compromise. As long as I scrubbed the blood-
sucking insects from her throat with a wooden nail, she
would listen to my words with deep sighs of happiness.

Life in such country districts as mine was a long unbroken dream, lasting thousands of years, in which the
same experiences, the same thoughts, the same life came
unceasingly, like the constantly reappearing flowers of
Spring, whose forms and attributes were the same, although the individuals were changing.

Having turned my cows out to graze, I lay in the
grass under a huge-leafed tree with my bare legs fanning
the air, reading the fascinating black characters of some
ancient book, dating back not hundreds but thousands
of years, but fresh and thrilling to me; dreaming of how
I should some day become a great *pak-sa* and how I
should sway others by my words. On one side lay Poohung, and on the other side, Dalksali, guarding me from
everything—even from insects.

What honest friends they were! It is very very unfortunate to hear the Christian doctrine preached that animals have no souls. I believe that the most intelligent
dogs have better souls than some dumb, insensitive, un-
stimulating human beings I have known. They say mon-
keys are also very intelligent, but I have had very little

chance to be congenial with them. I had perfect under-
standing with Dalksali and Poohung, however, and here
I know what I am saying. They had souls, souls that I
could understand, through their expressions, their movements, their playful dancings, their snarls and barks and
tears. The very eyes, the very mouthlines beneath the
nose, the very wiggling of their ears and tails spoke eloquent language to me. Of what good is language, if it is
only understood mechanically, and is not understood in
the deeper way by reaching the soul? Human beings are
hard to understand, not dogs.

It is a subject which has made many oriental writers
almost mad, the inscrutability of the human heart. Even
with the human beings we know best, we only think we
know them and they continually baffle us. Many orientals have killed themselves because of this very terrible
enigma—the human heart. It is the subject which made
Lord Houghton write his poem "Strangers Yet."

> Oh! the bitter thought to scan,
> All the loneliness of man!
> Nature, by magnetic laws,
> Circle unto circle draws,
> But they only touch when met—
> Never mingle,—strangers yet!

Did not Marcel Proust write his famous novel of fifteen
volumes upon the subject? And this seems to be the
universal experience. My father used to quote from an
ancient Chinese writer:

> Fish may be hooked though deep in the water;
> Birds may be shot, though high in the air;
> The human heart only can not be fathomed,
> Beyond all reach, beyond every snare.

> The heaven above us may be measured;
> The earth beneath us may be surveyed;

> Only man is beyond all wager;
> Only a man's heart can not be weighed.
>
> You may paint the tiger's stripe, outer tissue,
> But how can you draw the hidden bone?
> You may know a man's face, feature for feature;
> But how can a man's heart ever be known?
>
> You may think you sit with a friend of your bosom's,
> You may think you talk as familiars do;
> As the landscape hid by a thousand mountains,
> The heart of that man may be hidden from you.

I could never understand these words until later in my life. Now I know that compared to human beings the inarticulate dog is simple and comprehensible. How often did I wander through the mountains picking strawberries, with Dalksali and Poohung beside me, baskets tied by strings to their necks! How often did these dogs try to eat strawberries, although I had told them strawberries were only for me! Yet how patiently did they carry the baskets without benefit! How often did I walk through the thick bushes of the mountain woods and through the enfolding, sweeping branches of the Pine grove with Dalksali and with Poohung at my heels! And when I climbed after pine gum, the two dogs stood below and barked, never taking their eyes from me.

"Wong! Wong! Yang! Yang! Be careful! Don't go out on that branch. It's too slender," they would warn me. Just like a human being, Poohung would stand on two legs, his ears and tail fanning the air, his tongue hanging out, breathless with anxiety.

We loved the snow together, and we loved the rain. They in their fur coats, I in my straw raincoat were amply protected from the Summer showers as all three of us walked barefoot through the wet and deserted streets of Song-Dune-Chi, when others stayed in their houses. For Dalksali and Poohung seemed to feel with me the perpetual miracle of nature, in their veins as in mine leaped the forest spring which dropped from rock to rock like a shower bath, and they moved, crowned like me with clouds and trees. Nor was gaiety, joy and hardihood ever lacking from their hearts.

Storm in the mountains after a long dry spell might be very dreadful. Then when thunder and lightning seemed about to rip the world apart, when your heart jumped away out of your mouth, when even cows were frightened, dogs ran to you to protect you. What terror you felt! You could only hug Poohung, praying him to save you from the fury of the storm. Nature was no longer your friend. You and Poohung faced the angry universe together. Presently you sought protection in a hollow tree, or under a great rock, huddled beside other cowboys in dripping straw raincoats and bamboo hats large as umbrellas, from which the drops sizzled into the quickly made fires.

Yes, the extreme terror soon passed. And when the sun came out, dazzling in the blue, it was easy to see that the mountains, the cows and the cowboys had all had a baptismal shower bath. But there was no towel to wipe off. The cowboys took off their short linen clothes and dried them over fires. I always burned my clothes when I attempted this. They turned a dark yellow color. I did not know they were burned until I touched them. Then wherever my finger went, it made a hole. I moved home with very slow quiet steps in order not to break them more, and I quietly changed and hid the burned linen under a basket or beneath a towel when nobody was looking!

Late in August came an unusually long drought which made the grown people anxious. Then it rained for the

whole of one week, a steady, tireless downpour, but unaccompanied by thunder or lightning. Cowboys did not
go to the mountains. In the mornings, cows were hastily
tethered near home. Quite contentedly, I read the Classics in my crazy-poet uncle's studio, while the rain whispered an ancient monody to the grass roof overhead. I
was deep in wisdom of the past when at my feet Poohung
began barking. I thought he wanted me to let him out. I
opened the door, but he seemed undecided and looked
imploringly into my eyes.

"Go, Poohung!" (I was impatient to get back to my
book.)

With an eager whine, Poohung darted off in the direction of the river, but soon I heard him at the door again.

"Wong! Wong-a-wong!"

He meant, "Come quick! Come quick!"

I understood, but still I thought he wanted me to come
to play with him in the rain. I shook my head.

"No, Poohung!"

Three times Poohung came back for me. The third
time he was dripping with muddy water. Then my eyes
were opened and lost the blur of characters I had been
reading. I remembered that I had tied my cow in the
willows by the river. Through a tiny pane of glass in the
silk-panelled window, I looked out at the flooded scene.
Without waiting to put on my straw raincoat I hurried
out. The river, increased by the mountain torrents, was
lashing like an enraged beast full speed down the valley.
My cow had been tied firmly in a low piece of land between two forks of the river. The two forks of the river
had joined and in the midst I saw my cow as in a mighty
rolling flood. Only her back and her nose were visible.
She bellowed and struggled with the rope which tied
her. Without thinking of the current or the distance to

her, I jumped in, imitating the frog with my legs. This always worked well for the frog, but it did not work for me. Yet I meant to save my cow. I grew tired and fainting. The last thing I saw before I drowned was my cow swimming to meet me; she had managed to pull loose her cord. At the same time from the other side of the bank, I saw my dog leaping down toward me with a graceful dive. Then I died.

          *   *   *   *

I awoke from the mysterious land of nothingness where perhaps wander the ghosts of those who are drowned and found myself under the willow bushes by the river-side among the sandy stones. The rain had stopped but the river still lashed onward with wild roaring. It had a menacing sound. Even the ruddy sunset above the rice fields looked ominous. There was no sign now of the rice plants. The sun was setting above a desolate lake.

I had not far to look for more familiar and more endeared objects. Not far from me my cow was lying, as if chewing gum, her disposition unruffled by her struggle with the angry waters. Poohung, exhausted and dripping, panted beside me. I did not know which had saved me, but I dimly remembered throwing my arms around my cow's neck, in the river. So now I hugged my dog and clung to my cow with grateful feeling and thankful heart.

In acting as he did, Poohung had prevented me from ruining the family, for we could scarcely have afforded to lose the cow at this time. The flood continued after that. The river was no longer clear but presented a ghastly spectacle, jammed with logs, branches and leaves from the mountains, and carrying on its surface chop-sticks, bathrobes, blankets, baby shoes, wash basins, all the trophies of its destructive powers. The villagers of Song-Dune-Chi were helpless before such mad hostility of Nature. In perfect accord with her luxuriant and out-going moments, kindling to her every beauty and inspired by her to an unceasing national poetry, they could identify themselves with her in all moods but this. They could not cope with this insane wrath of a universe beyond their control, and they succumbed to the same misery year after year without doing anything about it, enduring the gloomy dark waters of the flood which robbed them of sustenance in a mute patience, and looking forward to the happiness which was theirs at all other times. My memory of Song-Dune-Chi just after that time I almost came to be drowned is sinister and dark, like the untamed river and like the bloody sunset I found upon awakening beside my cow and my faithful Poohung. For a certain undependability of nature and of man was suddenly revealed to me, owing to a deep childish loss I now had to experience.

During this season of greatest hardship, the wandering ghosts were worshipped in Song-Dune-Chi, and in the neighboring villages. To the Korean life was not a passing shadow as to the mystic Hindoo, but a reality most of the time. His joys and his sorrows were simple sensuous things, and Korean ethics stressed the duty of man to man, rather than the duty of man to the transcendental forces. But always in the gaunt time of the year ghosts were remembered by annual sacrifice. The feast was given them without stint then, even though the donors went hungry for weeks after. The superstitious farmer gave in order to get material blessings. The innately religious, like my grandmother, symbolized

their natural piety toward ancestors and the unseen
world by bowing before these suffering dead who had
no peace. All those who haunted around the tree-top
from which they had fallen, those who had drowned and
left their soul in the water, all who had died of hunger or
of violence, was it not a pitying kindness toward them, to
feed them now,—now especially, when hearts were
anxious and the outlook dark? For what other hope had
the living of being cared for by the powers behind this
inscrutable nature, kind one moment and cruel the next,
than loyalty to the dead and faith in the unborn grand-
child of the future? A scholar and a poet like my crazy-
poet uncle, though his intellect disdained the popular
superstition, and though his mind perhaps found not
enough the simple metaphysics of my grandmother on
this subject, obeyed her in all things and wrote down
reverently in his most beautiful style the wishes she
wanted remembered to the ghosts in regard to the living
whom she loved.

At the annual ghost worship each family killed a cow
or a pig or a dog, which they offered to the ghosts first,
then ate of it what the ghosts left. For the Koreans eat
dogs, and consider that the meat is very good food. I myself feel that it is not right to eat dogs, because they are
so intelligent and so faithful. But for that matter I would
not eat a sirloin steak from my cow, if the butcher told
me in time. None of our own dogs were ever killed and
eaten at home. In other homes this might be done, but
with us, some sentiment forbade. This year however my
family needed money very badly, and food was getting
more and more scarce. Just before the flood my prodigal
uncle had run away from home again, and my father,
thinking of the young bride, had made a vow to go after
him and compel him to come back. My father was all at

once very angry with his prodigal-son brother. The little aunt had been very small and flat when she came to live with us, but as time went on she seemed suddenly to come up; in fact near the New Year's time she was given sea-weed soup, which was the right medicine in Korea for every new mother. Owing to a load of anxieties, my father now sold Poohung to a man in a neighboring village for a very good price, the equivalent of something like four dollars in America, for all food was scarce at the time, throughout the countryside. With this money we would be enabled to buy a pig for the ghosts, on which we could live for some time.

When I learned that Poohung was to be sold for sacrificial meat at the ghost feast, I broke my heart. I cried and cried and argued with my grandmother. It was no use speaking to the men. Ok-Dong-Ya cried too, and joined her pleas with mine. My grandmother cried, but said that she could do nothing, she had to have money and the family must be considered. Besides, Poohung was growing too intelligent. He was almost like a man. She also argued that there must be some end to all living creatures, and Poohung had already lived long enough; it was better for him to go before he got old and blind and too much endeared. I understood my grandmother's view, and if dimly my mind rebelled against sacrifice of the living in offering to the dead, I was hardly aware of it then. But her words brought the blight to my soul. All living creatures must come an an end. But not only that. They were to be assisted out of this life by the hands they had served, and their best friends were powerless to aid. Here was some brutal and unfair necessity which I realized for the first time and felt crushed before. My grandmother's logic was irresistible. But when I looked at that muddy river, it seemed like a relentless dragon

which had come down from the mountains to swallow up
Poohung and all my contentment. It had taken Poohung,
not Dalksali, though Dalksali cheated and Poohung
never did. Poor Poohung, so innocent and sincere, who
had saved even me from the river's blind rage!

I am glad that Poohung after all was not unjustly offered up to the wandering ghosts, and that his fate was
the fate of the rebel. For this intelligent animal seemed
to understand what was going to happen to him. A few
days before the annual ghost feast, he disappeared into
the forest at the further end of our farmlands. There he
concealed himself for many days. All the while I sought
for him to offer him my sympathy. I sought him on the
Eastern mountain and in the Western hollow, through
the Northern Vale and along the Southern shore. I wandered fearless through the ghost's place across the river,
looking everywhere for Poohung. Whenever I glanced at
the black muddy river, I was reminded of my dog and his
faithfulness to me. At the same time, I collected bones
for him, and scattered them wherever I went, in the
hopes that he might find them by night and so not starve.
I myself lost the taste for food. All this while my soul was
dark and my heart ached. His purchasers appeared to
take him, but he could not be found and their schedule
had to be cancelled, the money returned. The time of the
Ghost Feast came, but the gay lanterns hung on poles
and strung along from tree to tree could not light my
spirit. The ghosts were fed in the yard, and candles
burned on their tables. My uncle read his petition for
the speedy return of the wanderer (junior uncle), for
the good health of each one of us there, and for the eas-
ing of the country's troubles, and the sorrows of the villagers. Then he burned the manuscript in the candle and
the rest cried with satisfaction as they saw the ashes go

upward, a sign that our prayers were favorably received. But I thought only of Poohung and heard the threatening sounds of the ruthless river.

Several days after that when I had despaired of ever seeing Poohung again, though now the danger to his life had blown over, I heard that in the village the boys had killed a mad dog. I hurried out my gate at once to the spot. And it was my dog, Poohung. Poor dog! He had not eaten for ten days. Of course he was wild and ravenous and ready to bite his teeth down on the first thing he saw. Dogs get like that when they have had nothing to eat for a long time, and so do men. Men may become cannibals under those circumstances. But when dogs do not act normally they say they are mad. For this reason the boys had killed Poohung. He was dead. There was blood in his mouth and in his eyes. I leaped to his side, and tumbled down upon his body, hugging and kissing him. I cried and cried all night and became very sick after that. In my delirium I thought I was again in the river and called on Poohung to save me. My poor Poohung! We were in different categorical kingdoms, but we were friends for all that!

Chapter 8

EBBING LIFE

I saw Eternity the other night. . . .
A Vision: HENRY VAUGHAN

ABOUT this time, my grandfather came home to be ready for death. He was very old, very beautiful, with gray hair and calm face and long gray beard; all his life he had taken everything just as it came. Now he took death like that too. I remember him as being very fond of singing a certain song:

> Mountains are green, sans words;
> Brooks run, sans etiquette, down;
> Winds are clear, sans being sold;
> The moon is bright, sans being owned.
> Sans sickness, with them I dwell;
> Sans thought of age, I grow old.

He had a beautiful death, quiet and peaceful, without wrestling. His married daughters had all come back to be there when he died. The tall doctor attended him on the mat, and as soon as the breath had passed, took a shirt of my grandfather's and went up on top the grass roof. There he shook the shirt three times, waving farewell to my grandfather's spirit, and each time he called out in a loud solemn voice the conventional good-by.

"Hyung-Ha!" (This was my grandfather's name.)

"Kyo-Shiu!" (Being the highest scholar's degree my grandfather ever received in his life.)

"Chuksam-kache kasiow!" (Oh, take with you this shirt!) Then the wailing began, low and rhythmical, mounting higher. To Westerners it would probably sound like a singing or chanting.

"Ai-kyo . . . ai-kyo . . . ai-kyo!"

And the villagers came too and cried with the rest of us, "Uyi, uyi!—sorrow, oh, sorrow!"

He was put in a coffin of thick strong pine in which only pine-wooden nails were used. Pine was to show the superior-mindedness of the dead, and also to keep him protected from the insects. High, high on the mountain he was carried by his neighbors and his family to the spot he had chosen as his grave, the grave which was to make his grandson a *pak-sa*. Lined up between our house and the Eastern mountain were hundreds of poetry banners of consolation. One was as follows:

The bright sun is falling behind the Western mountain
As the yellow river enters the Eastern sea.
From old old times until now, heroes and flowers
Have all gone down to their graves in the Northern snow.
Let be. . . . All things bloom and are scattered.
Why sorrow? This life is so . . .

And another:

The hill is the same hill always.
But it is not the same rill always.
By day and by night running onward,
How could it be the same, always?
The Hero resembles the rill—
He passes not this way again.

A Korean grave is always beautiful and my grandfather's was especially well chosen. As usual it was made in the shape of a half-moon, I don't know why, with no other graves anywhere in sight. When the half-moon is dug, the coffin is put down very deep, and the mound at once covered with grassy turf so that it never looks bare, like the new graves in an American cemetery. In the solemn peace of nature the sleeper rests alone in his box made of the wood called eternal. A stone table was placed beside my grandfather's grave to receive the offerings of meat and wine, to be made by his sons, and likewise a stone lion to be his guardian; besides these there was the plain stone pillar where his name and genealogy were carved. This spot was all for him, this grass was his, these mountains and these trees; no one else could be buried here but my grandmother when she should come to die; then these two would be left in their natural solitude forever.

After he was buried in this propitious spot, my future as a *pak-sa* ought to have been assured; except that conditions began to change so rapidly after my uncle *pak-sa* came home from Seoul. Having grown disgusted with politics, he had given up his life at the capital, said good-by to all the beautiful gishas, and came back to Song-Dune-Chi to retire. All men retired at about his age and for a while no one thought anything of it. According to the universal idea in the Orient, the age of sixty years is life at its very best. Before this a man is distracted by the five lusts. Now you are all over with the five lusts: life should be suave, easy, luxurious.

The first thing he did when he got to the old home was to celebrate his sixtieth birthday feast. This is a very special kind of birthday in Korea. The Korean calendar is arranged in cycles of sixty years and after the sixtieth birthday, an individual begins life anew, he lives time over again. A great festivity should be prepared, especially for a successful man like my uncle *pak-sa*. The individual's destiny has now been accomplished, he knows for good and all if he has a success or a failure.

It is a far grander occasion than that of his wedding, and quite rightly: no one knows if a wedding is going to be a success or a failure.

More than one village came to my uncle's birthday feast, which began in the morning and lasted all day and all night. It was held on the lawn between his house and ours. My uncle wore his Korean tuxedo over a green silk suit such as might have belonged to a fresh young bridegroom. This was because he was sixty and young again. On his exquisitely combed hair was the official *pak-sa* cap which entitled him to entertainment free of charge throughout the land of Korea, so that wherever he went, as soon as he arrived in a village, he was given the finest quarters there, with a sumptuous feast, and when he left a purse was collected for him from the whole village. This my uncle never refused, because he was a *pak-sa,* a kind of poet-laureate, to be supported by the whole country of Korea. My uncle *pak-sa* and his wife were seated on thick mats on the grass, and she too wore green: his wife, she reflected him and became young again too. He sat in the official way, that is with one knee drawn high over the other; those of middle station were sitting just naturally; while the very young or the very low sat on their heels.

My uncle *pak-sa* was a rich man and always had a great many servants while he lived at the capital. In Song-Dune-Chi, there was no such thing as a servant because all were relatives together, going by the same name Han, even though in the case of the low-born their relationship with the very respected was lost in the antiquity. My uncle *pak-sa* had one or two family slaves, but in my family, the only servants we had were the volunteers, who received for their work food and provision of various kind. One such servant, I remember, was an old woman who had no means of providing for her numerous children except through selling the fruit of an apricot tree. My grandmother felt sorry for her, and generously repaid all her efforts in our kitchen by a small share in the produce; all the onions and sweet melons and cucumbers this old woman earned she would carry to her apricot tree to sell, saving her pennies for a certain cause. The cause was somewhat in the interest of woman's rights, and somewhat in the spirit of Epicurus' philosophy. Her husband was another volunteer servant who often did work for my father since he had no land of his own, a ne'er-do-well who could talk to you about anything and about everything: he chose his own subjects. How he loved the treats of beef-steak with strong wine, and the exhibitions of the gisha whenever he could contrive to be on the outskirts of a wild party! When this happened and his wife knew, she would always manage to get a chicken somehow by means of pennies saved from sales off the apricot tree; she would cook it tastily and feast on it all by herself. When he came home she would say, "Well, I had chicken!" In this way she thought to balance up. Perhaps this was the reason why his family was always poor and lived every day on smelling fish, of the kind used for fertilizer. The children, too, never had any clothes of their own, but the girls wore old clothes of Ok-Dong-Ya, and the boys those of mine or of Eul-Choon; all their stockings had been one time mine or Eul-Choon's, all the girls' ribbons one time Ok-Dong-Ya's; and their parents had not even the forethought to have them to be our contemporaries.

Among my uncle *pak-sa's* domestics at Seoul was an orchestra of seven or eight pieces and several beautiful young men dancers. In Song-Dune-Chi on his birthday, these entertainers played for the last time before being disbanded. The chief dancer and actor, Sung-Han or Blooming Fellow, was famed for his delicate face and exquisite physique; his glossy hair-knot and turned up side-burns were always given the best attention and he dressed in silks of the finest weaves, almost like those of nobility. He could relate stories with great skill.

On my uncle's feast day, Blooming Fellow entertained us for many hours with extracts from "The Cloud Dream of the Nine," the gay and witty love story of a young Buddhist monk who grew tired of the monastic life. For his carnal desires he was condemned to a love-life in the world. There it was said of him that he liked beautiful ladies so much that he must be the reincarnation of a man who had starved to death: eight beautiful Celestial fairies became his two primary wives, his two secondary wives, his two gishas and his two concubines in a single marriage which was the happy climax of his life. The nine loved each other very much and lived with great harmony, yet in the end all agreed that life on a Buddhist mountain was superior to the most this world could afford, and were rewarded at last with a return to nirvana. The Western missionaries have thought the work an example of how immoral Koreans are. This Korean Boccaccio wrote it many centuries ago to entertain his mother whom he loved very dearly.

With vigor and enthusiasm, Blooming Fellow enacted the scenes. His movements were not stylized, as those of the Chinese stage, but realistic, and he improvised them as he went. Throughout he was accompanied by an orchestra of wild and beautiful Korean music, as natural as the mountains and rivers of his native land.

And Korean music, I may say, really is natural—like the song of the nightingale. Westerners have been known to complain that it does not "keep time," but who

cares about "keeping time"? Does the nightingale? Korean music at least holds impulsive sincere emotion, like
a Keats, like a Li Po. As a matter of fact, every note and
cadence is produced according to a fixed rule made by
teachers of music thousands of years ago, and the laws
behind its composition would be hard indeed for a West-
erner to grasp. Every instrument in the orchestra has a
long romantic history, several thousand years old. There
is the jade flute of the seven holes, producing the nearest approach to the unheard melodies. There is the enrapturing throat of the *kumoonko*, like a long narrow
bass viol, well adapted to express the sorrows of love.
There is the *hageum*, resembling in appearance a large
croquet mallet with a short head, a hollow handle and
two strings, and emitting a sharp melodious twang of
violin quality (the man who plays the *hageum* carries
a whistle in his mouth also, and sometimes it seems as
if he is only pretending to play the *hageum*, but is making the sound with his lips). There are cymbals and tam-
bourines, and many drums, or *boobs*, as they are called,
of varying shapes. The orchestra dances vigorously,
while playing, keeping time not only with the arms and
head, but also capering with the legs. There is one large
boob or drum, three feet in diameter, too big for the
musician to carry and to dance with at the same time,
so a boy always carries it on his back, while the musician
dances along in the rear, beating it according to the
rhythms of the rest of the orchestra.

Immediately after his dramatic rendering, Sung-Han
or Blooming Fellow took off his overcoat and shinnied
up a pillar of my uncle's porch, which was about sixteen
feet high, and danced out on a rope stretched from the
pillar to a tall pine. His black gauze stove-pipe hat worn
by all Koreans of no caste, and always balanced cliff-like

on the top of the head, did not even tremble in the breeze. He spread a pink-flowered silk parasol, and performed ballet steps high in air. For his art was not confined to one medium—drama.

In the evening festivities continued. Under a lantern pavilion, the children and young men of the village danced before my uncle, wearing dance-costumes which had come from the amateurs' chest and which had been handed down for several generations. Ok-Dong-Ya yielded to a child's ecstasy and whirled across the grass, pretending to herself, with scarves of deep rose, red, and pale pink, that she was peach blossoms in Spring. She was still allowed to dance by my father because she was only ten, and her movements, being spontaneous, were more beautiful than those of a gisha. But her dance, like the dance of a humming bird, was over so soon that it could hardly be enjoyed by others. She was shy and her shyness was only conquered by her love of grace, rhythm, music, which appeared to her soul like natural language; so as soon as she had whisked across the yard in her rose-red scarves, she laughed and hid her face in her sleeves, vanishing quickly behind the older girls and women.

In imitation of Sung-Han, I danced the dance of knives, taught me by an amateur of the village, who never got paid but sometimes held dancing class just for the fun; the people clapped my agility and fieriness of motion. Again, when I appeared with folded arms on the tip-top of a pyramid of dancing young men three stories high, the smallest and most gayly clad, I received much laughter and applause. My dance with the green, the red and the white scarves was called for the most; in that it was said that I resembled a ballet of the elements, water, fire and air.

"Why don't you take this pretty boy with you to the

market-place the next time you go?" Blooming Fellow suggested to my uncle with a bow. "He should see something of a *pak-sa's* life."

My uncle sighed, and uttered these ominous words:

"He is as bright mentally as he is agile, yet I fear the time for a really handsome scholar's career is almost over. With Japanese overrunning the court, there is no future for anybody in the country."

I overheard these words. An agonizing feeling came over me.

From this time forward I often heard such thoughts voiced. My community was retired and isolated. Now my illustrious uncle had returned with grave tales of the political situation. For hours he would discuss it with friends, sitting in one of his garden chairs, a rocky or tree-root seat under the peach and the pear trees, and smoking a very long pipe—the length was a mark of his dignity—which was always lighted by a grandson or a servant, since the bowl was entirely out of his reach. Over the Russo-Japanese war, when the Japanese first swarmed into Korea, and over all their tricky ways of deceiving the Koreans afterwards, my uncle shook his head and pulled his small goatee. Japan was trying devilishly to suck blood. Where would it end?

One old man recalled what his father had told him about the message the emperor had sent to the Japanese after their alliance with the Barbarians, and our repudiation of the Japanese then as unworthy to be associated with. Had not those Japanese cast off all cultural ties by taking the Barbarians for allies? Was not the emperor right to state that the country of Korea was well satisfied with civilized people's ways and did not propose to change? Better for us, the old man said, if we had stood by the message of our former emperor.

And still my uncle *pak-sa* shook his head. Was it possible to stem the river of Song-Dune-Chi in time of flood? he asked. What had happened to the Empress Min, when she strove against Japanese alliance in the Capital? She had been murdered, hacked in small pieces within her own inner chamber, by command of Miura, the Japanese emperor's envoy. The Japanese influence at Seoul had grown strong. What was there for a Korean official to do but commit suicide or retire? The former course had been taken by his friend, General Min Yong-Whan, minister of the war cabinet, my uncle *pak-sa* mournfully recalled.

"But what is to happen to our poor children," lamented another old man, "if the culture of a thousand years is to be taken from them, and they see only the bad example of these Japanese, and their allies?"

My uncle pulled his goatee, and rolled his eyes toward the old men with long grey beards, and spoke somewhat of his experience with Westerners in Seoul. Cautiously at the last, he gave his opinion that after all the Westerners seemed an unusual people, and perhaps much could be learned from their ways, national and military. One should keep the open mind of a gentleman and a scholar. The Westerners were not Japanese, and might they not even be as the life-saving rope to the man in the flooded river?

The old men of Song-Dune-Chi, his contemporaries, but not his equals in social distinction or worldly experience, were too polite to contradict the *pak-sa*, but looked the other way. My uncle appeared harassed, until he caught sight of his grandsons juggling grass on their toes, turning their graceful little bodies this way and that in a wrestling and leaping contest, casting each his penny with the square hole in the game of "muk-dong." Then his brow cleared in spite of himself. What peace was to be compared with the peace brought by grand-sons? He sighed and recalled that after all he had come home to celebrate the sixtieth birthday, and to retire from politics, amid the constant mountains, the inde-structible river and perennial trees. How could the Japa-nese take this part of his country away from him?

So my uncle returned to depths of nature. This en-forced retirement brought mingled pleasure and regret. Regret for past officialdom, for in the Capital, he had been a very happy man, delighting in the joys of the nobility, the royal excursions from province to province, the sunrise picnics amid renowned scenic beauties, the expeditions to Buddhist monasteries outside Seoul for afternoon tea with raw eggs: pleasure to find himself once more by the side of the winding river in the clear quiet atmosphere of Song-Dune-Chi, where he had spent the sunrise of his youth, and still hoped to pass the sun-set of his days, content to remember as a thing of the past his high noon of fame, wealth, honor, friends in the Capital. My uncle *pak-sa* after having been a devout Confucian and man of the world even became inclined toward the mysteries of Buddha and toward the crazy-poet's Taoist quietism. For he reflected that whatever the state of politics, his very fortunate and happy life was almost over and it had seemed to him as a one day's journey. Now like my crazy-poet uncle, he realized that life could be sweet in Song-Dune-Chi; it was sweet to linger entirely alone in the moonlit garden after even the wan lantern was blown, listening to the autumnal sounds, and the long pounding rush of the river, which was un-usually high. His desires now were so simple: to compose his songs of peaceful old age, his grandchildren around him, to meditate about his approaching disappearance from the ordered pattern of the world, and to speculate about his more permanent place in the abiding fabric of all things. Thoughts of his past were very pleasant to him. If he relived at times in the memory certain more exotic raptures with beautiful flower-like ghosts who had no home in this spot, and asked for none, except the casual remembrance of a bounteous perfume scattered on the winds of Spring, these had no power to intrude upon his meditations with sense of overwhelming loss or regret. Yes, my uncle had got into the national habit of happiness.

What was the ghost then that visited him under the moon, in those cold morning hours before the crow of cock? What menace could he feel in that autumnal blast, although it pierced his bones, from the antique mountain hollows around Song-Dune-Chi? What did he fear in the billows of merciless force which hurled against the shores of the everlasting pine grove, from out that very river which he remembered as one of the laughing guardians of his youth? What prevented him from sleeping the sleep of retired scholarship which he had earned, what night after night caused him to hold his poor head, reflecting upon the king and the royal family at Seoul?

There was one particularly bitter thought reserved for the last hour of his night wandering. The lament of that old man, his contemporary, himself a grandfather, "What is to happen to our poor children deprived of the culture of a thousand years?" Must all become allies of the Barbarians? He understood the strength of Japan. That other elder did not. The strength of Japan was as the torrent, it pounded upon the shores of Korea like that flooded river, but the strength of Japan was not really the strength of Japan, it was the strength of the West.

Next morning through the long quiet hours of day,

hearing the "cock-o-dack-o" of the hen, and the droning song of the woman beating fresh clothes, he almost forgot. He walked abroad, seeing in place of the weird humped beggar whining for alms outside the palace doors, the newly married bride drawing water from the well, in place of the pushing bustle of shrewd-eyed trade, well-shouldered, deft-footed young men bringing in fuel from the mountainside on the bullock's back. He thought, "Did a ghost really nip my heart last night?" For what could overcome this peace as of things eternal, preserved by the lowing kine, the song of men in the field? But the river, still swollen, sullen, spleen-colored, and glutted with spoils, would not let him forget. This new strength of Japan, was it not drawn from the West? And as he strolled through the village, he strolled too restlessly. Should a scholar of Confucius bow then to the learning of the West?

I remember this uncle *pak-sa* as a slender, aristocratic man with exquisitely cared for hair and hands, dressing always in immaculate white silk, with an extra coat or two even in the warmest weather to denote his high rank. He was so gifted with social ability! He was a better bluffer than a match-maker, yet he always had the goods, two essentials for a successful career. He had always been much cleverer in adopting a situation than my crazy-poet uncle, who was so busy writing verses that he never knew he was a poet: a very great failing; but my uncle *pak-sa* had a more practical turn of philosophy and poetics, and by adding scholarship to pull and pull to scholarship, *he* reaped the golden reward. So he found it particularly hard to believe in this spectre of a national failure which dogged his footsteps every night. What could defeat Confucius, the renowned Chinese re-

former of the fifth century B. C., the profound philosopher of human relationship problems, teacher of the
permanency of the practical?

No, it must be some reckless ghost which kept him
from sleeping, perhaps one of his own dear sons, who
died unnaturally before his father. He took long walks
to the mountains to visit the grave and offer a cup of wine
there. He noted how tall was the tree planted at the time
of death, and everything reminded him that he had come
to the Autumn of his years, and soon his own spirit must
be worshipped by posterity. What consolation had the
West to offer equal to that? Coming back to the pillared
porch, he observed his grandchildren with renewed
hope, placing on them his faith in the eternal order,
through them calming his fears.

"Chung-Pa!" he would call. "Chung-Pa!" And I would
run to light my uncle's pipe. Presently I would confide:
"I want to go to Seoul one day and get this country
straightened up. I will drive out all those Japanese."

In reply he did not mention the learning of the West,
which he proposed perhaps to foster, but reminded me
of the classics with an appropriate gravity:

"Cultivate yourself in body and mind, first, according
to the wisdom of Confucius. Next administer a family
well, and only after that is accomplished, seek to administer the nation."

Eventually the weather cleared. The river became
radiantly placid once more. Song-Dune-Chi was far from
the capital and few rumors came beyond that of dead-
lock between Japan's emissaries and the old Emperor.
During the crystal Autumn season when all sounds could
be heard with the distinctness of far away bells in the
remarkable atmosphere, I travelled a good deal with
my uncle *pak-sa* through mountain scenery, very tran-

quil and harmonious but woven of gorgeous colors. My gray donkey trotted sedately along on mats of red and yellow leaves behind my uncle's mule. This donkey of mine, relying on his white hairs and his expression of dignified old age, constantly tried to deceive me and force me to get down and walk, although I was very young and light and the donkey was used to carrying grown men. Except that he was more genteel, being a scholar's donkey, he resembled a certain donkey of our village which my grandmother liked to tell about.

This other donkey was taken to market to bring home two large straw bags filled with salt. They seemed to him very heavy. When he was crossing the river, he had a bright idea. He ducked under the cool flowing stream, and of course the salt was all melted away by the water. The owner was a kind man and did not beat the donkey overmuch, for he reasoned, "How could a dumb brute know about that?" Presently the donkey was again taken to market. This time the farmer filled the straw bags with cotton batting for quilts. When they came to the river, the donkey remembered how he had successfully lightened his load before, and he ducked under the water. Then how surprised he was! He was hardly able to rise, and all the way home could hardly drag himself and his load.

My grandmother always ended her account by saying:

"Remember that donkey, Chung-Pa. Little boys who are too shrewd always get cheated themselves before long, as that donkey did."

As we travelled the ancient roads across mountains, my uncle *pak-sa* would tell me:

"A certain sage passing over these mountains wrote a poem like this once."

Then he would quote, remembering all the poems he

had ever read, accurately. Or he would relate how a great poet once met a tiger. The tiger advanced, roaring on his victim. But the poet looked him in the face and recited a verse from the classics, and the tiger bowed and let the scholar pass. Even wild beasts, said my uncle, had to respect poets and scholars.

If the journey was long and dusty, one of my uncle's slaves walked behind us, carrying for each a change of white clothes. This was the case of course when my uncle *pak-sa* was reader in the great Confucian temple of the whole province. The Temple of Confucius was an impressive structure of red stone with two roofs like tiled boats, for the ends turned up like keels. It was set in the heart of nature; the services were very ceremonious, and all about it, the atmosphere seemed solemn. One quiet night in New York City, looking down Madison Avenue at Grand Central station, I was suddenly reminded of the Temple of Confucius, by I don't know what of massive gravity and power. But noisy trains enter there, and not the ghost of the immemorial sage, Confucius, quietly. When the priest carried the cup of wine up the long steps, he went very slowly. His ceremonial robe was very long with wide sleeves and tassels sweeping the ground; it was white or sky-blue in color, and he wore a kind of mitre with two ears, which symbolized the mountain on which the father of Confucius once prayed for his birth. While the wine went up the steps no one dared to breathe loudly. Lined up below in the big yard, standing in ranks on the steps, were the other priests, all clad in this same way. Of course there were a number of priests, for everybody who worshipped was a priest, but he must be a poet and a scholar. The common people took no part in the rites; they only looked on,

and prepared the food the day before for the offering.
My uncle *pak-sa*, when younger, used to carry the wine
cup. Now he was usually the reader, standing close to
the wine-bearer. All the poets and scholars looked up to
receive the ghost of the learned Confucius, while my
uncle read from a long scroll of white silk the first stanza
of the Chinese hymn:

> Great Prince, Confucius, hail!
> First wise man, first of seers!
> Power ranked with Heaven and Earth,
> Saint, of ten thousand years!
> Adored of flower-wreathed unicorn!
> Drawn by our music's golden thread!
> You harmonized the Sun and Moon;
> You made the man's and women's realm!

Then one of the scholars held up some rice on a Korean
spoon to feed Confucius, and my uncle continued the
hymn:

> Ring loudly, chimes of jade!
> Praise this superior man,
> Unique among mankind,
> In wisdom universal.
> Bring harvest feasts and greens of Spring;
> Seasons on thousand seasons roll
> Since first the crystal wine was poured
> As these fumes rising from this bowl.

After the benefits of the ghost were received, the spirit
was escorted away, while my uncle read these words:

> Fount high on Mount Ah-Ah!
> Choo-Choo and Sa murmur,
> Rivers that never run dry
> Although the source is far.
> In order should our rites be done
> To hymn the Lord Confucius' fame,

> He who refined the inner man
> And gave all scholarship his name.

The poet-priests then disbanded to write verses in the rooms provided for them; and I wrote some too in the old classical vein.

Chapter 9

VILE BUT NOT OBSCENE

I dream of a red-rose tree.
Women and Roses: ROBERT BROWNING

MY uncle *pak-sa* took me with him also when he went to attend the Fall meeting of his club of *literati* called the "Orchid and Chrysanthemum Society." It met twice a year, Spring and Fall: that was why it was called the "Orchid and Chrysanthemum Society." Constantly my uncle was disturbed at this period. Although he was living life at its best, for the age of the sixties is the only time your ears are obedient to you, Confucius says; he still worried, from patriotic motives, and intended to join a radical movement to promote the opening of a new school.

A mile outside the gate of the market-place we were met by Mai-Cha or Plum-Child, the mother of Blooming Fellow. She was beautifully dressed in voluminous silks, the expanse of her face more white than the moon, the lips and the cheeks more red than the peach, with hair oiled down and nails rounded out; I would have thought her some very rich and honorable lady if she had not been waiting all alone there for my uncle with head uncovered. She had been the concubine of a great scholar, now deceased, the father of Blooming Fellow and the friend of my uncle *pak-sa*. She bowed and bowed to us, showing by the suggestion of art that she had been a dancing girl in her youth, though now somewhat fat. It was a ripe-fruity fatness, and I thought her extremely beautiful, and her impulsive desire to please very refreshing.

"Come to my house please, for your entertainment," she insisted.

My uncle replied with the easy etiquette that a man could use to the concubine of an old friend; afterwards he seemed abstracted and kept looking at the sky. We rode on into the market-place, followed by Plum-Child on foot, who never failed to bow and lower her eyes with great artfulness whenever she encountered the eyes of my uncle.

The market-place was built in the shape of a horseshoe, around the sea. The mountains formed natural walls on three sides, and whenever the cliff-line was incomplete, masonry had been supplied. Koreans always made the most of natural boundaries to protect, for we had a very strong sense of "Monroe Doctrine," and still liked to be isolated. On top of each of the mountains was a park of natural flowers with a pleasure house for poets and scholars, reached by such a sinuous road that you might hold a long philosophical conversation with a friend who was going down at the same time you were going up, without halting the foot. There were many forests, thick bushes and inviting recesses leading off from the main path, where young men retreated with bottles of wine, kumoonkos, and gisha girls to have a good time. All the houses in the market-place were one-storied, and of unpainted natural wood having a warm sun-brown tint. Only the king at Seoul could have a two-story house by law. At the foot of the three mountains, in various rambling wine-halls, or sometimes in their own establishments, lived the gisha girls.

Mai-Cha, of course, had her own house, very clean and

cozy. The walls were hung with a great many poems made by poets of her acquaintance. Those of my uncle *pak-sa* were given the most honor. There were also four paintings, of Plum, Orchid, Bamboo, and Chrysanthemum, representing the four great sages. Mai-Cha seemed to use more on her walls than high-class women, just as she used more on her face. She had a small panel containing the "Story of Spring Perfume and of Master Plum"—a novel which American missionaries have called obscene—and other native Korean works. Scholars somewhat despised these, but Plum-Child read the native novels all the time, revelling in the stories of beautiful and learned concubines. She was also an accomplished letter writer in native Korean script, and even knew many Chinese characters. She took off my uncle's shoes and mine, and brought us wine and dainties immediately. I had never tasted such highly spiced delicious dainties.

"Sing me your wine-cup song, Mai-Cha" my uncle asked, after he had had a bowl or two of wine. There had been rather an austere look in his eye before that.

So Mai-Cha took her kumoonko and sang to its sweet wailing chords:

> Take, pray take my cup of wine,
> For it brings miracles of blessing,
> Ten thousand times, ten thousand times!
> For even heroes and great men
> Lie buried in the backyard yonder,
> Take, pray take, my cup of wine!
> Ten thousand times drink happily,
> Ten thousand times, ten thousand times!

As she sang about the heroes and great men, she looked roguishly at my uncle. She entertained us very pleasantly all the afternoon.

In the evening several of my uncle's poet-friends came

in and there was a feast of luscious and expensive foods served by Mai-Cha and her adopted niece, the young girl, Nan-Cho, or Lily-Grass—food rather over-rich and over-costly like their clothes. Later Nan-Cho went off to entertain a younger party of poets and Bohemians, and Mai-Cha after singing a song or two and bringing in her son, Blooming Fellow, to juggle balls before the guests, sat a little apart from the now serious-minded scholars, and listened, contentedly, only springing up to light their pipes, which they smoked in luxurious mood.

My uncle's *literati* club was to begin at dawn next day. We spent the night at Mai-Cha's house. Mai-Cha and Nan-Cho took their mats to the kitchen. I saw that Mai-Cha admired my uncle *pak-sa* very much, even to an unusual degree. The golden-threaded coverlets were piled high on his couch of mats. Mai-Cha herself brought in the bedtime stove, all glowing with pine-needle ash, from one compartment took the hot wine and from another the bedtime repast which she served with pleasing smiles and words. She arranged the screen comfortably around his bed. I was to sleep in the little back room which opened off from my uncle's and looked out on a flowery garden. Mai-Cha politely suggested that I might sleep in the outer reception room if this seemed too small, but my uncle said firmly no, it would do very well for me.

"Chung-Pa," said my uncle solemnly, after Mai-Cha had bowed herself out. "I want to tell you something. Women are very, very dangerous creatures. We may shoot a prowling tiger that we meet in the mountains, or we may abash wild beasts with our classical poems, but there is no weapon against the menace of Woman to scholars. Even a hero, if he is not constantly on his guard, may find himself hypnotized, and one fall for a woman may be enough to ruin a great man for life."

If he had been familiar with the story of Genesis where a whole career depended upon one apple, and Mrs. Adam spoiled it all, would he not have been even more positive?

My father had recently returned from Russia with the prodigal-son, whom he had got by the nose, and my uncle *pak-sa* used sometimes to preach to the prodigal-son in this same way:

"I don't blame young fellows for running out with beautiful women," he would advise, "but you must have some limit. You should imitate me. Of course there have been days when I have made blundering mistakes, but when Plum-Child comes around me, just see how I be-have *myself!*"

I somewhat think my *pak-sa* uncle inconsistent in these words. After he had taken a good deal of wine with his contemporaries, he would tell them that Plum-Child had long wished to become his concubine, but he gave as his reason for not taking her that he did not think it would be respectful toward the ghost of an old friend. What I really think is that my uncle actually preferred now to lead the simple life.

My father was different, a very rare type. He alone always practised what he preached. When under the influence of wine, he used to sob about his beautiful lost wife, and I have always believed that he loved my mother very much and that was really why he did not care to marry himself to a new wife. He thought gisha girls were feather-weights, and that it was much more important to take care of the family than to indulge your Bohemian side. There was no compromise in my father as in my uncle *pak-sa*.

In the morning, before I was risen my uncle went up to a pleasure house in the mountains to hold his *literati* meeting, and I was left in the care of Mai-Cha and Nan-Cho who indulged me in everything. Although twenty-five or twenty-six, little Nan-Cho was not much bigger than I. She treated me like a big sister, or a little aunt, except that she did not use the language spoken by elders to children, but only high respectable language to show that she knew her station with a child of the official class. Yet all that she did for me was done with fresh spontaneity and interest. She pulled up my stockings and tied my shoes and wrapped my trouser ribbons artistically about my ankles, and parted my hair very neatly and helped me wash my face and hands. She exclaimed at my new clothes; since she did not like to see them become spotted with water, she fastened one of her own robes around my chin like an old man's napkin, before she would let me dabble in the water-basin.

"Now you look like a beautiful young prince," she commented enthusiastically when it was finished. "See, Mai-Cha. Isn't he cute? How well the green ribbons become him!"

Remembering my uncle's words, I asked her why she was a gisha girl and not some boy's little aunt. Mai-Cha replied for her that one day when Nan-Cho was young, her mother was told by a fortune-teller that she was too beautiful to be a man's wife, for she was born to make many men love-sick; therefore she must be trained as a professional gisha, so that numerous youths might behold her beauty and enjoy it.

I remembered my uncle's words, yet Nan-Cho did not look to me like a dangerous tiger as her dainty little figure ran hither and thither with the wash basin that morning, her robes fluttering about her heels, her long hair in disarray, reaching below her knees. She was a typical dancing girl of Korea, with very white skin, long straight eyes and jetty hair. Her mouth was tiny and pleasant, and her feet exquisitely small. Ah, Nan-Cho! Where is she now? Is she still a gisha girl? Is she some scholarly gentleman's concubine? I hardly think she would make an emancipator for her sex.

When Nan-Cho had finished with me, I went out into the peppy, salty air of the market-place, full of all sorts of rich odors, and I threaded my way through the straw baskets and straw trays filled with every kind of commodity, dried fishes, sea-weed, savory herbs, strips of vivid colored cloth and crisp white linens, broad farmer's hats, laundry sticks and many more objects. I had been given twenty or thirty cents by my grandmother to spend in the market-place on *cook-soo*, or material for kites, on strings for skates and so forth. I went straight to a book store and in the end spent all my money on a beautiful blank notebook in which to write poetry. It was bound in scarlet leather, fastened with a green strap, with an inside pocket for cards and a hole in the binding through which was secured a big thick Western lead pencil.

While still in the shop I wrote on the title-page with the thick lead pencil, the characters "Myung Chul Lon," which might be translated as: "Bright Philosophizing Discussions." Then I wrote beneath:

"Someday I will grow and become a big man:

"This is that I may recall the fruitful thoughts of Yesterday!"

I showed my inscriptions to the shopkeeper and he was much impressed. Afterwards I sat down on the street and began some categories which I entered in the thumb index in my most perfect caligraphy. *Things I Love to Remember*, such as a beautiful little girl who passed just then through the market-place with her aunt or grandmother, or my crazy-poet uncle's saying, "man comes out of woman, as salt out of water, when he nears her, as salt by water he is melted again"; and *Things I Feel Sorry Having Done*. Foremost in the latter category was an experience I had had a few days before, which I still deeply regretted. I was sleeping in my crazy-poet uncle's studio, as usual, and I awoke with a poem about a chrysanthemum in my head. It was very very early and nobody seemed to be stirring. I ardently desired to pick and smell a chrysanthemum. So I leaped up from bed and ran out into the garden. But in warm weather I slept naked, and I had not yet put my Winter pajama on. I was running as fast as I could toward the chrysanthemum bush when a woman stepped out of a door, a newly-married wife of one of my cousins, come recently from a distant village. *She saw me naked.* I turned and fled into the studio, filled with a terrible shame, and hid my head under the pillow for an hour. Whenever I saw that woman's back for a long time, I would turn and run, and I could never bear to look at her face.

I spent the whole morning wandering around the market-place and writing about things I saw in my book of "Bright Philosophizing Discussions." In the afternoon Nan-Cho asked me if I would like to make an excursion with her to the Isles of Fairy Dreamland. She was going to entertain a group of young poets and scholars, she said, and I could listen to the mirth and partake of the dainties. She was all dressed up now in gisha-girl costume, quite different from how she had looked in the morning. Now she was a gorgeous thing, with painted hands and lips and simpering face, long gauzy butterfly sleeves and a gold sash tied under the armpits, but not nearly so attractive as that innocent morning Nan-Cho. Yet she wore prettier stockings and shoes than any woman I had ever seen; her shoes were of red leather with yellow chrysanthemums on top, and they turned up at the end like inverted question-marks. She wore her overcoat just like a man. Women of the better class always wore theirs upon the head, as if they were expecting rain; this almost completely covered the face. Gisha girls however did not cover the head.

We went down to the sea. Nan-Cho loaded me with presents, candy, and a Korean water gun of bamboo which she bought in the market; then we were joined by another gisha girl who was taller and stronger than Nan-Cho and who laughingly carried me on her back. Her name was Shun-Hi, or Happy Virtue. We embarked on a boat which was close to the surface of the water, and pointed at both ends. If you were cold there was a place to go in, and if you were warm, a place to come out. There were cushions and under the seats were the round-bellied earthen-ware jugs with long necks, full of wine, and the supplies of raw meat with pickles and spices to be eaten with wine. There was an orchestra, the members of which were known to Nan-Cho and Shun-Hi.

The boat was manned by hired oarsmen, who knew all the secrets of weather, tide and current, so that the bark glided over the waves like a black swan. These men could predict when a dark and spotted cloud went by that five hours later there would be a shower, or that a white bank in the shape of a camel meant twenty-four hours of fair sky. They had not learned their lore from books, but from study of the elements direct, and by a natural adaptability to the sea.

O that sea, over which ten thousand fleets rolled without making marks! How many minds it had fascinated and souls it had hypnotized to become wanderers: It was not just a Korean sea, but the greatest Bohemian of the world. I felt so even then. Very high and far away on the sky I presently saw five or six specks which I recognized as those same wild geese of Autumn I had seen but a year back with such poignant feelings. Today I felt only the exquisite joy of excursioning on the beautiful waves. Above my head the sea-gulls sailed up and down, in curving flight as different as possible from the high straight course of the wild geese. *They* fly like an arrow straight at the heart, making wanderers cry out for the old home, but sea-gulls know how to weave mazes of enchantment that wrap you like a magic veil in dreams of some strange beauty never yet attained by anyone, and perhaps if you judge by their hungering and lost cry, wholly unattainable. O bird with the Bohemian soul flying on insatiable quest, dreamer, romanticist, adventurer, I love you above all earthly birds!

The young men who had hired the pleasure boat were full of enthusiasm and holiday spirit, the orchestra played, Lily-Grass and Happy Virtue made languorous, swaying movements of hand and waist, so artificial as to be slightly ridiculous, but having that elusive style and grace known only to the gisha girl of the Orient. The men at the oars sang with the orchestra. The boat leaped over the green sea toward the Isles of Fairy Dreamland, and the big round fish, jumping into the air before our boat, their scales glittering like precious treasure of the deep.

Some of the young men withdrew to a corner to write songs and others gathered about the gisha girls for jazzy, jolly, happy, flippy flirtation. The difference between East and West in this respect is that a young Western man takes to a party the kind of girl who can give him a good time, and a young Eastern man finds a trained girl there when he arrives. I watched the young men with the gisha girls because I was curious, and also, being shy, I intended to hang to Nan-Cho's sleeve all the way.

> My soul is as blue as the sea,
>> But my experience is as green as the grass,

sang Nan-Cho in an artificial baby-squeak,

>> Also my heart is as large as the sky,

she finished, laughing heartily.

"And are you good to eat?" asked one of the young scholars.

"O very nice and fresh."

"Let me put some salt on."

I had not minded at all when one of the men put his arm around Happy Virtue and played with her hand, but when the young man who was paying for the party (being a rich man and not so good a poet as the others) came close to Nan-Cho with his lips, I brought out my water gun and shot at his hat. It was a new hat too, and all his clothes were new. Nan-Cho was the only one who saw me do it, and she laughed behind her fan when she caught my eye. After that whenever the man made advances to Nan-Cho I shot him again; once it flew between their approaching lips like a sea spray. He looked at me, but my hand with the gun was over the side of the boat in the water, as I stared at a cloud in the sky. Finally he reprimanded the oarsman for throwing water so high: oarsmen are never supposed to answer poets back.

The Isles of Fairy Dreamland had great rocks at the edge of the sea, and between the rocks, mats of velvet-

like grass on which rich Autumn wild flowers were growing, with fragrance heightened by the salty mist linger-
ing about them which freshened petals and hearts.

The young men took off their overcoats, and went out
on the farthest rocks where they caught crabs as big as
three months' old babies. They built a fire and had a
shore-roast, and everybody drank the wine and the raw-
meat dainties brought from the boat. While the gisha
girls, in their long dance skirts and sleeves, postured on
the beach, and the waves seemed a dancing chorus of
accompaniment, the poets drank their wine, smacked
their lips and sang songs like this:

> When maple leaves are threaded with red,
> And the golden chrysanthemum heaves perfume,
> Ah, but the wine that is made from new rice
> With the silk-scaled fish eaten raw tastes nice!
> Here, Child, give that kumoonko to me,
> For myself I will sing, and get drunk as can be!

Then they would take the gisha girls' kumoonkos and
sing other songs such as this:

> In the blue waves, ten thousand furrows
> Could not have washed out my ancient sorrows,
> But in this jug of wine to-day,
> My sorrows are all washed away!
> Was it for this that Li Po lay
> Forever drunk, in a swoon all day?

Or Happy Virtue sang plaintively to the man with
whom she was flirting:

> This cup I pour and proffer you,
> O please, do drink not less than all!
> For is not this the happy time
> That flowers bloom and little birds call?
> And in another season's hours,
> With whom may you and I see flowers?

We all had such a good time that the concluding episode was especially unsavory. Returning over the sands to the pleasure boat after sundown, we came on a Japanese woman of low caste, entertaining a Korean. As the wind blew, it swung her one-piece garment high across her thighs, showing her naked body underneath, for she made no effort either to stand or to move modestly. The Korean women, even gisha girls, wore many layers of clothes; on the banks of the stream on wash-day in my village were to be seen all sorts of things you never saw in your life before. But the Japanese, men and women, wear only one garment, which is exactly what you see on them, and of course this is no exception with the Japanese gisha girls. Koreans found this painfully shocking. Nan-Cho and Shun-Hi looked at each other and hung down their heads.

"The Japanese," they muttered.

The woman was with a man, and had not even a kumoonko; she had only her naked body, and a pack of cards.

Shun-Hi and Nan-Cho were so far removed from the Western or the Neo-Japanese prostitute that the women whom the Japanese were steadily importing into Korea shocked and bewildered them as well as more serious members of Korean communities. For the profession of the Korean gisha girl was the very ancient, highly skilled one of entertaining officials of the land, that is to say poets and scholars. Gisha girls were trained artistically from early years in dancing, in writing verse, in painting, in reciting stories. They were specialists in solacing the Bohemian side of man's nature. In the old days a Korean wine house would not keep gisha girls who were lacking in a certain decorum and self-respect—both necessary to the artist, even a poor dancing girl. It is true, gisha girls never became respectable wives, although they often became poets' sweethearts, when they continued in the pleasant task of flattering their patron's caligraphy and entertaining his verse-making friends, as no wife busy with serious baby-manufacturing, in obeying the mother and in instructing the young daughters for dignified household affairs had the time to do. Nor was a wife jealous of these gisha girls usually, even of a concubine. Why? She did not marry a man out of love for his Bohemian side, but out of reverence for parents, Confucius and the past. It was the same with a man; a man's marriage loyalty was toward parents, around whom his home revolved, not toward a wife. It was all, I confess, less complicated and less confusing than in the West, as people seemed to do and to say the same things about moralities.

But the Japanese girl was a new product. The young poets I had come with laughed among themselves, but were as uncomfortable as Shun-Hi and Nan-Cho and myself.

"Ugh!" they exclaimed with a contemptuous glance. "The Japanese."

I shuddered as I saw the Japanese gisha's face. She was like an artificial dead body. Neither she nor the man seemed to have that thing called soul, and if I ever heard of opium I might have thought they used it. She made some smart sally in Japanese about Shun-Hi and Nan-Cho who passed with crimson faces, for if obscene, these girls were never vulgarly obscene. The Japanese gisha began laughing mechanically, but there was no spontaneous gaity nor sparkling good spirit behind that laughter.

A little Japanese girl of about my age got up now from behind the rocks, to gaze after us. She was with her older friend to learn the trade of the Japanese gisha, for the Korean began insolently singing to her a line from a Japanese street song, and she pertly answered back. I once heard that song on the streets of Japan and suddenly recognized it years later. The words could be translated as follows:

He sings:

As patriotic souvenir, I'd like a bit of that gay flower.

She replies:

My will to give it you is great, greater than a mountain, mountain.
But the blossoms are not ripe, so I cannot give you yet.
Come to me again, again, I will give first fruits to you, when the flowers open.

We tried to forget the Japanese as soon as possible, but going back on the boat, over the moonlit waves, everybody cried more than usual. Nan-Cho's scholar suddenly chanted the philosophic poem:

> Think of our human life—
> Only a bundle of dreams!
> Good things, evil things,
> All are dreams within dreams.
> But as we dwell in dreams,
> Why not enjoy good times?
> What else could you do?

And Shun-Hi's scholar seized her kumoonko and sang fervently:

> Embarking over the golden wave,
> Cool winds under the yoke,
> Where tales are told to a piping flute,
> Floating down the river,
> So carousing with the moon,
> Call good-by to sorrow.

But in spite of himself the tears ran down the poet's face, and tears of sadness kept mingling with tears of rapture over that Korean moon, cool and bright in the waters. Even Nan-Cho and Shun-Hi cried heartily, and they had not had much to drink lately, and probably did not know what they were crying for.

Chapter 10

DECENT BUT DUMB

. . . Of the past world, the vital words and deeds
Of minds whom neither time nor change can tame,
Traditions dark and old whence evil creeds
Start forth, and whose dim shade a stream of poison feeds.
The Revolt of Islam: PERCY BYSSHE SHELLEY

THERE was a certain school by the North mountain of the Market-place, where immemorially the pine trees had been standing. The building was formerly a Confucian temple and my uncle *pak-sa* had gone there to worship many times. He himself advocated that it be made into a new Western school with black-boards and high Western chairs, and apparently saw it transformed without bitterness. Not so my grandmother. She was always annoyed at me for watching the low-class boys at their physical training when I came with her to the market.

"Butchers' boys!" she would say indignantly. "Sons of hat menders." (Slayers of dogs and cows were the lowest class in our society, and after that menders of hats.)

When she dragged me away, I cried and cried. I was particularly fascinated by gymnasium drills: one-two-three-halt. Arms up. Arms down. The Korean boys, although many of them were of the lowest station, for no discrimination was shown against them in the new learning as in the old, were very graceful at this mechanical performance, and made it a thing of life and beauty, in which their harmonious bodies, grown in an environment to have been appreciated by Rousseau, showed to the greatest advantage. All seemed to delight in the precision and discipline, the *tautness* required. Martial training was practically unknown to us: Korea had not even a police force.

But my family wished me to associate only with aristocracy and discouraged my interest in the West. *Pak-sas*, my father said, were not acquired by Western magic but by hard work on the classics.

Before my uncle *pak-sa's* retirement from Seoul, I was taught by my crazy-poet uncle, and I lived always in his studio. Every spare moment was spent with a book, some classic of Chinese literature, of course. The beautiful characters that I drew with the fine brush-pen filled my whole heart. My grandmother was equally interested in my education and usually sat in the studio with us, her needle in her hand, listening closely to the explanation of every poem, in order that she might help me in my studies when my teacher was not by. My crazy-poet uncle commuted by walking to a neighboring village where he had charge of many pupils. But his duties were not heavy, and he had a great deal of leisure to spend on me, while sitting before his low reading table, or perhaps at that large inlaid desk with the Chinese chair which the studio contained. All about were panels for books, many of them open, exposing volumes of thin beautiful paper simply bound with little cord-thongs. My grandmother sat somewhat apart. She was very careful not to let her skirts touch any of the books, because books were sacred and her skirts were not. Also women, it was thought, brought bad luck to scholars, if they came around too near. My grandmother, who idolized me, wanted to put no trouble in the way of my becoming a *pak-sa* like my renowned uncle, and perhaps a great official in the land, which all depended upon scholarship and good-luck. For this reason my grandmother reminded my little aunt to be most careful and respectful in dusting books. My little aunt was not so reverent toward books as my grandmother, but always had a very practical instinct about dust. She was better than my fat aunt however. My fat aunt, the wife of the crazy-poet, sometimes even stepped on manuscripts, and put all books in upside down, so for my sake she was rarely allowed in the studio.

In my family all the women except the fat aunt could read, but Ok-Dong-Ya was about to become the most educated of them—at least now that my remarkable childless aunt was no longer at home. Ok-Dong-Ya had picked up a lot of my learning and loved me to recite for her the classics by the hour. At the age of nine I knew the Four Books and Two of the Five classics by heart, and had won so many prizes at county examinations for poetry that I was famous in the country around.

When my uncle *pak-sa* came home, he too took my education in hand. But he said little to me about the new Western learning which was sweeping over the country, only remarking that I had a genius for the classics.

While I was with my uncle *pak-sa* on a trip to the Confucian temple I met my first real friend, Sur-Choon (or Slow Spring), just my age. When I saw him, he was hanging on the long sleeve of his grandfather, just as I was hanging on the corresponding sleeve of my illustrious uncle, for we were both very young and shy. He was then a lovely child with a handsome round face of a sweet and refined expression, and I always think of him so, for he never lost his child-like clarity and spontaneous ways. Already he had an infinite eagerness and curiosity for the distinguished and the beautiful.

With us it was love at first sight. We learned all about Confucius together. In many ways we were alike; I found in him the maximum of identity, the minimum of difference. He was brought up in a much richer house than mine, consequently his people were not quite so scholarly, for it was rare for the *literati* to be wealthy; my uncle *pak-sa* was an exception. But Sur-Choon's grandfather had been the governor of a distant province. Four years is not long enough for a good governor to straighten out a province, but it is too long for a bad governor, who sometimes in reaping the golden reward, impoverishes the people. His own grandfather was a very good scholar, however, and a friend of my uncle *pak-sa*, whom he revered highly until he discovered my uncle's growing tolerance toward the West. The grandfather of Sur-Choon was an old fashioned conservative.

Of course he lived so far away that he and my uncle *pak-sa* did not often get together. There were few Confucian temples where they both were priests, but when this occurred, Sur-Choon and I did a dance for glee. We did not waste our time in stealing pears or persimmons from the trees around the temple—at least not often; we were well-fed, for my uncle *pak-sa* and the grandfather of Sur-Choon were always feasted with the best and we were so indulged by the old men, that we were allowed to attack first the private tables served to them, piled two feet high with turkey-legs, big ripe dates and everything good—in fact the main thing to remember while on a trip of this kind with my uncle *pak-sa* was not to fill the rice in first. But we spent most of our time wrestling with literary and philosophical problems, just like our elders.

Our elders sat in a cool paper-sealed room adjoining the temple and played chess on a low table before a *mah-hah* plant, and discussed poetry and literature. We sat at a smaller table and played chess too. Poetry and litera-

ture were discussed at both tables; the only difference
was, Sur-Choon and I did not smoke the long pipes as
we talked, and we wore our little boy ribbons instead of
the dignified official caps of our elders.

"We must receive what is best, and we must give out
what is best," my uncle *pak-sa* preached to the grandfather of Sur-Choon. This was about the Western school-
ing. Yet even here my uncle *pak-sa* showed his weakness
for the compromise. He was really not a radical at all, but
was very cautious, at a time when strenuous action
should have been taken by the official class all over
Korea. He seemed to feel that by just keeping an open
and scholarly courtesy of mind all would be well. "The
past perhaps holds evil as well as good."

"The past hold evil?" exclaimed Sur-Choon's grandfather, scandalized. "But where can we get our models
if not from the past? No! Civilization must stand or fall
with the culture of Confucius. If this is the death of civilization—well this is the death!"

He now became very angry with Sur-Choon because
we two cared to discuss nothing but heretics and for that
purpose secretly studied all those classical non-conform-
ists who did not agree with Confucius. We did not know
much about the Westerners yet. But our minds seemed
preternaturally eager and questioning; already we were
as if vitalized by currents of rebirth that did not touch
the elder scholars. My uncle *pak-sa* looked at us with
frowns of perplexity, and not wholly of disapproval.
Then he sighed as Moses sighed, beholding a promised
land for his descendants denied his enfeebled old age.
But the frowns of Sur-Choon's grandfather were wholly
condemning. And soon, alas! he and my *pak-sa* uncle
were debating in civil war. It seemed that all over the
country now there was revolting, reforming literary so-

cieties, and other societies that opposed. Sur-Choon's grandfather joined a reactionary literary society, and my uncle joined a society which somewhat believed in schools for the Western Learning.

When Sur-Choon and I parted, we pledged each other to see who could read the most by the time of our next meeting. But that interval was long. Our elders were no longer intimate. Ah, Sur-Choon, my friend! Always I was thinking of him, and he of me, our congenial talks, the walks we had had by the sea-shore, our delightful wildwood excursions as we wandered over the hillsides, bathing naked in clear mountain pools and tanning under the sun's rays. Among a thousand people, we two had been accustomed to keep always close together. He would wear my hat, I his. Now we were severed by elders and this was all over.

The next Fall I was more than thrilled when my village selected me and one of my older cousins as their quota to go to the Western school in the market-place established by leaders of the province in reluctant agreement to the situation. My uncle *pak-sa* insisted that I accept the scholarship. My grandmother and my childless aunt prepared my dresses with expressionless faces. My father made no comment.

I was nine years old when I was sent to the market-place, a boarder at the new school. It was my first time to be away from my grandmother, Eul-Choon and Ok-Dong-Ya and the fat aunt's baby, for weeks without coming home. Yet I was not home-sick. I leaped to those studies with all the pep and enthusiasm I had, and they seemed like food I was hungry for. It was a very poor and half-hearted Western school. We studied Japanese, Korean and Chinese authors. My foundation in Chinese, owing to classical studies with the crazy-poet, was so good that I was bored by the Chinese lessons, but put all my time upon the Japanese. Through these Japanese authors, superficial though they were, I got my first hints about the West. Every night I went down to a Japanese store in the market-place in order to practise my Japanese. There was a young Japanese girl in charge there, with the exquisite charm of some Japanese women. After seeing the prostitute I did not think that any Japanese woman could be pretty, but this one really was. She had a quick tongue and exchanged many Japanese poems with me: in Japan, poetry was not confined to the upper class as in Korea, where our ideas of a poem somewhat differed. I was only pretending to buy from this pretty saleswoman, however. Nothing I bought except a toy once to send to Ok-Dong-Ya. But I made great progress in the Japanese tongue.

Before the end of the school year my father came to a decision: he told my uncle *pak-sa* that I was going to be spoiled, living with rough and impolite people near the market-place, and that he thought I was even becoming pro-Japanese. I made my good-by to Shina, the Japanese girl, and she felt so sorry to see me go that she went at once to her father and persuaded him to ask me to work in the store: both thought my Japanese accent very good.

When I told my father that if it cost too much to keep me at that Western school, I could work in a Japanese store, I have never seen him get so angry. He trembled with rage. His eyes shot fire. He ran into that Japanese store, and all that saved my father and that Japanese from a terrible fight was that neither understood the other's language. According to Korean, Chinese, and Japanese social system of the old days, business almost was the lowest occupation, the order being scholars, agriculturalists, artisans and merchants, coolies and dog-

slayers. Korea had been the longest conservative of the
three separate oriental nations. While very deeply admiring the Chinese classics and many aspects of the Chinese
character, Koreans in the past have been proud of their
differences from everybody including both Chinese and
Japanese. They have considered themselves far closer
to eternal nature than the Chinese and more unchang-
ing; the Japanese they have never been close to and have
thought of as upstart primitives. Now all the way back to
Song-Dune-Chi my father talked to me of the glorious
past of Korea, and spoke of Japan with intense hatred.

"There never was a friendly feeling between Koreans
and Japanese," he stormed. "Since the Korean scholars
like Wangin went to Japan to give them language, culture, paper and clothing, they have never been thankful,
but always aggressive. If we did not have our great admiral Yi Shoon-Shin, with his iron-clad tortoise, to defeat
them in the sixteenth century, what would have happened? My son, you had better look out for these flattering Japanese. They have a purpose in being here. But
we will defeat them and drive them away from Korea
as we always have before."

I did not go to a Western school for some time after
that. Instead I was sent to the old village school, to
counteract my bad manners. Here only the Confucian
classics were taught.

It was a pleasant old building behind a high stone wall.
Inside were willow trees, Odongs, pines and oaks, and
there were rose bushes and many kinds of flowers planted
and all was quiet. The pupils sat on straw mats upon a
carpet of oak ribbons, and the mellow sunlight came in
through the paper windows. The teacher was a lazy incompetent old man whom I will call by the vulgar name
of Co-Mool or Nose-Water. This was not his real name:

only a sort of pen name. In fact he would not have known it was his name at all. He was very unsanitary and seemed to consider it scholarly to be so. He washed his face—his eyes that is, enough to see his students. He combed his hair—but not often. (Perhaps he was not as bad as I am describing him, but it seemed to me he was.)

Having been taught by two renowned scholars, the crazy-poet and my uncle *pak-sa*, I had a sounder knowledge of the classics than his own, though I was only a child. I loved to put him in hot water by my questions concerning the classics. There was nothing more he could teach me. He did not know what to do with me, but at once made me a monitor and set me to teaching boys sixteen and nineteen years old. In private I continued my lessons in Japanese, all by myself.

A Korean school was always run on aristocratic principles. The teacher spent more time on the bright boys, because he felt that the progress of society and its future leadership depended upon these, and naturally these generally came from the homes of scholars. He judged the bright ones by those students who had the best caligraphy and could write the most skillful verse. Whenever he gave anyone an "A" the whole school was supposed to celebrate and applaud the young scholar, who had to send out for wine and dainties and treat the schoolmaster. Co-Mool gave a good many "A's," sometimes undeservedly.

We assembled in the morning before breakfast, by six or seven o'clock, and at first we read by the light of the lamp, which burned an oil made from fish. All day we read aloud until we became hoarse, only stopping for lunch which was served in the school-room. If we stopped making the reading noise, Co-Mool's birch-rod descended on our heads. Some boys sent messages to neighbors in the form of reading. About an interrupted "muk-dong" game, Shak-Doo-Shay would say, while shaking his head as if he were reading: "Yun-Koo, you owe me five pennies, and next is my turn."

Then Yun-Koo would answer in the same classical rhythm: "No, Chak-Doo-Shay, *two pennies* I owe you, and next is my turn."

The only fun I got was in the poetry contests. But there was really no competition. How I longed for Sur-Choon! I could find no friends nor rivals to sharpen me. I thoroughly agreed with Kim Sagat, the humorous poet, when he came into the school during a poetry contest and saw all the young scholars trying to write verse, then satirized them in a lampoon:

"All day you *heundeul, heundeul* [a peculiar untranslatable word, meaning to sway the body and hum for the muse to come].

"But the paper still is blank.

"Here comes the *cook-soo:* hool, hool [noise of eating rapidly].

"At once the bowl is emptied."

I very soon began to argue with Co-Mool, the schoolmaster, all the time. I insisted that the Western method of mathematics taught in the market-place was much better than that taught in his school, and I preferred to use it. He said, no, the counting rods or short chop-sticks used by our excellent forefathers were far superior to any method known by foreigners. He made a very serious didactic speech on how our Korean method had lasted thousands of years. This was his one great argument always:

"But our way has lasted, hasn't it? It is much, much older than the new."

One time I said to him:

"Confucius was wrong when he said the earth was flat. The earth is round."

"Where did you get the nonsense stuff? Earth is flat and heaven is round."

"No, because I saw a globe in the Western school. On the other side from us upside down is a continent called America, on which missionaries live."

"But why have we never fallen off? We have existed here since the remotest times," Co-Mool looked at me over his pipe, as if to say, "Deny at your peril."

"That is because we are too small. A little ant going around that branch would not know if he were upside down, or rightside up," I explained as I had been taught in the Western school.

"A Korean scholar with the learning of Confucius would know. We are not so small as all that. The Japanese have been talking to you."

At another time I asked him: "Do you know why the peaches fall to the ground?"

He looked at me blinking, and then taking his long pipe from his mouth, he spit on the carpet, which was an unsanitary way he had.

"Why peaches fall to the ground! Because it is natural —it is the natural road of peaches that become ripe."

"But don't you know why it is natural?"

He became red.

"It is because of the law of gravitation," I suggested.

Then Co-Mool sharply told me I was impolite.

"This younger generation is becoming rotten, vulgar, obscene," he said, "and I can see that this world is going to be Hell."

He was very much upset and trembled as with rage. Shortly after, he gave some conservative an A. And when the wine came, Co-Mool drank too much, and after that began to weep.

"Decency is a thing of the past. The world has no more respect for ancestors and old men. Oh, why are my two sons worthless? Why do they not take care of their old father so that he doesn't have to work among young scoundrels and ingrates?"

I began to be regarded as a bad element in Co-Mool's school. All this did not put me on better terms with my own father, and blinded me to the fast-disappearing merits of this Classical Korean school. Its most pleasant and unique feature was the part it had always taken in the life of the seasons, during the countless generations of students. In the time of Autumn, the whole school, headed by the schoolmaster, issued to the fields to celebrate the harvest festival with the grown people of the village. Just before the worst spells of Winter the school ghost would be fed with delicious rice cakes of all kinds, brought by parents and consumed by pupils and school teacher (after the school ghost had taken all it wanted, which was only a smell). At this occasion the school ghost was petitioned in verse to look over all the students, to allow none to get sick, and to brighten all their intellects that they might conquer their rivals in the next provincial examination or poetry contest. There was also the annual fight with straw candles which took place with the scholars in the school of a neighboring village, when the snow was heavy on the ground. The fight was always very hard, for if your village won, it would surely have the finest crops during the next year. Sometimes the bigger boys used unfair means, and a kind of dried fish with head that stunned like iron, and fins that cut like a knife, was put inside the straw candles, and the fight was with real weapons not with sparkling fire. Once in a while even some boy would be killed in the contest; then the old men of the two villages would get together and decide that there must be no more fire fights, but this custom had persisted through the ages, none the less. In the time of the Spring-fever there were always excursions to the mountains made by the school in a body, accompanied by the schoolmaster. The purpose of this outing was partly to pick azaleas, which the Koreans used dried to make delicious spice cakes, but it was not looked on exactly as utilitarian. After the red and white and purple azaleas were gathered, we dried the petals in the mountains on sunny grass or warm rocks, and their delicate, baking perfumery drifted faintly on the air. In the wind-trembled sunshine, surrounded by smiling azaleas, with the scent of crisping petals in our nostrils, we ate picnic food and drank wine and talked of poetry, and made verse, just like the older poets.

This was education as favored by my father. He believed that so all great *pak-sas* were made, and those who thought otherwise, even my illustrious uncle, were degenerates. As he would hear nothing against Co-Mool, and insisted that he loved him very much, my hatred of Nose-Water became for me a serious ethical problem. Confucius said, "Those whom the parents love, the son must love, even if they should be his worst enemies." For the son belonged to his parents, even the *body* of a son, his flesh, his limbs, likewise his hair. More and more I began to get into trouble with elders. I taught mathematics and Japanese to some village children, in secret, for my heart and my head were full of the subject. Some of the old men came to my father about it, and one woman told my grandmother that I was making her boy just like a Japanese; at the dinner table he talked in an unknown tongue. I had taught this boy a few phrases like "Give me some rice," and doubtless he had wished to practise his Japanese at the dinner table. The woman insisted to my grandmother that her son had forgotten how to speak Korean and it was my fault. All the villagers agreed that Chung-Pa, the son of the most just man of Song-Dune-Chi, and nephew of the renowned crazy-poet, was Japanizing and degenerating.

So the hopeless disagreement between my father and myself began. According to his view, somehow, by some means, the foreigners could all be made to leave Korea, she would return then to her days of golden peace, satisfied as before with her peculiar culture of an immemorial age and an antique harmony. He could not see that the Land of Morning Calm, as her people used to call her, was in process of passing, never to be recalled, and that isolated Utopias do not exist nowadays.

Chapter 11

DOOMSDAY

Then a great cry, as of one who suddenly sees a black phantom, rang out loud in the room, jarring my brain with the madness of its terror, and striking as with a hundred passionate hands on all the hidden harps in wall and roof;

And the troubled sounds came back to me, now loud and now low, burdened with an infinite anguish and despair, as of voices of innumerable multitudes wandering in the sunless desolations of space, every voice reverberating anguish and despair;

And the successive reverberations lifted me like waves and dropped me again, and the waves grew less and the sounds fainter, then fainter still, and died in everlasting silence.

A Crystal Age: W. H. HUDSON

In the late spring when I was almost ten I came home from the village school, sick, and under that pretense, I refused to go there any longer. My grandmother was worried about my stomach-ache. She called in a witch. Ordinarily my grandmother seemed to be a Confucian, and had raised her children by the ethical codes of that sage. Temperamentally, of course, she was a Buddhist, loving to meditate to herself, or to tell the stories of Buddha and its legends. Also she had her idea of God as the supreme ruler of the Universe: she was a monotheist like many Koreans. But when somebody was sick or anything went wrong in her life which required some practical measure, she called in a fortune-teller.

This witch, or fortune-teller, was an old woman of the lowest class, bent over, dressed in dirty mud-colored clothes, and walking by a wrinkled cane. I have always thought that when a woman is very very old, she must be very beautiful, for there is the record of many true and sincere movements on her face. On the other hand, if she has spent her life in ugliness and tricky ways, there are few objects more vile to see than the furrows telling of her past. I always thought the women I saw in Song-Dune-Chi had good-looking faces, even my fat aunt, until I saw this woman, who pretended to be friends with the spirits of sickness and ill-will and destruction; she bargained to put them favorable to you, if you gave her something for the service.

She often came around our house, for two reasons. If my grandmother accepted her, the other women in the village would too, for my grandmother was a criterion. Then my grandmother was so emotional that she almost lost her mind when anyone she loved was endangered. This time the fortune-teller advised that the shoes, socks, coats and trousers I had worn when I got sick, be given away at once; and then she took them home with her for her own son.

Yes, she was always very shrewd. She was careful to speak with my grandmother alone, when nobody else was near, for my grandmother was the only one she could deceive. None of the men in our house believed in these spirits, but they did not contradict my grandmother any more than a gentleman in the West contradicts his mother when she wants to believe in the Fundamental Doctrine. If she desired to send up a wish to the village ghosts, my crazy-poet uncle would write it for her in elegant verses, but with no enthusiasm; and all he would say was once in a while, "O Sug!"—inside. Now my grandmother was not exactly superstitious, and seemed to have plenty of commonsense when nobody was sick, or needed anything badly. Still, it is a fact, she always listened to the fortune teller, and when told to destroy my clothes, she reasoned:

"It couldn't do any harm to Chung-Pa's stomach-ache. It couldn't possibly make him any sicker. So why not do it and feel more comfortable? If he grew worse, and I had not done everything possible, how bad I should feel!"

But my stomach-ache did not go away, because I did not intend to return to Co-Mool's school. So the old witch came back. I saw her come in at the bamboo gate, and enter the kitchen door. I was very angry, because she had taken my clothes. I went running into the kitchen to show I was not sick, just as she was trying to make my grandmother give my best long ribbon over to her. She said the evil spirits wanted that, in addition to the rest.

"Get out!" I cried. "Get out! You dirty Devil-woman. I am not sick. Where do you get your stuff? Go to hell, you fake!"

She seemed to be really frightened, and cleared out, not saying a word. But she came back one day when I had gone fishing. She told my grandmother that I would surely bring the ruin on my family, if I were not sent off to study the doctrines of Buddha at once. This seemed to my grandmother a very good idea. My father, though he had no affiliations with the Buddha, did not object. Buddhism when compared with Western civilization was at least honored and ancient. Besides, though my father was the theoretical boss, my grandmother, in matters like this, was the practical boss.

The week on which we set out to make our pilgrimage had been very hot and still, in our village, as if in the heat of Summer. No one felt like doing any work. Everybody sat in chronological groups, discussing the political situation. All this discussion just made my father angry, and he alone kept right on working. My crazy-poet uncle sat under the broad leafed Odong tree, and drank wine, and looked worried, but said, "No—O no! Japan will not take Korea. In spite of all her new ways, she respects the ancient culture too much, and besides she has promised not to."

Before setting out, my grandmother and I had each a complete baptism in the bathtub. This was a round wooden tub, painted bright red, a nice place to sit, but sometimes too hot on these occasions. Our complete cleansing of every hair was symbolic, and the water was boiled first, to make it holy and pure. We started, before the sun got up, for the journey was thirty miles and we must walk steadily all day in order to do that amount on foot. The air was sweet and hushed and ghost-colored, so that it too seemed purified for the journey. My grandmother's eyes were shining; she was very happy to be going away, leaving all family and national troubles behind, for a while. Her mood was that of the old Korean poem:

> I take up my green budding rod,
> I turn up the rocky path-way,
> To three or four heavenly vales
> With halos of clouds.
> I shake off the world's dust to-day,
> To gather the pine's scarlet cones.

(The pine to the oriental is the symbol of immortality.)

My grandmother had her cane, and I my little bundle of clothes with paper and pens. Behind us my grandmother's servant followed with the food. This was a little girl of fourteen or fifteen who was named Keum-Soon, or Child-of-Gold, the daughter of a poor widow. There was not much to do in her house, so she came to us for food and clothes and to help my grandmother and her daughters do all the work of washing and of sweeping and of ironing clothes with the laundry stick. That old woman who owned the apricot tree and thought that the best thing in life was good chicken was an excellent helper at an ancestor festival, or for any feast of food, but was not much good for everyday at our house.

The morning grew only more calm. Ten miles below the monastery we entered no-man's land. Here was no house, nor any human. No horse could be used here. We travelled along a narrow walk of stone slabs, with silent greenery on every side, stretching for miles, always upward. Some of the stone slabs were carved with Chinese characters and my grandmother and I read them aloud to each other. Once in a while we saw a squirrel being caught by an eagle, or a big bird having a bath in the stream. Late in the afternoon a monk parted some bushes and passed us on his way to the heights. He took no notice of us, but walked in silence like the monk in the poem about:

> A shadow is made in the water.
> On the bridge a monk is passing.
> Stop . . . O monk, talk with me,
> Which is your way?
> But his hand points to the white clouds . . .
> He goes stilly by. . . .

All the way up, my grandmother talked of Buddha.

"You know," she said to me, "Buddha was a very very great man. You should do what he says, and follow in his footsteps."

"Why, Grandmother?"

"A great man always does what he says he will do. When he makes a resolution, he follows it to the straight, through floods, fires, mountains and every danger."

She told me a tale about Buddha. She believed it was actually a fact.

"Buddha was born a great prince, in an aristocratic family, where he had honor and servants and wealth. But he was not satisfied, because he wanted to understand about life. One day he heard a baby crying and he asked his guardian:

" 'Guardian, why is that baby crying?'

" 'Why, Master, it is being born, and that is the beginning of sorrow.'

"And Buddha thought, 'This is strange. Why is the baby crying? Where did *he* come from?'

"He went under a willow tree, and he saw an old man, gray-headed and wrinkled and ghost-like. He asked his guardian:

" 'Guardian, why is the old man ugly like that?'

" 'All men, Master, must grow old, in this life. It is the way of sorrow.'

"And Buddha thought, 'I wouldn't like to be old like him. That would be Hell.' (This is the nearest translation to my grandmother's and the Buddha's expression.)

"Then Buddha came on a man who was groaning with pain. And Buddha asked his guardian:

" 'Guardian, what is the matter with that man?'

" 'Master, he is in pain. Every man must know pain at some time or other in this life. There is much much sorrow here.'

"Then Buddha thought, 'I want to avoid *that!*'

"Presently he found people crying in front of a house.

" 'Guardian, why do the people cry?'

" 'Master, there is a man dead in there. At last he has gone away from this earth for good. It is the end.'

"And Buddha thought: 'Where did he go to? Why did this man die?'

"So Buddha thought and thought: 'What is it all about?' and all he wanted was to solve the problem. Finally he gave up his beautiful wife, his beautiful baby, his beautiful home, and he went up to the great Snow Mountain, still trying to solve the problem. After many many years he was enlightened. He saw how every living creature was making a pilgrimage to reach the no-life again and every soul that did wrong had to go back and begin all over again. After Buddha had solved the problem, he resolved never to do two things: He would not tell a lie, and he would kill no living thing, for everything, he saw, was his brother.—This," said my grandmother, "is why the good monk, Kim, never eats chicken when he comes to our house, you know."

"But the monk, Pak, did, Grandmother."

"Well, there are true monks, and false monks," explained my grandmother, "like everything else in this world."—And she went on with the story.

"And you know when you decide to be a great man, God always sends you a messenger to examine you. So after Buddha came down from the mountain and had made his two vows, God sent his messenger to examine Buddha, and his messenger was a deer.

"As Buddha was walking along, the deer ran out of the forest, and he cried to Buddha:

" 'O save me, save me, Buddha! A hunter is trying to kill me!'

"So Buddha thought, 'If I am to keep my resolution, I must save this deer.' He dug a hole in the ground and put the deer down there and covered it with oak leaves and told it to lie still.

"By and by a hunter came along.

" 'Tell me, did you see a deer? Where did he go? I am going to kill that deer right now.'

"What was Buddha to do? If he said no, he would be telling a lie, if he said yes, he would betray the deer, and the murder would be upon his soul. So he said nothing.

"The hunter kicked him on this side, then kicked him on that. But Buddha stood very firm on his rocky foundation. The hunter cut off his right arm and then his left. Still, Buddha said nothing. Then the hunter fell down and worshipped Buddha.

" 'Ah! Here is a great man!" he cried.

"And he became Buddha's convert, because Buddha had met the test and stuck to the resolution."

So the time passed delightfully with my grandmother until the sun went down and the mountains became soft and shadowy, with blue white mist here and there, like the Bodhisattvas, or future Buddhas, waiting to receive us. We did not reach the monastery until almost dark; so it was generally with pilgrims, for the monasteries were far away from the villages and had little to do with them.

It is a beautiful experience to come upon an old Buddhist monastery by twilight. There are many poems in the native literature of my country about this.

> From the boom of the drums that temple
> Must be close though they say it is far—
> Far over the green mountains,
> Away at the foot of the clouds. . . .
>> But I cannot see;
>> Thick mists obscure the way. . . .

At one time many centuries ago, they were a very powerful factor in the state, and even the king was compelled to put on monk's dress, as a sign that he was only an official of abbots. But by and by the country became corrupt under the rule of the abbots. A certain platform on which pretty young women worshipped would fall through the floor by a miracle. Far down underground these women got betrayed by monks. At last the monasteries were exiled to remote mountain sites where they could not work any more miracles. But those whose mystical natures could not be satisfied by the practical ethics of Confucius, like my grandmother, still made pilgrimage once or twice a year, and confided their prayers to the monks.

Up here in the Yellow Dusk the antique monastery seemed to melt into the summit of the green mountains, bounded everywhere with stone tigers and marble lions, singing streams and holy groves. These statues of fantastic shapes had been fashioned I suppose by the hand of man, but nothing here looked artificial; it seemed as if all must have sprung out of the ground. The rich dim colors of the shrines bathing in sun and rain, wind and storm of the mountain for countless centuries—all natural, natural the gray of the steps, natural the deep red of the pillars, all in tune with the natural rocks and natural trees, bound together it seemed, by invisible, indivisible unity. The song of the evening bird grew imperceptibly out of the sound of the running brook, and vanished again in the long sobbing of the pines. But somehow it was all ethereal and unreal like a mystic's dream.

In a series of cloud-like pictures, I recall my three months' sojourn at this monastery which belonged to the Meditation School of the Buddha—the darkness of the mountain hollows by dawn and by twilight, the hushed, almost buried stillness of everything by day, the mysterious greeting which the monks all gave one another, and which I soon learned to say: "Nam moo ah mi to pool" (I honor you and resort to you, Amitabha), or the prayer "Po che choong saing" (for the salvation of all living things), the cool silent ghost-chamber where I studied, with walls gorgeously painted with the heroes and sages who had lived in the past, the Buddhistic scriptures of the library in which I read and read, and the gray abbot, my teacher, in his mournful, mud-colored robes, and his transparent face free from all worldly care or desires.

He tried to teach me the way of Nirvana, which means a "blowing out," like a candle. We sat in his large empty room with pillars which held the engravings:

> Make no evil deed,
> All good obediently do.
> Purge the mind of self,
> This is all Buddha's teaching.

When I went out in the beautiful gardens I was rebuked for slapping the gnat to death which landed on my ear or my nose.

"Even gnats," sad the monk, Kim, "may have within them Buddha. They too may attain to Nirvana, and the state of never being born again. Endeavor to be more calm, do not become the evil fate of any living thing."

So I was taught how Buddhists kill neither mouse, louse, nor cows.

When I returned to my home during the last week in August, I found a shocking contrast to the mystic world I had just left. . . .

It may seem strange to the reader unfamiliar with Far-Eastern politics that Korea, an independent nation for over forty-two centuries, should have been so helpless those first ten years of the twentieth century before the stealthy but persistent encroaching of New Japan. But Japan's strength in the East is due to rapid Westernization, especially in regard to armament. That alone, perhaps, she thoroughly learned, since the time of Perry's entrance, and is thoroughly competent to proselyte. With the vigor of a younger nation, engaged already in enormous changing, inherently imitative, it is easy for her to slough one borrowed culture and to absorb another in its place. Yes, comparatively, easy, as it was not for the older nations, China and Korea. Clinging closely to the old Confucian nature, and each in an exhausted era of their history, they were truly stunned for those first decades of world-wide intercourse.

That little Japan won over the million millions of wise deep China, first. After her victory, she began to make her demands upon Korea, during the Russo-Japanese war. She must be allowed passage for her troops through Korea, and she signed a treaty stating that she had no designs upon the Korean state as a whole. These troops were never withdrawn. They remained to shelter the swarms of low-class Japanese adventurers who followed, and to uphold them in all they mis-did. Japan moved deliberately step by step. She first seized the silent control of the incompetent and bewildered government at Seoul, in 1907: hemmed in by spies and Japanese generals, the old emperor was made to abdicate to a minor son; then at last Japan spoke plainly, the 29th of August, 1910, when all treaties were annulled and Korea was publicly declared annexed. . . .

When the news reached the grass roof in Song-Dune-Chi, my father turned a dark red, and could not even open his mouth. My uncle *pak-sa* became suddenly very old, and he shrivelled and fainted in his own room. My crazy-poet uncle sat staring straight ahead of him until far into the night. My first thought was a selfish and immature one.

"Now I cannot be a *pak-sa* or the prime minister of Korea."

I burst into tears. But my elders did not cry, not yet. So I ran crying out of the house. I looked up at the sky, to see if there were really a black doom up there. Were a final thunderstorm and a flood about to come which would wipe us all out? But the sky was blue and serene, and the river had only a sunny crystal foam as it whirled past. Children were standing around with scared blank faces. The village was quiet. Nobody spoke. Later on, in the afternoon, there was a general weeping, everywhere the sound of mourning, as if each house in the village were wailing for somebody dead. Some men began to drink and drink, shouting:

"The doomsday has come! We have all gone to the Hell!"

My father lurched out of the house, although he had had nothing to drink, and nothing to eat since morning.

"My poor poor children!" he cried out, and tears now streamed from his eyes. He held out his hands to us, as if we were all his eldest sons. "Now all are going to die in the ruined starvation. The time of the unending famine has come down upon us. Who knows when we may be happy again?"

And with tears running over his face, and mingling with his beard, he put up the Korean flag over our gateway and bowed down to it.

There was no supper that night. My grandmother sat up by candle-light, in the same dress she had worn in the morning. Again and again she took a cup of rice tea to my father, but he lay heavily on the mats, and he would not accept it.

In the morning, it was found that several of the young men who had been among those drunk the night before had committed suicide. Their bodies lay along the banks of the stream where the women usually did washing on this day.

A Japanese policeman came to our village, at the head of a band of pale-blue-coated Japanese, each armed with a long sword. Of course they knocked at our gate, and asked why we did not have the sun flag of Japan instead of the red and white flag of Korea betokening the male and female realm, and in accordance with the Confucian philosophy of the Book of Changes, sun and moon and all the elements used in geomancy. My father shrugged his shoulders and pretended not to understand. The small Japanese policeman then flew at my father, kicking and striking him, with menace of the sword. My grandmother saw from the window, and ran out without even stopping to put her coat over her head and screen her face from vulgar eyes.

"Don't you touch my son!" she screamed, stepping between, "because he has had nothing to eat for these two days and doesn't know what he is doing."

As soon as she came between them the policeman knocked her down. He kicked her fiercely with his Western boot. Her sons seeing it, gasped. In the eyes of Koreans to touch an old woman, the mother of sons, was a crime punishable by death. Even criminals were safe behind her skirts. My father would have strangled him, but saw that my grandmother had fainted with pain. He at once lifted her on his back and started off toward the market-place where there was a fairly good doctor. But her ankle was broken and she was sick for many weeks.

That night I went into my crazy-poet uncle's studio and lay down on the mat, crying miserably. By and by I heard the crazy-poet walking around and muttering in the next room. With my wet finger I made a hole in the paper door and looked through. He stood there at the outer door and just shook his fist in the face of the sky.

"Oh, stars and moon, how have you the heart to shine? Why not drop down by thunderstorm and cover all things up? And mountains, with your soul shining and rustling in the green leaves and trees and grass, can't you understand that it is over now? This national career of the people who have lived with you all these many ages, who have slept in your bosoms, whose blood you have drunk, whose muse you have been for the countless years? You spirits of water, you ghosts of the hollows, don't you see how death has just come to this people established among you for the 4,000 years since the first Tan-Koon appeared on the white-headed mountain by the side of the Sacred Tree? Don't you know the soul of Korea is gone, is passing away this night, and has left us behind like the old clothes?"

I knew that my crazy-poet uncle was as if saying good-by to a ghost, just as the tall doctor had given the farewell to my grandfather's spirit on top the grass roof. . . . Was Korea ended then? A pristine country, contemporary of Homeric times and of Golden Ages—far, far removed from the spirit of the Roman Empire and all later modernity until this day. . . . I cried and cried myself to sleep. Outside all night I heard an unnatural day-sound—the jingle-jangle of cows which had not been put up for the night, and their astonished moos.

THE YALU FLOWS

THE YALU FLOWS

A KOREAN CHILDHOOD

MIROK LI

TRANSLATED BY H. A. HAMMELMANN

WOOD ENGRAVINGS BY JOHN DE POL

CONTENTS

I. *Suam*

S UAM was the name of the cousin with whom I grew up. The first of our joint experiences I can recall was not a happy one. I forget exactly how old we were then; I may have been five and he five-and-a-half. I can still see us sitting one evening with my father, who kept pointing with a little stick at a difficult character in a Chinese primer. Suam was to explain it. He had learnt the signs in the morning, but now on being examined he seemed unable to remember anything. There he sat, neither moving nor uttering a word. My father, who was an ambitious man, had determined to start Suam's Chinese lessons as early as possible because the language was so difficult.

"This character means 'vegetable'. What is it called in Chinese?" he asked impatiently.

"*Tsai,*" my cousin replied at once.

"Right," said my father, "and what about the next?"

1

This character seemed more difficult than the first. Suam remained silent, stealing forlorn glances first into one corner of the room and then into the other, and looking desperately even at me who could not possibly help him, because I had not yet begun to read at all.

"What a fool you are!" my father scolded him, and suddenly Suam's narrow eyes began to fill with tears, which rolled down his cheeks until they dropped on the enigmatic character itself. This made me very sad.

Fortunately, just at that moment our mothers came in to fetch us.

"Don't drive the children," my mother said to Father; "they'll learn it anyhow once they go to school."

Gratefully we slipped out of the room.

Suam was my comrade. We played together, had our meals together in the morning and in the evening, and went together everywhere. There were many other children in our house: I had three sisters, and Suam (whose father was dead) had two, so that there were altogether seven of us. Then there was Kuori, chambermaid, laundress, and nursemaid rolled into one; she, too, was counted among the children. But all of them were older than the two of us and all of them were girls, no good for anything. So we two were inseparable. We even wore, if I remember rightly, the same pink blouses with a dark brown belt, the same grey trousers, and the same shoes of black leather. Though Suam was only half a year older than I, there was no danger of anyone taking us for twins. Suam was a strongly built but fat little boy, with round, smooth cheeks. He had strikingly narrow slit eyes, a small, almost lipless mouth, and a graceful nose. I, by contrast, was thin and tall, had large eyes, and a big nose. For all that, we made an inseparable couple and usually laughed and cried at the same time.

The sun shone beautifully in the Rear Court where we played all day. In this quiet, wide court we were left altogether to ourselves, for hardly anyone came there in daytime. When it was hot we would take our clothes off and run about naked. We were surrounded by a high wall; none of the neighbors could see us, and of our sisters or the maid Kuori, who came over occasionally to pick vegetables, we were not shy.

Suam dug a long, straight ditch and covered it with flat stones which I got together. One end of the ditch he made into a stoke-hole, at the other he built a chimney. When that was done we burnt dry sticks in the hole and watched the smoke drifting slowly away through the chimney. We filled in all the slits between the stones with earth until there was no other escape for the smoke. It was a lovely game. Certainly Suam was not a fool, whatever my father had said. He was a good and clever boy.

Another time he showed me how to catch dragon-flies— a thing every boy in our country had to know. You tied together the ends of a thin willow branch and fastened this hoop to a long handle. Thus equipped, you went to search for cobwebs and covered the ring with them as tightly as possible. As soon as we saw a fine dragon-fly, we would chase it, swinging our net about wildly. Suam often made a good catch; he would remove the dragon-fly from the net with great care, holding her by the waist with thumb

3

and index-finger and bending her body forward, until the insect actually bit its own tail. When he caught a cock-chafer, he sometimes laid it on its back upon a broad, smooth stone, where it danced about for a long time, fluttering it wings. We thought that lovely.

When we got tired of running about we sat down on a straw palliasse to sun ourselves. The outer yard was not only our playground. There were also a vegetable plot, a shallow well without water, and a large barn. Balsamine bloomed on the wall, and in the kitchen garden we had cucumbers, pumpkins, and melons with their white and yellow blossoms. Here, too, stood a big pomegranate tree with countless flaming red fruit. We never picked them, for they tasted so bitter.

Our house had several courtyards. The main building, consisting of six rooms, a kitchen, and a covered veranda, was laid out in a circle around a large open space: the Inner Court, where the women lived. Here were a small duckhouse, a dovecot, and a few plants in flower-pots. In front of the house lay two more courtyards, separated only by a low wall with a door. The one on the right-hand side, through which one reached my father's room, was called the well-yard, because of a deep well there; on the lefthand side was the Outer Court, with a high gate and a number of guest-rooms. We were allowed only in this court-yard.

One fine afternoon Suam interrupted our game and led me to the Inner Court and from there into what was called the maid's closet, a room we very rarely entered. I followed my cousin eagerly, because his schemes were always wonderful and exciting. For a while he stood in front of a tall

4

cupboard looking up wistfully at a shining brown pot. I had seen the pot before, but did not know what might be in it. Suam got some cushions, placed them one upon the other, and tried to climb the cupboard. I helped him from below as best I could. He tumbled down several times, because Korean cushions are long and round, not flat, but he did not give in until at last he reached the top. There · he remained for a long time, making odd little sounds as if he were sucking or eating something. I asked him what he had found. He made no answer and just went on. Finally he announced that he would bring down some honey for me. He put his right hand deep into the pot and then tried to climb down, holding fast with his left. In the end, alas, he toppled over, for the cushions rolled away; trying to steady himself, he reached out with his honeyed hand, and left smudges everywhere, so that little remained of the beautiful yellow syrup. Even so, I licked his hand clean, and then we made off, quite contented and without suspecting in the least what was before us.

In the evening we had to pay the penalty of our sins. We were already in our beds, Suam in his mother's bedroom and I in mine. Suddenly someone called us. Hoping for a sweet melon or a pear, we entered my mother's big room full of expectancy. Our reception was by no means cordial. Kuori, the chambermaid, was examining one cushion after another, while my mother looked decidedly stern. With a glance of dismay, Suam conveyed to me that the cushions had given us away. My aunt asked whether we had climbed the cupboard. Suam said nothing, squinting grimly at his mother, who had taken up a bamboo stick. She did not, fortunately, use it to punish, and only slapped our cheeks with her hand, right and left. It hurt me very much, and I started to howl, but from Suam there was not a sound. He seemed to appreciate the justice of the proceedings. He neither cried nor protested, but gently drew me out of the room.

II. *The Poison*

EVERY morning Suam had to learn four new characters. I sat beside him in my father's room and waited until he was dismissed. Suam was very slow at learning. It took him a long time before he was able to repeat the four characters, first separately, then all together, and to explain their meaning.

Soon lessons began for me, too. One morning my father placed a new book before me and said: "You have looked on long enough; now it is your turn."

My book was just like Suam's, bound with blue string into a yellow cover. I opened it, and my father taught me the first four characters. I felt very solemn and sat in deep awe; but Suam was delighted, because from now on we would learn together and he would no longer have to struggle alone.

Much better than reading we enjoyed our writing lessons, which began a little later. We each had our own writing-box and a few sheets of paper; the first job, however, was to grind the Chinese ink. You poured a thimbleful of water into the hollow of the black grindstone and rubbed the ink-stick to and fro until the water became

7

thick and oily. The intoxicating smell of it! After that we got down to it, painting with our coarse brushes, line after line, according to a pattern set before us. Much patience was needed. To start off with, we wrote only one character, "heaven," and practiced that well over a hundred times. We clutched the paint-brush with the whole hand, the way a charwoman handles a broom, and besmeared the beautiful paper from top to bottom. Soon our fingers were coal-black. We wiped them carelessly on our trousers and went on writing. Suam, more impetuous in everything than I was, wrote rapidly, and within a short while his light grey trousers were covered with a criss-cross of black smudges. Even our pink sleeves became blacker and blacker. After the first of our writing lessons all the women in the house were horrified, but there was no punishment. My father defended us and said with good humor: "These are marks of honor for young writing-masters."

Our hands fared worst, because the ink settled in the countless tiny grooves of the palms and could not be removed. We became known as "the two ink-boys," and Kuori, whose task it was to wash me in the morning, gloated over it.

"What I should like to know is this," she used to say, smacking her lips. "Which is blacker—your hands or a crow's foot?"

After we had mastered the character for "heaven," we wrote, or rather painted, the sign for "earth," then for "blue" and "yellow" in the order prescribed by our primer. All writing had to be done on the veranda of the Inner Court, for in the rooms we would have dirtied the clean mats. We did not care. Soon we had learnt to write "sun," "moon," "stars," and "planets."

When our lessons were over we had to leave my father's room at once and were not to enter again unbidden. In no circumstances were we allowed to disturb my father or the guests who often came to visit him. It was difficult to obey this rule because it was just in his room that there were so many beautiful things which we longed to see.

One afternoon, however, the room was empty. My parents and Suam's mother had gone out. That was our chance to examine everything at leisure. We had a good look at the embroidered cushions and bolsters, inspected the writing-desk, peeped into the tobacco jars made of wood or pottery, and finally opened the sliding door of the corner cabinet, where we made the most exciting finds: picture scrolls, a hat-box, and a hollow games-board which you could beat like a drum. Next to the cabinet stood a large, mysterious chest of dark wood with seemingly countless drawers, all of them, alas, locked fast. We dragged, pulled, and pushed as hard as we knew how; but all our efforts were of no avail—the chest just would not yield its secrets. At last Suam discovered a little key, and now we were able to unlock one closet after the other and finger the magical objects which lay hidden there. That was where our luck turned.

Without the slightest suspicion that anything here might be unwholesome, we began to taste of the contents of each drawer. There were leathery white bulbs, thin twigs, little brown capsules, and all sorts of other things. I stuck to the little twigs because they had a faint sugary taste, but Suam was much more thorough and ate many black pills and whitish tablets. After a while he became curiously quiet and sat down in silence.

"Miak," he called out softly, as he always did when he had something special to tell me. He couldn't say an R nor a proper open O. "Miak, fetch me some water!"

I brought him a bowl full, and he emptied it in one gulp. Then he sat still for a while, rather dazed.

"Miak, look at my throat!" he said plaintively, opening his mouth wide. His throat was red and swollen. When I told him, tears came into his eyes. "Die," he announced sadly.

We left everything and ran into the Inner Court. My sisters sent Kuori to fetch the parents. Suam's throat seemed to swell and swell. He could hardly breathe; he suffered terribly. My poor Suam! Never had I seen him so unhappy. Breathing heavily, he lay on the ground without taking his eyes off me, as if he really meant to say good-bye for ever.

At last my father came. He brought with him the doctor, who questioned me closely about what he had eaten and proceeded to prepare a cup of black broth.

That black broth did miracles. Suam was well again next morning, only a little more subdued than usual. He willingly went on drinking the bitter medicine. The doctor seemed to have discovered all sorts of other things which were wrong with him; from now on my friend had to be examined often and to take medicine all the time. He did it without a murmur, knowing that only the black drink had saved his life.

The evil day came when Suam was to receive real pun-

ishment for his greediness. Nobody wished to punish him
as long as he was so ill; for my part, no amount of scolding
and slapping could make any impression on me, anyhow.
I was too pleased that Suam had not died. But now something terrible was in store for him.

One hot afternoon he was taken to see the doctor in
Father's room. The doctor explained to him that he would
light on his back two little heaps of medicinal herbs, so
that the heat could enter into his skin and heal him. When
he had been shown everything, Suam thought it over for a
second or two, and then bent down before the doctor.

"You won't leave me, will you?" he implored me.

"No, I won't go away," I assured him.

The two mothers held his hands, to make sure that he
would keep still. The doctor formed two small pyramids
of a greyish-green substance on his back and lit them at
the top.

"It's smoking," I told Suam.

"Does it hurt already?" the doctor asked.

"No," said Suam bravely. After a moment or two he
added: "Oh, it's getting hot!"

"Just a little longer," the doctor replied. "The strength
of the herbs must enter into the skin." He described a
circle round the burning mound with his finger.

"Oh, oh, it burns!" Suam yelled. "Miak, take that stuff
off my back!"

"A little longer still," the mothers cried, holding me
back.

"Do take the stuff away," Suam howled desperately once
again. "It burns my skin."

11

"I can't, Suam!"

"Quick, take it away, Miak, away, quick! Miak, Miak! Oh, Miak!"

This heart-rending scene ended with a terrible outburst of invective.

"Oh, you wretch!" Suam screamed; "you doctor, you dog!"

.   .   .   .   .

During all this time we went on learning from our Chinese primer. It was called *A Thousand Characters,* and that title was written on the cover. There were exactly one thousand characters in it, always four in a row. Beneath the proper title was another, "White-Hair-Script." When at last we got to the end of the whole book, my father explained to us this expression.

The author of the book, so we learned, had been a criminal condemned to death, while still a young man, by the Emperor of China. But he was also a great poet, and for that reason all the citizens begged the Emperor to spare his life. So the Emperor set him a very difficult task; if he could solve it, his life would be spared. The task was this: that in a single night he was to compose a true poem out of a thousand characters arbitrarily chosen by the Emperor himself. The condemned man succeeded in his task, but when he presented himself with his poem the next morning, nobody could recognize him. In that one single night, while he had struggled for his life, he had become an old man. The poem, however, was most beautiful; the Emperor recognized in him a great poet and gave him his life.

We sat at my father's feet and listened to the story

breathlessly. True, we didn't really know what a crime was, nor what sort of crime the poet had committed; but to think that in fighting for his life his hair had turned white made us profoundly sad.

. . . . .

A big change came into our life when my father hired a teacher for us and opened a sort of domestic school in the outer courtyard, to which the children of friends were invited. From now on both of us were to go every morning to the strange teacher, writing and reading the whole day long under his supervision. We didn't care for this new life at all, because we had to sit still and learn until the evening. The only thing we enjoyed were the breaks, when we could play with the other children, who taught us many new games.

The most popular game among boys was called *zbegi*— a kind of shuttlecock. We made our own balls out of coins (which had slits in the center) and a bit of silken paper. You kicked the ball into the air with one foot, caught it again with the other before it touched the ground, and kicked it up again. Whoever could do this most often without dropping the ball was the winner. Usually we played just for the honor of winning, but among other children the winner was sometimes allowed to chide and rail at the loser, or even to hit him with two fingers on the arm near the wrist. Suam played *zbegi* passionately, but he often started to quarrel when he got excited, and the game would end in kicks and blows.

III. *First Punishment*

SUAM sat in the chamber behind the big visitors' room. He was working diligently, splitting a long bamboo stick into fine slivers and shaving the splinters with a sharp knife until they were smooth. He cut a round hole into a large sheet of paper given to him for his writing exercises, and then painted beneath it an ink butterfly. He made a frame of slivers, glued the paper to it, and let the whole thing dry. The result was a paper kite. Often we had seen other children flying such kites on the town walls in front of our house, and longed for one of our own. Alas! this was a wish which our parents failed to grant us. Having thoroughly inspected a kite, Suam was making one of his own. I was full of admiration for my cousin's skill and helped him glue and dry the paper, in the hope that soon our own kite might soar into the sky.

The next day, in secret, we made our first attempt in the backyard, but the kite would not rise; again and again it fell clumsily to the ground. Countless times I ran, throwing it up into the wind, while Suam with the line dashed full speed in the opposite direction. The kite would not move. Suam was disappointed, but he set to work anew with still thinner slivers and even finer paper. He was not in luck. One kite followed after another. He had plenty of paper, for each day he received three new sheets for his writing, and of these he took one for his kites. Moreover, whole piles of the most beautiful paper lay arranged in rows in the chamber, and that, too, he used occasionally. Since nobody came there in the evening, he was able to work quite undisturbed. I returned tired and a little discouraged to my room.

.   .   .   .   .

Lying in bed I used to love looking at the pictures on the wall-screen. It had no fewer than eight panels. There were mountains on it, rocks and flowers, rivers and bridges, and a seashore with wild geese moving across the horizon, and in the candle-light the whole had a wonderful glow. The picture I loved best was that of a shepherd boy riding on a cow and playing his flute. He was just passing a tall weeping willow on the way back to his hut, which was barely visible in the distance among the hills. The sunny road pleased me and the slowly moving cow; the sound of the flute seemed to reach me with its infinite peace.

As I lay there alone I was often joined by my third and youngest sister, who was only two years older than myself. Setye was a strange girl. She did not care to play with the other sisters and cousins when they got together at night in the back court for their various girls' games. Instead she came to me and told me fairy-tales. She knew countless sagas and tales of the stars, of sun and moon, of the swallows, the hares and the tigers, of poor peasants and woodcutters.

One of her stories was of a simple wood-cutter who went into the mountains to fetch fagots. Suddenly a hazel-nut rolled down the slope. "That is for my mother!" he said and as he picked it up, others came tumbling down until his pockets were full. When he reached home all the nuts had turned into pure gold.

Another fairy-tale told of a poor fisherman who was fishing in a big stream. The whole day long he was out of luck, and he was worried that he might not be able to bring home anything at all. At last in the evening he caught a carp whose scales shone like silver. As he was putting the fish into his basket, he noticed that the carp was crying bitterly. This made the fisherman very sad, so he threw it back into the water. Next morning he was sent for by the King of the Southern Seas and received a present of a charmed wishing-barrel, because the carp whom he had spared was the King's only son, the Prince. The wishing-barrel brought forth every good thing the fisherman could ever wish for.

Like my other sisters, Setye did not go to our school, which was only for boys. Daughters were to be taught the female accomplishments by their mothers and the older women. Setye was still too young. She did not yet know how to sew or embroider, nor how to cook, and spent her days prattling and playing. Sometimes I saw her sitting in the garden twisting squeezed balsam leaves round her little finger. This was to make her finger-nail red, which she considered beautiful. At other times I found her lying in a corner engrossed in reading a fat book. She loved reading stories and romances.

The books she read were written not in the difficult Chinese, but in the easy Korean script which consists of some twenty letters. As Setye explained to me by and by, the individual characters were not called, say, "heaven" or "earth," "sun" or "moon," but A or O, E or K or N. Setye had learned them very early from her foster-mother, and since then she was able to read all tales and romances, which were printed in these characters, so that there should be something to read even for the women who did not usually go to school at all.

Setye enjoyed teaching me. From her I learned counting, the names of the feast days and anniversaries, and many other important things. When she was not telling me fairy-stories, but lying silently beside me, arms under her head, I knew that she was just about to examine me.

"What are the four directions?" she began.

"East, west, south, and north," I replied.

"And what are the colors called?"

"Blue, yellow, red, white, and black."

"And how do the seasons succeed upon each other?"

"Spring, summer, autumn, and winter."

"Which are the beauties that the spring brings?" she continued. She had taught me many proverbs about the beauty of the seasons, and these I was expected to recite.

"On the mountains the flowers are blossoming, and the cuckoo calls from all the valleys."

"Yes, that is so. And what makes the beauty of the summer?"

17

"A fine rain sprays the fields, and the green leaves of the willows hide the walls."

"And what is beautiful in the autumn?"

"A cool wind sweeps across the fields, dead leaves fall from the trees, and the moon shines into the deserted courtyard."

"That is good. And what does the winter bring?"

"Hills and mountains cover themselves in white, and you will meet no strange wanderer on the path."

"You are very clever!" she praised me.

.   .   .   .   .

One evening I decided to go back to the secret chamber to see how Suam was getting on. He had in the meantime made countless smaller kites; now he wanted to construct a really big one. He told me to paint two large butterflies in black ink below the round hole, while he himself prepared the bamboo sticks. The glue was being warmed and the iron had been placed in the red-hot fire-basin. We were just sticking the bamboo slivers onto the paper, when suddenly the door opened, and there was my father. We were completely taken by surprise and did not know what to do. In the hurry Suam had no chance to hide the kite. My father had already seen it. For a short while he looked with amazement at us, the kite, and the used roll of paper; then he called out angrily:

"Come out of here at once!"

We crept out of the room, and the beautiful kite had to be left behind.

"He only watched me!" Suam spluttered, to save me from punishment.

And that followed next morning. Kite-building alone might not have been so bad; the worst crime was the mis-use of the paper which was given to us for our calligraphy lessons and the opening of the precious paper rolls. The teacher was told of our misdeed, and it was he who pun-ished us. We had to pull up our trouser-legs and were beaten on the calves with bamboo sticks. At all times a few such sticks, of the thickness of a finger, were within the teacher's reach, but never before had he made use of them. Now we two were to be the first of the whole peaceful school to serve as a warning example to the rest. All the children were placed round the walls to watch, while we two delinquents had to sit in the center of the room. It was very solemn—painfully solemn! The teacher put his gradu-ate's cap on his head, once again carefully explained our misdeed, took up one of the sticks and tested its toughness. Oh, how awful! He commanded Suam to free his calves. Suam gave the sticks a suspicious glance and remained stiffly seated.

"Won't you come here of your own accord?" the teacher called out.

Suam sighed, stood up before him, and pulled up his trousers. Three strokes came in rapid succession and Suam, my friend, began to cry. Then he declared that I was totally and absolutely innocent, that I had only watched him make the kites. Even so, I too received three strokes, which hurt very much. Yet the pain was not the worst—that I was able to bear. Much more unpleasant was the shame of being beaten in front of all the children who watched us with so much pity.

IV. *At the South Gate*

ALMOST all the school-children were older than the two
of us and therefore further advanced in their lessons.
A few already knew the greatest poets of the Tang dynasty
and wrote exercises in rhyme, much to the envy of the
others. These verses invariably spoke of flowers, rain,
moonlight, or cups of wine. Most of the other pupils were
studying the great historical work called *Tongam,* which
extended to no less than fifteen volumes. It made most fascinating reading. Nations were at war with each other,
dynasties were overthrown, and others arose to replace
them. The two of us—Suam and I—and the smaller children were still on the modest boy's book which taught the
five so-called moral laws and a concise version of Korean
history. At last, to our delight, we were through with this
primer and received the first volume of the big history.

In the morning, when the teacher entered the classroom,
every child had to make a deep and solemn bow. Then
followed questions to discover whether we remembered
yesterday's lesson. A new task was given to those who
passed the test; anything forgotten had to be studied again.
When all the children had been examined, each got out
his rubbing-stone to prepare Indian ink and practiced calligraphy from a new sample provided by the teacher. After

a short interval we read the lessons prepared for the day. Since every child read aloud, and each one from a different book and from a different place, the whole classroom hummed like a beehive.

In the afternoons we had more recesses than in the mornings, and in summer-time we were often sent bathing. Many fine brooks passed through the gorges of our Suyang mountain, and here we ran about, bathed, and played. The very road to such a stream was beautiful. As we left our town behind us we came along a shady path lined on both sides with stone monuments, until we reached a large, deep pond. At once we threw off our clothes and jumped headlong into the clear, cool water. We stayed until the worst heat was over and the air had become less heavy. Then we walked back along the beautiful path. In the trees the cicadas rasped their repetitive refrain.

After supper our mothers allowed us to go for a little while to the South Gate. This we loved. The two-storied tower-house presented a glorious sight in the setting sun. We hurried through the narrow, winding lane between the town wall and our row of houses and climbed the seemingly countless stone steps to the open square in front of the tower building, where the children of the neighborhood were already gathered to play. Some threw old worn coins on the ground and tried to hit them with little flat stones, some played feather-ball, and others hopped back and forth over a given stretch on one leg until they collapsed. They chattered, boasted, quarreled, and fought each other; yet as soon as the opening bars of the music from the Three Gates reached us, all fell silent. The Three Gates were a long distance away, right in the center of the

town by the Governor's official residence, but in the calm
of the evening the heavenly sound was carried marvelously
and clearly to the South Gate and lulled us slowly into
the dusk. It was the evening salute offered by the Governor. The day was drawing to a close, night was falling, and
all citizens of the town could go to rest free from fear.
Peace was over our country!

Yes, the peace of evening had come. Smoke rose from all
the houses, and the grey roofs slowly dissolved into the
mist of the summer night. Only the highest summits of the
mountains still shone brightly into the blue sky. At this
time I often felt sad, perhaps because one more day had
gone and inexplicable night now enveloped us.

While we sat in self-forgetting, a tall man slowly began
to mount the stone steps, entered the tower hall, unlocked
the gate of the bell house, and took up a heavy hammer.
For a while he stood quite still and listened to the music.
When it had died away, he swung the hammer back and
struck the giant bell; a roar thundered out deep into the
mountains. We stood around the keeper and counted on
our fingers the number of his strokes. First we bent in all
the right hand, from thumb to little finger, and then we
stretched them out again in reverse order. That made ten
—quickly we bent in the thumb of the left hand to start
counting once more with the right. Every evening there
were twenty-eight strokes, because the evening bell was
devoted to the earth, which is ruled by the twenty-eight
gods of destiny.

Now the gatekeeper was content; he descended the steps,
not without admonishing us to go home at once, before
the little evening goblins would throw stones at us. The

children obeyed him; they squatted on the broad stone balustrade and began to slide down. We did the same; much sliding had made the stone quite smooth and clean, so the bottoms of our trousers could not become any dirtier than they were already.

We walked up to the archway to make sure that the South Gate was firmly closed and that the pie-man had set up his stall in the usual place. His delicious slices, round, square and oblong, were laid out on a broad board, arranged according to size and ingredients. Near them were a small lamp and a pair of scissors with which to cut the slices. From time to time the pie-man would praise with melancholy chants the various spices which he had mixed into his wares, beating the rhythm with his small scissors.

Satisfied and at peace, we made our way home through the darkening lane. We were not afraid of the goblins. A weak light from some of the houses already fell across our way, and within we still felt warmed by the sweet melody of the evening music.

I went for a short while into our back court-yard to watch the girls at their games, but Suam sometimes stole away, not to return until late. The boys of our quarter of the town assembled in some lane or on a square to fight the children of another district, who, being inhabitants of a strange quarter, were considered enemies. Mostly they fought only with their fists, but occasionally sticks or even little stones served as weapons. The cooler the evenings became and the brighter the moon, the more frequent these fights. On such occasions Suam's jacket often looked grim.

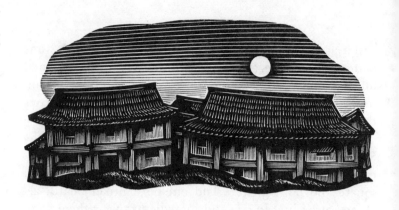

V. *Seven Stars*

WITH his relatives my father did not seem to have much luck. His brother died young and left him his widow and three children to look after. Then the husband of his sister died, and she came to join us at the end of her mourning years with her only son. He was about ten years of age and the eldest of us three, a very good-looking boy, with his red cheeks, slender and gracefully built, like most boys at that age. His beauty was marred by one flaw only: his lips were extraordinarily thick and hard. We were told that they had become like that after a serious illness. His eyes were bright and lively and his ears marvelously rounded. The color of his face was so delicate and that of his cheeks so rosy that he might have been taken for a girl had he not worn boy's clothes. What surprised me even more were his inordinately clean hands. When I looked at my own, I realized the big difference between him and me.

24

One evening we were playing our usual game of feather-ball in the Fountain Court when he suddenly appeared. Walking up, he asked which was Suam and which Mirok. We knew immediately who stood before us. It was Seven Stars, the new cousin who was to live with us from now on. I liked him at once because he was so beautiful. Immediately I asked him to join us. Suam did not seem to care for this; he leant against the fountain and refused to continue the interrupted game. "It is too cold to play here," he said, and viewed with disdain the new-comer who looked so frail.

After we had continued our game of *zbegi* for a while, Seven Stars took from his pocket a short bamboo flute and began to play on it. Through his thick lips he blew first a smart, lively tune, and then a slow, melancholy one, which brought back pleasant memories. I felt a marvelous lightness in my limbs, and soon I saw that Suam's body was moving with the rhythm. I, too, began to dance, and Seven Star's music became more and more passionate. He blew and blew; intoxicated by our dance, we failed to notice that my father and an old gentleman, the grandfather of Seven Stars, had appeared on the veranda outside my father's room and were smilingly watching us.

My father had never seen me dance. I could not remember him in my mother's room any of the evenings when we performed there under the direction of my grandmother. My two older sisters would beat the rhythm on a small drum and sing childish melodies, while we moved our arms and legs as best we knew. But never had our sisters sung so beautiful and moving a song as this one.

It was a tune from the so-called Valley Dance, a popular pantomime which was performed in our town once a year. One fine spring morning, several seasons ago, Kuori had taken Suam and me to the town to watch this spectacle. There we joined the throng which was following about thirty masked dancers accompanied by a band through the whole town to the open-air stage outside the North Gate. All around the theatre the spectators sat packed on the town walls, on the gatehouse, and on the slopes under the tall shady trees.

The first person to appear on the stage was an old priest who had left his monastery to come to town. Here he fell in love with a beautiful woman, and this filled him with such happiness that he felt compelled to dance. He was joined eventually by a gay fool with a cluster of bells which jingled at every movement he made. In the end the fool confused the priest's wooing so much that he was able to elope with the beauty himself. Nothing remained for the poor old man but to return again to his mountain and his monastery. His leave-taking—a dance full of rhythm but very sad—formed the end of the performance which had lasted the whole day.

This final dance began as the sun was setting and continued well into the dusk. It moved me deeply. To see the old man swinging his all-too-long sleeves back and forth to the nostalgic melody, to watch him set his tired feet slowly and deliberately, to see his back, now erect, now bent, as he moved in a sad circle—all this so penetrated my heart and mind, that on this occasion I was able to repeat the dance myself. My father openly shared our joy that we three cous-

26

ins had spent so harmoniously our first evening together.

We had, indeed, a very peaceful autumn and winter. My elder cousin taught us many novel games which delighted us. As soon as school was over we went down to the ice-bound river and played with our spinning-tops until darkness. At home we carved all sorts of toys: tops, bamboo flutes, bamboo sticks, little tobacco boxes, and ashtrays.

. . . . .

At the turn of the year we celebrated the biggest family feast of my homeland. It began around midnight, when sacrifices were offered at the altars of our ancestors. Then we children were called into my mother's big room and regaled with the finest dishes and fruit; we could stay up as long as we pleased. Next morning, dressed in our best, we were sent out to pay New Year visits to all relatives and friends. The cold was severe, the roads were ice-bound and very slippery, a biting wind stung our faces, but, full of excitement and joy, we ran from house to house to give messages which we had learned by heart. Everywhere our hosts received us with words of kindness and offers of sweets and fruit. What a happy feast-day that was, when one heard only friendly and flattering words and was offered nothing but sweets to eat! At home, everybody, from grandmother down to Kuori, was in his best garments, all wore smiles throughout the day, and no one spoke an unpleasant word. Even rough Sunok, who lived with us as bailiff and always called me a good-for-nothing, proved cheerful and gentle that day and remarked that perhaps I might become a proper man one day after all. Everybody joked with us and gave us presents, and as we went to sleep late at

27

night—for some time now Suam and I had shared a room —my mind became blissfully aware that there were still a whole fifteen days without lessons ahead. "How beautiful the world is!" I said to myself. But Suam was already snoring.

After the children, it was the turn of the adults to pay their calls. Numberless visitors—girls and women, young and old men—came to our house, which was filled with gaiety and laughter. In this way feast day followed feast day in unending succession.

While I lost count of time in this festive mood, Suam would quietly disappear in the evenings and return home very late. Among the boys New Year battles had begun, and he could not resist the temptation of taking part. His beautiful clothes bore traces of kicks and nose-bleeding which he attempted with great care to remove. One evening he returned in a terrible state. The two sleeves were half torn off and his head was bruised and swollen in many places. He told me that, when they had taken him prisoner, three hostile boys had beaten him until he was freed by a comrade. This experience seems to have cooled somewhat his ardor for battle; during the next few evenings he remained quietly at home, although the fighting became more violent than ever and the decision of the whole war was but a few days off.

Instead we began another battle at home among the three of us. This battle was brought about by none other than my father himself. One evening when there were no visitors in the house he called us to his room and showed us a remarkable game. All the ranks and titles of officials, from the highest to the lowest in the land, were drawn up on a stiff roll of paper. We were to begin our career at the bottom of the ladder, and he was the winner who first achieved the rank of senator. Father took up a book and opened it at random. The first word of the page was chosen as the rhyme word, and each one of us was to recite a classical poem which ended on this word. Whoever succeeded was allowed to begin his career. Seven Star's first word was "ruler." For a long while he remained silent, for he knew no poem with such an ending. Then it was Suam's turn; his word was "spring"—so common a word in verse that we envied his good luck. After a little stuttering he said: "Along the lanes nested the spring." "Good!" said my father and appointed him to the rank of Scribe of Literature. That was a great performance of Suam's, but unfortunately it remained his first and last. He received no further promotion because he did not receive another easy rhyme word. He had read only one volume of poems, and even these he no longer knew by heart. Seven Stars and I did not make a great deal more progress: his promotions stopped after the third and mine after the fourth. There was no winner.

A few days later we resumed the game, but this time not as a contest of poets but as a struggle among dice-throwers. It was Seven Stars who had discovered that this made the game much simpler. We all became officials at once and received continuous promotion; the whole game was decided in half an hour. Each victory was worth one copper coin. My father did not in truth like this way of playing, but he helped us none the less, and gave fascinating explanations about the rank and power of each individual official and how one reached such a position in real life.

Suam was very keen on the post of Governor of our province ever since we had seen his solemn entry into the town the year before. This powerful man had been received by his staff of officials some three miles outside the boundaries. There he had partaken of his first meal within his future domain before riding into the town. We, accompanied by Kuori, stood among the crowd who had taken up their position in front of the houses. From far off we heard the glorious music, and then, through the South Gate, we had our first sight of the cavalcade. Ahead rode five double rows of musicians on chestnut horses, followed by about forty mounted maidens in gay silk costumes and ten pairs of high dignitaries in their solemn black attire. They were Deputy Governnors of our province, which was still divided into its twenty-three sub-provinces. After that the Governor himself rode past with two beautiful young men, his personal servants. His steed was as white as his hair. The hat he wore was a kind of top hat crowned with snow-white feathers and fastened under the chin with strings of amber. Behind the Governor followed countless clerks and officials. On little Suam the great man had made an immense impression.

For myself, I was more taken by the so-called *Osha*. This was the man who travelled all over the country to straighten out injustices and see to it that all the King's subjects did their duty. By a mere report to the king he could dismiss the mightiest official or promote the humblest. Of course he walked across the country unrecognized, usually disguised as a beggar, so that nobody knew when he was near. The stories we had already been told about this *Osha* were innumerable. He had brought rice and money to many poor families and given freedom to innocent prisoners. I wished to become such an *Osha* who looked like a beggar, had a train of many hundred unrecognized servants, and was yet a man of power without equal. When I held this position in our game and threw a six, all other officials were exiled until they themselves succeeded in getting a six. Meanwhile I was able to continue my career alone— in the comfortable post of Senator I awaited the runners-up and had no more rivals to fear.

To suffer banishment of this kind, on the other hand, was gravely resented, especially when it occurred more than once in a game. Suam was often sent into exile, and at this he flew into a terrible rage, particularly, I noticed, when this penalty was inflicted by Seven Stars. In the long run his anger became quite personal, so that almost every evening we went to bed cross. Suam always lost, and soon there was nothing left of the riches he had collected during the New Year days. I lost, too. Seven Stars won everything. Actually, my two cousins had never got on very well. The one was too temperamental, the other too calm, and on top of that Seven Stars was always held out to Suam as a model child. And indeed he was always just too clean! After months his clothes looked like new, while nothing Suam ever wore remained clean for more than three days. Thus the eldest cousin had become a thorn in our flesh. Threatening clouds had long been gathering over our heads, and the smallest spark was sure to release the most violent thunderstorm. This game was the very thing. By the end of our school holidays I had also lost all my money. We were playing for my last copper coin. My father was not at home. Seven Stars had sent me into exile. I came back, was banished again, and came back once more. Suam, whose money had run out long before, was merely watching us. Seven Stars threw up the dice to send me back into exile. Before the dice landed, however, Suam fell upon him violently and caught hold of his long hair. On the ground the two rolled from one corner into the other. I helped Suam a little. Oh, how good it was to see that model boy for once with a bloody nose and a torn jacket.

That was the end of our community.

Judgement came swiftly, but it was not very just. I had thought that Seven Stars ought to receive the worst punishment because he had won everything and thus caused the quarrel. Suam deserved the punishment next in severity, because he had done most of the beating. But in the end the opposite happened. Seven Stars was acquitted and left my father's room unmolested. Suam received from my father three strokes on the calves, which he accepted without crying.

"And now it is your turn!" said our judge.

I, however, refused to bare my legs, for how could I understand why Seven Stars should go scot-free and only Suam and I should be punished?

But Suam poked me in the ribs to tell me to bare my calves. I did so with much hesitation, and already my father began hitting. My opposition availed me little, for he was strong and held me so fast that I could not escape.

After three lashes I turned to tell him that it was high time for the other cousin to have his share. Immediately I received another stroke, and this time it was on the shin, which hurt awfully. I screamed. Suam rushed in and tried in vain to wrench the birch stick from my father; but he, too, received a painful blow on his back quarters and retired whimpering. I got many more strokes—ten at least.

Then my father said: "Now you have had what you deserve!"

But I did not go away.

"Go on," I said stubbornly.

"What!" he called out, and began to beat me again.

Now Suam threw himself once more between us; after a real struggle he snatched the stick out of my father's hand and ran away with it. I was removed from the room by force.

"Be off with your obstinacy and take it where you like, you pig-head!"

VI. *Two Mothers*

I N spring Seven Stars and his mother left us. They moved into a small house in a neighboring lane. Whether Seven Stars' mother wanted a larger household of her own or whether it was our quarrel which put an end to our living all of us together, I do not know. In any case, the separation was very salutary. We did not quarrel any more when we met. Suam and I were even ashamed of having beaten up our elder cousin. True, he was provokingly clean, but that was not his fault.

Shortly after they left, a very strange visitor, an old woman from a distant province, arrived at our house. She spoke of me as her little son. My mother told me to call her Mother. Although she had not given birth to me, it was explained, she had prayed on behalf of my mother for a son and heir, and thus had helped to bring me into the world. She was, in other words, a woman who intercedes and prays for those who desire a child. She was by no means to be confused either with a soothsayer, who goes from home to home with her book of oracles and her painted fan to tell fortunes, nor with a *shaman* woman who conjures up spirits through music and dancing. Her rank was far more exalted, and had nothing to do with the lesser things of life. She prayed directly to the Master of Heaven in the name of Buddha and of one of his disciples. No sooner had my mother heard of this woman than she set out on the road to beg for her intercession, for she lived in great anxiety that she might become old without having borne a son. She found the intercessor, who came to our home to say this prayer which was to take her forty-nine days. It was addressed to Buddha's disciple, the blessed Mirok, whose name I was eventually given.

One evening, a few days after her arrival, I went into the forest with my two mothers. There, before a statue of Saint Mirok, we were to say a prayer of thanks. Far from the town, deep in a remote valley, stood the little shrine with the life-size likeness of the saint cut in stone. My spiritual mother fetched the key from the nearby village, unlocked the door, and lighted a candle. Darkness was already upon us; uneasily I stood between my two mothers gazing upon the statue, which shone brightly in the candlelight. The saint's expression was calm and peaceful. His eyes were lowered. His ears were remarkably long, his arms closely pressed to his body. His hands were tightly interlocked, while his legs had remained unshaped and their actual form was only hinted at by the sculptor.

My second mother set fire to a thrice-folded sheet of paper and, looking into the face of the stone image, began her prayer. I did not understand all she murmured, for I was too deeply moved by the sight of the white shining saint in the dark forest and by the thought that to his kindly meditation I owed my existence on earth. On our way home, after the prayer was ended and the shrine had been closed, I felt a great sense of gratitude to the good spiritual intercessor who had made possible my entrance into this world. Without her prayers I should have been born somewhere else and would have had to grow up without Suam, without Kuori, and without my sisters. I tightened my grip on her hand, and she repeated from time to time: "My beloved child."

She gave me many presents. Before going to town she never failed to ask whether there was anything I wanted, and there was not one wish which remained unfulfilled. One day she brought me a large Greek tortoise which was to give me immense delight. I had never seen anything like this animal. The back resembled a beautifully carved ink-box, and I was awestruck when I noticed, clearly engraved on the belly, the Chinese character for "king".

My last four-legged friend had been a small lovely squirrel which became quite tame. Every evening when I came back from the school-yard it had jumped around my face and neck and tumbled about in my sleeves until I gave it a peanut or a chestnut. After I had told my second mother of all this, and also of my regrets that the little squirrel had finally run away, she brought me the tortoise.

Only rarely, and then most cautiously, did I touch the tortoise on the back. Nor was there much else I could do with her. She was so very different from the squirrel. She neither jumped nor screamed, but only moved slowly about the veranda, or might not stir at all for hours on end. She looked most distinguished and regal, and appeared to be deep in thought. My spiritual mother explained that the tortoise was meditating on the fate of man and was able to forecast good and ill fortune. The way to discover the future was to bend forward until one's back was absolutely horizontal, then to place the animal on one's spine and wait until it crawled down. A descent on the right-hand side was taken for a good omen, on the left hand for an ill one. Suam and I bent our backs right to the ground each morning and waited until the tortoise, often after considerable deliberation, made up her mind to climb down. I could not help feeling somewhat uneasy whenever she began to crawl towards the left. Suam advised me to raise my left shoulder very slightly so that it was easier for her to move towards the right. Once the oracle had spoken, we left the tortoise alone; for the rest of the day she lumbered on her solitary phlegmatic round through the two courtyards. She lived on cucumbers and melons, of which we brought her ample supplies. We were told that in the southern land where they grow up these miraculous animals live only on the dew which falls on their lips each morning at sunrise.

. . . . .

It was midsummer again. My second mother had left us. The heat was so intense that there were lessons only in the mornings. In the afternoons we could go to the brooks and bathe as long as we liked. By then we had become good swimmers and dared even to go into deep water. The water of all the mountain streams was crystal clear, so that one could see the pale gleam of rocks and sand many feet below. Sometimes we swam like frogs, dived to the bottom, or floated on our backs at the whim of the current. At others we would stretch out on the rocks, close our eyes, and listen to the lapping waters.

Suam and I invariably brought the tortoise, for she, too, enjoyed a good swim. On the way there and back we wrapped her in a big melon leaf to protect her from the hot sun. Only once did we forget to take her. That was the day on which the tragedy occurred. It seems that she had a great desire for water, and being left alone, had sought it everywhere. When we returned in the evening to feed her, she was nowhere to be found. We searched the whole house; everybody helped. Gradually dusk fell and it bcame dark. The melon-flowers stood out brightly against the night, and bats flapped about close to our heads. But the tortoise was nowhere to be seen. Everyone carried a candle or a wick, and we searched each room in turn, the corn stores, and the ditches in the garden. Finally, Kuori discovered the missing animal in a cooking-pot. She had ceased to move and lay motionless whichever way one put her on the ground. She was dead.

Next day Suam took his spade to the backyard, where he built a little earth mound on which to bury our friend. In those days there were no graves on the flat in Korea; every family owned its own mountain, and on it was one's family graveyard. We, too, therefore wanted to bury the tortoise on a mound. Suam spent the whole afternoon digging until the heap was almost three feet high. I constructed a rough bier of two thick branches and a piece of rope, and on this we carried the animal to her grave. There she lay throughout the whole day. We offered a bowl of water (in the place of wine) as a sacrifice to the mountain spirit and to our dead playmate, so that the soul of the departed would find peace. At sunset we buried the corpse. By the time the tiny grave was closed we were profoundly sad.

Tortoises are said to have a long life, sometimes several thousand years. The death of such a miraculous animal in our house was sure to augur ill for the future.

VII. *My Father*

SOME months later my father fell ill. He had gone on a
journey, but returned again within a day or two, and
the whole house was set in great commotion. What his
illness was I did not know. I only saw that he lay motionless in his room. He kept his eyes closed and did not speak.
My mother, my grandmother, and my aunt—Suam's mother—sat around his bed. Many doctors came into the house,
but they were unable to do anything for him. Throughout
the whole night and the next forenoon he never stirred,
yet he was not asleep, for he understood my mother when
she asked him to take his medicine. Towards dusk all
hope of recovery was abandoned. My mother fainted and
had to be carried to her room. The silence of death fell
over the whole house. The women were assembled in my
father's room, the men on the veranda just outside. No
one spoke. Only my aunt attempted again and again to

give him the medicine which he was no longer able to swallow.

My mother rested in her room. She had recovered, but would not speak, and only held my hand tightly in hers. When my grandmother came into the room she exclaimed: "This is the end of us all, Mother!" Grandmother did not hear her. She sat down and mumbled to herself. Just then Osini, my second sister, joined us with the news of the arrival of yet another doctor for whom we had already sent in the morning. Suam and I hastened to my father's room.

This new doctor was a man of high reputation and much in demand. He had been in our town for several weeks to visit his patients and was just about to return home. Only the persistence of our messenger brought him to the house. The doctor did not look at my father for long before he spoke to the aunt.

"He is lost," he said. "I would rather not interfere."

"Please try once more!" my aunt whispered, and I saw that she was paler than the patient himself. She held the strange man by the sleeve and prevented him from leaving. "You shall have anything you can ask for."

The doctor sat down again; he examined pulse and heart and then the body of the sick man.

"I will do what I can," he said, "but don't reproach me if the attempt fails."

He drew a leather case out of his pocket and took from it a long needle, with which he pricked first the upper and then the lower lip of the patient. Then he pushed the needle deep into the stomach immediately below the curve

41

of the ribs, left it there for a moment and slowly drew it forth again.

"If the patient is to live, he will give a sign of life before the evening," he said, and walked out of the room.

Evening came; the whole family took hope, for it seemed a promising sign that Father was no worse. He still lay quietly, as he had done in the morning. Outside it was already dark when he moved his hands a little so that they touched. We watched each one of his movements eagerly. Suddenly he opened both eyes and looked around. A sigh of relief went through the room. Then he closed his eyes again and turned to the left so that his face was hidden from us. He fell asleep, breathing like a man in good health.

"He is alive!" said my aunt and burst into irrepressible tears; she was no longer strong enough to rise and had to be helped back to her room.

Meanwhile my mother had heard the good news. She came into Father's room, and could hardly believe that he had taken a turn for the better. She herself looked almost dead, and trembled all over. Gradually she grew calmer and sent us all out of the room with orders for the kitchen and a message to the doctor. Suam and I had to go to bed, and fell asleep at once. When I woke after midnight and ran into the sick room, I found my father sitting up, talking to Mother. I rushed up to them, and he held me on his lap until my mother drew me to herself. I could not keep my eyes off him; again and again I had to reassure myself that he really was alive. At last I settled down beside his bed and fell asleep again, while my parents continued to talk softly of the doctor who had performed this miracle.

Indeed, what a doctor! He was a true miracle-man. Later I heard that he had given new life to many people in our town and all over the country. Once he even returned to life, so it was said, a man who was just being taken to his burial. Alas! the fees he demanded were so exorbitant that the poor could not afford to call him. One day, returning from a visit to a rich patient, he was struck by a stone weighing more than a hundredweight. His crushed body was found just below the town wall. Nobody knew who had done the deed. There were those who said that his heavy sack of gold had turned into stone.

My father recovered very slowly. Throughout autumn and winter he was looked after with the greatest care. He even had to give up the work which hitherto he had been able to do despite his gout. Now he shut his home firmly against the outside world. Social commitments were given up and none but his closest friends came to see us. At first he was very loth to obey the instructions of the doctor and the insistent appeals of the family, but gradually he himself came to realize that he needed rest. He retired more and more into himself. In the end, he even changed the life of the household; the private school was given up and the pupils returned to their homes, never to come back. Once again the outer court lay almost deserted. Only Sunpil, the young clerk, Pang, the old servant, and Sunok, the bailiff, were allowed to live there.

A family council was held. What was to happen to Suam? It was decided that he should continue at school so as to learn Chinese. He was to move with his mother to the country, to a village with a school which gave good classical teaching. My aunt was to look after the management of one of Father's farms which had hitherto been under his personal care. For the two of us, after a whole childhood spent together, this was the first important leave-taking. I walked with Suam all the way to the Dragon's Pond, a bay more than an hour from our town. A boat took him across the sea to the wild craggy shore on the other side. Sitting between his mother and Dulche, his sister, he looked back to us anxiously while the sail was being hoisted and the boat slowly drifted on the restless blue waves.

Once our household had been reduced, our life again took up its old course. My father, however, underwent a great change. He began to introduce Buddhist literature and ceremonies into our house, and from then on he spent several hours in prayer every evening. No rain, no wind, no visitors, no domestic disturbance would hinder him. I could not understand a single word of the prayers because he said them in Sanskrit. I assumed, however, that they were all concerned with his future life.

My mother was pleased, because she herself believed wholeheartedly in the Buddhist teaching. When summer came she suggested that we should visit the temple "Light of God" to say our prayers there. She invited a priest from this monastery to teach her about the various ceremonies and offerings. Eventually the plan had to be postponed until the next summer. I was very sorry about that.

Although the mountains around our little town were dotted with countless monasteries and shrines, I had never seen a temple. Never once had we brought offerings to Buddha, and the big prayer had never been said for us in a temple. The mendicant monks who called at the houses and ran through their prayers outside our gates hardly helped to make the mundane townspeople more religious. Only once a year, on the eighth of April—the day when the divine Buddha resumed his baths after his nineteenth meditation and began to preach—festive Buddhist celebrations took place in our town. High trees, often four times taller than the houses themselves, were set up all along the main street. The trunks were swathed and decorated with multi-colored pieces of cloth, and from the branches countless gay ribbons were spread out to the roofs and to the ground. At night colored paper lanterns hung from the ropes and ribbons, and made you feel as if you were walking through a garden filled with iridescent flowers.

I was very anxious to see a temple, especially the temple "Light of God," which my parents had mentioned so often. One fine morning, on a sudden impulse, I joined two other boys on an excursion to the temple. I had met my old school friends near the West town gate as I was about to return home from my morning walk. I asked them where they were going, and was told quite briefly: "To the 'Light of God'!" The name, when I heard it, went right to my heart, and without hesitation I accepted the invitation to go along with them.

I stepped out bravely and did not worry about anything that was to come. And what a beautiful walk it was! Soon we left our little town behind us, penetrating deeper and deeper into the gorges, until we were hemmed in by mountains on all sides. The sun was beating down upon us, and we sweated heavily. This did not prevent us from walking steadfastly on until at last in the distance we saw a courtyard surrounded by trees. Grey roofs were gleaming through the leaves. They were the roofs of the monastery "Light of God."

It was not until after our arrival that I noticed with alarm the long shadows thrown by the trees; already the sun was low in the west. I begged the others to be on our way home again at once, lest we should be too late. Their answer was that it was too late anyway, and that we should have to spend the night at the monastery. Since my parents did not know where I was, this was the last thing I wished to do. I pressed for our return, but without avail; they wanted first to see the temple. While we were arguing, the sun sank lower and lower, and the young monk who had received us insisted that we could not possibly return during the night along the dangerous paths. I had to give in, and thus it was that I spent my life's first night of sorrow in these mountains.

I hardly saw the glorious halls with their countless statues, did not hear what the monk told us about them, could not eat of the dishes which he brought us. My eyes were fixed upon the mountains which robbed me of the sight of our little town. Nowhere did I discover an open valley, nowhere a glimpse of the familiar sea. Steep summits towered above me, and the evening peal of the temple bell died away forlorn among the mountain crags. Now monks dressed in yellow robes, with prayer-beads

46

fastened round their hands, entered the courtyard to perform their evening rites. Out of the halls of the temple poured light from the thousands of candles on the offertory tables placed all round the walls. Here the monks and descendants of the dead said the big prayer for the souls of the departed.

Broken only by short intervals, this prayer went on throughout the night. Towards dawn the worshippers stepped out into the open and began to circle the courtyard in stately procession; the monks, more than a hundred of them, in their gorgeous vestments, the women in garments of mourning. Each one held in her hands a wooden tablet on which was placed a sheet of paper rolled in the shape of a cylinder, the abode (so I was given to understand) of a departed soul. From the centre of the large circle the sacred log fire threw a mellow glow into the dawn. The muffled bells sounded out their solemn, slow rhythm, while the choir of the monks sang the prayer for the departed and the Namuhamitabul. Now at last was the time for the souls of the dead to be freed from this earth and to enter another existence. Enraptured by the steady drone of the wooden bells and the rhythmical song, we three boys joined the moving circle. Day was slowly breaking, the faces of the men became clearer, faint light fell upon the mountains. The fervor of the prayer reached exaltation and an ardent intensity seized the worshippers. Now in the east a red light rose above the mountains and the first rays of the sun touched us. While the monks continued their chant one woman after another approached the fire and threw the abode of the

47

soul into the flames. The women sobbed and wailed, for this was a last farewell for eternity. We boys also burst into tears. Sombre and mellow the rhythm of the wooden bells rang into the morning and unceasingly the monks carried on the Namuhamitabul.

. . . . .

Much moved by the experience of this night, I took my leave of the mountains and started on my way back.

At home I accepted every reprimand and punishment without a word of protest. This religious experience had strangely shaken me; I felt far more grown up than the day before. My father soon forgave me and asked to be told of everything I had seen. He appeared pleased by it, and from then on even allowed me to pray with him a small part of his evening prayers. After that he told me of the monasteries and temples which lie scattered among the ravines of the Yangtse valley and of the many famous poets who had visited them and praised them in their songs.

Just then in my Chinese lessons I was reading the poets of the Tang dynasty. But rather than read narratives and poems out of books, I preferred to hear my father tell his own stories—sagas and anecdotes of the Tang dynasty. In those days there had been so many unhappy poets, so many beautiful maidens who, tortured by longing for their lovers, sought death in the waters of the river. Nostalgic melodies floated across from the rocks and the groves into deserted valleys, and sad parting songs hovered in the rising evening mist over Tungting lake.

On fine moonlit evenings a seat was prepared for my father under the peach-tree in the fountain court. The

48

stories he told there were his most poetic; he never tired of telling them and from time to time even made up his own poems. All trace of paternal severity was gone. He joked with me when he succeeded in finding a good rhyme. Once he even enticed me to drink a few bowls of wine with him.

This happened one lovely moonlight evening. It was as well my mother was not with us for she would never have allowed me to drink with my father. She was strongly opposed to wine, while my father greatly enjoyed it. Now and then this led to a little friction between the two, but my mother proved good-natured and accommodating on the whole and did not begrudge my father his jar of rice-wine at night. When we sat together, a small table with the wine, two bowls, and a basket of fruit was placed before him. My mother usually remained with us until it became late and the jar was empty. That summer evening, however, she was not with us, because the women were at their reading circle.

Already the moon had risen over the roof of the empty school building and gave light to a cloudless night sky. The wall between the two courtyards cast a hard shadow. There was nobody to be seen, not a voice to be heard. Nothing moved in the big house. All life, all consciousness radiated to me from the smiling face of my father, who could tell such wonderful tales. The longer the evening progressed, the more he drank and the more thrilling his stories. How many poems he could recite and sing!

"Have you ever heard of the great Korean poet Kim-Saggaz?" he asked me.

"No," I replied in happy expectation of another story.

"His father was an important official, the Governor of a province in the South. His King was a bad ruler and soon fell into disrepute. The powerful Governor in the South commanded thirty thousand archers, all excellent marksmen. With them he marched to Seoul to overthrow the King. Three provinces had already declared for him and there was no one to stop his progress to the North. As he entered at the head of his troops into a newly gained town, he met a man who was waiting for him in the street. The man was unarmed and his hands were empty; yet he ran up to the horse of the victorious conqueror and snatched the bridle."

My father looked into his wine-bowl and emptied it. I tried to fill it again, but the jar was empty.

"Nothing left?" he asked, and as he asked he became a little—I'm not sure whether I may call it that—yes, he became a little sad.

That saddened my heart.

"I'll fetch some more," I said eagerly and stood up with the jar.

He laughed and took hold of my hand.

"You are very bold," he said; "ask your mother as nicely as you can! Perhaps she will let you have a little more!"

"Of course I'll get you some more wine," I replied.

I came back with a full jar and poured for him. He was delighted.

"And who was this opponent?" I asked.

"That is just what I wanted to hear from you. Who could have been so brave?"

I thought for a while and then answered: "The King himself?"

"Well done!" he said, "and it would have been best for the King himself to come and face his enemy unarmed. Perhaps another king might have done it. But this one was a great coward. No, it was not the King, but the son, the conqueror's own son. It was the famous Kim-Saggaz! You didn't expect that, now, did you? But it was really his own son. 'Turn your troops back to the south!' he begged of his father. He, however, replied: 'Become my officer and I will give you a thousand men.' 'No,' said the son; 'you have broken faith with your King and I refuse you my obedience!' With these words he allowed his father to proceed. Kim-Saggaz remained loyal to the King, but did not raise a hand against his father, and became a mendicant poet."

"I should have helped the father," I said when the story was ended.

"No," said my father; "you are too young to understand. Once one has promised allegiance to the King, one may never fail him."

"Kim-Saggaz had promised obedience to his father too, so he could not refuse that."

"That's true," my father admitted, pleased by my logic; "that is why he did not act against his father, but became a poet and left the world."

"I should still have helped my father," I said. I could not comprehend how one could leave one's own father for the sake of the King.

"How pig-headed you are!" my father exclaimed.

"No, it only looks like that to you. I do not know whether you, as a grown-up, understand this better than I do!"

"Well spoken! Now then, my clever son, drink a bowl of wine with me!"

He filled the second bowl which stood there empty, just for the sake of etiquette.

The offer threw me into great confusion; hitherto I had looked upon intoxicating drink as an enemy, because my mother spoke against it. Now, however, I did not hesitate long and took up the bowl.

"Now drink!"

I emptied it in one draught. Soon, alas, tears filled my eyes, for the wine was very potent. Quickly my father put a date into my mouth, and I felt better.

"How did you like it?"

"Well," I said.

"There you are, then take another bowl!"

I nodded. Speak I could not. Everything inside me was in turmoil and my throat seemed sealed. Even so, I strove to sit quietly and not to complain while my father recited one poem by Kim-Saggaz after the other.

As we were emptying the second bowl, I already had two dates in my hand. This time it wasn't so bad. Gayly and bravely I chewed my dates. Soon, nevertheless, my head began to swim in strange and unaccountable fashion. Still I did not give in and remained sitting as if all were well.

At this moment my mother came to join us and noticed immediately that something was very wrong with me.

"Quite true; yes, indeed," my father told her. "He has had two bowls of wine."

Mother was appalled; yet she did not say anything and her looks were not severe and angry, but rather ironical.

"May I have one more bowl?" I asked my father.

"For heaven's sake!" my mother burst out and quickly took away the bowl.

"Oh, don't be so cruel," my father begged of her: "a little wine can't do him any harm. I must have a friend in my solitude."

"All right, but just this once," she said and filled the bowls.

Very proudly now I emptied my third. I felt quite grown-up. I was accepted as a friend of my father's, who was so wise a man and could tell such wonderful stories.

"If only, Father, Mother could understand how essential wine is to a poet!"

"Quite so," said my father, while my mother half closed her eyes and gave me a sidelong glance.

I could not tell whether she was admiring me or making fun of me. I did not care—not in the very least! The moon was shining so brightly, the air was full of the scent of the peaches, I was sitting there drinking wine, and was my father's friend!

VIII. *The New Learning*

I HAD often heard of the school for what was called "the New Learning," and since last autumn my parents also had begun to speak of it. This extraordinary Institute, founded only a few years before, was in the northern part of our town, in a building distinguished for its many sparkling panes of glass. The subjects taught there sounded odd. It was rumored that the pupils learned neither the classics, nor script-writing, nor even poetry, but altogether new-fangled sciences introduced from a distant Continent named "West of the Ocean" or Europe. Where this continent was situated or what exactly was its science nobody seemed to have any clear notion. Some said that the school taught advanced arithmetic and obscure occult arts, others even spoke of the science of the earth and the heavens: all were afraid that it would undo and corrupt the children because they would not learn the classics.

My father, who seemed to know much more about the Institute, had formed quite a different opinion. After long consultations with my mother and the whole family, he decided that I should receive lessons there for a year. For a boy of eleven, he explained, I had read enough of the classics. Tsung-yong and Mang-dsa, whose works I had

54

been studying for the past few months, would have to do for the present, and the next books were in any case too difficult for my age.

I felt rather uneasy when I was asked whether I would like to go to this school. Being an only son, I had no wish to be corrupted and, what is more, I enjoyed reading the classics and loved classical poetry. But I trusted my father and said that I would try if that were his wish.

Thus one clear, cold spring morning I followed him out of the house into the town. I was wearing my best suit and carried my lunch in a neat basket given to me by my mother. We walked up our little lane and into the main road. "Is it true," I asked my father, "that we will learn the science of the heavens?"

"That is what people say," he replied. "Listen carefully whenever the heavens are spoken of. It is the highest knowledge."

"Will I be able to understand it?"

He nodded as if to encourage me. "See to it that your heart is always pure," he pronounced, gravely.

We walked across the street of the bell-tower, took one or two turnings, and soon stood at the gate of the big building. This, then, was the formidable, much-talked-of 'new' school, its name inscribed above the entrance. I gave a quick glance into the court, which looked vast.

"Come along," my father called, for he had gone ahead. "You aren't, by any chance, afraid?" he asked when I hesitated.

Slowly I crossed the threshold. Inside the gate I stopped again to look at the many rooms, but he pulled me along by the hand and led me to one of them. An old gentleman came out of the door, and Father told me to make my bow.

"This is the head of the school," he explained with a smile. "Be grateful to him and obedient."

While he was talking to the Principal, I was taken into a sombre and sunless chamber to a young teacher called Song. I bowed deeply to him also, and he invited me to sit down. I asked whether I was to sit on the chair which stood beside his. I had never sat on anything other than mats and a chair struck me as rather too grand. He gave me permission and I took my seat with great care.

"What have you learned so far?" he began to question me and, noticing that I was still too shy to speak, he went on: "Have you read Tung-sam, for instance?"

I nodded. "Up to the eighth volume."

"And what else have you read?"

Once again I sat there, dumb. I could not think, for the moment, what I had read after that. I was too confused.

"Shak, perhaps?" he asked.

I nodded my head.

"Mang-dsa, too?"

I nodded again.

"Have you read Tsung-yong already?"

"Him, too, I have read.."

"That is much." He fetched a book from his case, opened it, and laid it before me. "Have a look at that."

I read.

"Can you understand it all?"

"Yes," I said, though hesitating a little.

"Now what could be the meaning of this word?" he asked, pointing to a character which meant "America".

"Perhaps it might be a country near England," I suggested. I had often heard the two names mentioned in conversation about Europe.

Teacher Song considered for a while and then determined that I was to join the second form.

My father had gone without seeing me again: there was nobody in the Principal's room. He had left me to my fate.

On the first day I learnt nothing about heaven. The natural history lesson was about a ball being pulled apart by four horses. Then we peered into a long glass cylinder where a copper coin and a feather were made to move from one end to the other. There followed an hour of arithmetic. Twice we had gymnastics. Towards evening we were shown a tube; when you lifted it to your eyes, objects inside glittered in a myriad of bright colors.

.　　.　　.　　.　　.

It was sunset. My class-mates were pouring out of the school gates. I was again called to teacher Song. He gave me two school-books, a satchel, some pencils, and a slate, saying that they had been brought for me by a tradesman. I looked at the books; one was called *The History of the Occident*, the other *Laws of Nature*. I opened them and examined the inside. The natural science book was full of pictures: of scales, a glass cylinder, sailing-boats, and a European steamship. The ball which had been discussed during the day was not there.

Teacher Song asked me whether I had a watch.

"No," I said.

"Has your father one?"

"No."

57

"That's a pity," he said, with concern. "'Do you know the new reckoning of time?"

"Twelve hours?"

"Yes, but twice twelve hours; twelve before noon and twelve after. Tomorrow you will have to come to school at eight o'clock. Today the sun just touched the wall of the southern playing-field as the clock struck eight. Come in any case right after your morning meal."

I was still searching through the nature book.

"I can't find the ball," I announced eventually.

"Which ball do you mean?"

"The one which is being pulled by four horses."

"For that you will have to ask teacher Ok. I only teach history. But go home now; it is getting dark and your parents will be waiting for you.'

.   .   .   .   .

In my father's room the men and women of our house were assembled, my mother and my sister among them. They all had a good look at the books, my satchel, and the writing things, while I ate what was left of my father's evening meal.

When the others had gone back to their rooms and my father and I were in bed, he asked me what I had learned.

"Many things, Father."

"Have you heard anything about Europe?"

"Indeed, but it was something very queer."

"Well, then, why don't you tell me what it was?" he said impatiently.

"I can't explain it properly. I listened very carefully, but couldn't quite make out what the teacher said. He explained how a ball was to be pulled apart by four horses. Toward the evening I saw a glass tube. Every stone in the school yard, the clothes of the people, the tiles on the roof, everything shone in many colors as soon as I put the glass to my eyes. I can't understand why that is so. Can you tell me?"

"Did they say that it had come from Europe?" he asked, after a long silence.

"Yes, I think they did."

"Who was the teacher who showed it to you?"

"They called him Ok."

"And what did he say about it?"

"He said that the light was being split, or something."

"Split the light? Split the light?" he repeated in a whisper.

After a while he asked me to light the lamp again and to take some books out of the low case in the corner of the room. These books he had ordered from the capital. They contained much European wisdom. He looked through them all, but then he made me put them back again.

"You must be more attentive at school," he said, disappointed. "Now blow out the lamp and go to sleep."

"I felt so queer today," I said. "Everything at the school was strange. For a long time I was afraid I would never like it there, because it is so different from what I am used to."

My father did not answer at once.

"Were you sad?" he asked at last.

"It must have been that. I could not help thinking of the old school and of home."

"Come into my bed for a while," he said, and I felt his hand drawing me close to him. "Do you remember the song of Sotong-pa?" It was the song of a sailor poet which I had read to him the year before. "Will you recite it to me?"

I did so without hesitating once.

"Could you sing me the song of Eternal Grief?"

I did that too. It took a long time before I was through all the fifty verses.

"Is your heart still now?" he asked.

I nodded and crept back into bed.

"Will you go to school again tomorrow?"

"Yes, if it is your wish, Father."

IX. *The Clock*

NEXT to me at the new school sat a boy called Kisop;
he was bright and good-looking and seemed to know
many answers. He was sorry for me because I understood
but very little and sat rather dejectedly at my desk. Of
natural history I could make almost nothing and of arithmetic even less. From time to time Kisop glanced into my
open copy-book and wrote down a few figures, to give me
the results at least of the difficult problems. This, unfortunately, was of very little use to me, for I had no notion of
how these results might be arrived at. Thus I sat there the
entire day, discouraged and longing for the evening. On
the way home, however, I did my best to get things straight
in my head: little odd bits of natural science and whatever
I had been told about Europe, so as to be able to tell my
father about it. Anything new, however slight, pleased
him. I told him word for word what I had learnt and

61

brought home everything that looked even faintly European: pieces of paper with European print or writing on them, pictures of the tall houses, the bridges and steeples. Carefully and deliberately he examined them all.

During the breaks and at the end of school hours some of the boys would gather in the play-ground and talk of the countries of Europe and of the profound knowledge of their wise men, whose names I could never remember because they sounded so strangely foreign. Puksori, one of my schoolmates, told of a rich Chinese who once upon a time had visited a European sage. Unnoticed, a valuable diamond ring slipped off the rich man's finger and fell into the courtyard below. When, during the conversation, he became aware of his loss and mentioned it to the sage, he received this answer: "Fear not, honored guest; in a European country no one will take that which does not belong to him"! Down in the courtyard, a servant was sweeping the ground. Looking through the window, the anxious Chinaman saw him pick up the ring and gently replace it as soon as he had brushed the spot where it had fallen.

Kisop told a story of a Chinese prince who had lived in Europe for a time. When he decided to return home, he went to pay his respects to the highest man in the land, to take his leave of him, and to thank him for his country's hospitality. Outside the castle he met a gardener who was weeding the gravel path, and asked him whether he could be received by his master. But the gardener answered thus: "I am myself the President of this country. In Europe we have neither servants nor masters, as the barbarian countries do."

How delighted my father was with this story: "You see," he said to me excitedly, "the Europeans, they are true human beings!"

. . . . .

The big wall-clock which my father had ordered a few days before struck midnight. Its chime boomed through the whole house; when it had died away, the clock continued her steady tick-tack into the still night.

My father sat by candle-light looking through my school-books. "There is nothing else you have heard about Europe?"

"No."

"Didn't they tell you who governs these countries?"

"No. But I think it must be the Presidents. They speak of them as kings."

"That might be possible."

He went on reading in my books, sometimes pausing to consider, sometimes smiling to himself. Then he put them aside and stared before him, as if intent on peering into a new world which was hidden from him.

. . . . .

One day, as I was about to go home, a boy stood waiting for me by the school gates. He belonged to a senior form and was called Yongma. "Are you the son of Kamtsal Li who lives within the Southern Gate?" he asked me as I came out.

"Yes," I said, "I am that."

"We are to go together to see a family and try to get their son to join our school."

I had heard that the pupils of the new school went about the town visiting other middle-class families to explain to the parents the advantages of the new education and to persuade them to send their children to our school.

"Teacher Song has chosen us two for tonight," Yongma continued when he noticed my hesitation. "Come along right after your evening meal and meet me by the willow bridge. And don't forget to bring some of your school books. We'll show them to the parents."

Dusk was already falling as we walked along the river. Only the water gleamed in the twilight.

"Do you know anything about Newton?" Yongma asked me on the way.

"No," I had to admit.

"But surely you've heard of the force of gravity, which makes things fall to the ground?"

Yongma looked at me with surprise. He could hardly believe that a boy of my age had never heard of gravity.

"I only know that the earth circles round the sun," I said.

"Good! You can tell the people that," he conceded with a smile. "Or you can speak of oxygen. Tell them that water is composed of two different substances—of oxygen and hydrogen. Our ancestors only knew that the Universe consists of two poles—Yin and Yang—but the Europeans have discovered that this principle applies also to individual things, to the water, the air, and the rocks."

His voice was very gentle, he spoke beautifully and with care.

"Many say that bad times have come over us. Then you must answer them: the times are not bad, it is only that new times have come, like the spring after a long winter

64

with much snow. The azaleas are in bloom and the cuckoo calls. That is how I feel our times."

The father of the family which we were about to visit was a brush-maker. The entire front of his house was covered with huge characters which indicated that writing-brushes were for sale there. As we reached the top of the stone steps, we met a young woman with a watering-can. When she heard what we had come for, she went into the house without a word and locked the door. We knocked repeatedly, but nobody opened. For a while we stood, listening to the rushing water of the little mountain stream nearby, and then we turned back.

"If you can find a wooden box at home," Yongma said, "stick some black paper on it inside and out. One side you must leave open, so that it can be covered with a piece of frosted glass. Make a small hole on the opposite side, no bigger than a needle's head. If you look through the box, you'll see all the trees and flowers reflected on the glass. Show it to your people and tell them that photographs are taken with a box just like that."

When we got to his home, he took me inside to see his many books. Some of them were bound in the European manner and decorated with gilt lettering. I hardly dared to touch them.

"It's only because in Europe they write with gold, while we just use black ink," he told me.

As I was about to leave, Yongma produced a thin book in a blue cover with a European title.

"This is a book which every progressive person ought to read," he said, handing it to me; "show it to your father!"

I ran home as fast as I could.

"Abraham Lincoln, Abraham Lincoln," my father whispered; "is that the name of a man?"

"That is what I took it for, Father."

He read a few pages, glanced through the others and examined the book from all sides. "Go to bed now," he said abruptly, without looking up.

"Is he a European sage?" I asked.

He nodded his head.

"Like Confucius or Meng-tse?"

"No, different."

"Or perhaps like our Yulgok?"

"He's something quite different."

My father's face showed plainly that he did not wish to be disturbed. I kept quiet and waited until he had read the whole book. The story had obviously excited him, but he said nothing to me. He sat in silence, staring at the book before him. Then he lit his pipe and smoked.

Was this European perhaps a poet? A hero, a loyal subject of a bad king? Were there even in Europe kings who governed badly?

I took my pictures from the drawer and examined the tall houses, a wide bridge and a high steeple. I wondered what the steeple might be for?

The clock on the wall struck the hour with its deep, low voice. It sounded as if coming from afar, from the inaccessible seat of wisdom which only now and then sent beams of light through rifts in the clouds.

． ． ． ． ．

Since his illness, my father received few visitors. He said

that he needed tranquillity. He gave instructions that all business callers were to be dealt with by Sunpil, the young clerk, and the peasants from our farms received hospitality and advice from Sunok, the bailiff. People came and went, bargained and argued, but only in the outer courtyard that had once been our playground. In the Inner Court, separated from the other by a wall and a gate that could be locked, all remained quiet throughout the day. In the morning a farm-hand swept the ground, and in the evening Kuori watered the flowers.

The only visitor whom my father saw every day was my mother. She came after the evening meal, accompanied by Kuori or one of the other servants, and stayed with us for some time. She discussed the household with my father, told him what went on in the Inner Court, and of the women who had visited her. Then she listened to the news I brought home from school, let down the rolled-up bamboo shutter in front of the open window, lit the lamp, and wished us a good night.

Of my three sisters, Knogi, the eldest, was already married, and the youngest, Setye, was still too shy to enter my father's room. Osini was the only one who came occasionally in the evening to sit with us when we talked. She was very interested in my school and liked to look through my books, even reading a passage here and there with enjoyment. From time to time she would take along a book which I did not need the next day, to study it carefully in her own room. Once, however, when my father asked her whether she, too, would like to go to the new school, she appeared quite frightened and quickly put down the book.

"How can you tease me so!" she said, blushing.

One evening, while I was alone in the little "east room" on the Inner Court, Osini came to see me. "These books are so strange," she began with disapproval. "They contain no classical words and no sentences of any profound meaning. Do you believe that they will one day make you a wise man?"

"I hope so," I answered.

"And what do you learn from these books?" she asked with an air of superiority, fingering one page after another. "I think it is a pity for you. You are, after all, gifted; you have read Tsung-yong. You have learnt many old poems by heart, and have even copied Yulgok's anecdotes. But now, with this new learning, you are wasting yourself on worthless things."

Osini was an intelligent girl. She liked reading and knew many of the anecdotes and novels written in the old style; her speech was rich in classical Korean words unfamiliar even to my mother. People considered her the cleverest of us children, and indeed she was the only one who often found fault with me. She thought my handwriting miserable, my language without beauty or dignity. For this reason I tried to avoid talking with her.

"It is just that the new learning is something different," I told her at last: "it teaches you how to build railways which will enable people to travel over thousands of miles. It teaches you to estimate how far off the moon is, or how to make use of the power of the lightning to produce light."

"That does not make you a wise man," she said with concern.

"These are the new times," I continued, "brighter ones after our long, dark sleep. A fresh breeze has awakened us. Now it is spring, after a long winter. That is what they say."

For a long while Osini seemed lost in thought and hardly listened to me. "And how far is it from us to this country which they call Europe?" she asked me at last.

"That I haven't learned yet, but it must be many times ten thousand miles."

"Once upon a time the Princess Sogun married into a country without any flowers. It couldn't be there, could it?"

"No; that was only the land of the Huns."

"Do you believe they have flowers in Europe like our lilies, forsythias and azaleas?"

"I don't know."

"Do you believe they have a south wind there? Do they sit in the moonlight drinking wine in order to write poems?"

"I cannot tell."

"Then you don't know anything worth knowing," she summed up, disappointed.

X. *Vacations*

At the old school we had no summer vacations, nor did we have Sundays free either. When it became very hot we learned a little less than usual and were allowed to go bathing more often. Only twice a month there were no lessons.

At the new school the Sundays were holidays, and now in summer we were allowed to be idle for a whole month. It was wonderful. My father was pleased, too, and allowed me to choose whether to go to a famous teacher of classic script who lived in a distant village in order to improve my calligraphy, or to stay at home and copy a classical work. He was disappointed with my handwriting and expected me to employ the holiday making it better. I decided in favor of the latter. I was given several fine brushes and an empty copybook which I had to fill with small letters the size of a grain of rice. Each morning I learned two pages of the text and proceeded to copy them. My father made me repeat many of the characters again and again, and it happened quite often that I had to do over an entire page.

In the afternoons I received instruction in *paduk*, a dignified board game played with numerous black and white counters. I noticed that the exquisite white pieces, of the thinness of paper, were fragments of shells worn away by the sea, with the mother-of-pearl coating still showing on one side. The black ones were squat and round and of slate-grey color. They looked as if they had come from the bottom of a brook.

"Now take up a black stone," said my father, as I examined the pieces, "and set it on the board as firmly as you can."

I did as I was told, and the box that formed our playing-board gave out a clear sound which lingered in the air. The inside of the box was strung with many copper wires, my father explained.

"When your opponent has moved a piece," he told me, "wait until the sound has died away. Only then is the time to make your own move, and let none be unconsidered."

I received a handicap of twenty points and the contest began.

"Slowly!" he called out, when I was about to send my little stone counter too precipitately to what looked like a favorable place. "Always think first. The opponent's weakness is very often only a delusion."

Once he told me that *paduk* was not fit for men to play, but only for the Gods who now and then came down from our mountains to while away their time over this game. "Can you imagine a God playing hastily like children racing with each other?"

"No, the Gods are very dignified," I said.

"Surely you have heard of the woodcutter who lost his

way and strayed into the realm of the Gods, where he watched them at their game. By the time he returned home his axe had rotted away. The game of the timeless Gods had taken too long for the earth-bound human."

We played on and on. Every afternoon, as soon as the worst of the heat was over, I had to carry the game into the garden and set up the board in the shade of a tree. We would sit on a rattan mat, the game between us. I always lost, but never ceased to believe that one day I should succeed in winning. We played until cool shadow lay over the whole garden and Kuori called us to our evening meal.

At night I was often fetched by Yongma at the hour when my mother came to join my father. We still went occasionally to enlist new pupils for our school; at other times we just strolled through the town to look at the shops. Walking along the main streets to the East Gate gave us the chance to see Japanese stalls.

I knew very little of the Japanese, who in our country were not quite accepted as civilized and had long been known by the none-too-flattering name of "Wai barbarians". Yongma, however, said that recently they had learned much from the Europeans and had reformed their country, so that Japan was now to be counted among the civilized nations. It was a fact that Japanese traders sold many strange articles which must have come from Europe: sweets, cigarettes, lamps, oil, dolls, and toys of all sorts. In front of one of the stalls was a tilted wooden board with many nails. For a copper coin one was allowed to run a ball down the incline towards slots which marked a score.

The big prize was a wall clock, and the Japanese dealer called out indefatigably: "Come and play, fetch my wall clock, *arâ arâ arâ*; I must lose my wall clock; my wall clock must go."

Another store sold and rented bicycles. Yongma stayed longer here than anywhere else, making a careful study of them. He reached the conclusion that the cycles really did come from Europe because they looked so strange.

"Why shouldn't I try to ride for once?" he asked me after he had watched the other children for a while.

"It is not exactly dignified," I replied, not quite convinced yet that this striking toy did come from so illustrious a place as Europe; "after all, you do belong to an educated family."

He nodded, gave it a little more thought, and abandoned the idea.

Until late at night all the stalls and booths were brightly lit. The salesmen were sitting on mats in front of their wares. In contrast to our countrymen, they wore black. The black material of their clothes often had white patterns like snowflakes or plain lines and dots. On their backs many even had large Japanese characters, which looked terribly gross. Not one was dressed in elegant white and not one wore shoes. All went about in clattering sandals with their toes turned inwards. Japanese women were also among the stalls selling goods; they were not carried in litters and they allowed themselves to be seen in the street unaccompanied by a servant, as if they were but servants themselves. We wondered whether all these people belonged to a dishonored caste or if they were just so poor that they had to send their women out into the streets like serving-maids.

I had never seen any pictures of the country from which these people came, neither of their villages nor of their cities. Even Yongma did not know much about them; he merely repeated that Japan was now reformed and had many trains and steamers.

"People say that there are now six civilized nations in the world," he told me once: "England, America, France, Germany, Russia and Japan. Japan, it is true, comes at the very end; for it has, after all, only imitated the others."

"And where does our country stand?" I asked with astonishment.

"Not among the civilized by a long shot," was his dejected reply, "because we still have too few railways."

"And China?" I asked.

"The Chinese seem to be very conservative," he replied after a long silence. "Yu, the cloth vendor, was very angry once when I suggested that he should have his hair cut because a pigtail is so old-fashioned. The old man flew into a rage and would certainly have boxed my ears, if I had not run away as fast as I could. The green-grocer behind the Namsan mountain is very old-fashioned too. Once I showed him my school books to find out how much he understood. I wrote in Chinese characters the question whether China would introduce European culture. He laughed and dismissed the idea with a sweep of his hand. Then he wrote on the ground with the bowl of his pipe: 'Europe is a land of barbarians. They have no Confucian morals.' "

74

The word "conservative" did not sound good. I thought it must mean something like stupid and obstinate. I was sorry for the Chinese, if they really were conservative, for to me China meant beauty, tenderness, and splendor. Only to think of the sound of the words "Yang Tse Kiang," "Tung Ting Hoo," "Suchow," or "Hangchow," or to repeat a few verses of "Sutung Po" or "Tao Yen Ming" was to see a splendid world opening out before me.

Setye and Osini, my sisters who had read many Chinese novels, thought and felt the same way. Although they had never seen the morning fog clear from the Yangtse valley, nor the moonlight over the Yoang groves, they loved the splendid Land of the Central Empire above all others, better even than our own homeland, which, with a faint tinge of disdain, they often referred to as "that little Eastern country."

.   .   .   .   .

Towards the end of the summer holidays we had a strange and eventful night. After our evening meal I was fetched by Kisop and another school friend with the terrible name of Horang, which means tiger-wolf. They told me to come with them to our school at once; there was to be a march through the streets because today was the birthday of the King or the Queen or of some other prominent person.

When we arrived at the school, the pupils—some two hundred, perhaps—were already assembled in the courtyard. In time the gymnastics teacher arrived and lined us up in four rows, according to size. Yongma was in front, for he was the tallest of us all, while I stood almost at the

75

very end of the whole column, next to Kisop. We were
addressed at length and admonished to march through the
streets in perfect order so that the citizens of our town
and the pupils of other schools should have reason to
admire us.

When dusk fell, each one of us received a colored paper
lantern with a burning candle. Then we were off through
the school gates, with drums and trumpets, singing patriotic songs. We marched to the Bell Yard. From the south
and east came other groups of scholars, also on their way
to the same place, singing and carrying lanterns. Two
more "new schools" had been created that summer. Kisop
explained that one of them was founded by Christian
missionaries.

Now all three schools were joined together, and we
marched backwards and forwards across the town until at
last, after passing through the Three Gates, we came to
the Governor's Palace, with its infinity of courtyards. It
made a veritable sea of splendid lights.

I fell into a most solemn mood. Many festive gatherings
had taken place here in earlier days, but I had never advanced farther than into the outer yard, through a slit of
a side door. From there I had admired the glory of the
light in the other courts and listened to the lovely music.
This time our procession moved boldly through the im-
posing Three Gates, past many halls, and to the Courtyard of the Lotus Pavilion, where we were received by
the Governor himself.

We stood around the big lotus-pond, drawn up to form
the shape of a plum blossom, the emblem of our Royal

Family. The light of countless paper lanterns was mirrored and reflected in the water. At that moment the most important man in our province appeared before the pavilion.

The Governor praised our sound judgement in recognizing so promptly the new times. Our homeland, he said, was a small nation, but our ancestors had developed a high degree of civilization and had passed it on to Japan. Now it was Japan which moved ahead and wished to help us reform our country; for this reason, we should strive hard to reach the same heights as the brother nation farther in the east.

Enthusiastically we greeted our homeland and our King with the traditional cheers of *"Manse! Manse!"*

At the end of the ceremony each of us received a batch of pencils and two copybooks as rewards for this demonstration of belief and interest in the new civilization.

We returned home content with ourselves. I thought it a wonderful evening. True, we were a small nation and lived in a small country—but our wisdom was more important than that. Big, glorious China had once called us "Little China," because our ancestors were so wise. And who but we had given Japan her writing, her philosophy, her religion, her architecture, and heaven knows what else! Now we were lagging behind Japan in acquiring the new civilization; but what harm was there in that? After all, we were wise—the Governor himself had said it. We were all uplifted by his words.

I thought it a really wonderful evening!

XI. *On the Okke River*

IN the autumn school took up more time, for now we
studied geography and what was called world history;
our lessons, moreover, had to be copied laboriously from
a blackboard for lack of text-books. Often it was already
cool when I left the school gate behind me in the half-light
of the evening.

It was on one such late afternoon that I was fetched by
Kuori, our maid. She had been sent by my mother because,
so she said, it was dangerous to be alone in the streets
today. Many Japanese soldiers were about the town, and
some had even forced their way into private houses.

I felt uneasy, although I had often heard that the Japanese had come to us not as enemies, but as friends and to
help us. We hurried home. When I heard Japanese soldiers spoken of, I was always rather frightened.

"What does my father say?" I asked Kuori.

"I don't know."

"And what does Mother say?"

"That there will soon be war again."

"And Sunok?"

"That this will be the end of the world."

We hurried on. Agape against the dark night sky stood the large south entrance to the city. The High Street was darker than usual. The fruit-vendors had abandoned the stalls where on other days they sold melons, pumpkins, pears, and pies by the light of their paper lanterns. The pie-man with his beautiful haunting tunes had made off too.

At home the events of the day were the subject of excited discussion. It was true that soldiers had turned up in every street and lane to search houses. Sunok had seen three soldiers forcing their way into the Bread House at the top of the main street. Nobody knew what they were looking for, because it was impossible to understand their speech, and no one was allowed to go near them. The general feeling was that something terrible awaited our town.

My parents conferred late into the night. My mother proposed that at least some of the children—Osini especially, who was already grown up, and I, as the youngest— should be taken to safety. My father would not consent, though he did not understand the significance of the searches any better. There was no reason, he said, to fear war, and the soldiers would do no harm to innocent citizens. We should offer no resistance and give up whatever they wanted. The soldiers were certain to have been sent by our King himself for some good reason.

My mother found it hard to regain her composure after

such a day of excitement, but she gave way with a heavy heart, and in the end only directed that I was not to leave the house for the next few days and should sleep in my old east room on the Inner Court. I obeyed her willingly, although I was no longer afraid now that my father had entirely dispelled my fears.

The next afternoon four soldiers armed with rifles actually did come to our house. They walked through all the courtyards, pried into every room and shed, and then left again as my father had foretold, without molesting us or taking anything. After that we all calmed down and I was allowed to go to school again. Only Osini, who had fled from courtyard to courtyard at the very sight of the soldiers, was upset and scared for weeks to come.

Such house-searches were repeated often, almost every day or even twice a day. Occasionally the soldiers appeared early in the morning; sometimes they turned up unexpectedly in the Inner Court during the evening and caused the women to run away in terror.

At the same time a sinister rumor was about: it was said that some of our countrymen—young peasants, hunters, and others opposed to the new times and suspecting the Japanese of evil intentions—had gathered in the nearby mountains to fight the invaders. This would explain the recurrent searches in our town for hidden arms.

At first my father took all of this for mere gossip. Yet there seemed to be truth in the story, for we saw more and more heavily armed Japanese troops pass through the West and the North Gates. They marched out singing and singing they returned to the town.

Later they brought prisoners. It was a terrible sight, terrible to watch our own peasants being dragged through the streets, beaten bloody and in heavy manacles, their features swollen and appallingly mutilated. Never had I seen a human being in chains nor one so flayed. I staggered home sick with fear and horror and a cold sweat ran down my face.

My mother again proposed that I should be taken away from school in order to go to a more peaceful part of the country. I was a young child, she argued, and ought to be spared such impressions. Father discussed the matter at length but in the end did not consent. He only sent Pang the laborer and our bailiff to the peasants on our farms; they were to warn our people not to get involved in any trouble with the Japanese. As for me, he said I should simply not look at the marching soldiers. Only an uneducated child could be so inquisitive as to stare into their faces.

The fighting became still more violent. Throughout winter and spring prisoners were brought into the town. Even women were among them.

Not until summer, with the onset of the rains, did things begin to settle down at last. The house-searches ceased altogether. Steadily the monsoon rains fell from morning till night.

One evening Kisop came to see me. He looked pale and wan. "Have you heard?" he asked me.

"No; what do you mean?"

He kept me waiting for a while. "I think we have been tricked after all," he said at last; "our country has been annexed."

"By Japan?"

81

"Of course by Japan."

"Where did you see that?"

"If you have time you can go to the South Gate later and read the proclamation. But be careful. A soldier is there. You must not make any fuss or tear down the poster."

After our evening meal I went to the South Gate accompanied by Kuori. There it was, a large printed manifesto illuminated by two big lamps. All around was still as the grave. Not a soul was to be seen near the gate or in the main street. Only two lights flickered in the darkness, and a soldier with a rifle stood beside the proclamation. I approached cautiously and saw impressed on it a large royal seal.

Yes, it was a letter from the King, the first and last I ever saw in my life. It touched my heart, for it was a parting letter—the parting letter of a whole race of kings who had given us their protection for half a millennium. When I had read it all, Kuori came up to me and pulled me out of the archway.

"What does it say?" she asked me. She was unable to read.

"Our King has gone away!"

"Forever?"

"Yes, forever."

"Why has he gone away?"

"I don't know."

At home I repeated to my father the text of the proclamation word for word.

He listened attentively, but made no comment.

"Is there still worse to come?" I asked him.

He only looked at me in silence.

Everyone in the house was silent, the men in the outer courtyard, my mother, my sisters—all were silent.

Late into the night my parents and Sunok sat over a jar of wine and spoke of the kings of the last dynasty. In the end my father came to the conclusion that the whole Royal Family had become too weak to protect us. Now we should have to wait patiently for a new king to come and rule over us. To me he said that I should go to my school unafraid and take no notice of worldly matters.

. . . . .

Before autumn was over they began to pull down the town walls, the town gates, and the official palaces, and to widen the narrow streets. Shops were dismantled, houses and courtyards broken up. Newly exposed heating-shafts peered through the rubble-heaps, and with difficulty I made my way to and from school across what were once our streets. Day and night the work went feverishly on. From all directions came the heavy crash of the battering-ram, the sharp bang of the hammer, and shrill whining of the saw; thick dust filled the air. Men shouted, gave orders, gesticulated, and quarreled. I was glad when our gate closed behind me.

But even our outer courtyard had been affected by this unrest. Incessantly people came and went. Expelled peasants, dismissed officials, refugees, and emigrants adrift across the country came to ask for shelter. Sunok offered them hospitality only for a few hours and then sent them on their way again. He had to explain the whole day long that our house was not as wealthy as it looked and that they should try their luck elsewhere. This went on throughout the long, cold winter. More and more beggars and refugees arrived to fill all the guest-rooms; Sunok sat in front of the house cross and full of bitter words: "Oh, these miserable times, this miserable world!"

Only the Fountain Court remained quiet; indeed it was more quiet than ever. The whole day long my father, with the help of an interpreter, was involved in discussions with the occupation authorities over the countless new regulations or the new taxes, and this so exhausted him that quite early in the evening he had to lie down and could not stand very much conversation. When I told him about my school he only listened for a short while and then asked me to lie down myself and to blow out the lamp because he was in need of rest. Quite often he interrupted me saying: "Enough of that now; go for a walk and come back to me later."

I felt I was becoming tiresome to him and held my tongue.

I did not care to go for a walk. The dismantled town walls, the unroofed tower gates filled my mind at night with unspeakable sadness and great terror. I preferred to stay at home. When I was with my father, I still felt somehow protected. I was his flesh and blood, he would surely be able to look after me.

.   .   .   .   .

Summer returned. One hot afternoon my father asked whether I would like to go with him to the Okke valley to bathe. I was delighted. The Okke was a fine, small river in a quiet valley full of old trees. In their shadow I had

84

spent many days of my childhood while I was still at the old school.

Kuori preceded us with a mat and a small tray of fruit and wine, while I with the *paduk* board under my arm followed my father. Outside the town we took the familiar path along the brook and gradually climbed through the defile to the mountain farm where the old pavilion stood. Kuori had already prepared our seats and left.

While my father looked around the countryside, I set up the *paduk* game and covered the squares with black handicap stones.

"Nothing has changed here during all these years," my father said with a smile. "Don't you feel that this is a world of its own?"

"Yes, that is so, Father," I replied. No human sound was heard, only the chirping of the cicadas from the treetops, and from the ravine the steady murmur of the brook. All the stillness of the day seemed to repose in the deep green shadow, broken once in a while by a cool mountain breeze.

I filled my father's bowl. "May you live a thousand years!" I said, repeating the salutation of the Singers.

He smiled. "Have you ever tried to sing a Shidso song?"

"No, how could I?"

"Try," he said and sang the song of the 'Mild South Wind.' It was a sombre ancient melody, usually presented by famous singers as a wine song. Speechless with admiration I listened, for I had never known he could sing so beautifully. For myself, I could not summon up the courage to follow his example. He looked at the games board. "Still ten points handicap?" he asked with a frown.

Reluctantly I took away two corner stones and only held the inner wall occupied with my pieces.

He took away another two counters. "Surely you can beat your own father with a handicap of six," he laughed and moved his first piece.

Naturally I lost the game.

"Well then, make it eight points!"

I lost again.

He looked at me with pity. "You have lost practice. There is nothing to be done but to give you two more pieces!"

"I don't mind," I said and continued playing with ten points.

"Let's stop playing," he suddenly said when he found that I put my pieces all too often on the wrong spot. "Take off your clothes and get into the water for a while."

I was sorry to have disappointed him. "You must remember that a tiger sometimes gives birth to a dog," I said to console him.

"Never mind; come closer and let me have a look at you! Stand straight; you need not be embarrassed before your father."

He looked at me from all sides. "You are still very skinny," he concluded with real concern. "How old are you?"

"Thirteen."

"Well, there is time. Now go slowly into the water. It is extremely cold here."

He took a bowl of wine and watched me wading clumsily from one rock to the next.

Then he came into the water. He seated himself cautiously under the edge of a big broad rock and let the water trickle over his shoulder. He had hardly been there for a minute when abruptly he leapt out again and sank into the sand, seized by a sudden spasm. He was deadly pale and shook all over. Quickly I got a towel and rubbed him, because I believed he was cold.

Gradually his face regained color and he got up again.

"What happened, Father?"

"Nothing, nothing has happened at all. Just fetch me my clothes."

We dressed, but the shock still made me shiver.

My father, however, said to me: "Don't be afraid; I shall live for a long time yet. I will live until after you marry a beautiful wife and present me with a grandchild."

But for me all the joy of living had been drained away. "Father, please let us go home."

"No, no," he said with a laugh, "you can see that I am quite well again. Let us stay for a while in this beautiful spot."

He looked at the mountains, still aglow in the evening sun. The farm itself was already lost in shadow and from the valley rose a cool wind.

"Will you try one more game?"

"No, please let us go home."

Fortunately, Kuori soon came to fetch us back.

"The life-force wells up unbroken from this brook," he said as we left; "take care if ever you bathe here again."

Hardly had he crossed the threshold of our house when

he was taken with a new spasm. He had to be carried unconscious into my mother's room.

The whole evening I raced from doctor to doctor.

Shortly before midnight my mother told me to kneel on Father's left and to take his hand into mine. She took his right hand and began to pray. We all joined in, while Kuori spread out a broad white cloth on the floor to prepare a way for his soul from the bed to the threshold of the house.

XII. *Years of Mourning*

OSINI had become very silent. She did not speak as often or as much as she used to. My father's death seemed to have changed her much. Silently she went about her jobs in the Inner Court, and it was only rarely that she entered Father's room, where she had appeared each day in his lifetime, despite my mother's admonition that she should not go so often to the men. Only when my mother had gone on her usual autumn journey and Osini had to take her place, would she come late at night into my room to see whether everything was in order. She watched me drawing and writing for a while, but without asking what I might be drawing and without criticizing my handwriting. "Go to sleep soon," she said softly. "Mother would wish it."

Often I pored over my books until past midnight. My studies were more difficult and consumed more time than of old, for we had to learn a great deal of Japanese, and all our textbooks had been replaced by others written in the Japanese language. History was to be re-learnt altogether; all events which had happened in the time of Korean independence were eliminated because the Korean people were no longer looked upon as a nation with its own history, but rather as an outlying community which should always have paid tribute to the Japanese Empire.

Other subjects, like geography and natural science, also demanded harder work, on account of the many changes in terminology and in the arrangement of the syllabus. The teaching of these subjects had been much curtailed in favor of Japanese language lessons; there was no time for them. Without much explanation or comment, we were taken perfunctorily through the curriculum such as we found it in our text-books. All the rest was left to the pupils themselves.

Of my school friends, Kisop was one who came often to talk with me for a while or to help me with my homework. He was often ailing and from time to time could not go to school for weeks on end. Even so he was still one of the best pupils in my form and never tired of lending me a hand in mathematics. He would sit down beside me and watch me solving the problems. Whenever I made a mistake he would correct me with a gentle smile, but without uttering one word.

Yongma arrived each night, but never for more than a few minutes, to ask invariably whether there was anything I had failed to understand at school. He was better able to help me than any of the others because he was the most clever and experienced of us all and knew more Japanese. He answered every question concisely and clearly and then went off again immediately, for there were many others in equal need of his help and he also had his own work to do.

Mansu, too, came to join us. For the past year he had sat close to me in our classroom and had become a friend.

He talked a good deal and often told me of his walks and of the strange old trees in the neighborhood of our town, of the lovely bathing-places in the mountain brooks and of the little temples and pagodas which he had newly discovered. Learning came easily to him and he understood many facts of natural science more quickly than I did, so that he was often able to help me.

Despite all my friends' assistance I had to work much harder than the others to keep pace. I could not tell whether the real reason was that I had been taught too long at the old school and was not yet accustomed to thinking in the new scientific way. A great deal I did not understand at all, and concepts like atom, ion, and energy meant very little to me. Now algebra was added to the rest, and it caused me a great deal of trouble. Equations were unintelligible to me, and I failed to see the purpose of the whole thing. Neither Mansu nor Kisop were able to explain it, and even Yongma had little to say except that these equations would be useful later in the study of higher physics. I pondered and brooded over them by myself, sometimes deep into the night.

As I sat late over my books, my mother would enter the room and gently take brush or pencil out of my hands, close my books and fold away my papers, and tell me to go to sleep. When I objected that my work was not yet done she would say quite briefly: "That is not necessary; do as I tell you."

One such night she stayed with me me for a while even after I had gone to lie down. "What is it that gives you so much difficulty in your studies?" she asked me.

"Everything—," I mumbled, "mathematics, physics, chemistry; none of it is clear to me yet."

"Don't be sad," she said after a long silence, "if you are not sufficiently gifted for this school. This new civilization, which is so alien to us all, just does not suit you. Think of the earlier years. How easily you learnt the old classics and the poets. There you always shone. Come, leave the new school which torments you and go this autumn to Song-nim farm to recover. It is the smallest of our estates, but the one I like best. Chestnuts and persimmons grow there. Have a good rest, get to know our peasants and their work. You will grow strong in this quiet village and fitter than in this restless town. You are, after all, a child of the old times."

This made me sad. I had always been afraid that my true bent was not towards the new sciences which my father had placed before me because nothing else would lead us to higher culture. To have to give it up after four years of working diligently, just because I was not gifted enough, made me very sad.

"Will you do it?" my mother asked as I lay on my mat in silence.

"Naturally, Mother, I will do as you wish," I said dejectedly.

"My dear child," she said and left the room.

XIII. *At Songnim Bay*

THE little village of Songnim was near a remote and solitary bay distinguished only for its oyster-beds. Along the coast, and hidden deep behind the bay, stood some twenty straw-covered farmhouses. During the day hardly anyone was to be seen about the village, for all the men and women were at work in the fields on the far side of the hills. This was the time of harvesting barley, wheat. and maize. I strolled about from field to field and watched the cutting of the corn and the binding of the sheaves until load after load had been taken back to the farm in ox-carts.

At night I returned to my room, the guest-chamber in the house of the local headman. It was a simple room with walls of loam and only a small rough-hewn wooden table in one corner. For a short period the whole village would come alive. Cows were lowing, and out of the houses came the shouts of mothers calling their children home from the beach for their evening meal. Soon all was quiet again and the whole village seemed to fall asleep. Only the head-man stayed in my room to talk to me for a while. He found the warmest spot in the room and prevailed on me to lie down and rest there. He himself sat by the rush-light to plait a straw rope which, he explained, would be needed to repair his thatched roof in the autumn. The lamp was a coarse pottery cup filled with clear vegetable oil and a wick unable to produce more than a very weak flame. The monotonous rustle of the straw and the heat in the room as I lay on my mat would often send me to sleep against my will. When I woke again the light was most often out and the Toldari uncle, as I called him, had gone. Silence lay over the whole house and over the whole village; only the night tide rolled and splashed in the bay.

.　　.　　.　　.　　.

When there was no important harvesting to be done, I did not trouble to watch the workers, and went fishing instead. I greatly enjoyed this, for it made a delightful change from the routine work in the fields. Fishing-rod in hand and basket on arm, I walked along the beach right to the entrance of the bay, to the oyster-rocks, which even at low tide were covered by the sea. Sitting on a rock I could fish undisturbed until the tide came up again. Every day the headman told me exactly when to leave the rocks and walk back along the beach without the risk of being overtaken by the rising water.

There I sat by myself fishing the whole day long. The so-called "line fish" were the most common fish to take the bait; they were no more than a finger's thickness and did not taste particularly good. Only rarely did I catch any-

94

thing better, and throughout that autumn I never saw a single one of the sea-breams which the peasants fancied so much. Nevertheless I returned day by day to sit patiently on my rock, not just because I enjoyed fishing, but for the wonderful view, which did me so much good. Here I escaped the enclosed bay and the sea spread before me into the infinite. On the horizon water and heavens seemed to melt into each other. In the west the solitary rocky Yenpin Island reached into the autumn sky, and to the north a narrow sandy strip around a low chain of hills lost itself in the distance. Far and wide not a sail was to be seen; a cool breeze now and then played over the wet oyster-rocks.

The peasants never went angling, even though fishing-tackle was to be found in every house. They caught their fish with nets which were laid out beyond the bay near the Main Creek. The haul did not consist of small "line fish," but of quite different and bigger ones, such as flounders, soles, bream, or the long white sword-fish which were highly thought of. Since I had never seen net-fishing before nor ever watched the nets in use, I eagerly accepted an invitation to come along one day when they were to be put out. The peasants had picked on a low night-tide. This at first made me somewhat apprehensive, but I soon learnt that it was just at night that the best fish were caught in the nets.

It was dark along the shoals as we went out, for the moon was not up, and the shallow water through which we waded was bitingly cold. Presently, in the brilliance of the starlit sky, the sea grew luminous. By and by I was able to make out sea-weed and crawling crabs against the background of the dark sea-bed. We crossed endless sand creeks through which at this time the water was still seeping out towards the sea. After much wading we reached the main creek, an immense mass of churning water. Quite close the net was set up like a screen in the form of a horse-shoe. Now and then a big fish as long as my arm would leap out of the water in a vain attempt to jump over the net. The farther the tide ebbed away the more desperate became the attempt of the hard-pressed fish to escape their fate. In mad confusion they thrashed about, leaping in greater frenzy than ever, until at last they found themselves flat at the bottom of the drained sea-bed, shining like quick-silver under the night sky.

Swiftly we gathered them into our baskets and made for home. A deep calm now lay over the shoals, for the surf of the breaking waves had receded. Now and again from the distance faint sounds reached us of people talking or shouting to each other. Probably they were other fishing parties returning with their catch, but we could not see them. One might have taken them for the spirits of the drowned, stalking the seashore and whispering to each other because the night was so beautiful and so still.

The fine autumn weather held. Threshing continued from early morning until late into the evening. Linseed, beans, buckwheat, and beet were brought in, and finally we had the rice harvest. As for the corn, the peasants, after cleaning the ears of the chaff with the help of a draught of artificial wind, filled them into straw sacks holding several bushels each. The headman took me to one farm-house after another and explained not only every aspect of the work but also the difference in quality of the various varieties of corn.

The Toldari uncle tried hard not to let me feel lonely in his village. So that I should have something to read during the evening when there was nothing else to do, he had placed several hand-written books in my room. There were four of them: a slender volume of poems, a collection of anecdotes, and two fat novels. The dark-brown oiled paper of all these books turned out to be so much fingered and worn that I could barely decipher the tiny characters by the weak light of my lamp.

"It is very quiet for you here," he said one day as he fetched me from a farm-house, "because you have lived in town until now. But remember the wise men of other times who retired to the mountains when evil ways came over the world. In daytime they stood behind the plough, and took up their writing brushes only at night. So you, too, must live here quietly until the barbarians go away again and the good old days return."

All the men and women of this peasant village believed that the good old days would return quite soon—as soon as a new Royal Family appeared to rule over our country. I was not able to share this view, yet I never said anything against it, because I could not myself imagine anything better for our people. Moreover, I should have thought it impolite to contradict adults whom I called uncle and aunt. It was an old-established custom for the landlord's family and their peasants to regard each other as relatives and to address each other thus. I liked the custom, and always used to add the name of each farm in order to distinguish between my many uncles and aunts. Thus one was called the Udgel uncle and his wife the Udgel aunt, another the Tuissem uncle and his wife the Tuissem aunt. I went generally by the name of "the nephew from town" and was treated like a real nephew. The headman told me that the custom was a good one because it made the peasants feel truly part of the family. All together formed one big clan headed by the landlord's family who might fittingly be richer than any of the others.

Autumn had gone and snow began to fall. Day and night the wind tossed big white flakes across the bay, the fields, and the roads. The harvest was over, and after the Thanksgiving Prayer the storehouse was made fast with a big padlock. The roofs had a new thatch and new silk paper covered the windows. The peasants now stayed in their warm rooms occupied with their home crafts. They made ropes, cords, plaited mats, nets, and sandals. The women spun and wove and the children were sent out to the village teacher, who also was a peasant and only called the children together in winter to teach them reading and writing.

Now and then neighbors forgathered with their work to gossip or to take turns in reading aloud. The books read were usually novels of the old style concerned with a hero in distress. Maligned and ostracized, he had to leave his homeland and tramp from place to place, enduring hunger and cold, until at last he came to a wise hermit who gave him shelter. In the end the hero himself became a philosopher and was called to the Court, where the King made him a powerful man. He married a beautiful prudent woman and returned home again, where, admired and respected by all who knew him, he lived happily ever after. All novels began and ended like that. This did not prevent them from being read over and over again, and each time the patient audience was roused anew to anger about the unhappy fate which befell intrepid innocence. The effect of the story was heightened by the solemn and half-chanting manner of reciting the novel, which called into play the whole range of voice and mood, now gay and then again melancholy. The deeper the snow and the stiller the night, the more full of pathos the readings, so that you could guess from afar just how serious was the plight of the hero. I often stopped in front of such a house and listened, not to discover how the tale might go on, but just to hear this tone of voice, which reminded me of my own carefree childhood when peace was over our country.

XIV. *Spring*

IN winter I often thought of my school years, of my former school friends, and of everything they had told me about the new world of Europe. I recalled the pictures I had collected as a child of the glorious houses and castles so tall that they belonged to the regions of heaven rather than to the earth. As I walked along the bay almost blinded by the driving snow, my imagination would conjure up all these buildings in the distant West and the gay, tall, blond people who lived in them. They knew no earthly cares, no struggle for existence, and no vice. They pursued the paths of wisdom and devoted their lives to investigations into Nature and the cosmos. If one was to become a truly educated human being of the new civilization, it was in the West that one would have to study. There one would see everything for oneself, experience everything oneself, and receive all the new learning from those who themselves had discovered it. Many beautiful sagas and anecdotes which I had heard of this wonderful world came alive again, and I began to consider how I could get there.

The snow-storms had now ceased. The ice-blocks in the bay broke loose, and soon they were gone. It became warmer.

One fine afternoon in March I sallied forth, bound for Shinmak. Shinmak, situated two full walking days from our village, was a small market town through which the railway was said to pass. If I were to board a train there, I would be able to cross the northern frontier of our country, and would surely find opportunities of making my way farther and farther west, until I was bound to arrive in Europe at last. That was all I knew for the time being. What a railway train looked like and how one boarded it, what kind of language one used to make oneself understood abroad or whether people in Europe used money—of all that I knew nothing.

I walked all afternoon and even through the night, for it was easy to find the way in the moonlight. I had to walk throughout the next day, too, till dusk, before I caught my first glimpse of the town far out in the plains. Even from the distance I could see that it was a place very different from our own town, noisy, bustling, and busy. All the best houses on the main street were occupied by Japanese. Their clattering sandals made me quite restless. Screeching, blowing their horns, and ringing their bells, rickshas, motor-cars, and bicycles plunged through dense crowds of pedestrians. With no little trouble I made my way through the throng to the railway station at the far end of the town, only to learn that the next train for Manchuria would not come through until early the following morning.

I tried to acquaint myself thoroughly with the railway buildings and the sidings, the like of which I had never seen before, and took careful note of the entrance and exit, so that I should not go wrong next morning. After a long search I found a bed in a native hostelry on the outskirts of the town. For the first time in my life I spent the night at an inn. Since I intended to rise very early, I went to sleep immediately after the evening meal. My fatigue was great, for I had been walking throughout the previous night without respite.

Although exhausted, I found no real rest. My legs hurt, and in my half-slumber the image of my mother forced itself upon me again and again. I had left a brief parting letter for her on the little writing-desk, so that she should not look for me in vain. I had to do this, for she considered me unpractical and would not have let me go. The thought of the letter had calmed me on my way and had made me almost forget my mother. Now I saw her before me most of the time as if she were really there. At last I fell into fitful sleep, but woke myself within a few minutes, dozed off and woke up again. I heard my mother calling for me and saw her sitting over my letter sadly and at a loss for words. Once she took my face into her two hands and smiled as she used to do whenever she came to Songnim to visit me for a few days. Thus it went on the whole night through.

I dreamt of my childhood. I sat on a straw pillow in our outer court and watched my mother coming out to hang up newly dyed silk cloth. The warmth of the sun filled the whole courtyard. I was thrilled to see my mother, ran up to her, embraced her from behind, and called out:

"Guess, Mother, who is behind you?"

She finished hanging her piece of silk, turned round, and lifted me to her breast.

"Now who could that be?" she laughed, holding me high over her face. "Yes, who is this? My golden bough, my jade leaf! Will you be one day a great poet or a great painter, a hero or the governor of our province?"

Towards dawn I saw her crying bitterly; my head was in her lap. I was upset and whispered: "No, dear Mother, I shall not go away!" I had only seen her weeping once before, and that was when we had come down from the high mountains after my father's funeral, to spend the night in a tent outside the house of the gravekeeper. When I woke again I felt feverish and cold in turn.

Dawn was now breaking, and outside a stinging wind blew across the plains. The small white-washed station hall was brightly lit and crowded with people. Most of them were Japanese, soldiers as well as women, standing about, saluting each other with their repeated deep bows. When finally the little office opened and the railway tickets were being sold, all the uniformed passengers arranged themselves at the head of the queue in order of rank. Next followed those in civilian clothes and sandals. I took my place at the tail of the queue, and when my turn came received a ticket to the capital of Manchuria.

Mist still enveloped the sidings. The ice-cold wind chilled the waiting crowd. At long last the train arrived, thundering, whistling, and smoking. All the passengers raced up to the carriages and pushed through the doors. In no time the whistle sounded and the train departed again, while I was left standing on the platform.

A railway official came up to ask why I had not boarded the train. When I could give him no reason, he took the ticket out of my hand and inspected it. "All the way to Mukden!" he exclaimed with astonishment and cast me a testy glance. Then he led me to the office and told his colleagues.

One of the older men demanded my name and age. "Have your parents consented to this journey to Mukden?" he asked suspiciously.

"No," I said.

"I thought so," he said, becoming sharp. "What did you want to do in Manchuria?"

"Go on to Europe," I answered, hesitating a little.

For some time he looked me searchingly full in the face. "That far you wanted to travel? And have you got a passport?"

"No; I never thought of such a thing."

"Well—and what about luggage?"

"I haven't got any."

"Do you speak English, or French, or German?"

"No, I haven't had time for it yet."

"How much money have you? Show it to me."

I put all my money on the table. He ran his eye over it and grinned. "So you expected to travel to Europe without luggage, without knowing English, without passport, and with so little money?"

"Yes, that is so."

He looked at me askance. "But why, then, didn't you get on to the train?"

I had no answer to that. The young official who had led me back interjected that this was the question I had not been able to answer from the outset.

"Tell me, then, why didn't you get on that train?" the older man asked me once more.

"It was too restless, too noisy, and in too much of a hurry," I replied.

The younger man sneered and said that he had heard the same thing before from Koreans. "The railway is not dignified enough for these people, too noisy and too fast," he remarked, and everybody laughed.

"But you can't very well travel to Europe on an ass," the old man said.

"No, that wouldn't be so easy," I had to admit.

"Will you try again tomorrow, to travel to Europe by our train? Once again, despite the noise?"

"I haven't made up my mind yet."

That was the end of our conversation. The official took back my ticket, paid me the money, and laid it with the rest of my belongings.

"Now go back home and continue your studies. In our country the schools are no worse than in Europe. If you are gifted and can leave the school at the top of your form or somewhere near it you may go to Seoul later and study at the university. Our universities are no worse than the European ones, and Seoul is full of the new civilization. All the public buildings are built in the European style, on three stories, sometimes on four, and the professors are dressed in noble European suits. Remember, though, that you may travel to Seoul only if your parents let you. If I stick to the regulations here I must arrest every runaway like you and send him home in police custody. With you I will make an exception, because you don't look like a bad boy to me. Take your money and go home. But be careful with it, for it is something most precious."

I returned to the inn and went to sleep. I did not wake again until the late afternoon. There was not a ray of sunshine in my room and I felt very cold. Even now the noise from the street outside disturbed me strangely. Coolies drawing rickshas were yelling, bicycle bells were ringing and the street traders shouted out their wares, especially the famous Japanese life-pills, *intan*. From the distance came the whistle of a train steaming into the railway station. There were screams and orders. A second train came from another direction with a deafening roar. Somewhere a policeman was beating a man; one could not avoid hearing his moans and cries for mercy. Sandals clattered on the pavements, a band struck up martial music.

That is how I started on my way home.

XV. *The Drought*

THE peasant headman did not know what to say when he saw that I had come back. He stood and looked at me silently for quite a while. He did not ask where I had been nor why I had returned.

"Go to your room!" he ordered curtly.

His wife, too, looked at me with wide, astonished eyes, as if I were now a different person. She brought the evening meal to my room. It was a pleasure to see her again, for she had always looked after me with great care.

"I am back again, Aunt," I said; but she left the chamber without replying.

I had been away for more than three days. The return journey turned out to be much slower than the way out. The lonely road dragged on endlessly through the unattractive countryside with its few low hills, until at last the chain of our mountains came into sight. Now I was back again in this quiet village which knew no noise. Only a cow mooed somewhere and the tide splashed against the oyster-rocks. When I opened my window around midnight, the bay right to the crest of the beach was alive with the surf of the breakers. The sandy shore was scarcely distinguishable from the silvery waves. The straw roofs asleep in the pale moonlight stood out white against the dark hill. I could not tell which was the dream: the events of the past few days or this village.

The peasants ploughed, sowed their seeds, and put out their plants. At home, the women bleached the twine, wove their cloth, and cultivated silk-worms.

From the distant ravines cuckoos called, larks rose high in the air, buttercups and wild roses were in bloom.

One sunny day followed another and we missed the usual spring rains. The weather was so dry early in the summer that it caused the farmers anxiety. The soil became powdery and the ricefields were getting parched. A bad harvest was feared.

Many of the peasants were convinced that the drought, like everything else, was the fault of the Japanese, because they had torn down so many walls, demolished so many historic buildings, and had ransacked the tombs. This last misdeed was by far the worst, for the Japanese despoiled the graves of the precious porcelain which went with the dead. It was said that all this ware was taken to Tokyo to be sold at a high price. There was not a mountain without its ravaged tombs bared to the sky. Ancient human bones lay scattered under the mountain sun. In the course of road-building, as well, the barbarians had desecrated and broken into many old graves. Often, as one walked along the slope of a mountain, some human bone or skull would come rolling down, causing people to run away in fright. I believed myself that heaven would take its revenge for such crimes.

The drought continued. Many fields were now without a drop of water, and here and there the earth showed deep cracks. The villagers began to carry water night and day. Our only source of water, the brook, dried up, and so the villagers had to walk for hours to bring water in all kinds of vessels from the nearest spring to save at least the young tender plants until the next day. Women offered prayers for rain, kneeling in their courtyards or by their fields in the starlit nights. By candle-light they made offerings of bowls of water placed on simple wooden stands and begged the heavens to spare the innocent peasants from this terrible scourge.

The heavens were merciless. Each morning the sun rose in the east like a fiery ball, only to sear the tortured earth the whole day long.

The peasants had long ceased to sing in the fields. In silence they went out hoeing during the day, while at night everyone desperately searched the skies for the faintest trace of a cloud. Even I never found proper sleep at night and often looked up to the sky. We all grieved, and cared little to speak to each other.

One morning I was woken early by the peasant with whom I lived and saw that the skies had relented after all. Rain poured down upon the whole bay. There was a burst of rejoicing in the village.

Soon after the rains, the weather became hot and close again. The rice meanwhile was saved and growing as it should. Hoeing went on from early morning till late at night. Every day I expected news from my mother. I had written to her and asked her forgiveness for running away without her permission. I was quite willing now to continue living at Songnim until I heard from her again. The headman told me that during the days of my escapade she had not slept one wink and refused to take any food. She had remained alone in her chamber, speaking to no one, so I was afraid that I had made her suffer a great deal. It was with a shock that I learned one evening that she had just arrived in the village. When I came up to her she received me calmly with a smile and merely asked after my health.

Next evening, when we were alone in my room, my mother asked me whether I still desired to study.

"No," I replied.

"Think it over carefully."

"Really not."

"Why have you changed your mind?"

"If I did study, I should have to go to Seoul eventually."

"Don't you want to do that?"

"No."

"Why not?"

"I don't want to go away from you."

"You may go to Seoul," she replied. "Come back to town tomorrow and resume your studies."

"No, I shan't do that."

"Come now. Try it. I want it so."

I did not understand why she said this and why she insisted. I had really intended not to continue my studies. I thought I had learned that the new times were alien to me and that I probably had no bent towards the new sciences. "All right, Mother, I will try," I said at last.

XVI. *Examinations*

MY school friends were delighted when I returned to my studies. We discussed at length how I could best make up for lost time and get to the university as quickly as possible. If I were to matriculate at our local school, and prepare for the university entrance examination at a secondary school in Seoul after that, I was bound to lose another three or four years. Everyone advised me to shorten this period by study at home and, with the help of correspondence courses, to start working for the examination immediately. This idea appealed to me. I ordered correspondence lessons from a well-known institute for my whole curriculum and began.

At first I got on well. The courses were not difficult to follow and I made tolerable progress in all subjects. After a few months only the English language was causing me trouble. However often I read them, I could not quite understand the complicated transcriptions into Japanese syllable characters nor the explanations concerning grammar. I had no previous knowledge of this language, nor were my school friends able to help, for they had none either. At our local school there had been no English lessons, for teachers in this as well as in many other advanced subjects were scarce. The few native teachers who spoke English were all claimed by the better schools in the capital. I was discouraged, for was not English the most important language to learn if one wished to approach true European civilization?

Yongma helped me over chemistry and physics, Kisop in mathematics, and Kasong, another schoolfellow, assisted me in European history, which I found difficult on account of all the foreign names. My friends came every evening and worked with me until I was tired. All of them had completed our local school, but for various reasons were unable to go to Seoul to continue their studies. This made them all the more determined to see to it that at least one of us should get to the university. Each night my room was turned into a proper classroom, with the difference that here were only one pupil and three or more teachers.

Mansu was the only one who did not help me ever. He had not changed. Seventeen years old already, he still went about visiting his friends without learning anything himself or thinking of a profession. Eventually he became a musician of the old tradition.

He also came to visit me every evening, but not until after the others had gone and I was alone with my books. He would watch me at work for a while and then ask me to come to his room to make music with him. He owned a *kayago*, a kind of string instrument which was always very popular with musicians and singers. Whenever I told him that I had not yet finished my work or was too tired and wanted to go to sleep, he would maintain that so much studying was bad for me. He always had a ready supply of arguments: that too much reading did harm to the human spirit, or that, as the only son of my mother,

I should take care not to over-tax my brain. When all this failed to convince me, he would wistfully appeal to me to go with him on the ground that I was his only friend.

I often went along to his room, which was off a narrow, paved courtyard and had its own entrance, so that you could go in and out as you liked, even at night. This room contained neither books nor writing-desk nor alarm clock, none of the things which every schoolboy owned. In fact the little room was almost bare. In one corner were folded sleeping-rugs, in another stood a brazier with a pot of glue on it. A wardrobe against the wall contained all his possessions, and from this he took a jar of wine and a little fruit in a copper basket.

"Now drink; I have bought this especially for you to-day," Mansu would say.

Then he reached for his *kayago*, laid it in my lap, and opened the bulky old manscript score which was reputed to contain all our classical music. I have no idea how he had been able to acquire this valuable instrument nor where he had found the music. He pointed to a particular place in the score and hummed the tune. I plucked the strings cautiously and slowly until my fingers had gained assurance and were able to play the piece without too many mistakes. Patiently he would continue humming the music and correct my fingering; as soon as he was reasonably satisfied with my playing, he would accompany me on his flute, and we would play until late into the night.

"Oh, Mirok," he once said, "must you really go to Seoul and study there?"

"Yes, that is what I shall do if I pass the examination."

"Wouldn't it be wonderful if you were to live here and

we could always make music like this? You would not have to work nor trouble about anything; you could live happily, as a human being should live. You could ask your friends to come and see you whenever you wished, and talk with them about the heavens and the earth, about the world and about human hearts. You might have a hut built in the mountains, and there you could listen to the splashing brooks and watch the passing clouds. Your mother would be happy, you would live serenely, and I could remain with you forever."

"No, I must study."

"You are strange, after all," he said with a sigh.

.   .   .   .   .

The year passed quickly and winter came on again—a very cold winter, but without much snow. It was then that fate put a tempting opportunity in my way. The medical faculty of the university issued an announcement about the forthcoming entrance examinations, which were to comprise five subjects only: mathematics, chemistry and physics, as well as the languages, Japanese and Chinese. English and history, the two subjects which I dreaded most, were to be left out. This entrance examination for the medical faculty presented a great temptation to me, the more so since everyone was agreed that I was better suited for medicine than for anything else. On the other hand, the examination of the Medical Institute had always been known as the most difficult of all on account of the large number of potential students. Candidates were drawn from the best pupils at the secondary schools, and even of these only one in ten was able to pass the exam.

I took several days to consider the question; eventually,

encouraged by my school friends, I yielded and handed in my application. Within a week word came that I had been admitted to the examination and that on a certain day I was to present myself at the municipal hospital with the other candidates from our town. I was instructed to bring brush and ink, a pencil, and a penknife.

It was still half dark and bitterly cold when I walked to the hospital early on the first day of the examinations. A nurse took me into a small room, where I found three other candidates huddled in the corner awaiting what was to come. I knew none of them. All three smiled when they saw me, but their faces were pale and anxious. Then the commissioner came in, called out our names, and compared us with our application pictures. He admonished us to remain calm when being questioned, to think clearly first, and then to write down the answers. Thereupon each one of us received a copy of the examination syllabus which was to govern the next five days.

The first day was given over to a medical examination only. We were led into one of the larger rooms of the hospital, where two doctors took our measures and weight, tested our eyes and vision, examined our spines, our lungs, hearts, stomachs, kidneys, and everything else they could think of. When the other three had been passed, my heart was once again examined more thoroughly, for some reason which I could not discover, and it was only after long consultation between the two doctors that I, too, was at last accepted as medically fit.

We had to arrive for the written examinations very early each morning at a small lecture-room where we wrote for several hours. One day was devoted to mathematics, another to the languages, a third to physics and chemistry. I found the mathematics test exceedingly easy, and there were no great difficulties in physics and chemistry, but the old Japanese and the classical Chinese texts which we had to translate into modern Japanese struck me as so difficult that I was sure few of the candidates would be able to pass in these two subjects. The commissioner sat quietly near the stove with his back turned towards us, perhaps because he did not want to prevent us from helping each other a little. None of us, however, dared to do anything but work quietly by himself. It was only on the third day that a tiny ball of paper came rolling gently across my table. When I gingerly opened it I found it contained the figures of the melting-point of yellow and red phosphorus.

In the oral exam on the last day the commissioner asked me why I had chosen medicine for my study. I replied that I would like to know the cause of life and death. He gave me a smile and played with his pencil for some time.

"That is a high aim," he remarked with approval; "but for the time being what we need is a large number of general practitioners, especially in your country, where general hygiene has been badly neglected."

In the middle of our talk he left the examination room for a moment, and I had the opportunity of reading his comments on the candidates. In several columns remarks had been written below our names. Under mine I could read: Language: simple, clear; Character: honest, gentle, courteous. Under "Purpose of Studies" there was a blank.

Soon the commissioner returned and, after a short silence,

he told me: "You have done a good examination. Your name will be on our short list, but even of those entered on this list, only one in five can hope to be accepted as a pupil at our institute. If the answer you receive should be disappointing, don't let yourself be discouraged. The final selection is almost a lottery."

As I left he gave me another smile and said: "Whenever you speak of 'our country' you should not think of Korea alone, but of the whole Japanese Empire. And whenever you speak of 'our countrymen' you should not forget that you are talking not only of the Koreans, but of all the people of the Japanese Empire."

I did not reply.

Some three weeks later the news came that I had been accepted as a pupil of the medical faculty at Seoul and that I should present myself there early in April. When I came home that evening I found the whole family and all my friends assembled in my room, engaged in animated conversation. Everyone stopped talking as I entered and Yong-ma came up to hand me the communication from the Institute. All congratulated me. Even my mother, though she said nothing, seemed to be pleased, for she touched my hands several times. After that there was no more talking.

My friends felt that the end towards which they had helped me evening after evening had now been achieved. Soon I would go out into the big world, while they would have to remain in our little home town. Our servants may have thought that I was now lost to our house for good. Kuori anxiously scanned the letter from the Institute, which she was unable to read.

One mild spring evening I went down to the Dragon's Pond Bay in the company of my friends. There, riding at anchor, was the steamer which was to carry me to Seoul. Mansu, Yongma, and Kisop, talking gaily, walked ahead, and I followed with my mother. She gave me her company for part of the way out of the town in order to send me off with advice for the journey and for my life in the big city.

"Don't think too often of the past," she said in the end; "times have changed, as you yourself have often told me. The others are ahead of us in the new civilization. It is true that they are often tactless, but you must remain gentle and put up with their crudeness if you wish to learn something from them."

My friends came with me right down to the shore, which was bathed in bright moonlight. The white steamer stood out magically against the dark rocks. I took leave of everyone and boarded a small boat which was to carry me across the water to the white ship. My friends remained at the pier, waiting until the steamer had turned about and, with a nostalgic moan of its deep siren, set its course out of the narrow bay. To watch the three of them walking home across the hill without me was sad. What might they be talking of? Did Yongma speak? Or Mansu? Were they discussing the journey, or music? Soon, passing between the South Hill and the Fairy Mountain, they would reach the beloved fields round our town.

I was greeted with enthusiasm by the other students on the steamer. Each one congratulated me on my successful examination and all promised to help me at Seoul.

The Dragon's Pond Bay vanished from sight. The tall Suyang mountain sank away. The Suab islands seemed to ride past us so close that you could nearly touch them. Soon we were out in the open sea. All around, from horizon to horizon, the moonlight fell only on an endless succession of waves.

XVII. *Seoul*

SOON after breakfast our steamer entered the harbor of Chemulpo. Here we all had to disembark; I followed the others to the station and boarded a train which took hours before it finally brought the Three Horn Mountain into sight. Hills, valleys, and villages sped past us as we approached the city which for more than five hundred years had been the residence of our kings. Here only a few years ago the nightly beacons converged from all the provinces of the land—those bonfires which, as small children, we had watched from the walls of our town; here the governors had received the royal orders to rule their people. Here had dwelt the most famous poets of our country, and here all the learned men and artists had gathered together. I closed my eyes, lost in thought. The train rushed through a tunnel under the river before it entered a vast station. Outside someone shouted that we had arrived at Seoul.

Picking up my luggage, I allowed the stream of passengers to carry me out of the station. An immense square faced me. In a deafening din of hooting and bell-ringing, rickshas, bicycles, and motor-cycles darted about the tramcars. We took a tram. After what seemed to me an eternity, we reached the main street, with its modern stores, banks, and hotels, and came to the northern quarter of the city, where most of us students intended to live. Here one met students in every lane, in every bookshop, and in every restaurant, all of them wearing uniforms identical except for the signs of their institutes and faculties on cap and collar. Nobody asked what you were reading, which school you came from, or what your home province was. All the students greeted each other and helped each other as if they belonged to a single big family.

Next morning I stood at the gates of the Medical Institute of Seoul, which was situated in the east of the city and consisted of several buildings in the European style. There was a constant coming and going of students in their dark blue uniform with its golden medical badge. Only the newcomers were still in their native costume, the Koreans in white, the Japanese in black. I went with them to the registry to receive my documents, the lecture plan, and the insignia for my uniform and cap.

The chemistry lecture was competent, well arranged, and with plenty of practical demonstrations. In physiology, on the other hand, we did not learn much that was new to us. Anatomy—the most important course of all—was little better. The lean Professor spoke indistinctly, without proper emphasis, and lacked zest. He would take a bone and point to its various outlines and cavities, explaining them as far as one could make out in Japanese, German, and Latin. Since he mumbled and spoke very fast, not even those who sat in the very first row were able to understand what he said. From time to time he would write something on the blackboard, but what he wrote was just as difficult to make out as what he said. One after the other we laid down our pens and sat in boredom until these two hours of torture were over and the lean face had disappeared.

"What a fool!" some of the students grumbled.

The more inquisitive ones among us walked up to the Professor's chair and fetched some bone or other out of the chest, in order to study it and compare it with the pictures in our books.

"Should we not also do that?" my neighbor asked me.

"As you wish," I replied, and fetched a carefully cleaned cranium bone, which I laid before him.

He examined it closely without touching it.

"This is a human bone," he said.

He stared at the bone for a long time before he took it up gently, weighed it in his hand and put it down again.

"Strange," he murmured; "this is part of a human being."

After that we nonetheless inspected the crevices, recesses, and protrusions, and corrected our copybooks in so far as we had written down anything at all.

My neighbor was a quiet and pleasant colleague from northern Korea. He was called Igwon. Medical students usually worked in pairs, since doing so enabled them to supplement each other's notes, to correct each other's notebooks, and to carry out joint experiments. Such a pair of students usually moved together to a pension, and many of them eventually became close friends. Igwon and I lived together in a large, cheerful room. Every evening we studied and argued, one day on physics, the next day on chemistry, then on anatomy, and very often about German grammar, in which we heard lectures four times a week.

For all medical students German was obligatory, as most medical textbooks were written in the German language. Even after we had gone to bed we would often continue to practice our conjugations and declensions.

Each morning we walked to the Institute together, and together we came home again in the evening to continue our joint studies. Together we went shopping, together we took our baths, together we went to the theatre. On Sundays we saw the sights of Seoul: the North Palace, the Park on the slopes of the South Mountain, the Zoological Gardens, or we made excursions on the Han river. Igwon knew his way about everywhere, for this was already his second year in Seoul.

Our Institute was one of the most important seats of learning in Korea. Every famous man who came through the country called there, and whenever some prince or great statesman visited Seoul, we had to march to the station to welcome him. Something of the atmosphere of school—indeed, an almost military tone—still clung to the whole place, as it did to all establishments set up by the Japanese occupation authorities. We were not free to choose the lectures and seminars we wished to attend; no one was allowed to miss a lecture without urgent reason, and even during the hottest days of July we were given no respite from our studies.

No wonder, then, that we were very pleased when the last day of term arrived and we were able to leave and pack away our uniforms for a time. We discussed what we might do during the holidays so that we should be able to continue working together in the autumn. Igwon thought that I was too far behind in optics, so I packed the physics book with my things. He sat at the desk and watched me. He had decided not to go home for the holidays, but to spend them at Seoul, for his parents were no longer alive. He was an orphan since early childhood, and the Christian family that had brought him up ceased to welcome him when he decided not to study at one of the missionary institutes, but to attend the State school instead.

We determined to spend our last evening together strolling through the town, because we had done that so rarely. A twisting lane led us gently along the high, mossy wall of the East Palace. It was this Palace which served as a prison for the surviving members of our Royal Family, and it was said that several hundred persons were still held behind these walls, counting in attendants and maids. Whenever I walked past, I stepped out diffidently and softly. Perhaps, so I hoped, I might hear the voices of the august Royal Family. Vain hope. Not a voice, no fragment of conversation, no footstep reached the outside world. The descendants of our proud ancient dynasty had become quite still.

At the end of the long Palace wall we came to the main street and to the south district of the city. Shops and windows with their Japanese and European luxury goods were brightly lit. Everywhere the sound of Western music was in the air, of violins and pianos, accordions and phonographs. In the garden of the Station Hotel a band played European marches and dance-music. We walked on to the district where all the bookshops were located and bought some novels as presents for my friends at home.

On our way back we walked through the night-fair in a broad side street of the city. There were many stalls and stands which sold old cheap odds and ends, tattered books, common writing-paper with blue and red lines, pictures, fans, pipes, tobacco jars, hats, women's shoes made of silk —all dusty and shabby and to be had for a coin or two. Old men in worn but still dignified silken clothes endeavored to entice passers-by to make a purchase. For all one knew they might have been former governors of some province or district. Deprived of office and function and impoverished, they tried to earn a little in this way to provide the essentials for their families. There was constant coming and going, an atmosphere of bargaining, haggling, and arguing.

On one of the last stands we discovered a large pile of thin bamboo flutes which were offered for two nickel coins apiece. Igwon stopped to examine the flutes. I advised him against a purchase, because they were obviously very roughly made and unlikely to give a pure tone, but he persisted. Whether they were good or bad would not matter much to him, he said, because he had never even handled a musical instrument. All he wished was to try a few simple songs when he felt lonely. So I looked among the many flutes for some which were reasonably clean, tried one or two songs, and told him which to buy. As Igwon made his purchase, a young stranger came up and asked me to find him a usable flute too. I did what he desired. In the end the young man was not the only one who wished me to test a flute for him. An older man and then two women followed his example, and soon Igwon and I were surrounded by quite a crowd of people who wanted to hear me play. I did not care for this. As I tried to push my way out of the throng, the old vendor approached me with quite a different kind of a flute, a true musician's flute made of hard bamboo core and decorated with simple and delicate ornaments. He himself had a similar flute in his hand and asked me curtly, almost in a tone of command, to play with him the Tariong, a favorite classical piece familiar to anyone acquainted with the old school of music. To judge from the flutes and from his way of speaking, the old man must have been a former music teacher or a musician from the Royal Court. Now that European music was being imitated everywhere, he had no job. He was evidently delighted to have found a young man able to hold his old instrument properly and willing to share with him once more the pleasures of a classical piece. Even so I was hesitant, for were we not, after all, at the night-fair in the midst of a vast crowd of people? Igwon had listened all this while to the songs with silent but obvious excitement. Now he whispered to me to do as I was told, the more so since we were not in our uniforms and I would give great joy to the old man. Thus I put the flute slowly to my lips and the old gentleman in his silken clothes began to play. All listened wrapt in silence. No one moved, no one spoke as the musician paced up and down and in a surge of recollection and feeling played before the crowd.

To the south the new Japanese quarter lay before us in a sea of lights; the old Korea in the north was asleep under a blanket of darkness. The night sky spread its black velvet over the Three Horn Mountain and silence isolated the ancient Tsangdok Castle.

XVIII. *The Old and the New Science*

Fᴿᴏᴍ the very first term I was aware that Igwon worked more carefully and more thoroughly than I did. I would be quite content when at the end of the day I had written down my lectures without serious omissions and had gained some notion of what they were about. He, on the other hand, would continue to think about them, discovering new ambiguities and new questions, so that we often had to go through the whole matter again and again in almost endless discussion. Igwon took all the subjects very seriously, but it was obvious that he gave most thought to the problems of physics and chemistry. His attempts to comprehend such difficulty concepts as ether, substance, or energy impressed me. He would sometimes spend a whole evening trying to understand a problem of this nature, with the result that we might not reach our physiological or anatomical lectures until the early hours of the morning.

At this time of night we both began to feel very hungry and eagerly awaited the cry of the pie-boy who passed through our lane each night offering his steaming pies. He knew exactly in which house and on which floor students might be at work past midnight, tormented by hunger. His chant reached us first from the distance, as if a mosquito were approaching. Then the sound became louder and louder, until right under our window it ceased altogether. We heard him put down his case and lift the lid. Igwon, with a smile of anticipation, opened the shutters and took in two slices of rice cake, filled with jam. Then the pie-boy's song would recede again down the lane and we returned to our books.

In addition to his scientific textbooks, Igwon's library contained quite a bit of light reading, European novels in Japanese translation above all, which I knew only by name. One day I discovered several books dealing with philosophy. I took down one of them, called *The Science of Being*, and started to read. That was on a Sunday when Igwon had gone to visit one of his school friends and had left me behind. I was so fascinated by the book that I read the whole afternoon until my friend returned. Seeing me so engrossed, he was pleased at first, but then remarked that I had better not occupy myself too much with the problems of philosophy because they would distract me from my proper studies. In any case, he believed that we Eastern people were too much inclined towards theoretical speculation.

Even so, I found it hard to give up the book because it dealt, so it seemed, with the most profound questions which human beings can ask themselves. It was little use to put the book away and to resolve not to take it up again, because I could not help thinking of what I had already read. Thus, a few days later I ignored Igwon's advice and took the philosophical work from the shelf again.

"The modern sciences in which we lag behind the Europeans," Igwon said one evening, "have not sprung from metaphysical speculation, but have been gained through practical knowledge of nature. That is true of natural science and it is equally true of medicine. Our ancestors always attempted to understand the human body merely from the point of view of the ancient philosophers; it was the Western scientists who boldly opened the body and inspected the inner organs with their own eyes. They ceased to speculate and consider, but tried to see instead where the heart and the intestines were located and how the veins and arteries were distributed throughout the body. It is to their boldness and courage that we owe all modern medical knowledge, which is a hundred times greater than anything that was known in the old times."

Neither Igwon nor I had any acquaintance with old native medicine. Hitherto we had looked upon it, as upon all the old traditions, as antiquated and useless, and had not troubled to learn anything about it. We knew nothing of the studies of the old medical school nor of its views on the sciences. All we had heard was that to become a doctor in the old medical tradition you had to study for at least ten years, so that in fact there never was a medical man of the ancient school whose hair had not turned grey.

Then a lucky incident delivered a rare old manuscript into our hands. Igwon once visited a friend whose uncle had been one of these old-fashioned physicians. The books he had left were to be burned, but one had been saved, and now Igwon brought this precious relic to our room. We looked through the volume, turning the leaves with great care, and found that the text dealt with a section of anatomical studies. The book was full of black brush drawings showing the human body from various angles. Each picture contained a multitude of lines and dots which covered the surface of the body and these were inscribed with complicated names. The lines were called the life-lines, although their course was not identical either with those of the veins or those of the arteries. At the very end of the volume there was a supplement of pictures dealing with internal anatomy, also drawn in black ink. The shapes of the various organs were indicated roughly and simply, as if the whole was but a preliminary sketch of an artist. The outlines of the stomach and the heart corresponded exactly with those given in our modern text-book. The liver, on the other hand, contained to our surprise seven small lobes suspended in a row from the left lung to the heart, which we took to be a symbol of the small circulatory system.

We smiled at this primitive anatomy, but could not help admiring the author for his skill in achieving this degree of accuracy in his drawings of organs which he had never seen. We knew that no doctor of the old school had ever performed a dissection. All their knowledge of what is inside the body was derived exclusively from the hands, from feeling and examining the surface of the body with the fingers.

These venerable doctors hardly ever touched the body of a sick man. They never put their ear to the patient's chest nor sounded his organs. They only looked at the face of their patient, listened attentively to what he himself had to say and felt his pulse. Then they would write down a prescription which their assistants made up at the time. All the necessary herbs, roots, and plants were kept in the consulting-room, so that pills, juices, and salves were always prepared under the direct supervision of the doctor. Nothing else was done for a sick man; the old medical science knew no surgery, no injections, no ray treatment. Just occasionally, when he thought an illness due to a disruption of the assumed life-line, a doctor might venture to stick a needle into the body and puncture it at certain points along the line.

Why study so long to learn such a simple art? Did the students philosophize and speculate all these years on the meaning of human existence? Or did they spend their time studying the efficacy of medicinal herbs?

Never before had we seen a book on the old medical science describing the anatomy of the human body. They were unobtainable in the book trade, and every doctor looked after his old books as if they were secret documents.

.   .   .   .   .

The human body was considered sacred, particularly so after the soul had departed. Then it had to be restored to the earth at a certain spot so that it might return to complete harmony with nature, and would not bring trouble and misfortune to the living or to later generations. For this reason, it was a sin against the law of nature and against the spirit even for a doctor to open a dead body. The early students of our Institute, all of them Koreans, had therefore refused to take part in anatomical dissections. They were quite willing to be taught the modern science of medicine because they were aware that it was far superior to the antiquated native methods; to dissect a corpse, a dead human being, however, they held to be a grave sin.

It had been just the same several decades earlier, at the time when the first attempts were made to introduce Western civilization into our country. But even we who had long rid ourselves of these old notions felt somewhat uncomfortable when one winter's evening we were taken for the first time to the grim building where the anatomical demonstrations took place. With six other colleagues, Igwon and I slowly approached the big table which served as the bier of a young man, an inert body helplessly facing what was to come. Some distance from the table we all stopped and stared at the pale human being which, instead of resting deep in the shadow of the earth, was obliged to lie on this metal board with the winter's sun falling upon his naked torso. Igwon gave me a bleak look and took my hand.

"Not even a little incense!" he muttered with disgust.

The Professor came up and explained that today we were to look at the organs of the abdomen *in situ*. Dissecting a human body was no violation of human dignity, he pointed out. In his view, on the contrary, we were doing a great honor to the dead by sacrificing their mortal remains on the altar of science. He called on one of us to be bold enough to begin cutting the skin from the vault of the ribs downwards. Not one of us moved for some time; at last a student deliberately brought forth his instruments and did as we had been instructed. After that each of us took his turn, and in the end we all worked together until we had neatly laid bare the *omentum majus*.

By the time we had seen all the organs under the flood-light of the operating theatre and were ready to go home, darkness had fallen on the town. At home we refused to eat and could not speak for the rest of the evening. Everything around us: our studies, our philosophy, nature, and human life, everything seemed meaningless and ugly. As soon as we left the Institute I had felt an immense desire to take a hot bath to cleanse myself. Yet at the same time I was afraid of seeing my body and putting my hand on my own flesh. I lay without moving and tried to forget the appalling impressions of the afternoon. Igwon sat at his writing-desk and seemed to finger in a distracted manner one book after another; now and then he uttered words such as "appalling," "barbarian," "awful." At last he found a book which held his attention. He never stopped reading. I fell asleep, woke up again, went back to sleep, and throughout the night, whenever I woke from my fitful slumbers, I saw him sitting over his book.

"Shall we really continue with medicine?" he asked me the next morning.

"I do not know," I said.

XIX. *Departure*

It happened during our sixth term at the medical school. One afternoon as I was leaving a lecture on ophthalmology, I was stopped by a fellow student called Sangkyu, whom I knew quite well. He asked me in a low voice whether I was prepared to come to an important discussion next evening at the restaurant "On the Southern Clouds." I agreed to go, but asked what was to be discussed. Sangkyu took me aside and whispered that local students had given him certain information which needed careful consideration. The Korean people were planning to organize a demonstration against the injustices of Japanese policy, and the students of all the native schools were to take part in it. Sangkyu wanted to ask a few reliable Korean colleagues from our Institute whether we thought the medical faculty would be ready to participate.

Igwon had also been asked by Sangkyu and seemed very preoccupied. He did not speak a word on the way home. We got our evening's work done as quickly as possible and then asked ourselves what the people might demand of the Government. Would it be the right to vote? Or their own army? Or might it be control of local government?

"In any case, it must be something political," Igwon grumbled.

"That's certain."

"Do you realize that we shall be punished if the authorities find out that we have been in on the demonstration?"

"Of course I realize that."

"We will be worse off than the others, because we are studying at an institute which is directly under the Government. Gratitude alone, they will say, should have kept us from taking part in any political demonstration."

There, then, was the big question: should we take part or keep out? We were grateful to the faculty which introduced us to the exalted science of medicine without, we assumed, demanding anything in return. At public expense we had been shown whatever was worth seeing and introduced to the most famous scientists, priests, and statesmen.

Igwon pondered this for a long while. "What do you think we should do?" he asked me.

"I don't know myself."

"If something is to be done which concerns the whole nation to which we belong, we must take part."

"It looks like that."

"What do you think, then?"

I remained silent.

"A wretched situation," he murmured. "In any case we must both do the same."

"Yes, that is obvious."

When we arrived next evening at the restaurant "On the Southern Clouds" we found about ten fellow students assembled there. Sangkyu told us that preparations for the demonstration had already progressed far and that the students of the public institutions had been unaware of them only because we, as "half-Japanese," were not being trusted. Everyone listened attentively and all favored participation. Not a single voice opposed it. None of us knew who had started the idea of the demonstration, how it was organized, or what it would demand of the Japanese Government, but all the students wanted to take part.

Later on we spoke at length of our own ancient civilization and of the cultural achievements of our ancestors and agreed that the Japanese were no better than upstarts. We spoke of the first printing with movable type, of submarines, of the art of pottery, of our paper, and of many other things which our ancestors had invented before anyone else in the world.

After listening all evening, even Igwon, who was the most quiet and thoughtful of us all, joined in with an "All right, then, let us go ahead with it."

We, the medical students, must have been the last to block the movement; now we had joined, it gained momentum and surged toward the goal which seemed so near at hand. Sangkyu often brought us news of more preparations for the demonstration, of flags, of leaflets, of marching orders. Finally he arrived with the important message that the rally was to take place on the first of March at two o'clock in the afternoon and would start from the Pagoda Park.

It turned out to be a fine, warm, and sunny spring day.

When I awoke, Igwon was already fully dressed in his uniform. This day I did not intend to go to any lectures because I had been given leave of absence on account of a slight infection.

"Come early to the Park," he said, offering me his hand, "so that we shan't miss each other there; we'll march together."

"Yes, of course."

He left the room with a smile on his face.

We had slept very little during the night. Leaden fatigue kept me on my bed and I found it very hard to rise.

.   .   .   .   .

When I arrived at the park at two o'clock the whole area was already surrounded by policemen and the small walled-in area was so closely packed that I could hardly make ten steps forward. Neither Igwon nor any other of my friends were to be seen anywhere. I stood by a corner of the wall and watched more and more people crowding through the entrance. Suddenly there was complete silence and somebody began reading the proclamation of the Korean people from the terrace of the pagoda. From where I stood it was impossible to understand a single word. At last the speaker finished, and after a second's pause for reflection a thundering *"Manse"* call broke loose and was taken up again and again by thousands of voices. The tiny park was charged with tension and ready to burst. Leaflets of all sizes and in many colors were thrown up and fluttered in the air as the demonstrators streamed out of the park to start on their march through the city, swept along by the threatening *Manse* call.

I got hold of one of the sheets and read the proclamation. The Korean people declared that the annexation by Japan had been a mistake and that from today onward it was no longer valid. The Koreans as a people demanded to be given back their right to determine their own fate. I read the proclamation over several times and joined the procession. At the park gate someone pressed a packet of leaflets into my hand and curtly commanded me to distribute them.

The street was densely lined by a vast, astonished, and curious crowd of people who eagerly took the leaflets. "At long last!" some called out, and others shouted, "That is the spirit of our students, our children!" Women in great agitation, some in tears, offered us food and drink.

The police did not interfere in any way with our march through the city. Only official buildings and the consulates were guarded by heavily armed soldiers, ready to prevent any excesses by the students.

It was not until much later that we began to feel hemmed in. Our freedom of movement became smaller and smaller. As soon as we had marched through any one district, soldiers and police closed in on it, so as to restrict the area of the demonstration. Finally, as we left the French Consulate, where we had declared ourselves a free nation without any interference, and made our way to the offices of the occupation authorities, we found ourselves in a cul-de-sac. Our advance was barred. The street was occupied on both sides by four rows of armed policemen, and in the centre there were soldiers. For a moment the two sides faced one another irresolutely. Then the first line of troops burst on the crowd with drawn sabres. Those at the head of the demonstration held fast, but behind them a panic developed and the whole crowd broke. Our cause was lost. After all the glorious *Manse* calls nothing remained but whimpering and whining. In no time the soldiers chased us back into the main street, where another band of soldiers was ready for us and continued the hunt.

I reached home unharmed and went to sleep almost at once. When I woke up again it was dark. Igwon had not yet returned. Restless with anxiety, I went out to search for him. The atmosphere in the city struck me as sinister; the streets were deserted and dimly lit. Everywhere soldiers were posted with machine-guns. Black armored cars raced past me.

I groped cautiously through the back streets to look up fellow students in their rooms; not one of them knew what had happened to Igwon. In vain I went from one boarding-house to the next. At last I met Sangkyu at a corner; he, too, was out to check upon his friends. He had been to see nearly all of them and found out that including Igwon five of our fellow students were missing.

Our room was still empty when I returned after midnight.

The night passed very slowly.

Next morning Sangkyu came with the news that Igwon and the other four had received minor injuries and had been arrested; he asked me to take some food to the prisoners.

Meanwhile the national rising had spread rapidly from the big cities to the smaller towns and thence to the market towns and villages. From my own home I heard that Kisop and Mansu had been taken to prison with other friends of mine. After the students and school-boys, the merchants began to join the movement; then the artisans and peasants, and at last even the Korean officials. The occupation authorities found their position increasingly awkward and asked for more Japanese divisions. Once again troops were continuously on the move, just as they had been ten years before, during the annexation of our country. There was bloodshed everywhere. In a village inhabited mostly by Christians all the inhabitants were locked up in a church and burnt alive. Old prisons and jails were being enlarged, new ones had to be built, and the police were known to carry out tortures day and night. After the fourth public demonstration the students of Seoul went underground and became engaged exclusively in secret service for the movement. I myself took part in the printing of leaflets. After the military suppression of the revolt Tokyo decided to dismiss Hasegawa, the Governor-General, and in his place arrived Admiral Saido, who introduced a policy of conciliation. He disarmed all the officials, who, whether tax collectors or teachers, interpreters or doctors, had hitherto worn uniforms and carried sabres. The secret police, the terror of the people, was dissolved and torture was prohibited. The salaries of Koreans were put on the same level as those of the Japanese, freedom of the Press was proclaimed, Korean schools received equal status with the Japanese, and an imperial university was set up at Seoul.

In strange contrast to this conciliatory policy were the severe punishments inflicted on all the participants in the March demonstration. The courts continued to sentence those whom they described as "disturbers of the public peace" and the police continued feverishly to search out and arrest anyone connected with the movement. Many of those persecuted fled abroad. I personally discarded my student's uniform and took a train home.

.   .   .   .   .

Throughout the period of unrest I had rarely been able to send word to my mother about the events in Seoul, and even then only in guarded language. Naturally, she was in great anxiety about me. Now that I was able to tell her all that I had seen and experienced myself she went quite pale; without saying a word she left the room.

I fell into a deep slumber. I had not had a quiet night for months and was quite exhausted.

In the evening my mother came to see me. "You must flee the country," she said.

"Flee?" I repeated without even catching the meaning of the phrase.

I was quite unable to think about anything; all I felt was immense and unconquerable fatigue.

"Yes, you must flee," she said once more. "I have been told that along the upper reaches of the Yalu the frontier control is not as strict as elsewhere. There you should still be able to get away to the north."

I remained silent. I had no courage for the flight because so many escaping students had been arrested or shot on the way.

My mother did not take so serious a view of the danger. She believed that many refugees had succeeded in crossing the frontier at the river and had made good their escape.

This was what I should do. On the other side of the frontier I would be able to get myself a passport and eventually continue my studies in Europe.

Even the word Europe did not give me courage. I knew that it was exceedingly difficult to study at a European university and that the language alone usually proved an almost insuperable obstacle to Asians.

Slowly my mother persuaded me, and I began to realize that I would have to try to leave the country in order to give her peace of mind. It was clear that I would cause her less anxiety by going away than by staying with her in constant danger. I almost regretted that I had ever taken part in the demonstration.

By the following evening I was ready to leave. My mother dissuaded me from staying at our home any longer. Nobody was to know of my departure until I had crossed the frontier.

She handed me a small wicker basket which contained a change of clothes, a silver pocket watch and chain, and a roll of money. This was all I was able to take with me on the long journey to that other world of which I had dreamt so much.

Despite fog and darkness my mother accompanied me a long way on my road out of the town.

"You are not without courage," she said after we had walked together in silence for a time. "You have often been discouraged, but you have always stuck to your ideas. I have great confidence in you. Be brave. You will easily get across the frontier, and I know that in the end you will reach Europe. Don't worry about your mother. I shall patiently wait for your return. The years pass so swiftly. And if we are not to meet again, don't take it too much to heart. You have given a great deal to my life, a very great deal of joy. Now, my child, you must make your way alone."

XX. *The Yalu Flows*

I WAS close to the wide Yalu River along our frontier with China. Progress across the country became very difficult. The rushes through which I had to make my way grew head high and it was only rarely that I could catch a glimpse of the rice-fields or of pasture. Patrols of armed soldiers were about; from early morning till late at night the crack of rifle-shots could be heard in the distance, most often at nightfall, when many fugitives seemed to be on the move. From village to village or even only from house to house I myself was guided by plucky peasants or fishermen until at last I reached an uninhabited hut. Here I was to lie in hiding and to await a ferry-man willing to risk the crossing.

The next night two more students joined me at the hut, equally anxious to be taken across the river. They appeared to be even younger than I. One of them, a pale, nervous boy of less than seventeen, obviously regretted that he had ever risked the escape. He sat on the floor dejectedly and just stared.

At last during the third night an old fisherman appeared and told us to follow him. It was bright moonlight. Afraid of being seen, we hesitated to leave the hut, but the ferry-man convinced us that when the moon was up the frontier guards would be less active. We trusted him, and so he led us by a difficult trail through what seemed a jungle of reeds and rushes. After more than an hour's brisk walk we reached a thicket. Our guide whistled, and soon from the undergrowth came the expected reply. Two more fishermen emerged and led us down to the river-bank. It was a terrifying sight. Here, quite close to its mouth, the Yalu was so wide that it had ceased to look like a river and was almost lost in the endless sea.

The fishermen whispered among themselves and then, as we were waiting without daring to move, they fetched three small dug-out boats from their moorings. Each fisherman took one of us into his boat, and at intervals, one after the other, we moved off from the bank. Paddling softly and noiselessly across the water seemed to take an eternity. When we were in mid-stream we heard shots being fired higher up the river. My ferry-man looked quite unconcerned, but gave me to understand that I must not speak. Later he whispered that these had only been warning shots fired from the railway bridge. Nobody would discover us here in the midst of this shining expanse of water.

We did not reach the other side until long after midnight. The fishermen gave us directions for the three hours' walk to the nearest Chinese frontier town and bade us a brief good-bye. For a time we stood to watch the three boats slowly making their way back to our homeland. Then, without a word, we set out on the rough path, the first time in our lives on Chinese soil.

It was already light when we entered the town. After a long and tiring search we found the Korean inn of which we had been told and went to sleep immediately.

That very afternoon we three separated. The younger one of my two companions left for Shantung and the older for Mukden.

I went for a stroll through the town. The narrow streets were crowded and everything was far more bustling and alive than in Korea. A strange smell of musk pervaded the whole place, and despite all the signboards with their lettering in golden characters the streets looked dingy, for the houses were not whitewashed and all the people were dressed in blue.

I left the town and climbed a hill to have one last look at the river. There it flowed in its sandy bed between the hills, calm and blue in the evening sun. At this point, upstream from where we had crossed, the Yalu was still narrow—hardly half a mile wide. I could almost make out the faces of the people on the other side. They were hanging up their nets to dry. Women and girls sat outside their houses, shelling beans for supper, and children were playing and chasing each other.

I watched the steady flow of the river which separated my homeland from this vast Manchurian country. Here everything was big, sombre, and serious; over on our side all was small and gay. Bright, straw-covered houses dotted the hillside. Evening smoke was already rising from many a chimney. On the horizon the chains of our mountains appeared one behind the other under the clear autumn sky. The mountains were aglow in the sunlight; then, before wrapping themselves gradually in blue mist, they shone out once again in the dusk. I imagined that far to the south I saw the gorges and brooks of the Suyang mountain and the two-storied tower building where every night as a child I had listened to the glorious evening music. It was as if I should be able to hear the heavenly sounds carried to me all the way from home.

Steadily the Yalu flowed. Darkness fell. I descended from my hill and went to the railway station.

POSTSCRIPT

FROM references to historic happenings it can be gathered that the story of *The Yalu Flows* takes place during the first two decades of the present century. Such, however, is the timelessness of this autobiography and of the experience which it re-tells that it is the ever-renewed conflict between the old and the new which holds the reader's imagination rather than the specific events which here bring about a clash.

Mirok Li never returned to Korea. His long journey into the heart of the 'new civilization' brought him to Europe at last, but as an exile from his own country. He made his home in Bavaria, where he lived and worked as a medical practitioner. Here he wrote, almost a quarter of a century later, his book of childhood reminiscences in simple German, a language which he handled with accuracy and immense tact, if not with any great freedom.

In his heart Mirok Li remained a Korean; and the picture which he paints of the joys and sorrows of his childhood has the qualities of an eastern brush-drawing, its warmth as well as its most sensitive delicacy which shrinks from all over-statement.

Mirok Li never saw his mother again. Six months after his arrival in Europe he learnt from one of his sisters in the first letter from home that she had died within a few months of his escape from Korea. He himself died in a small Bavarian town on March 20th, 1950, while engaged on a continuation of his book which was to have described the impact of the reality of European life on one who was so deeply rooted in the ancient civilization of the East. Of the second manuscript, unfortunately only a few fragments survive.

H. A. H.